THE LONER

THE LONER

The life of Xavier Aislado
as told to

Quintin
Jardine

headline

First published in 2011 by
HEADLINE PUBLISHING GROUP

1

Cataloguing in Publication Data is available from the British Library

ISBN 978 0 7553 5716 1 (Hardback)
ISBN 978 0 7553 5717 8 (Trade paperback)

Typeset in Electra by Avon DataSet Ltd,
Bidford-on-Avon, Warwickshire

Printed in the UK by CPI Mackays, Chatham, ME5 8TD

HEADLINE PUBLISHING GROUP
An Hachette UK Company
338 Euston Road
London NW1 3BH

www.headline.co.uk
www.hachette.co.uk

This book is dedicated to Robert Morgan Skinner, QPM, who played a big part in its being written. **QJ**

And to Paloma Puig i Garcia, who had an even greater role. **XA**

And finally, to Mia Abernethy Teixidor; guapa, pure guapa. **QJ/XA**

Co-author's note

Xavier Aislado has been a part of my existence for around three years, although I suspect that he's lurked in the background for rather longer than that, without either of us being aware of the fact. We were introduced indirectly, by a friend we have in common, Bob Skinner, whose acquaintance with Xavi goes back even longer than does mine with the man who's currently chief constable in my city of Edinburgh, and my near neighbour in Gullane, my home village.

When finally we did meet, I suspected from the outset that this massive man was going to play an appropriately large part in my life. Then he vanished, and I guessed that I had been wrong.

Xavi's an impressive and imposing guy. People who've met him will never forget him, and they've all tended to make assumptions about him, some well founded, others less so. However, there were two things about him on which everyone agreed. One was that from his youth he was a naturally sombre individual. The other was that an air of sad serenity enveloped him like a bubble in the last fourteen years of his life in our community. Its cause was a matter of record, and so when he did leave our midst, without warning, without farewell, many of us thought that he simply couldn't stand being him any longer.

I was among those, I confess. I shared that foreboding. My fear was that he had sought a way to end it all, and that if Lord Lucan was ever found, the remains of the late managing editor of the *Saltire* newspaper, the monument he left behind, would be close by.

Nevertheless, when the post lady rang my doorbell one morning, asked me to sign for a package, Spanish stamps and postmark, and I saw the sender's name, on the back . . . Sr. Xavier Aislado . . . I wasn't really surprised. Indeed, I berated myself for my own foolishness. That great, serious totem of a man is far too big in every respect ever to have done away with himself, and I, of all people, one of his few confidants, should have known that all along.

However I was taken aback when I opened the parcel. Inside I found a four gigabyte memory stick, and a covering letter from the big fella, printed on personalised stationery. It read:

Dear QJ

I've read your work, and I believe that you're the guy to help me. My life is on this gadget. I'd like you to take it, consider it, and then do what you can to give it book form, in the hope that it might interest others, and even more, in the hope that it will provide a fitting tribute to those who have made me what I am, for better or worse; my dad, and his mother, the greatest and most remarkable human being I've ever met.

If you're prepared to undertake this task with me and for me, go ahead in your own time and get back to me when you're ready. If not, please shred this letter and destroy the stick.

Yours ever

Xavi

When I plugged the device into my computer, I found a Word document and two MP3 audio files. I listened to those first and they scared the shit out of me, especially the shorter of them, the second in order. After that I could do nothing but go on. I read Xavi's documentation. It was a series of notes and recollections, a very long series at that, the kind a journalist would compile in researching a story. It told a remarkable human story, long and ultimately tragic. For all that he might appear to be now, and for all that he might possess, this man has borne a share of ill fortune that would have broken a lesser being.

Of course, I knew some of the tale; so did most of our city, and a good chunk of the rest of the country. It couldn't be otherwise, as Xavier

Aislado was his country's leading journalist in his time. Yet behind those headlines, behind those 'exclusive' tags, there was a secret world, one that's been hidden until now from everyone who didn't live in it, or through it. I was amused, surprised and, finally, shocked, as I read his largely unreported saga, and I'm sure it will have much the same effect on you.

I've done my best to tell this life story in the manner in which Xavi hoped I would. Mind you, I haven't followed his instructions slavishly. I wasn't content simply to be his sub-editor. In preparing this work, I've spoken to those who were part of the Aislado years, those who've survived, that is: the recently retired John Fisher, his mentor at first then his right-hand man, Tommy Partridge, his friend and counsellor, Alexander Draper, who helped set him on the road, Simon Sureda, a distinguished scribe whose example Xavi set out to follow, and of course Bob Skinner. Much of what they've told me has found its way into the following pages, which include a series of objective interjections among Xavi's account of his life. Some are direct quotes, from my own knowledge, others are conversations that I've assumed took place, while being fairly certain of their accuracy.

Xavier Aislado has been many contradictions in his time. He has been gentle, yet his physical appearance, his genetic inheritance, has made him seem, unknowingly, fearsome. He has been naturally kind and caring, and yet he has been unintentionally cruel, by failing through his single-mindedness to appreciate the needs of others. He has been a great reporter who shone light upon many scandals and many crimes, and yet he has been blind to those closest to him.

He has been the keeper of the flame of truth for many, and yet he has dwelt alone in darkness.

This is his life.

One

There was a time when a few of the sun's rays shone into my life.

There was a time when I supposed that people were inherently good. There was a time when I lived in a world where my first instinct was to trust, rather than suspect. There was a time when naivety was an endearing trait rather than a potentially lethal character flaw.

There was a time in my schooldays, in a different life, when I was almost gregarious, and my friends laughed at the irony of my name, Xavier Aislado, or in English, Xavi the Loner. Now I have few friends beyond my own front door. Because I seek none. Because friends ultimately mean hurt and I've known too much of that. Believe me, I'm Xavi Aislado now . . . in every respect, locked in my own world, because that's the way I want it.

I was given my prophetic name by my dad, a childhood refugee from the Spanish Civil War who grew up in wartime Scotland and stayed there for a while after that, since his father had been violently anti-Franco and was in exile for a lifetime . . . either his or Franco's: the former as it turned out, since he died in November 1961, three months before I was born. Grandpa was Xavi the First. (The Catalan 'X' is pronounced 'Ch', by the way, as in 'Chocolate'.) My dad was christened Josep-Maria, but the second of those forenames remained his secret, in Scotland, at any rate. There, everyone outside the family, and these days that means almost everyone but me, calls him Joe, the name he was given when he arrived from Spain as a four-year-old, in 1936.

I can't remember a time in my formative years when I truly liked him. My dad was born a son-of-a-bitch, and he'll probably be that way till the day he dies. He's perversely proud of it too. He says that his

1

nature was his gift from my grandmother. I have memories of her from my infancy. They are of a grim-faced old harridan . . . when we are very young, every adult is very old . . . with a scowl like a black flag draped across a coffin. Those images are still imprinted in my memory, sixteen years after she went to dance the great Sardana in the sky. They make me smile now, for I have others, the product of acquired knowledge in our later years.

My dad inherited some of Grandma Paloma's (that's what I called her from infancy) thunderous nature, and the running of Grandpa Xavi's business. I'm told that the old guy called himself a socialist, and that's what put him on the Caudillo's death list. Whatever the truth of that, like all Catalans, he was a capitalist in his heart and soul. Grandma told me, when I was ten, once she had decided that I was ready to absorb her wisdom, that he made his first fortune by opening a string of hotels in the cities of Girona, Figueras and Olot, then selling them to an idiot French investor in 1935, the year before the Civil War erupted. As I say, that's what she told me; I didn't learn the whole truth until several years later.

Grandpa Xavi and his little family unit arrived in Edinburgh with enough money to buy another hotel, but instead, grasping the essential nature of the people amongst whom they had chosen to settle, he went into the pub trade, and as a result, became even more prosperous than he had been in Spain, while Europe tore itself apart. By the time he died, he owned a chain of forty-five boozers across central Scotland, and a small brewery which supplied them. Yes, that cunning old fox had the foresight to anticipate the real ale craze . . . or so I thought for much of my life.

After he was gone, my dad developed the business shrewdly, carefully and very profitably, for fifteen years. One of his first acts was to sell the brewery to a couple of Asian entrepreneurs for an eye-watering profit. He used the money to double the number of outlets in the pub chain, and to move them upmarket, with carpets on the floor rather than cigarette ends and empty crisp packets. After that, he kept on expanding;

his business philosophy has always been: 'To settle for what you have is to embrace stagnation.'

I knew nothing of this as I was growing up. I have very few early childhood memories of him; he seemed to be always at work, leaving me in the care of my mother, a quiet unsmiling woman from Falkirk, maiden name Mary Inglis. I didn't know it at the time, not surprisingly, but she had been a clerk in my grandfather's office when the eye of the son and heir had fallen upon her, followed by the rest of him. Yes, there was a lot I didn't know.

I didn't want for anything as a kid. That wasn't down to my dad, who was never there, or my mother, who was entirely indifferent to me and gave me nothing but the occasional slap across the legs when I annoyed her. No, it was all Grandma's doing. She was a proud woman, with a small circle of acquaintances from the Catholic Church, with which she had a fitful relationship over the years, and from the Scots-Italian merchant community . . . the closest she could find to Spanish, I suppose . . . that thrives in Edinburgh, and she made damn sure that I lived up to the image of our family that she wanted to project. At her insistence, I was enrolled in George Watson's primary department when I was five, over my mother's fairly limp protestation that she had wanted me to be educated in the state system. I wasn't bothered either way; school was the means for me to meet other kids, as I hadn't until then, and I didn't care whether they wore fancy uniforms and spoke nicely or were snot-nosed, with their arses hanging out of their trousers.

Watson's was a relief to me, although I was too young to recognise it as such. For a start, it got me out of our loveless house in Merchiston. (It didn't take me long to realise that's what it was. The very first time my best class friend Bobby Hannah took me home for tea, aged seven, I knew that the way his folks behaved towards each other was the way it was supposed to happen.)

I did very well at school, almost from the start. I might have lagged behind in English initially, thanks to Grandma Paloma's habit of speaking Spanish and Catalan to my dad and me . . . and even to my mother when she was reproving her for something . . . but I caught up quickly, and I was always ahead of the game numerically.

I found that I was popular too; it didn't mean anything to me at the time, but looking back, I must have had something going for me. Nobody ever bullied me, or made jokes about my name. Mind you, I was a big lad even then. When teams were picked for playground football, I was an early choice, until eventually I became one of the pickers. In truth, I sailed through junior school, and when I won the medal for top boy in the final year, nobody seemed surprised. I thought that might have drawn a small smile from Grandma Paloma, but it didn't; she seemed to take it as a fair return on her investment, no more.

My mother wasn't around to congratulate me. When I was nine, she gave up; I assumed it was in the face of my dad's disinterest and Grandma Paloma's undisguised contempt. I arrived home from school one October afternoon and she was gone, back to Falkirk, back to the dour and ill-tempered Inglis grandparents whom I had met eight times in my life, at their place on each occasion, for they were never invited to Merchiston. For a couple of years she sent me birthday cards, then she gave up on that too. For the rest of my childhood, she was lost to me; not that I missed her.

There was one thing that Grandma deigned to teach me herself, and that was music. She had been raised in the era of real home entertainment, the kind that you make for yourself without the aid of computer game designers or television production companies. She was an accomplished pianist, and began to teach me almost as soon as I was old enough to sit on the stool and reach the keys of the baby grand in the music room of our big house in Merchiston. My dad was tone deaf; when I was eleven years old, she told me, once I had attained a standard of proficiency that satisfied her, that I was a second chance, given her by God, to pass on her skill. Actually, He'd had help, but I was too young to point that out to her at that time . . . indeed maybe I was never old enough! She taught me to play in her own classical style, but when

I was twelve, I discovered Thelonius Monk, and that was it for Chopin.

In 1975, when I was thirteen years old, Franco died.

You should understand this; I had never heard of the Generalissimo until his death was reported on telly, and Grandma Paloma roared, 'Yes!' from deep within her armchair.

'Who's he?' I asked.

She glared at me. 'The Devil,' she replied, 'gone to hell.'

I remember thinking, but being smart enough to keep it to myself, that there was an element of contradiction in what she had said, since by definition, if he'd been Satan he'd been there all along.

My dad always played his cards very close to his chest . . . literally, as one of his old poker buddies told me many years later. He sat tight for two years after the old Caudillo was put in the ground, watching as King Juan Carlos led Spain to democracy. And then, with no warning, without a single leak to Scotland's ferret-like business press, he sold the booming pub chain, one hundred and twenty outlets by then, to a major UK brewer for a sum that might have made Grandpa Xavi burst out of his grave with pride . . . or perhaps that would have been astonishment.

As I should have expected in my family, I found out about the sale at school. I had just started my fourth year in Watson's secondary when the news broke, with a bang that was loud enough to make the front page of the *Scotsman*. Scott Livingstone, another of my class pals, although not as close as Bobby, thrust a copy of the paper into my hand as we walked into morning assembly, folded so that the story was all I could see.

'You're a dark horse, Xavi,' he said, loud enough to draw a few others towards us, including the delectable Grace Starshine, a blonde Jewish girl whose Hebrew name had been anglicised a few generations before.

Grace and I had started school in the same class, on the same day. We were both chubby kids aged five; she was as fair as I was dark. But we grew at the same pace, shed our puppy fat at the same time and entered the adolescent world together. Grace hung with the girls and I

5

hung with the boys, until the time for kids' play was past, and then quite naturally we hung with each other. A few years later, Bobby remarked that we had been joined at the eyes from the start. He was a good objective judge, for he had no interest in Grace himself, nor in any other girl, or woman.

As I took the paper, I stared at the headline, then scanned the first paragraph. (I was on the editorial committee of the school's semi-official newspaper, and knew even then that every good story stands on its intro.) 'Fucking hell,' I gasped as it sank in, drawing a tut from Grace. 'If you think I'm secretive, mate,' I told Scott, 'you want to meet my old man. This is news to me, and I've just had breakfast with him and my grandma.'

'They never said?' Grace exclaimed, forgiving me for the first of many expletives that I was to utter in her presence.

I shook my head. 'Not a fu . . .' I strangled the second before it emerged. 'Not a word.'

'So when do you think you'll be going?' Scott asked.

'Going?'

'Read on. It says your family's moving back to Spain.' He glanced out of the school hall window at the September rain. 'Lucky sod.'

'You reckon?' I muttered, as I thrust the paper back at him.

I wasn't at my best that day. It was all I could do to keep from bolting out of assembly and running all the way to my dad's office. But it wasn't his office any more, was it? He'd sold the bloody place, and as I saw it, he'd sold my inheritance, without a murmur in my direction. So, instead, I festered through classes until mid-afternoon, when I cut rugby practice (rugby was the winter team game for boys at Watson's), with the approval of a sympathetic games master, and walked the short distance back to Merchiston, my mood growing darker with every stride.

As I stalked up the drive, I saw my dad's Mercedes in the garage: he'd left the up-and-over door open. There was another car, parked to the side, one I hadn't seen there before.

Grandma Paloma spotted me coming, from her upstairs eyrie in the small sitting room off her bedroom. She rapped on the window which overlooked the front garden, and beckoned to me, a summons to her presence. As I'd grown older, the old lady and I (actually, she was only seventy-three at that time, but in Scotland she always dressed like an ancient) had developed a degree of mutual respect. She might have been stern, but I recognised that she was fair with it, and maybe even kind, although she'd never have admitted it if I'd put that accusation to her.

She was no miser, that was for sure. Whenever there was shopping to be done for me, clothes, for example, or other school stuff, she took care of it. We'd get in a taxi and head for Jenners, or Aitken and Niven, where she had accounts, and that would be that. (I didn't set foot in Marks and Spencer until I was eighteen years old.) She made my twice yearly appointments with the dentist, and took me there until I was old enough to go by myself, and could be trusted to turn up. She handed out the pocket money too. Periodically she'd ask me how much my school friends were getting, I'd pick the highest weekly amount that I knew (Scott Livingstone was my usual benchmark; he claimed to be market leader in that department) and she'd give me a little more than whatever it was, from a stash that she kept in her sitting room. As a result I was always flush; there wasn't a Stones, Clash or Sex Pistols album that I didn't have. (Looking back, I suspect that my incipient dark side had made me reject the clean-cut freshness of the Bee Gees, the Eagles and the like, for their anarchic rivals.) She paid the domestics from the same cash box. We'd always had a gardener, and since my mother had left, a cleaner. My dad could have afforded a cook, but that was out of the question. Grandma Paloma was old-style Spanish: the kitchen was hers and hers alone. Not even her son was allowed in there, although I got to watch, and help, occasionally.

I knocked lightly on her door . . . she expected that, even when she'd summoned me . . . and went in at her call. She was standing in front of the window, looking up at me, but not by much. Even in her seventies her back was ramrod straight. Me? At fifteen I was six feet one, on my way to being one centimetre over two metres tall.

'You've seen the newspapers, I suppose,' she began. She spoke English, and so I knew we were in for a serious discussion, not the household chat.

'Yes, Grandma Paloma,' I replied, 'I've seen them.'

'I thought so, for you arrive home with a face like thunder.' Coming from her, I took that as a compliment.

'He never told me, Grandma,' I said . . . or maybe I growled.

'That was his choice. I might have done differently, but I wouldn't tell him what to do. It's grown-ups' business, and you're still only a child.'

I bridled at the word. I was a teenage hormonal maelstrom, capable of some very grown-up feelings, especially when it came to Grace Starshine. 'I'm fifteen,' I protested.

'Exactly,' she snorted.

At some point Grandma Paloma and I had crossed a line, on the other side of which intimidation didn't work. I sensed my dad was a little afraid of her, but I wasn't; I knew his mother better than he did. 'Exactly nothing,' I shot back. 'It said in the *Scotsman* that we're moving to Spain. I don't want to.'

Her natural frown turned into the scowl that I'd known since infancy. 'Xavi, what you want is not the most important thing in the world.'

'It is to me.'

'Then you are selfish, boy,' she snapped. 'Your father did not choose to come here, neither did your grandfather, and neither did I. We were forced to, by the devil Franco. Now he's gone, and with King Juan Carlos, Spain is safe for us again, so we can go back.'

'But I'm not Spanish!' I protested. 'I'm Scottish; I was born here and all my friends were born here. I've got a British passport,' I added for good measure. That was true; I'd been on a school cruise in the Mediterranean two years before, and had visited Rome.

'You are your father's son,' she said stiffly. 'That makes you Spanish.'

'I'm my mother's son as well, and that makes me Scottish.' That was the wrong thing to say.

'Your mother will not be mentioned in this house,' Grandma Paloma hissed. 'She was happy to leave it.'

'And . . .' An older version of me tried to retort that I was capable of making the same choice, but she was right; the child that remained in fifteen-year-old Xavi Aislado couldn't get the words out. All I could do was glare back at her, knowing that I couldn't win. Much of what I grew into may have come from Grandma Paloma, but at that stage I was still a shadow of her.

'Your father has made his decision, *nino*,' she said, more gently. 'He is with his lawyer now, telling him to sell this house. We are going to live near Girona, and we may also have a place by the sea.'

'And me?'

As I asked the question, I heard knuckles tap the door behind me. 'Come, Josep,' Grandma called.

My dad stepped into the room, unsmiling, stocky, three-piece-suited. He looked me up and down . . . no, probably just up, since I was four inches taller than him, even then. 'You're angry,' he said, simply, in the almost-but-not-quite-refined Scots accent that he'd acquired in his childhood. 'You're standing there like you want to banjo somebody.'

'I don't want us to go to Spain, Dad,' I repeated for his benefit.

'So what do you want? Do you want to move in with those folk in Falkirk? Your mother's married a fucking policeman.' That was complete news to me. He nodded a quick apology, for his language, to his mother; it was a token that I'd seen a few hundred times before, and learned myself, the same gesture I'd made to Grace a few hours before. 'Maybe he'll take you under his wing,' he added. I said nothing but I must have blanched, for he gave me a grin that might have been a sneer. 'No, I didn't think so,' he said.

The half-smile melted. 'Here's the deal, Xavi,' he continued, bluntly. 'You're in your fourth year, and you've got exams coming up. If I

9

withdraw you from Watson's now, then all the money that Grandma Paloma's made me pour into the place will have gone down the crapper. So you'll stay on there, as a boarder. I've checked with the headmaster; you can do that. You'll have your own accounts at Jenners and at that other place. You'll get the same allowance your grandma gives you, with a bit more for books and stuff. Pass your O grades, and you'll stay on to do your Highers. After that, we'll talk about university.'

'In Spain?'

'Not unless you want that. As I'm sure you've told Grandma Paloma, you're Scottish. Fuck me . . . sorry, *Madre* . . . so am I, to all intents and purposes.'

'Then why are you going?'

'Because I promised my father, before you were born; he made it a condition of his will that when the time was right I'd take your grandma back to Spain, and he made me sign a declaration that I'd do that.'

'But not me? I wasn't mentioned?'

'I just said; you weren't born at that time. Plus you'd been conceived on the wrong side of the blanket. He didn't give a fuck . . . sorry, Ma . . . about you.'

And that, I suppose, is when Xavi Aislado started to live up to his name.

'How did a miserable cunt like him ever get to be managing editor of a paper like this, Mr Fisher?'

'Mitch, son, if you listened to him, rather than throwing a paddy every time he rips a piece off you, you might just make a journalist. But if you carry on like that, then next time he tells me he wants to fire you, I'm not going to say a word to talk him out of it. You just got your arse kicked because you filed a story yesterday that we put on page three when the Scotsman and the Herald ran their versions as page-one lead. We are pissing against a hurricane like we always have; we're the Saltire, the independent voice of reason that strikes a balance between the two establishment Scottish blacktops. We don't just have to be as good as the opposition; we have to be better. That piece of yours will have them both laughing their rocks off at us.'

'I didn't put it on page three, Aislado did. The story was okay. The company's gone bust and the workforce is on the dole. That's the important part.'

'That's Mister Aislado to you, chum. Your story was deficient in one major fact . . . Mister Connor. The business in question, AlgeBra, the one that's just gone belly up with the loss of two hundred and fifty jobs, is owned by a guy who's the subject of a Canadian arrest warrant, and who hasn't been seen since he was bundled into a car outside his house in Toronto last Sunday afternoon, by two guys who were definitely not the Mounties. You missed that.'

'The police never told me!'

'They didn't tell the other papers either. They found out because their people followed up properly, and made inquiries in Canada about the guy. You made yours in our cuttings library. Now I'll answer your question. Xavi Aislado got where he is because he's the best journalist I've ever met in my fucking life.'

'Aye, sure, plus his old man owns the place.'

'And you know why? Because Xavi made him buy it after that Russian bastard ripped off the pension fund and had the banks about to close us down. Xavi didn't have to do that. He's turned down better jobs than the one he's got now. He could have gone anywhere, even to bloody Spain. But he didn't; he stayed here and he leaned on his dad . . . a guy he's always fought with, by the way . . . so that ungrateful wee shites like you could stay in work.'

'And you too.'

'Aye, and especially me. I'm sixty-two years old, boy, and my pension was stolen by that fucking Russian. Remember what happened? No, maybe you don't, maybe you were too wrapped up in yourself even then. Xavi found out that something was going on, and he did an investigative job on his own boss. Then he ran the story, in the man's own fucking newspaper, no less. The Russian did a runner to North Cyprus, and the finance director went to jail. All the assets had been stripped out of the company, and out of the pension fund; the Saltire was bust. Then, just when it looked like we'd all be out on the street, InterMedia Girona stepped in and bought the show off the receiver. They couldn't save our pensions, though, so I still need a job and I need Xavi and his dad to make the profits that are going to fill up the fund again, so that maybe, just maybe, one day I can retire. Now fuck off out of my sight and think about being a proper reporter while you've still got the chance.'

'Okay, John, I get the message. You sound like you and he are really good friends.'

'Xavi wouldn't say that. Xavi has colleagues, and that's the way he wants it.' But he calls me Jock, he thought. Only my friends do that. 'You called him miserable, and I can see why. But he's not. He's sad, the saddest man I know, in fact.'

'What's he got to be sad about? He's a millionaire's son and he runs a successful newspaper.'

'None of that makes you happy, lad, not by itself. Now fuck off and get to work. I mean it.'

Two

My dad could have chosen a better time to put a Merchiston mansion on the property market, especially at the sort of money he was after. It was 1977 and as the media reminded us every day, the British economy was the laughing stock of the developed world, as was its failing government. Times were tight and cash was even tighter. The situation was complicated further by his Catalan heritage, emphasised by Grandma Paloma whenever he showed signs of wavering, which forbade him from even considering a compromise over the price that he had put on the place.

Eventually, though, the following spring, he found one of those suckers that are said to be born every minute, an advertising magnate who had just sold his agency to an international operation, and was looking for somewhere to dump some cash, other than into the tremulous stock market, which had still to be convinced by the Saatchi brothers that the Tories really were coming.

The delay didn't affect me. Grandma Paloma had decreed that I should move into the school boarding house straight away, rather than face the disruption of a change that might come, for all any of us knew, right at the time when I would be cramming for my exams. There was no debate over the matter, but had there been I'd probably have agreed with her.

My new situation brought with it a subtle change in my status within the school. My friends didn't desert me, but I realised very quickly that they were looking at me in a different way, not as a freak, but as someone who was no longer normal in the way they were. Only Bobby Hannah and Scott Livingstone had ever been invited to Merchiston.

That was at my grandma's insistence, since I'd been entertained by their parents and such hospitality should be returned. I'd been wary in advance of their visits, but they had been more amused than awed by the old battleaxe, and had been seriously impressed by her cooking. Once I became a boarder, and the house went up for sale, our social relationship seemed to change; we stayed pals, but there were no more home visits. I'd become Johnny Foreigner.

But it was different with Grace. Looking back, I should have guessed that her hormones were rioting too, but at the time my only assumption was that she was sorry for me. As I've said, we'd always been chums as nippers, but as we grew we became more so, without either of us realising it was happening. (No, that may not have been true; she probably knew all along.) While Grandma Paloma was still there . . . my father spent much of his time in Spain, even before the house was sold . . . and the house was stuck in the buyer's market of the time, I'd go back to Merchiston at the weekend, and hang out there, alone, but towards the end of the year Grace invited me for Sunday lunch, with her parents.

Her dad, Rodney, was a businessman; Grace had told me that he made pharmaceutical products in a factory out in West Lothian, but it didn't mean much to me, since at that time I didn't know what they were. He was very polite, asked me about school, and seemed genuinely interested in me. All through lunch, I was expecting to be questioned about my dad and my grandmother, but that never happened. He seemed more interested in my sporting interests than in my family. Her mother, Magda, was nice too, still in her thirties then, a blonde looker like her daughter, and such a pleasant woman that she made me think of my own mother, something I hadn't done in six years. She had been so different, so dull, so uncaring; for the first time I began to ask myself whether I might have been responsible for some of her unhappiness.

Grace and I had our first official date, at the Dominion Cinema in Morningside, in January 1978, three months before her sixteenth birthday, and one before mine. It had taken me weeks to pluck up the courage to ask her, and God I was nervous. I wore a rugby top I'd just bought on my tab at Aitken and Niven, and Wrangler jeans from Jenners. She wore a white blouse and a fairly short dark skirt. I didn't want to blow anything, so I didn't even try to hold her hand; Scott had told me that should be my minimum objective. I just sat and watched the film. It was *Star Wars IV*, the original; it had been running for months, yet neither of us had seen it. Yes indeed, I behaved immaculately; too immaculately as it turned out, for Grace eventually kissed me, rather than the other way around. I remember: it was just as Han Solo decided not to run off with his reward money, and joined the battle instead.

She turned out to be pretty good at kissing, a natural. I wasn't too bad either, once she'd persuaded me that it wasn't supposed to involve eating her face. It was something we did a lot after that.

Some other things in my life changed that year. Academically, I wasn't troubled. I was going to cruise through my O grades; I knew that and so did everyone else. But on other fronts, my new domestic independence began to show through in my thinking. Most dramatically, I chucked rugby. This came as a great blow to the games master, when I told him at the beginning of February. I'd already played for the First XV, in the back row of the scrum, and he'd been counting on me for another couple of years, but in truth I didn't like the game. There was no real skill required, not by my kind of forward, at any rate, and as a spectacle it was ugly; I didn't particularly like hurting other people either, as I did once or twice, accidentally, when clearing them out of the way to win the ball. The coach did his best to make me feel guilty with a few choice phrases that boiled down to, 'You're letting the school down, Aislado.' I told him that I wasn't going to be anyone's conscript. I could have told him also that I'd discussed my decision with my grandmother, and that her opinion was that the school was there to serve me as best it could, and not the other way round.

Scott Livingstone wasn't impressed when I told him what I'd done.

He didn't quite have it when it came to rugby. He lacked the self-discipline that the game requires and was sent off a couple of times in the junior grades, once for the unforgivable sin of eye-gouging, but he had been enjoying being a pal of the rising star, the future Head Boy. On the other hand, Bobby Hannah was delighted, as my decision pretty much guaranteed his place in the first team once we all moved up to Fifth Year. As for Grace, she was pleased too, since she reckoned it would mean she'd see more of me. Her father may have thought so too, for he gave me a piece of advice that wound up taking even more of my time.

'A young chap like you should always do some kind of sport, Xavi,' Rod insisted one weekend when I was at their place, supposedly studying with Grace. 'I have a friend who's on the committee of Tynecastle Boys football club. Would you like me to get you a trial?'

Why not? I thought. *I'd be rude to refuse.* Grace said nothing; she knew I hadn't played with a round ball since primary school.

What she didn't anticipate was that the club's head coach would take one look at me and put me between the sticks. In those days that's what you did with a six-foot two-inch, still growing, sixteen-year-old. To my surprise, I loved my new role in my new game. I had big, safe hands, I'd learned enough playing rugby to be able to dispose of physical challenges, and there was something about being a goalie that appealed to my solitary nature. In no time at all, by the end of the season, I had leapfrogged my age-group team and was in the under-eighteen side, and I'd had a trial for Heart of Midlothian.

My old man was in the middle of selling the house when that happened, and I was in the middle of my O grades. I didn't bother to tell him until Hearts had come back with a contract offer, and I probably wouldn't have if I hadn't needed his signature on the form, because I was still a minor. When I called to tell him, he asked me only one question. 'How much are they going to pay you?'

In fact they were going to pay me nothing at all, not till I was seventeen, and little more than bugger all even then, but the offer was enough to make me feel better about myself than I ever had before. I was a living paradox: my family was leaving me behind, and yet I felt more settled than ever I had, unencumbered by close ties other than the one that was binding me to Grace, and that one I'd chosen for myself . . . at least that's what I believed.

There was very little time between the end of the school term and the start of pre-season training. I spent all of it in Spain, helping Grandma Paloma move into the country house that my dad had bought in a village a few kilometres from Girona, and where he'd been living for a few months, adding muscle to my growing frame by helping the guys from Pickford's heave the massive furniture that she had brought from Edinburgh, as she barked orders at us.

'She's fucking ferocious, your granny,' one of the movers whispered to me as we took a break, under parasols set up beside the swimming pool that I reckoned would never be used by anyone but me.

I remember having to mask a smile as I nodded agreement. 'Aye,' I concurred, 'but I bet you think it's an act.'

I hardly saw my dad in the time I was there. He would disappear in the morning and return in the evening, leaving Grandma Paloma and me to get the place sorted. It was another monster, bigger and much older than the Edwardian place in Merchiston had been. Grandma told me that it had been built in the eighteenth century by the Count of Somewhere-or-other. She called it *la masia*, the farmhouse, and indeed that's what it was. The walled and gated grounds were at the very least six times the area of Hearts' football stadium, with orchards, lawns, water features and flower beds. When I saw it for the first time, I wondered how she was going to be able to manage it, but that turned out to be no problem. In a far corner there was a cottage which housed the gardener and housekeeper, Pablo and Carmen, a middle-aged husband and wife team that my old man had inherited from the previous owner. There was a daughter too, in her early twenties, I judged, also named Carmen, a girl as dark as Grace was blonde, but she was very much in the background. My imagination cast her as a vacationing student like me, but I didn't get round to asking her whether I was right.

During that stay, my only proper conversation with my dad didn't take place until he drove me to Barcelona Airport (it was pretty rudimentary, in those pre-Olympic days) for my return flight. By that time, the boy he'd left behind in Edinburgh was long gone; I had never been afraid of him, but he had always been distant from me and maybe I had lacked the confidence to reach out . . . or found no need, with Grandma filling the roles of two parents. There on the edge of adulthood, I found that I was bolder, and able to be blunt.

'What are you up to?' I asked him as he steered his new left-hand drive Mercedes . . . the marque was his personal statement . . . carefully down the hazardous road south.

I saw him frown, in profile. 'What d'you mean?'

'You're supposed to be retired, but it's just like it was in Edinburgh. We have breakfast and then you're gone.'

'When did I ever say I was retiring, Xavi boy? I'm forty-seven years old. Do you expect me to sit on my arse for the rest of my life?'

I realised that he was right. I had assumed that he had settled for playing golf and poker through his twilight years; but I had never asked. I looked at him, more closely than I ever had before, and saw that in reality he was younger than the mental picture I carried around in my head when we were apart, which was, of course, most of the time.

'So what are you doing?' It was strange; as I put the question I was aware of the curiosity in my own voice, and aware too that I had grown up without actually giving a toss about my old man's life, just as he had seemed to take little interest in mine.

'I've bought a newspaper group,' he told me, his tone matter-of-fact, as if he was saying he'd bought that day's edition of a newspaper. 'It's called InterMedia, all one word. It's based in Girona, owns a daily there . . . it's called GironaDia; not the most imaginative name, I'll grant you, but what the hell . . . and a few smaller titles along the Costa Brava. There are a couple of radio stations too.'

'Are you that rich, Dad, that you can do something like that?'

'Yes,' he nodded. 'But it was quite cheap, as it happens. The company was on its uppers; Franco didn't care for the owners, so the papers all had to be po-faced and their circulation was lousy as a result. I've been in control for six months and the figures are up already.'

'What do you know about running newspapers?'

'Fuck all, but I know how to run a business. It's all about keeping the income higher than the overheads, that's all, and the higher the better.'

'What do you know about Spain?'

'Not much more than I know about running a newspaper. But I do know this. I've cut the payroll by thirty per cent; the people who are left are all the more motivated, so they're selling more advertising, more newspapers and attracting more radio listeners.'

'You sacked people?' I bellowed. I'd never raised my voice to him before, but that didn't occur to me then. 'You put them out of work?'

'No, they did that themselves, by being useless at their jobs. You're indignant, Xavi, and that disappoints me. Business isn't for poofs . . . not that I'm calling you one, mind. You have to be tough. When I ran the pubs, I operated what I called an acceptable level of pilferage in each one. It goes on in that trade, endemically, and you'll never eradicate it, so I tolerated a wee bit, usually three per cent tops, although it varied from area to area. But if it went over that in any unit I sacked everyone in the place.'

The weirdest feeling swept over me; I was having an adult conversation with my old man, and I knew that I had to keep my end up. I recalled a phrase I'd read in *Private Eye* a couple of weeks before. 'Dad,' I told him, more calmly than before, 'that's called shooting the wounded.'

He gave a strange growling chuckle. 'My secretary in Edinburgh used to call it "flushing the brownies".'

I blew up again. 'Then she was as big a cunt as you,' I yelled. 'Those are people you're talking about, with families, wives and kids and stuff.'

'Hey!' he shouted back at me. 'You watch your . . .' He stopped, in mid-sentence, then surprised me by laughing. 'No, don't do that at all. You're starting to talk like me and I should like that. You're not starting to think like me yet, but time will change that, make you less of a bleeding-heart liberal. I've got to admit you're right about Esme Waller. That's exactly what she is; that's why I've got her learning Spanish back in Edinburgh. I want to get her a work permit, bring her out here.'

'Who is she, exactly?'

'I told you, she's my old secretary.' He paused. 'Ah, I bet you're wondering if I'm shagging her.' The bastard had been reading my mind. 'Well, the answer's no, for two reasons. One she's wee, fat, and fifty, with a face like a bag of arseholes, and two, if I did that I'd be putting too many cards in her hand. Never shag the hired help, Xavi son; it gives them power over you and you mustn't have that. I learned that the hard way.'

'Dad, you're . . .' My sixteen-year-old vocabulary betrayed me. I couldn't tell him what he was, so he did it for me.

'Unbelievably crude, blunt and thoroughly distasteful? Yes, my lad, I am, but I am also right, and you will come to recognise that in time. This wee football adventure of yours will help. If you think I'm a bastard, you wait till you really get to know some of the people who work in that game. And it's not just in football. You should hear the way some of my journalists talk to each other.'

He paused again, twisting his head to look at me for a second . . . in those days it wasn't safe to take your eye off a Spanish road for any longer than that. 'How are you and Rodney Starshine's girl getting along?' he asked.

If I'd been old enough to be behind the wheel, we'd have been dead, for I'd have taken us right off the road. 'How do you know about Grace and me?' I demanded. 'Grandma Paloma doesn't even know that.'

'Do you think I'm not interested in you at all?'

'Never mind that. How do you know? Have you had that Esme woman spying on me?'

'No, son,' he replied quietly. 'The school gives me reports on you; it was part of the deal when you became a boarder.'

'Bugger that! I think I'll leave.'

'We both know you won't. It's fair enough; pastoral care, I think they call it . . . or some such. They're *in loco parentis* on my behalf; they would be failing in their duty to me if they didn't know about your relationships.'

'Okay, Grace is my girlfriend. So what?'

'So you're both sixteen.' Suddenly he seemed awkward with me; that was a first. 'Look, Xavi, we're never had the wee chat, man to man, but if we had, I wouldn't have been talking to you about the birds and the bees crap. That's a ridiculous bloody analogy. I'd have been talking about the boys and the girls and the more or less permanent hard-on that lads your age walk around with. All I'm going to say to you now is that you may have been baptised into a church that insists that French letters are a sin, but that's a part of its teaching you should ignore. Either keep your cock in your pants, son, or keep it encased in rubber when you have to. That's all I have to say on the subject, but if Grace's mother hasn't said something similar to her by now, I'll be surprised.'

It wasn't a discussion I wanted to continue, and not only because I didn't want to prolong our mutual embarrassment. I didn't want to tell him either that he was behind the times; Grace was on the pill, courtesy of the Brook Centre in Fountainbridge, where patient confidentiality was guaranteed, as maybe it wouldn't have been if she'd gone to her GP. 'Point taken,' I said, then I changed tack. 'How do you know Grace's dad?'

'I've met him. Mostly at Tynecastle; his seat was near mine.'

Still more of a journey into the unknown. 'I never knew you were a Jambo, Dad.'

'You know fuck all about me, son.' Then he shrugged. 'But that's not your fault. As it happens, I'm not, but I always bought a couple of seasons through the pub business. Mostly I used them as sweeteners for managers, or suppliers.'

But never for me, I thought.

We drove on in silence for a while. He had run out of things to say; but I hadn't. 'What about Grandma Paloma?' I asked him as he turned on to the road that circled Barcelona and led to the airport, south of the city.

'What about her?'

'Who's going to look after her, if you're never there?'

He bellowed with spontaneous laughter. 'Look after her? You're kidding me. She is, Xavi; she'll look after herself, just like she always has, even when your grandpa was alive. I'm not saying that my old man was an idiot, far from it, but he wasn't the sharpest blade in the knife drawer either. He never did a fucking thing that she didn't tell him to do. It was her father that owned the first of those three hotels in the old days, and when he died and she inherited it, it was her who told my father how to run the business and grow it. When the Civil War clouds were gathering, she saw them in the distance when hardly anyone else was looking, and she found the gullible French bloke that took them off their hands.'

He risked another glance in my direction. 'After the three of us moved to Edinburgh, your grandfather would have bought a fucking boarding house somewhere and that would have been the end of it. It was my mother that told him to get into the pub trade, and it was her that made sure that I was trained to take over, eventually. Even the brewery was her idea, because it was going for a song at the time. Trust me, you don't want to worry about Grandma Paloma. She's got what she wants, the thing that's driven her for over forty years; she's back home in Spain, and she can die happy . . . not that she's any plans to do that. She's even dancing the Sardana again, that strange Catalan thing that Franco banned, with the other old harpies, in the village square on the saints' days.'

He chuckled. 'Who do you think wrote my father's will for him? Who do you think got me to sign that agreement? She did. No, you shouldn't worry about her, Xavi son, you should be happy for her, and for yourself. You may not realise it, and she doesn't either, to be fair to her, but all your life she's fucking suffocated you. Now she's cut you loose and you can breathe your own air.'

'What's up?'

'They're kids, Magda, just kids.'

'Yeah, aren't they just? Does she remind you of anyone?'

'Who?'

'Wrong answer, Rod. "Yes dear, she's just like you were at that age, and that big serious lad might have been me in another time." That's what you were supposed to say.'

'I'll go with the first of those, but I was never like him. Was I?'

'You were to me. You still are, in your intensity. Oh sure, you're many things that Xavi isn't. You have a clear sense of purpose; he hasn't, not yet at any rate. You're devious when you want to be; he hasn't a sneaky bone in his body, and I hope he never has.'

'What do you mean, devious?'

'Don't deny it, now. I know damn well why you introduced the boy to your friend at the football club. You wanted to give him a way of burning off his energy, or maybe should I say, another way.'

'Nonsense. A big lad like that, he should be involved in sport.'

'Sure, whatever you say.'

'I'm not devious.'

'Okay, let me put it another way. As a parent, you're more conservative than you like to admit.'

'No I'm not. When have I ever denied Grace anything?'

'Never. You've been the soul of generosity, all through her childhood. You've raised her with gentleness and love, tended her with even more care than you give to those tomato plants in your greenhouse. But she's in fruit now, and the picker's come to harvest her. You're not ready for that though, Rod, are you?'

'I'd like to think I am, but like I say, they're only sixteen, the pair of them, plus . . .'

'Go on.'

'No, it wouldn't be fair.'

'You've started, so you'll finish, chum. What were you going to say?'

'That I'm not sure about this picker, that's all.'

'Then you're damn right it's not fair. Xavi's a nice boy; he's intelligent, he's popular at school, he's courteous . . .'

'And he's sad, too. I'm not sure he's bringing the right sort of baggage for our kid.'

'Why do you say he's sad? He looks happy with Grace.'

'Look at his family background.'

'Rod, his dad's a multimillionaire . . .'

'. . . who's pretty much abandoned Xavi in Scotland. And his mum?'

'I don't know anything about her, other than that she left his dad and him a while ago. Xavi never talks about her.'

'Exactly. Don't you find that just a wee bit sad?'

'I would if I was in his shoes, but I think that he's adjusted to it.'

'I wish I was as sure. Joe Aislado got rid of his wife at the first opportunity, that's what they say. The marriage was a disaster from the start. That's not a healthy environment for a boy to grow up in.'

'Maybe not, but he's made a damn good job of it, as far as I can see.'

'And maybe I see further. He's still got issues to sort out.'

'Then our daughter is the ideal girl to help him. Because she loves him, and he loves her.'

'Magda, I repeat: they're sixteen years old.'

'And you're patronising, as well as devious. When we were their age . . .'

'I remember what we got up to when we were their age.'

'Ah, double standards as well; another in your list of faults. You remember getting into my knickers then, but you're not prepared . . . Rod, you've had sixteen years and more to get ready for this time. Live with it, for you know what? If Xavi was your son and Grace was someone else's daughter . . . Need I say more? Honestly?'

'I suppose not.'

'Good. We're making progress. Worry if you will, I suppose you see it as your job as a dad. But don't worry for Grace; she's unbreakable, that one. Worry for Xavi.'

'Why should I do that?'

'Because apart from us, I doubt if any others will. His upbringing has been so narrow, I'm not sure that he'll be ready to cope when life kicks him in the balls, as one day it surely will.'

Three

I had a lot of thinking to do as that 737 climbed slowly over the Pyrenees, heading for the Heathrow stopover. In a day of weirdness, I found myself in a strange situation, looking in on my own life from the outside, analysing each phase, my early years, as far back as I could remember, my progress through school, my choice of friends, the solitary situation to which I had come.

My dad had been spot on about one thing: the entire course of my life had been plotted and shaped by Grandma Paloma, even those decisions that I had believed I was taking for myself as a young adult. Yes, even they had been discussed with her, her view on each one taken and invariably followed, up to and including the signing offer from Hearts. The saving grace was that as far as I could tell she had been right about every one.

But did I feel suffocated by her, as my dad had claimed? No, I didn't. Instead, I realised what a lonely little boy I would have been without her attention to me, whatever had motivated it, whether she had been genuinely interested in my well-being, or had been merely using me as a means of asserting her own status, establishing bragging rights within her small Edinburgh circle about her grandson at George Watson's College. Whatever my dad had said, I had never felt stifled by her. When it came to him, though, that was another matter.

He had power over me, as I saw it; he controlled my life, for that time at least and for my university years, should I choose to take that road. Yes, I'd be making money from football with a bit of luck, but I'm talking about the seventies, not the noughties, and it wasn't going to be great, unless I turned out to be the new Gordon Banks. My dad had me by the shorts; I loathed much of what he stood for with the righteousness of youth (although I was grudgingly pleased by his new business direction, even if his philosophy offended me) and I had just told him so. He could pull the plug on me any time he chose, casting me out to make my own way.

But couldn't I do that? Couldn't I pull the plug on him instead? I asked myself the question. If I did that Watson's would have to go, but Hearts had a good reputation for looking after young players, and I was sure I could continue to study for my Highers at a state school, maybe James Gillespie's, then on to the arts degree that I had been contemplating, all the time flat-sharing with other students.

Sure, I could do it, I convinced myself. And then I thought of Grandma Paloma, and of how she would react. I had no idea of her motives, but I was pretty sure that as long as she was alive my dad would continue to support me . . . or else. A grand gesture on my part would only have one effect; I would be spiting myself. I might also have considered the possibility that it would hurt her, had I not been certain that she was immune to hurt.

By the time my second flight touched down in Edinburgh and I was met by Grace and her parents, my head was sorted and I could see a road ahead. I even felt a surge of pleasure as I checked back into the school boarding house. I was one of only two summer residents, the other being a lad called wee Dave Colquhoun, a year younger than me, the son of a widowed army officer who was on a tour of duty in Northern Ireland. I was closer to living independently than I had ever been in my life. Grace even came to visit, although we had no opportunity for privacy, as wee Dave and I were under the shrewd and watchful eye of a conscientious den-mother, or matron, as I declined to call her, who, I had no doubt, had seen it all before, many times. It wasn't just her presence that kept us celibate, though. As the son of a one-parent family I sympathised with my little housemate, and so I'd often include him in what Grace and I were doing, to the extent that by the time the rest of the boarders arrived back for the new term, we'd become a regular threesome at the Dominion.

Pre-season training with Hearts went well too, although I found out very quickly that my father hadn't been kidding when he'd warned me about workplace attitudes and methods in the football industry. The physical side was harder than I'd expected, even though the trainers made allowances for the fact that I was still a growing lad, and the goal-keeping coach was not a man to use a conventional adjective . . . or even a hyphen . . . when an expletive would serve. He was very quick to give me a sense of perspective, and of my place in the pecking order, telling me that I would be lucky to get more than a couple of starts with the reserves and that I could look forward to a full season in the youth squad. But if he was trying to give me a competitive edge he was wasting his time. They weren't paying me at that stage, so I still saw the game as a hobby, not a career, and intended being fully focused on my school work, for another year at least.

These shared low expectations, the coach's and mine, didn't stop me having hero status when the autumn school term began. I was even more of an oddity than I had been before: a budding professional footballer, at a rugby-playing school. Watson's had spawned a few of those over the years, but nobody could remember one who was still a pupil. Even Scott Livingstone seemed impressed with me once again, until Grace, Bobby Hannah and I were made prefects and he wasn't. The signs of renewed closeness disappeared overnight, although he stayed chummy with Grace, and continued to treat Bobby as Piglet to his Pooh. Where did I fit in that analogy? I could only have been Eeyore.

And that was it with the changes, for a while. My life fell into a comfortable pattern of school, study, evening training, Saturday games and weekend evenings with Grace, usually at the movies or at her place. Her mother and father seemed to have accepted me as a permanent fixture, although I wondered if that might have changed had they known what happened on the odd occasions when we had the house to ourselves.

On the field, I did a little better than my coach had predicted; I started the playing season with every goalie's dream: a string of clean sheets behind a crap defence. As a result, the assistant manager took an interest in me, and I became a regular starter in the reserves, playing at some of the biggest grounds in Scotland, even if they were empty of all but a few spectators.

My football commitments meant that I couldn't go to Spain for Christmas. For the first time in my life I received my own Christmas cards at my own address, and one of them was from my grandmother. I was astonished when I opened it, even though I'd sent one to her, and another to my dad. (No, I didn't get one from him, and I never have.) I was amused too. She signed it 'Paloma Puig i Garcia'; Spanish women don't change their surnames on marriage, and during forty years in Scotland she had never allowed herself to be called 'Mrs Aislado'. In theory, that Christmas Day was an oddity, in that I spent it with a Jewish family, but since its highlight was, as always, the *Morecambe and Wise Christmas Special*, it wasn't any different from others I'd known . . . apart from the warmth around the dinner table.

It was a nice day. It would have been perfect, if Magda Starshine hadn't raised a subject that I had told Grace was off limits for discussion. 'Xavi,' she began, with a look in her eyes that told me something awkward was coming. As she hesitated, my instant suspicion was that she had found a stain on the sheets. Wrong. 'Can I ask you something?' she continued. I nodded. 'Do you ever contact your mother?'

I felt myself go tense. It must have been obvious, for she continued quickly. 'I'm not prying, you understand. It's just that with your father and grandmother having gone to Spain, she's all the family you have here . . . apart from us, of course,' she added quickly.

I didn't reply until I was sure of what I wanted to say, and how I wanted to say it. 'My mother left me when I was nine, Mrs Starshine,' I replied, when finally I was ready. 'She hasn't spoken to me since then, or tried to make contact.'

'I appreciate that, Xavi. I just wondered, as a mother myself . . .'

'Can you imagine going eight years without seeing Grace?' I asked her, gently.

'No,' she admitted.

'She can contact me any time she likes, Mrs Starshine. All she has to do is call Watson's, or get in touch with my dad. That wouldn't be difficult for her; she must know who his lawyer is. My name's in the papers sometimes; she even could call Tynecastle if she wanted. But she hasn't. If I wanted to contact her, I wouldn't know where to start. I know that she's married again, to a policeman, but I don't know what her new name is.'

'If she did get in touch, would you turn her away?'

I hadn't asked myself that question before but my answer was automatic. 'I don't suppose I would. But I wouldn't know what to say to her either.'

'Maybe listening would be enough.'

I felt my eyes narrow. 'She hasn't been in touch with you, has she?' I asked; I sounded a little suspicious, I realised.

'No, she hasn't.' She took my hand and made me look into her eyes. 'And I promise you, I would never try to contact her, unless you asked me to. You're a mature young man, Xavi, and I respect your right to make that decision.'

I nodded. 'Thanks. If I change my mind, I'll tell you.'

Life rolled on for the rest of the academic year, and the football season. Hearts began paying me in February 1979, although my wages were less than my allowance from Grandma, once tax and National Insurance had been deducted. The Higher papers were even easier than I had hoped for, and I left each exam in no doubt, even if I was tactful enough not to tell anyone, that I'd passed every one I sat: English, Spanish, French, Maths, History, Physics and Chemistry.

But my sporting season ended on a downer and in a degree of uncertainty. I'd done well in the reserves, but the first team had been a disaster. Hearts, traditionally one of Scotland's top sides, were relegated from the Premier League for the second time in three years. There was talk of a player clear-out and for a time I wondered about my own situation. That was resolved quickly; the coach took me aside after the last reserve match and told me I was okay. I was a low earner, and potentially a tradable asset, he said. I didn't care for being described as a commodity, but I kept my mouth shut, for the money gave me the illusion of independence from my father. Also it would come in even more handy, since I had decided to leave Watson's after only five years and take up the provisional place I had been offered at Edinburgh University. I had no serious idea of what I would do outside football, but even at that stage of my fledgling career, I had seen too many players completely unprepared for the day when their legs or lungs or talent gave out on them.

I went back to Spain as soon as I could, for again my free time would be limited by training for the following season. I was a year older, a couple of inches taller, more confident, more arrogant, no doubt, and all the more ready to show my old man that I would never stand in his shadow. As if to emphasise this, I took Grace with me . . . with her parents' approval and my grandmother's agreement, there being a subtle difference between the two.

The pair of them had met before, but never as women on an equal footing, for that was how Grace and I saw them. I reckon that even my dad was fascinated as we watched them adjust to each other.

Strangely, Grandma Paloma seemed younger to me; I had never seen her with a tan before, or dressed in anything that was not predominantly black. Her hair was different too; in Scotland it had always been wound so tight that it had been bereft of any lustre, but in Spain she wore it loose, hanging down to her shoulders, and it shone like pure polished silver.

She and Grace behaved very politely towards each other, very formally at first, until they settled into each other's company and began to relax more. It had been almost ten years since I had seen my grandmother interact with another woman, and that had not been a happy experience. As far as I could tell she took to Grace, although as always, her approval was expressed by the occasional nod, rather than by anything as expansive as a smile.

The sleeping arrangements were, of course, formal. We were allocated bedrooms that were well apart and on either side of Grandma Paloma's suite, above the front door as it had been in Edinburgh. The floors were polished stone, so there was no question of squeaky boards, but I suspected that the old bat would be listening at the door for the sound of shuffling feet long after we had all retired. My dad lived in another part of the house, on the ground floor. It comprised a study, bedroom and bathroom, and had its own entrance. He spent much of his time there; visits were by invitation only, and very few were ever extended.

There had been a lot of change since my last stay. The great old house now had air conditioning, and central heating, but its walls were so thick and most of its windows so small, that for all but a few weeks of the year neither was necessary. Pablo and Carmen, the gardener and his wife, were still in residence . . . and so was the dark-haired daughter . . . but they were living in new, larger accommodation, built in another corner of the estate. What had been their cottage had become a store. There was a new truck, too, a long wheelbase Land Rover. By that time, I had a provisional licence, but I didn't reckon I was ready for the Spanish roads.

With my dad, though, it was business as usual. He was polite to Grace, making a point of having breakfast with us each morning, something he had not always done with me on my previous visit, but as soon as Grandma Paloma and I had cleared the dishes he was off to Girona, and his office.

We had been there for a week when I asked my grandmother how his business was doing. We were in the garden, drinking her home-made lemonade under a parasol, watching my girlfriend swim lengths of the pool, in a bikini that had drawn a raised eyebrow when it had made its first appearance.

'Are you telling me you don't know?' she exclaimed, sternly. She'd have made a great lawyer, would Paloma Puig. She never asked a question to which she did not know the answer already.

I looked at her, and then I smiled. It had taken me seventeen years and a bit to realise it, but I enjoyed the old lady's company more than that of any other person in the world, save Grace, perhaps.

'Don't mock me, boy,' she warned, in formal Castellano, 'with that silly grin.'

'I'm not,' I told her, in the same tongue. 'I'm admiring you. You're well aware, aren't you, that I've got a subscription to Dad's main newspaper.'

'I'd have been disappointed if you had not. So you tell me, how do you think my son's new business is getting along?'

'I think the paper's improved since the start of the year. It's bigger for a start, and that must mean he's selling more advertising. The sports pages are more interesting than they were, and there's a business section. It looks better too.'

'All of that is true, as it is of all the smaller papers he owns. And the radio stations also. A year ago, he had two of those; now another is open and there will be three more next year. Why do you think this is? Come on, you helped produce your school newspaper, so you should know this.'

I did. 'Well,' I ventured, 'my old man couldn't write a story or lay out a newspaper if his life depended on it, and he doesn't strike me as a natural salesman, so it must mean that he's employing the best journalists and the best advertising people.'

'And?'

I thought of the Watson's headmaster's hands-off attitude towards the editorial committee of which I'd been a member. 'And leaving them to get on with the job without interference.'

'Exactly. Now, if he'd just carried on after he bought the business with the people who were there before, do you think it would still have been as successful as it is?'

I could see where she was taking me. 'No,' I admitted.

'Then why were you so hard on him last year when he told you what he had done to improve things? He told me what you called him. He was hurt, you know.'

I didn't buy that. 'My dad's never been hurt in his life. When I called him that he laughed and said he liked me talking like him.'

'How little you know. Your father has seen hurt.'

I stared at her, sceptically. 'Whoever hurt him?'

'Your mother did,' Grandma Paloma replied quietly, 'but I'm not going to talk about it. You might be a giant, but you're still too young.'

'Grandma, I might be only seventeen, but I'm not as young as you think.'

She gave me a very long, down-her-nose, look. 'Xavi, just because you're making the beast with that young lady in the pool, that doesn't mean you know everything about being an adult. The dogs in the street do that, but it doesn't make them Einstein.'

'Grandma!' I protested.

'Come on, son,' she said, 'you can't kid me. I'm fifty-eight years older than you are. I can tell by the way a man and a woman look at each other whether they are lovers or not. I can tell anywhere, and when I see it in my own home . . .'

'Nothing's happened in your home,' I pointed out. 'You made damn sure of that with the way you arranged our rooms.'

'Of course. When you are at her home does her mother say to you, "Go on, Xavi, it's all right that you sleep with my daughter, even though she's still at school and the two of you are not married"? No, of course she doesn't, and it will be no different here . . . except I know that it will, sooner or later when my back is turned, for you know by now that I take a siesta every day from two until five, and when I go to bed at night I never leave my room until I rise at seven next morning. As for your father,' she paused, 'well, he has his own interests.'

I would have asked her more about those, but two considerations stopped me; one, I was still digesting the very broad hint she had given me that she didn't care what we got up to as long as she didn't know, and two, Grace had climbed out of the pool and was walking towards us, with a towel wrapped around her. I looked at her and felt myself stir.

'Enjoy that?' I asked.

She smiled. 'Too right. It's a big difference from the Commonwealth Pool in Edinburgh.'

'You mean there's no hair or toenail clippings floating on the surface?'

'Don't be disgusting, Xavi,' said Grandma Paloma in English. She rose from her chair with the dexterity of a much younger woman. 'I'm going to make some lunch.' She nodded to Grace. 'You may help me if you wish, my dear, once you have put some clothes on.'

She strode off towards the kitchen. I followed my girlfriend to her room. 'What are you up to?' she asked as I stepped inside, after her, just as she dropped her towel to the floor. She smiled as I explained my understanding of my grandmother's house rules. When I thought about it, they weren't too different to those that applied at Starshine Towers. Grace's parents were responsible, but we were both children of the swinging sixties and I had grown fairly sure that her mother was a woman of her time.

Most of our holiday was spent loafing around, although we did go with Grandma Paloma when Pablo drove her in the Land Rover to the street market in Girona, shopping for those fruits and vegetables that weren't grown on the estate. In truth, there wasn't a lot on offer. In 1979, the quality and range of produce in Spain's food shops was pretty poor, and so were most of its people. Few of them could afford imports.

The break in the routine, well mine, at any rate, came on the eleventh day of our stay, a Friday morning. My father had breakfast with us, as usual, but when he was finished, instead of wishing us a good day and leaving, he turned to Grace. 'If you don't mind, lass,' he said, 'I'd like to borrow the boy for the day.'

'And if I mind?' I asked.

'You don't have a vote. You're coming to the office with me. It's time you saw what I'm doing now.'

'I know what you're doing now,' I told him. 'I'm on holiday; I don't want to spend any of it in an office.'

'Humour me,' he insisted. 'Come on.'

I looked at Grace. She grinned and nodded. 'You do as your dad says. I'll help Pablo in the garden.'

I surrendered. 'Okay, then.'

'Put on a white shirt, and trousers,' my father told me.

'You want me to wear a tie as well?' I asked him, sarcastically.

'Oh no. This is Spain, Xavi. Only the boss wears a tie. Most of the guys who work for me don't even know how to make a proper knot.'

He told me I could drive to Girona. The Mercedes had picked up a couple of bumps since the previous summer. If it had still been pristine he might not have been so cavalier. I was nervous behind the wheel of a left-hand drive car, on the 'wrong' side of the road, but there was no way I was letting him see that.

We made it without incident, although not having to change gear helped a lot. The newspaper office was in the centre of the city, not far from the Ramblas. 'Where's the car park?' I asked as we approached.

'Just find a place in the street,' he instructed. 'We need all the space round the back for the delivery vans and the paper lorries.'

'Where do the staff park?'

'Wherever they can; the few that have cars, that is. Most of them just have bikes.'

'Is that why the profits are so high?'

He frowned, and I sensed exasperation. 'Are you still on about me being a capitalist vulture?' he grumbled. 'My people are better paid than any journalists outside Madrid. If they weren't, they'd all fuck off to the Barcelona papers, and I'd be left with the dross of the profession. What you need to understand, kid, is that Spain's still like Britain in the forties and fifties. The average family doesn't even aspire to having a car. But at least Franco made the trains run on time, and because of him the economy isn't screwed up by wild-cat strikes and wanker shop stewards who think they're more important than the fucking Prime Minister! This place is on the up, while your country's headed for the buffers at full speed ahead, unless this woman Thatcher can sort things out, which I doubt since the rest of Europe's laughing at her.'

The closest I ever came to liking my old man in those days was when I provoked him into an argument. 'My country?' I retorted. 'A couple of years ago you were telling me how Scottish you are.'

'And part of me always will be. But I have two passports now, Spanish and British, and to tell you the truth, I'm grateful to my old mother for making me come back here. If she hadn't I'd have frittered the rest of my life away in the fucking casino in Edinburgh, playing poker with the Chinese waiters who flood the place after midnight. I tell you, Britain has ten years, tops, to pull itself out of the shit. Maybe this new woman will be the answer after all. Christ, I hope so.'

'Where do you play poker now?'

'I don't. This business is my gamble now. Why do you ask that anyway?'

'It was something Grandma Paloma said, about you having your own interests.'

'That old bitch! I'm pushing fifty, and she's still trying to run my life.'

'What do you mean?'

'Never mind. Come on, we're late for the news conference.'

He led the way into the building, a three-storey, stone-fronted relic from the twenties, or possibly earlier, uttering a crisp, *'Bon dia,'* as we passed a uniformed security guard, and up a wide staircase. We stopped at a varnished door, which was slightly ajar; he pushed it fully open and held it for me to go before him.

A woman looked up as I entered, from behind a massive desk; she had small, piercing blue eyes and her hair was jet black, almost certainly dyed, I judged, and frizzy. 'Morning, Esme,' said my dad. So this was the hard-hearted secretary of whom he'd boasted the previous summer. 'Wee, fat and fifty,' he'd said. *Correct on every count*, I thought as she stood, although he may have knocked off a couple of years out of some sense of gallantry. He'd been right about her looks, too; she had a face that was . . . let me put it this way. Formidable? Esme could have worked the door of any pub I've ever been in.

'So you're Joe's wee boy,' she said, in a warm, musical voice that was her saving grace. 'I've heard enough about you over the years, but he never said you were this size.' I was a foot taller than her, and then a little more. 'Well seen you're a goalie.'

She continued to appraise me as we shook hands. Hers was small and pudgy and disappeared into mine. I looked back at her, with the same curiosity. I hadn't expected to find her there, since my father had said nothing about her having made the move from Edinburgh. I had expected to dislike her, based on his remark the previous year, but I found that I couldn't, not at first encounter at any rate.

'Pleased to meet you,' was all I said; but I said it in Spanish.

She nodded and replied, 'And I to meet you.'

'You two can make friends later,' my dad interrupted. 'Xavi, come on.' He backed through the door, beckoning me.

'Where are we going?' I asked as I followed.

'Editorial conference; I sit in every morning. But I never say anything unless I'm asked, so neither do you . . . not that anyone will ask you anything, except maybe the sports editor.'

He led the way again, up the next flight of stairs. It took us, not to another landing, but straight into an open-plan work area, lined with desks, of which no more than half were occupied. There was a glass-walled room at the end on my left, in which six men and one woman sat round a rectangular table.

The woman sat at the head of the table; she looked to me to be in her mid-thirties, but it's more difficult to put an age on someone when you're only seventeen yourself. She saw us as we headed towards them, nodded in our direction and said something that I couldn't begin to lip-read; whatever it was, it drew a laugh from the rest.

'My apologies, Pilar,' my father began, 'if we've kept you waiting.

This giraffe with me is my boy, Xavier; you can blame his driving for the delay. We won't extend it further.' He pointed to two empty chairs on the far side of the table from where we stood. 'Over there, Xavi,' he murmured.

The editorial conference began. It wasn't an entirely new experience for me, although it was on an entirely different scale. The team that prepared the Watson's newspaper had been organised along the same lines, with individuals responsible for subject areas prioritising items for the next issue, in a group session. As it progressed I began to work out who was who. Clearly, the woman named Pilar was the editor, and I could see why. She had a dynamism about her, an intensity that communicated itself to the others without being threatening. All the men, even my dad, looked at her with respect. The guy on her right, he was in her age bracket, she called Simon; he had to be the news editor. Beyond him, older, bearded, Angel was soon revealed as the sports editor, for his main contribution was a proposed story about the American debut of Barcelona FC's departed hero, the Dutchman Johann Cruijff. Of the other four, Miquel was business, and another, Marc, headed the features section; what the other two did, or what their names were, I wasn't sure, not until the conference drew towards its close.

'Tomorrow's Saturday,' said Pilar, 'our biggest sales day and the one when most people will read our lead editorial. Isn't that right, Jordi?' The man nearest me nodded, but everyone in the room must have known that, so I imagined that she'd said it for my benefit. 'So what will the subject be?' She looked at the sixth man. 'Ramon?'

'I am concerned,' he began, portentously. I reckoned that he was the oldest person in the room, even including my dad . . . yes, I know that he was still short of fifty then, but in those days that was late middle age, at best, to me. 'I am worried about the direction of the government. They are talking about introducing a bill to make divorce legal, in defiance of the Church, and also in defiance of the feelings of a substantial group within the UCD.'

My dad leaned towards me. 'He means the Union of the Democratic Centre,' he whispered, 'the main governing party.' I knew that, but I wasn't ready to let him know that I was one of his subscribers.

'Spanish democracy is young,' Ramon continued. 'It is in a fragile condition, and it is still vulnerable to action by the military, especially if the King supported it. Now I am not saying that Juan Carlos would lead a coup d'etat, but if it was a fait accompli he might feel that he had no choice but to give it his blessing. Suarez,' ('The Prime Minister,' my dad whispered again. I knew that too), 'is a clever man, but he must plot his course very carefully. My gut feeling is that he wants to reject this divorce bill, but he is afraid that it will destabilise him if he does. This newspaper has great influence upon UCD members in Catalunya. I suggest that we support him by publishing a leader condemning the bill. I have already briefed Jordi, here, on what it might say.'

'How would the majority of our readers react?' Pilar asked, quietly.

'Our readers are, in the main, conservative Catholics.'

'But not all.' I said it without thinking. My father glared at me and grabbed my arm, as if that would silence me. 'I'm sorry,' I continued, in Spanish. 'I know it's not my place to speak at this meeting, but I'm one of your readers. I can tell you that I'm not conservative, or particularly Catholic, and if you look at the content of your correspondence columns, you'll find that I am not alone.'

'Young man,' said Ramon, 'the people I'm talking about do not write letters to newspapers.'

'Then how do you know for sure they read them?' I found myself countering.

'I know because I speak to them. It's not just Spain, you know. European politics are fundamentally conservative. Look at your own country.'

'My country's had Labour governments for eleven of the last fifteen years,' I pointed out. 'Yet Thatcher wasn't elected to halt the advance of social progress; she's there on a promise to speed it up.' I could feel my father bristling alongside me. 'I'm sorry, Dad,' I told him, in English. 'I'll shut up.'

'Too fu—'

'No.' Pilar's firm voice cut across his retort. 'It's good to have a fresh viewpoint in this room. What do you feel about the divorce bill, Xavi? Let's say you were Spanish and old enough to vote. Would you want it?'

'I'd demand it,' I replied, without even thinking. 'The Church should not lay down the conditions under which a democracy can operate. It has a right to oppose, but not to veto.'

'You sound very firm about that.'

'I am. My school debating society discussed a similar principle last spring, only our motion proposed a ban on contraception. I spoke against; it was put to the vote and rejected by a hundred and six to three.'

'So should we simply ignore the subject,' Ramon growled, 'because the Church is against it?'

'No.' This time, to my surprise, it was my dad who interrupted. He looked along the table. 'Pilar, you know I'm always reluctant to intervene in your discussions, but here I must. I'm a divorced man myself. Xavi's mother left me eight years ago. That being the case, it would be hypocritical of me to oppose this bill, or for any of my newspapers to be seen to do so, or even to prevaricate on the issue. I would not wish to see an editorial that did anything but support it.'

'Me neither,' said the editor. 'As it happens, I have a sister who can't wait to get rid of her miserable goat of a husband. Jordi,' she asked, 'would you have any moral objection to writing a strong leader article in support of a divorce bill? If you do, I'll respect that, and write it myself.'

'I'm fine with it,' Jordi told her. 'I'll get on it right now.'

'In that case,' Ramon began, but my dad raised a hand to stop him.

'Hernández,' he barked, 'if you're about to resign, don't be a clown. You're far too valuable to this paper for me to lose you. If you walk out,

I'll let the world know that it was because you lost an argument with my son and couldn't handle it.'

'I'll consider my position over the weekend,' the man muttered.

'I've been considering it for a while,' my old man retorted. 'I'm promoting you to associate editor; you'll be responsible for circulation, government relations, at all levels, and public relations, reporting directly to me.' He glanced at the editor. 'Don't worry, Pilar, it won't affect your authority; not at all.'

It didn't hit me like a thunderbolt, but now I know that it was right there, right then, in that room that I decided I had to be a journalist. While my budding football career still had my attention, I knew within myself that I wasn't actually going to be the new Gordon Banks, or the next Lev Yashin. (The new Alan Rough, maybe, but the original was going strong in the Scotland goal at that time, even after the National Disaster of 1978, so there wasn't a vacancy.) I hadn't done any serious long-term planning at that stage. My intention had been to take the broadest based arts degree I could, and go from there, that's all.

Yet as I looked around as the conference broke up and the department heads went off to begin the task of putting together the next morning's newspaper, I felt as if I could touch the atmosphere, the tension, that had gathered in that room. I didn't realise it at the time, but indeed it must have been tangible, for as I breathed it in, it found its way into my bloodstream and took root there, an insidious virus that in time would spread through my system and trigger an infection that would come to dominate my life.

Someone I respect once tried to tell me that journalists are born, not made. Maybe that's true, but we all have to find our vocation, or it can lie dormant. Once we do, though, my kind, we're junkies; from our first fix, we're addicted to the unique authority that our profession gives us. By uncovering the news, then reporting and expanding it, by putting our own spin upon it . . . and hell, we do: for all that some of us might express contempt for those whom we christened 'spin doctors', we feed off those people as voraciously as piranha upon a drowned carcass. Yes, we're information junkies and they're our street corner, back alley, dealers . . . we mould popular opinion, we make or break those who aspire to rule us, we play the face cards in the game that decides the fate of nations. We're the harlots that Stanley Baldwin berated when he stole his cousin Rudyard Kipling's line 'power without responsibility' in a desperate defence against an onslaught from Beaverbrook's *Daily Express*.

I wish I could say that Baldwin was wrong, that unlike harlots, we can't be bought, but that isn't true, as I knew from the start: some whores do walk among us, and offer themselves on the street corners of our world. I knew at once, instinctively, that Ramon Hernandez had been bought: he was in his fifties, his career had spanned much of the Franco era and he had emerged from it with a formidable reputation as a political fixer, and with a solid gold ring on the little finger of his carefully manicured right hand. It had a diamond set in it that was bigger than any that Grace and I had seen when window shopping in Laing's or Hamilton and Inches. He had sold himself to the old guard, and he was still doing its bidding, as he proved that morning. Yet I learned something very valuable from Ramon; I learned to look out for guys like him and to value all the more those who are truly incorruptible. And they do exist; for most of my career I believed that I was one of them.

I was deep in thought when I followed my father back into his office, and so I was unprepared for the volley he fired at me as soon as the door closed on us. 'What the fuck did I tell you?' he shouted. 'Why did you open your big Scottish gob?'

'As I said in there, Dad, I'm sorry. That pompous old twerp was talking shit; I couldn't help myself.'

'Everyone else in the room knew that too, but they kept their mouths shut. Do you think what he said came as a surprise to Pilar and me? Not a bit of it; Jordi tipped us off two days ago. Yesterday we had Hernandez followed to a café where he had lunch with one of Franco's old chums. What you saw in there was us letting him help himself to enough rope, not just to hang himself, but to make sure that the drop would rip his fucking head off. The game was that Pilar was going to say exactly what you said. She was to slap him down hard, and that when he threatened to quit, I was going to let him. Other than that I wasn't going to open my mouth.'

'So why didn't you accept his resignation?'

'Weren't you fucking listening to me in there? I couldn't have him walking out of here shouting about Josep-Maria Aislado's kid interfering in editorial affairs and insulting a senior journalist, especially when there was a room full of honest witnesses who'd have been hard pressed to deny it. That would have been a huge loss of face for me, and politically it would have cost me a bundle. I was within a minute of getting rid of the reactionary old bastard, when you stepped in and saved his fucking bacon!'

'Why did you have to promote him?' I asked him, out of my depth, but standing up for myself as best I could.

He had calmed down a little; he sighed. 'Xavi, lad, if I'd let him stay on as political editor the day after we found out that he's taking backhanders from the Francoistas, Pilar would have quit on me, and I couldn't have that. She's the lynchpin of this place. So I had to get him out of that job in another way.'

'And now you're stuck with him,' I said, 'and it's my fault. Fair enough: I apologise, Dad, but if you'd told me all that stuff before we went in there, I'd have known to bite my tongue.'

'I told you to say fuck all in there, didn't I?'

'Yes, but—'

'Is there any part of "fuck all" that you have trouble understanding?'

'No, but—'

'Ach son, go on.' He pointed to the door, dismissing me. 'Get back upstairs and spend some time with Angel. He said he'd like to talk to you about Scottish football. I told him you were a global expert on warming your arse on a bench with Hearts' ham and egg team, but that didn't put him off.' I glared at him, but just as I was about to stalk out of the room, he held up his hand.

'Hold on,' he called out. 'In case you give a shit about having cost me money through keeping Hernandez on the payroll, don't worry too much about it. He's going to find out that "reporting directly to me" means accounting for every single minute of every single day. He won't stick that for longer than three months. Next time he quits, I'll let him, give him a glowing reference, then put the word out among my fellow proprietors that he's a stooge. Pretty soon he'll find that what he's really done is take early retirement.'

'What if the Francoistas get back into power?'

'They won't, not through the ballot box. They might try it the other way, but they won't succeed. The King's very clever; he's commander in chief of the military and the military fucking knows it.'

(I have to give that one to my old man. Eighteen months later a mid-ranking army officer named Tejero was the figurehead of an attempted coup, which collapsed after the intervention of Juan Carlos. Ramon Hernandez, by then an ex-employee of the newspaper group, was implicated in the plot, and spent some time in prison. He was lucky; a regime like the one he espoused would have shot him.)

I left my dad, and Esme, to his in-tray and went back up to the editorial room, in search of Angel Esposito, the sports editor. He didn't speak a word of English, but he could name four Scottish football teams apart from mine (he'd read up on that): Rangers, Celtic, Aberdeen and, to my surprise, Dundee United, who had beaten Barcelona in Spain back in 1966, and would do so again a few years later. He asked me if I knew any Scots players who might do well in Spain. I told him that I reckoned Kenny Dalglish, Graeme Souness and Martin Buchan would be stars anywhere, but that after the Scotland squad's traumatic performance in the Argentina World Cup the year before, most of the rest would never want to set foot in another Spanish-speaking nation, not even on holiday.

Angel was a nice guy; he even offered to fix me up with a trial for

Barcelona while I was in the area, courtesy of a B team coach who was a friend of his. I thanked him, but I had to remind him that I was a registered Hearts player, and that the football authorities took a dim view of even an obscure youngster like me being tapped up by another club. (As it turned out, if he'd made the offer a few years later, I might have accepted.)

Once he had picked the little that was in my football brain, I moved on and spent the rest of the morning with each of the department heads . . . apart from Ramon Hernandez. They were all courteous, but hard pressed, so much of my time was spent simply watching them at work, without really understanding much of it. It wasn't until I reached Simon Sureda, the news editor, that things began to click. He had just despatched all his reporters on assignments, and had some time on his hands.

'What do you want to know?' he asked, simply.

'What is it that a journalist does?' I replied.

'A journalist seeks knowledge,' he replied, without a beat. 'A journalist seeks the definitive version of the truth about each situation he investigates, from the many that might be put to him. Then he will express that truth to the people through his newspaper, or his broadcasting station. He must have integrity, because he must be worthy of the trust of the people who read his words or listen to them. Equally, those who give him information must be certain that he will report it accurately and also that if they ask him to maintain their confidentiality, he will do so, even in the face of the severest threats. He must have understanding of all sides of an argument. He's not a judge, he's an analyst, and so he must resist any urge to condemn. He must not mock or doubt the beliefs of others, unless they are unarguably false. For example, he must recognise that those who follow the Cross, those who follow the Crescent and those who follow the Star of David are all sincere, and deserve respect, even though personally he might reject the beliefs of all three. He must have the determination and the skill to uncover secrets which are wrongly hidden from the people by those who rule them, or crimes that are committed against them by the state or powerful individuals, and he must report such wrongdoings with courage and eloquence. He must never think of himself as a master, always as a servant. Finally, he must have an insatiable hunger for the truth, and the will to hunt it out even at the risk of his very life. Recent history is littered with the bones of journalist martyrs, and he must be prepared to join them.' Then he smiled. 'How's that?'

Impressive, I thought, but I didn't say so. 'I always thought that journalism was a relatively safe profession,' I ventured. 'I thought they were off limits.'

Simon frowned, and shook his head, slowly. 'My uncle was a reporter, thirty years ago, on a paper in Barcelona that no longer exists. He uncovered a story about some guys, friends of friends of Franco, who had built a property on the Costa Brava, near Palamos, without permission. It was poorly constructed, it collapsed and people were killed, but because those responsible were who they were, the cause of the disaster was all covered up by the authorities. My uncle had a source within the Guardia Civil who told him all about it. He wrote his story, gave it to his editor, and waited for it to appear. It didn't; that same night he was taken from his home by some men with their faces hidden, but their guns waved in my aunt's face. His body was never found, but his friend in the Guardia, he was shot in the street a couple of days later. His killer got away in the crowds, they said, but there were more police than civilians around at the time.' He reached out and put a hand on my shoulder. 'Xavi,' he said, 'what you are suggesting, that journalists are a protected species, that might be true in a democracy, but even there it is sometimes no more than a balance of risk. Is the risk of letting a troublesome journalist live outweighed by the risk of discovery if you kill him?'

He was taking me to a place I'd never imagined. 'There are people who think that way?' I asked him, incredulous.

'Sure. The Mafia, for a start.' He paused. 'But sometimes journalists are not troublesome at all. Sometimes they are very useful. I spent a couple of years in London, at the beginning of this decade, as the

correspondent of one of our national daily newspapers. I saw there
that some journalists, some well-known people at that, allow themselves
to be used by the politicians as vehicles. The same is true of some
of those who cover the business community. I believe that there are
even people in Britain, and in Ireland, who are virtual mouthpieces for
terrorists.'

'And that doesn't happen in Spain?'

'Spain is different; Spain is just emerging from a long dark period
when all that appeared in the press was what the regime wanted to see
there. Like the Soviet Union, but at the other end of the political
spectrum. That story I told you about my uncle was not an isolated
incident. That recent history has imprinted my profession with a strong
sense of public responsibility. Most of us are determined that we will
never allow our country to go back to those days.'

'Most but not all?'

He knew that I was talking about Hernandez. 'There will always be a
few lice in the woodpile,' he said, his face impassive.

I was still thinking about everything that Simon had said as I ambled
into my dad's outer office, heading for his door.

'You'd better wait, son.' Esme called out. 'He's got Pilar Roca with
him. He doesn't like being interrupted when she's in there.'

There was something in her tone that suggested an unwitting
disclosure. For all my dad's strictures against 'shagging the hired help',
from the year before, I couldn't help thinking back to my grandmother's
casual remark about him having 'his own interests'. The notion made
me feel strange, a little queasy, perhaps. But when I did think about it,
hell, the guy was forty-eight years old, and I had spent enough time with
the coaches and senior players of Heart of Midlothian Football Club to
know there was no cut-off date for the pastime that the club's
physiotherapist referred to as 'horizontal jogging'.

'How long has she been editor?' I asked. 'She seems young for the
job.'

'Since your father bought the paper,' Esme replied. 'Joe fired the guy

who was here, and his deputy, and all the other senior executives apart
from Angel and Ramon. He recruited Pilar and Simon from the biggest
of his Barcelona competitors. Obviously I wasn't here at the time, but I
gather it caused a wee bit of a sensation.'

'He must have taken a hell of a chance, sacking the other people all
at once. What did he do until Pilar arrived, edit the paper himself?'

As she smiled, her little eyes almost disappeared into her pudgy
cheeks. 'Your father doesn't take chances, Xavi. The whole deal was
put in place before he pulled the chain.' I recalled the unpleasant
lavatorial remark that my old man had quoted and felt another surge
of dislike . . . maybe I should say a flush of dislike . . . for the woman.
'Pilar and the new team were waiting in the coffee place on the corner
as he broke the news to the outgoing lot. Within half an hour they
had swapped places. The security guy told me they passed on the
stairs, literally.' I glowered at the door. 'Hey,' she said, 'don't look like
that. Your father was generous to them; they all got a better pay-off
than they'd have had anywhere else. I know this; I've seen the accounts.
I know you think Joe's a bastard, but he was kinder than those
people deserved. He told me you accused him of shooting the
wounded . . . we had a laugh about that, by the way . . . but what he
really did was show clemency to the guilty. The old guard ran a lousy
show; they nearly killed this paper. They were holdovers from the
Franco times. In fact, Angel told me that the real power in the place
was Ramon Hernandez.'

'Then why didn't Dad get rid of him with the rest?'

'Because he was plugged in everywhere in this city, in this province,
aye, and maybe in Barcelona too. Joe wasn't, not then. He couldn't risk
cutting him loose, so he played on his great big ego and let him carry
on until he was ready to ease him out the door.'

'And that would have happened today, if I'd kept quiet in there.'

'Yes, but he should have warned you more clearly than he did.
Either that or he should have chosen another day to bring you into the
office.'

'He probably wanted to show me how powerful he was,' I muttered.

Esme shook her lump of a head. 'God, you really don't like him, do you? Your father's a rich and powerful man, yes, much more so in Spain than he was in Scotland. The amount he sold the pubs for, that raised a few eyebrows in Scotland, but here it made him a very big player. But he doesn't flash his wealth or show his power. I don't know why he chose to make you a witness to Hernandez being brought down, but I tell you one thing: he wasn't showing off to you. Why the hell would he need to do that? Do you think he craves your approval?'

I looked at the woman, still trying to weigh her up, still trying to work out how I felt about her. 'You tell me,' I shot back at her. 'You seem to know everything he thinks.'

She didn't answer me, not directly. 'I've known Joe since before you were born. I know that he's interested in two things, business, and a wee bit of poker now and again, although never for stakes that would put people off playing with him. He's never been a family man, but that's understandable.'

'What do you mean?' I snapped at her.

'There was never room for him in your family; all the available space is taken up by the old lady.'

'Have you even met Grandma Paloma?' I asked, indignantly.

'Just the once,' Esme replied. 'Going on eighteen years ago, the only time she ever set foot in the office.'

'How long have you worked for my father?'

'I worked for your grandfather before him, lad. I went to work for him as a bookkeeper in nineteen forty-eight, after my husband was killed.'

The revelation took me by surprise. 'What happened to him?' I asked.

'He was in the navy. He was working on mine-clearing, and somebody made a mistake.' Her mouth twitched a little, in one corner, and her eyes went somewhere else for a second or two. 'They could have sent him home in a bin-bag. I went to work for old Mr Aislado a few months after that, after I'd recovered from my miscarriage.' Jesus, another shock: I was in the early stages of discovering a truth that has guided me since, and cursed me too, that there is usually a hell of a lot more to other people's lives than one ever supposes. Much of my career has been spent uncovering such secrets . . . and even my own.

'Your dad was your age then,' she continued. 'He was in his final year at George Heriot's . . .' (I was beginning to feel like a foundling, an alien within my own family. Until that moment I'd had no idea that my father had been educated there. I had assumed that he'd gone to Watson's, but I'd never asked.) '. . . but he used to come into the office on Saturday mornings to help out. No five-day week then, son.'

'What was my grandfather like?'

'There was no harm in him.'

I detected a note of caution in her reply. 'What's that supposed to mean?' I pressed.

'You should really be asking your grandmother about him,' she said, stalling.

'Maybe, but I was asking you.'

'For the times,' she replied, finally, 'he was a good boss. The money was decent and the work wasn't too taxing, not in those days anyway.'

'But?'

'But he didn't have the spark about him that your dad has. In business terms he was a plodder. Even then, I used to wonder if most of the decisions about the business were being made at home, and not by him either. Now I know from your father that they were.'

'And so do I,' I told her. 'But I didn't mean what was he like as a businessman. I don't know anything about him as a man.'

'He was a good man.'

The reply was too simple. 'Go on,' I insisted. 'What else about him?'

'He had an eye for the girls,' she said, quietly. 'And having seen your grandmother, I'm not surprised.'

'Don't you say a word about Grandma Paloma,' I snapped at

her. 'You don't know a bloody thing about her.' She was taken aback by the sudden anger in my retort. In truth so was I; it was entirely instinctive.

She went on to the defensive as quickly as I'd gone on the attack. 'I'm sorry, son. You're right. I did only meet her that one time; everything else I know about her came second hand.'

'You mean my father talks to you about her?'

'Yes. He says she's a difficult woman.'

I found myself smiling. 'He's not telling you the whole story, then. Grandma Paloma can be a lot more than difficult.' And then I thought about what I had said. My grandmother was formidable, that was for sure. I suspected strongly that she had scared my mother away; I didn't know how, but I was pretty sure of that. And yet I had never been afraid of her, and when I thought of the way I was treated by her I could find no fault with it. In Scotland, more so than in Spain, it seemed, she had kept a barrier between herself and the world. But there was a key to its solid gate, just one, and it was mine. It wasn't made of metal; no, it was forged out of something intangible: understanding. I had never asked myself the question before; it's not one that occurs to a child, but it was an adult who had that exchange with Esme and in its midst I dared to confront it, not out loud, only in thought. '*Do you love the old bat?*' The answer was an unequivocal, '*Yes.*' My smile widened. Esme looked at me, saying nothing.

'You and she would probably get on like a house on fire,' I told her, laughing as I did so.

Since then, I've given a lot of thought to the relationship between my dad and his secretary. For all that he had denied it, I took a while to dismiss the notion that it might have been physical, then or at some other time. It took me even longer to realise the truth: Esme was a substitute. Josep-Maria Aislado never understood his mother when she was alive, not in the way I did. He interpreted her lack of warmth as a rejection of him, and he couldn't handle it. He took it personally, when there was really no need. He still does, for all that I've tried to show

53

him. He couldn't talk to her about his feelings, his worries, and I know now that he wouldn't have shared them with my mother. His secretary was his confidante; she was his closest friend.

I returned to Esme's earlier disclosure. 'Why did my grandma come to the office that time? Was it when my grandfather was ill?'

'Nobody ever knew your grandfather was ill. He just died.'

'Of what? People don't just die.' I had never asked my dad or my grandmother, and neither had ever volunteered the information.

'He had a massive stomach tumour,' Esme told me. 'He didn't know about it until it haemorrhaged, and . . . that was that.'

'So why did Grandma show up there? Had something happened in the business?'

'No, nothing like that, not in the sense you mean, anyway.' She frowned. 'Listen, I shouldn't have got into this. Ask your father if you want to know any more.'

'Ask him what? Why my grandma paid her one and only visit to the office? Maybe he doesn't know why.'

'Oh, he knows, but the fact that you don't . . . No, you'll have to ask him.'

'What's the bloody mystery? What happened eighteen years ago?' And then I thought about the time frame. I had happened. 'I'll tell you what, Esme,' I said, 'I won't ask my dad, I'll ask Grandma Paloma instead. Of course, she'll want to know why I'm asking. Do you fancy meeting her again?'

The little eyes screwed up tight. 'Are you threatening me, son?' she murmured.

I gazed down at her, considering her question. I think I am, yes, I decided, and told her so.

'You and your father, eh. Two of a kind.'

I frowned. 'No, I don't think so.'

'I do. Okay, I'll tell you why she came in. It had to do with your mother.-She was pregnant.'

'So? Why would that bring Grandma into the office?'

'Because that's where your mother was,' she said, patiently, as if she was humouring me.

I felt my eyes widen. 'Eh?'

'You never knew that?' she gasped, genuinely astonished. 'Nobody ever told you that your mother worked for your grandpa?'

'No. Esme, when I was a kid, nobody ever told me anything.'

'Obviously they still don't.'

'Fine, but I'm still asking, why would my mum being pregnant bring Grandma Paloma into the office?'

She sat silent, staring up at me as the extent of my ignorance sank home. Then she looked across at the door of my father's office. I guessed that she was hoping it would open and rescue her from her interrogation; but it stayed solidly shut. 'Your mother and your father weren't married,' she continued, in a whisper, as if she was afraid she might somehow be heard through the door.

I was surprised, but well short of stunned. I recalled my dad's lecture on condoms, a year before, and understood his vehemence. 'These things happen,' I replied.

'They do, but in nineteen sixty-one, most people looked at them in a different way. Your grandma did, that's for sure. She was incan-fucking-descent, Xavi. She came into that building like the wrath of God. Your father was about thirty years old at the time, yet he was hauled into your granddad's office like a schoolboy going in for a belting off the headmaster. Then your mother was sent for. The rest of us just sat there, none of us saying a word, until your grandpa came out and told us we could all go home early.'

'How did my grandma find out?'

'That I do not know.'

'What happened afterwards?'

'We never saw your mother again, not in the office at any rate. A couple of weeks later Joe let it be known that he and Mary were married. I said that I'd organise a whip-round for a wedding present, and asked him what he wanted, but he told me not to.'

'How did you find out that my mum was up the duff?' I asked.

Esme shrugged. 'She told me. I was her best friend in the office, her only friend, when I think about it. I knew that she and your father had a thing going, that they'd been out on a couple of dates. If I'd known they'd got to that stage, I might have warned her.'

'About what?'

'About Joe. She wasn't the first, Xavi. He had a few flings with girls in the office before her. When he got bored, he chucked them and they wound up leaving. Mind you, if I had told Mary about them, there's no saying it would have made any difference. She was only nineteen, and very quiet with it, but there was something about her, underneath the surface. I've always had a suspicion that she had an eye to the main chance, and that getting pregnant by Joe suited her fine.'

'If it did, she found out different,' I murmured.

'How come?'

'You may have suspected that about her, but looking back, I can see that my grandma was certain of it. I was only a kid, but even I realised that things were bad between them. Grandma Paloma treated her like shit, and my mother took it. Occasionally I'd hear her shouting at my dad, but she never stood up to Grandma.'

'Were you sorry when she left?'

'My mother was never interested in me. Why should I have been sorry?'

'Then I'm sorry for you,' said Esme. 'A lad should always be close to his mother.'

'I didn't have any say in it. I don't remember her ever trying to be close to me.'

'Maybe she wasn't allowed to.'

'We lived in the same house for nine years,' I rumbled, releasing my bitterness, 'and she wasn't locked in the fucking attic. Yet I never once remember her coming into my room at night to tuck me in. Even my dad did that sometimes. She never as much as slipped me a Penguin biscuit. Even my dad took me to the pictures now and again, and bought me ice cream.'

'See?' she challenged. 'Your father's not so bad.'

'He grew out of it, though. The last picture he took me to was *Beneath the Planet of the Apes*. I was eight at the time.'

'He was a very busy man.' She was loyal, that one, if nothing else.

'And he's been busy for nine years since then. He was never there, Esme. Grandma Paloma was. She might be a bit stern, but she looked after me when nobody else could be bothered.'

'Maybe nobody else was allowed to look after you.'

I recalled what my father had said, at the end of my first visit to Spain, about breathing my own air. I still didn't buy it, though. 'My parents had the opportunity,' I replied.

And then the door opened: Pilar Roca came out, smiling. 'Hello again,' she said, as she saw me. 'Have my colleagues been looking after you?'

I nodded. I told her that Angel had even offered to get me a trial for Barcelona, but that I had turned him down, with regret.

She laughed. 'It's maybe as well you didn't accept. Angel's influence may not be as great as he thinks. But other than that, has your education been complete?'

As she spoke, my father followed her into the outer office. I glanced at him, then at Esme. 'By God, has it ever?' I replied.

'Habla Castellano?'

'Hardly any. Xavi's always on at me to learn, but I've never made any progress; if he spoke more Spanish to me, maybe, but . . .'

'I know. You have other things to study than languages.'

'You speak English, though. And it's good.'

'It's okay.'

'Where did you learn?'

'I studied it; at school, and then I worked for my aunt for a while and she taught me much more. She's Welsh, from Cardiff. She and my uncle Emilio have a restaurant in Tossa, and most of their customers are British.'

'Do you still work there?'

'If they're very, very busy, my aunt sometimes calls me and I'll go and help out, but otherwise, no.'

'So what do you do?'

'Do?'

'What's your job?'

'This is it. I don't like the restaurant, so I help my parents, any way they need me to. Here in the garden, looking after the car, cleaning the big house, cleaning our own. Do you like our new house? Don Josep, Senor Aislado, had it built for us over the winter. The other one was very old; he said it was easier to replace it than fix it. Now we have proper hot water, new things in the kitchen. We are very lucky. And the salary he pays us is far more than we'd get anywhere else.'

'You work hard for it.'

'Still I'm lucky. We're country people . . . What's your name, senorita?'

'Grace.'

'I'm Carmen, like my mother. Carmen Mali. People like me, Grace, we're not used to such luxury, especially not here in Catalunya. The old ruler was not kind to us; he didn't like our people.'

'So Xavi's told me.'

'You and the young senor, have you known each other long?'

'Since I was five. We're at the same school . . . or were, for Xavi's just left. I'm staying on for another year.'

'What's he like?'

'Xavi? Dark and mysterious, my friend Jill calls him. But he isn't, not really. If anything, he's not mysterious enough, not dangerous, unlike . . .'

'You're attracted by danger? Be careful what you wish for.'

'I know, yet . . . it's crazy, but sometimes I . . . Oh, nothing. Hell, what am I talking about anyway? I suppose that mysterious is exactly what Xavi is, until you get to know him. He doesn't talk much, to anyone other than me, not even to his father.'

'How do they get on?'

'I don't know. That's true, I honestly don't. They're not close, that's all I can say.'

'And his abuela? Sorry, I don't know the English word.'

'His grandmother? I'd say that Xavi worships the ground she walks on. I would say it, but he never would. They have an amazing relationship; they're so careful with each other. I think it's because they're so alike.'

'Silver and mysterious. Yes, that would be a fitting description of Senora Puig. My father, he thinks she's . . . again I'm not sure of the words . . . he has great respect for her. He says that she's like a figure from the past, a great lady. I have to take his word for that, for I don't get to speak to her very often. I only get to clean downstairs in the big house; my mother does upstairs and the kitchen.'

'Grandma Paloma's nice. I can see why people find her forbidding; she spent more than half her life in a foreign country, after all, and she never really settled there. But she's very polite to me.'

'She has to be.'

'Why?'

'Because you're with her grandson; you're his choice, and she wouldn't cross him over you. But don't worry; she does approve of you.'

'How do you know that?'

'*From my parents, of course. How else? Hey, he's a big boy, your Xavi.*'
'*He's still growing. I don't know when he'll stop.*'
'*My God, and I said that I was lucky!*'

Four

Grace was in the garden when I got back, picking green beans with the caretaker couple's daughter. The woman . . . I'd guessed her age as early twenties, generously as it turned out, for Grace told me later that she was ten years older than us . . . glanced up as I approached. Although it was my second visit, it was the closest I'd been to her. She was a looker, no mistake, with dark brown eyes to match her hair, high cheekbones that lent her a touch of the exotic, and a straight nose that gave strength to her face. She didn't hang around, though; with a quick word to Grace she picked up her basket and headed for the cottage. She was wearing shorts; her legs were pretty impressive too.

'Made a new friend?' I asked.

'It seems so. Her English is good. Her aunt's from Cardiff.'

'Does she speak Welsh too?'

'We didn't get that far.'

'I wonder what the hell she's doing here?' I mused. 'A woman like her.'

'Fancy her, do you?' she asked, with a worldly smile that added, 'For anything she can do . . .'

'No.' I may have lied about that, for if there was one thing that Carmen was, it was fancyable.

'It's just that you don't expect to find someone like her buried in the heart of the country.'

'Well, she is. She does the same as her parents, she says.'

'There you are. A woman like her, working as a domestic?'

'I don't imagine there are too many openings for Playboy bunnies around here. How was your day?' she added quickly, and for a moment

I suspected that maybe she was keen to divert my attention from the gorgeous Carmen.

If she was, she was being too cautious. Grace was blooming herself; just turned seventeen, but she was all woman, a natural blonde with a body that was losing the gawkiness of her mid-teens. She commanded attention every time she walked into a room. When I'd taken her to the Hearts' reserves informal end-of-season do in the Tynecastle social club, I'd had to give a couple of my teammates a polite but serious message.

'Interesting,' I told her. 'I caused a major diplomatic incident, had the offer of a trial for Barcelona and discovered what I want to do once I leave university, or once I've finished with football, whichever comes first. I'm going to be a journalist.'

'A journalist?' she exclaimed. 'A newspaper reporter? You're not serious, are you?'

'I've never been more so.'

'But aren't they all boozers?'

'That's not a condition of employment, especially not in Spain.'

'You mean you're going to work for your dad?'

'No fucking . . . sorry . . . way. I'll look for a job in Edinburgh.'

'As a sports reporter?'

'I don't think so.' I told her about Simon Sureda, and how he had described a journalist's raison d'être.

She looked doubtful. 'I don't want you doing it if it's dangerous,' she said.

'Don't be daft. I don't plan to be a war correspondent or anything like that.'

'But what about the hours? Don't journalists work late?'

'As far as I can see they work a five-day week, fixed hours, just like anyone else.'

'As long as you're not coming in at midnight.'

I smiled. Grace and I hadn't got round to discussing the future at that stage. We were kids, living for our furtive moments and not much else. 'Coming in where?' I asked her.

She looked me in the eye. 'Home,' she replied.

'Whose home?'

'Ours.'

'Does that mean we're engaged?'

'Aren't we?'

'Am I not supposed to ask you to marry me first?'

'Don't you want to?'

'Well, yeah. Okay, I love you, and I always will, so will you marry me?' That's how big a pushover I was for her.

'Of course. Now kiss me.'

I did, for quite some time. 'When?' I asked her.

'Whenever we feel like it. Once we're both through university.'

It occurred to me that there was something else I was supposed to do. 'Eh, don't I have to ask your dad for permission?'

'If you want, but he'll say yes.'

'He won't mind me not being Jewish?'

'If he minded about that you'd never have got over the door.'

'What about your mum?'

'My mum's well on your side. Who do you think told me about the Brook Clinic?'

'Where do you want to go for the ring?'

'Wherever you like, but only when you can afford it. I want you to buy it with your own money, not to go asking your dad or your grandma for the cash. I'm marrying you, not your family.'

I liked the sound of that. Much as I liked her folks, I'd grown up to be fiercely independent, and I didn't want to become a cog in someone else's domestic machine. Grace and I would form our own nuclear unit, thank you very much. Would we ever.

'Hey,' I said, 'now that's all sorted, is it okay if I'm a journalist?'

'I suppose,' she conceded, 'if you don't grow out of it before you get that far.'

'I won't.'

Of all the things I said and did that day, and in the time that followed, that's the one that has remained my only constant, unchanging truth. My vocation will see me to my grave. I will never lose it, even if, ultimately, I have betrayed it.

But no, there is another unshakeable truth. I may try to reject it, I may have denied it on the odd occasions when Jock Fisher, or my dad, has drunk enough to dare to bring up the subject, but ultimately it's the one thing that I can't lie to myself about. For all that happened, a part of me still loves Grace; and it always will.

You may come to be shocked by that admission. Well, too bad if you are; I don't give a shit.

'What do you think of her?'

'Who?'

'Xavi's girlfriend. Who do you think?'

'There's more than one answer to that question, as we both know, but . . . As I've told you before, Grace is Xavi's choice, and he is hers, so we have no choice but to respect it.'

'We do, Mother. If we didn't approve, I could threaten to cut him off.'

'And that would be an empty threat, even if . . . You know as well as I do that whether his birth certificate was issued in Scotland or here, Spanish law doesn't let you disinherit him.'

'That's true, I'll grant you. Ah, they'll be fine, I'm sure. From what I know of her parents they're good people, and they care about him. As long as he keeps his powder dry for a few more years . . .'

'Don't be so crude. Anyway, young people today are sensible in that respect.'

'So was his mother. Very fucking sensible.'

'Enough! She will never be mentioned. Grace is entirely different. Her horizons are broader, her vision and her ambitions are greater. She can see further than the end of the boy's pene.'

'Christ, and you tell me not to be crude.'

'Sometimes even I have to use the sort of expression you understand. She is a very capable young woman and I'm happy that she doesn't seem to have an eye on our family fortune, since her father has his own valuable business.'

'Fuck all good . . . sorry, Madre . . . that would do her anyway even if she had, with you guarding it. But how about answering my question for once?'

'Which one?'

'You know damn well. What do you actually think of her?'

'I prefer to keep that to myself.'

'Mother, for once, humour me, please.'

'Very well, if you insist. I have one big problem with her. I don't know why, not at all, but she scares me.'

'You what? Run that past me again. She scares you?'

Five

I tried to persuade my dad to let me go to the office again, but he told me that he didn't want Ramon Hernandez to see me around there. Instead, he drove Grace and me down the coast to one of his radio stations and had the manager give us a tour around. A few months before, we'd been on a school visit to the BBC's Edinburgh head-quarters, in a rambling, confusing building on Queen Street. My dad's place looked to be much better equipped than that had been, and the music playlist was mostly stuff that we recognised.

On the way back, I asked him where the newsroom was; we hadn't seen it. 'There isn't one,' he told me. 'The news, sport and weather coverage comes from the paper in Girona. They send it by telex to all the stations and the presenters read it. Why keep two dogs when one can bark loud enough for everyone to hear?'

I wasn't sure about his metaphor, but I saw the sense in it.

We had three weeks there, before pre-season training started to loom up. The closer our departure day came, the more I found myself thinking about a problem I'd have when we were back in Edinburgh. I'd be homeless.

I'd every intention of finding a room in a student flat, but we'd gone to Spain before I'd been able to do anything about it. I knew that Grace's folks would put me up if I was stuck, but I wasn't too keen on that idea, and I didn't reckon her father would be overjoyed either. Then I had what passed for a brainwave; I called the assistant manager at Tynecastle, and asked him if he could sort something out for me. I knew that the club sometimes placed young players with landladies.

He sounded optimistic, but by the time he called me back with good news of digs in Oxgangs, I was no longer in difficulty. On our last Saturday, two days before we were due at Barcelona Airport, my dad gave me one of those rare invitations into his private apartments. 'I've bought a flat,' he said, abruptly, even before I had a chance to sit in the chair he offered me.

'That's nice. Where?'

'In a block out on the Queensferry road, just across the Dean Bridge.'

'In Edinburgh? I thought you meant in Girona or down in the south of Spain.'

'What the fuck would I want that for? Your grandma and I have everything we need here. Of course it's in Edinburgh. I was brought up there, after all, and your grandma thinks I should keep some links with my Scottish roots, that I should have a bolthole there, somewhere I can go for a break if I feel the urge . . . and, she says, because she's lived through it, if the politics here go bad on us again.'

I nodded. 'She's right, I suppose. So? What's it got to do with me?'

My dad looked at me with half a grin on his face. 'How did you get to sit all these fucking Highers, Xavi? So . . . When you get back to Edinburgh on Monday, Willie Lascelles, my lawyer, will meet you at the airport, take you there and give you the keys.'

'Eh?' My old man had surprised me before, but never on such a big scale.

'Here's the deal,' he continued. 'It's quite a big place, four bedrooms. One of them's en suite; that will be mine whenever I decide to use it, and when I'm not there nobody will sleep in it other than you. If you want to rent out two of the other three rooms to people you can trust . . . no fitba' players, all right . . . leaving one for you when I come over, that's okay by me, but you'll be responsible for them. It'll be on the understanding that if I say I'm coming over, they move out for that time. I'm not living in a student den. Willie's employing cleaners to look after the place for me, so you don't need to worry about that, but there will be no rowdy parties to piss off the neighbours, there will be no boozing, there will be no dope smoked. Ever.' As he spoke he poked a finger into the arm of his chair to emphasise each point. 'Understood?'

My mouth was hanging open by then. 'Sure,' I gulped.

'One more thing. No sleepovers with Grace. She's still at school, and the pair of you still have a bit of growing up to do before you start playing house. So every evening she's there, she goes home. Clear?'

'Clear. As long as she's still at school. She plans to move into a flat when she goes to university, so . . .'

'Okay, cross that one when you get there. But remember what I told you last year. I've got shares in the London Rubber Company and I need the dividend to stay high.'

We talked some more, mostly about the coming football season, before I went back to the garden. When I told Grace, she was a lot less surprised than I had been. 'Your dad's a very rich man,' she said. She was in the pool, supporting herself with her forearms, on its concrete edge, at the deep end. 'And he is your dad. Why should you have to live like a scruff when you don't have to?'

'Do you really think it was my dad's idea?' I asked. 'Grandma Paloma put him up to it. He said as much. He hasn't shown any interest in going back to Scotland since the day he left.'

She shrugged her shoulders, almost slipping under the surface in the process. 'Who cares whose idea it was? Either way it's good news for you. Who are you going to move into the spare rooms?'

'Nobody I don't know, so they'll be Watson's guys. Bobby, if he wants, wee Dave; they're both leaving this year.'

'What about Scott?' she suggested, taking me by surprise. 'I know he's staying on at school, but he's in an awful situation living with his mother.'

'I don't think he'd fancy moving in with me,' I pointed out. 'He's never been my best mate.'

She shrugged, pouting a little. 'Your choice. As long as it isn't one of your football groupies.'

I dived into the pool and pulled her under. 'Hearts reserves don't qualify for groupies,' I told her after we'd risen to the surface again. I paused. 'Mind you, my dad didn't say I couldn't let a girl stay there.'

'Apart from me? Don't you dare.'

'I don't know any girls apart from you,' I reminded her.

'Can I stay? At weekends, at least? My mum won't mind and my dad won't ask.'

'Mine says no, not yet. Let's keep him happy for a year or so.'

'I suppose. Anyway, he might decide to move a girl of his own in there, or bring one over from here.'

I laughed. 'My dad? You're kidding.'

'I thought you said he was chummy with his editor.'

'Not that chummy.' I remembered a detail. 'Besides, she wears a wedding ring.'

'Aw, Xavi,' she exclaimed. 'How naive can you get? So did Caro Livingstone, Scott's mother, and she shagged half the men in her street before his father found out about it.'

I'd known that Scott's folks were divorced, but none of the colourful details. 'Where did you hear that?'

'Girl talk at school,' she said, vaguely.

'Well, you can forget that as far as my old man and Pilar are concerned.' I explained his views on relations with the staff.

Grace raised an expressive blonde eyebrow. 'You reckon?'

I nodded. 'He isn't a man to let his cock get in the way of his business. He learned that the hard way.'

She was seventeen, but she had the smile of a thirty-year-old. 'Nice choice of adjective,' she murmured.

The flat was all right. Hell no, that's what I said when I was seventeen. It was a great deal better than all right. It wasn't in a Georgian or Victorian block as I'd expected, but in a much newer building, which Willie Lascelles described as art deco, a phrase that meant precisely bugger all to me at that time. It was on the top floor, the fourth, with comfortably proportioned apartments, their doors and ceilings appropriate to my height. The living room, which had a television, a music centre and, to my great delight, an upright piano against one wall . . . the clearest evidence possible of Grandma's influence . . . looked out over Queensferry Street, while the two biggest bedrooms, the en suite and the one I decided I wouldn't be renting out, had a view to the north, across the Forth to Fife, and had less traffic noise at night as a result.

Everything about it was fresh and spotless; there was a smell of new paint about it and all the furniture looked to be straight from Martin and Frost. As a matter of fact it was, as the lawyer was quick to tell me as he showed me round. I liked Willie Lascelles, not least because he treated me, regardless of my youth, with the respect he would show any other client. 'Your father spent a lot of money on this place,' he said. 'He's had it completely refurbished, rewired, replumbed, the lot. It's a fine property, one of the nicest I've been involved with. I'm sure you'll enjoy it. You'll be fine here, and if you should have any problems, I'm a phone call away.'

With or without company I was going to like it; I knew that at first sight. What I didn't know, and couldn't have guessed, was that I'd still be living there almost thirty years later. Most of that original furniture has been replaced, some of it more than once, and the decoration was refreshed a couple of times, but essentially it always remained the home that Willie Lascelles first unlocked for me. The flatmates went in time, of course. I came to prefer it that way, but in 1979, I couldn't fill up the place fast enough. Wee Dave Colquhoun . . . in reality he didn't stop growing until he reached five feet ten, but he was always called wee Dave . . . jumped at the chance. He hated Watson's, and he'd talked his soldier father into letting him transfer to Basil Paterson's College, an independent set-up that caters for young adults rather than kids of his age, but which had agreed to take him on and get him up to Oxford entrance standard. I'd no worries about Dave as a tenant; he'd been raised on military lines, so he was always neat and tidy, almost to the point of obsession.

I'd given Bobby Hannah first refusal, of course, the day after I moved in. His face fell when I made the offer. 'You bugger,' he moaned. 'I've just turned down the place they offered me at Heriot Watt. I'm going to Aberdeen instead, the main reason being that my folks were being difficult about me leaving home if I went to uni in Edinburgh. I'm sure they'd have been fine if they'd known I was living with you.'

'Is it too late to change?' I asked him.

'By about a week. If you'd only phoned me . . .'

'I didn't know myself until Saturday, Bobby.'

So Scott Livingstone took the room instead, after I'd explained to him what the house rules were and that anyone who broke them would be given no second chances. I've never been one to make threats; they're always promises, and Scott knew that. I felt sure of his good behaviour, for I had another hold over him. As Grace had reminded me, for the three years following his parents' divorce, he'd been forced to live with his mother, and to endure a succession of 'uncles' who had passed through his life. The stable jockey of that moment was only nine years older than him, and Scott was in the bad books for knocking out one of his teeth in an argument over rights to the dregs of a Corn Flakes packet. He knew that if he fell out with me, or let me down, he'd be back there.

Nonetheless, it wasn't plain sailing at the start, for all our good intentions and impeccable conduct. When it became clear to the neighbours that three teenage boys were living above them, without parental supervision, it caused a bit of a stir on the lower floors. Nothing was said to us by any of them, but after a couple of weeks I had a visit from a small middle-aged man in a crumpled suit. I was still wearing a Hearts tracksuit after a training session, and I'd barely opened the door to him before he advised me that he was the factor of the building and demanded to 'inspect the premises'. Willie Lascelles had told me that maintenance of the common area was managed by a firm of surveyors and that each owner paid an annual community fee, so I knew at once that the guy was effectively my employee, and was overplaying his hand by a long way. I told him that I couldn't let him in at that time, as the boys and I had booked a trio of strippers for that afternoon, and that he should get in touch with my father's solicitor if he wanted to make an appointment to visit. He stood his ground, glaring up at me, until his neck began to ache. 'Go away,' I told him quietly, 'or my father will be getting in touch with you himself.'

I watched him from the front room window as he climbed into his Cortina and drove off. Its blue exhaust fumes had barely cleared before I changed out of my training gear into a white shirt and slacks and began a round of visits to our neighbours. It took me the rest of the day to catch them all in, but by the time I was finished, I'd introduced myself to each one, told them who my father was and why I was occupying his flat, and promised them that we'd all be good boys. Most of them were taken aback by my call, but they all gave me a hearing; one guy was crusty to begin with . . . maybe he was the culprit who'd set the factor on us . . . but he turned out to be a Hearts supporter, so he was an easy convert.

Once that teething problem was smoothed, the three of us . . . three and a half really, for Grace was there at least two evenings a week during school term and every Sunday (on Saturdays less so, for her father had a burst of Jewishness, perhaps inspired by the prospect of his daughter moving out of his influence for good, and insisted that she observe the Sabbath at least once a month) . . . blended into what was, I have to admit even now with all that water flowed under the bridge, a happy little family unit. My reservations about Scott faded away quickly, for he was as tidy as I asked him to be . . . although we both struggled to live up to wee Dave's military standards . . . and was never aggressive about the Corn Flakes or anything else. We were each of us students, and although Scott's school workload was less than Dave's at his cramming college, or mine, as I juggled football commitments and university work, there were few moans over the restrictions on television viewing that we'd agreed. At the time, our accord surprised me: I hadn't expected it to be such plain sailing. Looking back, now I can understand why it was. We were three lonely boys. None of us came from a family background that had ever approached normality, neither Dave nor I had any siblings, while Scott's only sister was twelve years older than him, and all three of us had absentee dads. Scott's was a surgeon, who'd taken the huff when the court had refused him custody and had little to do with him, Dave's was still operational in the army and his son didn't know where, and mine . . . I didn't care to talk about. Together, we were the closest thing to a family any of us had, and if you could line the three of us up today . . . difficult: you'd need a shovel . . . and ask us the same question, it's probable that each one of us would admit that for that year, that first shining year of adulthood, we were truly happy, happier, indeed, than we had ever been. The other two guys both had girlfriends. Scott had three or four, in fact, a succession of girls from school, who, as he put it, came and went, but Dave's was more enduring, Lina, a Chinese student he'd met at college. She was three years older than him, and had been sent to Scotland from Hong Kong by her parents, to live with an uncle and broaden her education. She was a nice girl, in every old-fashioned respect.

'Like two kids on a Sunday School trip,' Scott muttered one evening in the kitchen, watching them through the open door as they sat side by side on the couch. 'Have a word with him, Xavi.' He glanced at Grace. 'Or you take her aside. Up to the Brook, even.'

I cuffed him lightly round the ear. Grace frowned at him. 'You know, Scott,' she said, 'if you ever need brain surgery, they'll prepare you by shaving your crotch.' I laughed, spontaneously, loud enough for Lina to look round at us, and know at once that we'd been talking about her when I cut it off short.

Dave's dad was so mysterious that Scott once speculated to Grace and me that he didn't really exist, that the wee chap was actually an orphan with a guardian and a trust fund, shoved out of the way to complete his education. I might have bought that, had Major Colquhoun not turned up out of the blue to visit his son for Christmas.

His name was John and it was obvious at first sight where Dave's early problems with perpendicularity had come from. The soldier was no more than five feet seven, but stocky with it. He was also tanned, darker than Grandma Paloma; that told me, although I didn't remark upon it, that wherever it was that he'd been operational, it hadn't been Ireland, not for a while at any rate.

He had booked himself into the Mount Royal Hotel for a week, but I wasn't having that. I insisted that he move into the spare room, the one that had never been used. He protested, but not for long. 'What are you guys doing for Christmas lunch?' he asked me as he carried his suitcase across the threshold . . . with no obvious effort, I noticed, although it seemed almost as big as him.

'Trying to choose from our freezer stock at the moment,' I confessed. 'Now you're here, I could go to Grace's, but that would mean Scott would have to go to his mum's, with the attendant risk of him shoving a drumstick up her boyfriend's arse.' That was no joke. Relations between my flatmate and the guy, who'd even had the temerity to describe himself as his stepfather (this would have made him younger than his 'stepdaughter', Scott's sister), were worse than ever. I was on Scott's side, all the way. The clown had called at the flat in late August, during the school day, when only I was there, to 'check that everything's up to standard' as he'd put it. I'd tolerated that, but when he insisted on inspecting Scott's bedroom, I showed him the door, indeed I showed him the street, and told him that if he ever came back uninvited I'd take him to Tynecastle and see whether I could kick him from goal to goal without a bounce.

'Let me take you all out,' Major John offered.

'Thanks,' I replied, 'but you wouldn't want to go anywhere in Edinburgh that you could still get booked into.'

'In that case we'll do it properly in-house.'

That's how it worked out. John bought and cooked the turkey and trimmings, I did a Spanish starter, a gazpacho recipe of Grandma Paloma's that I'd copied, and Lina did the fish course, something in a wok involving soya and bean sprouts. There were seven of us round the table; Grace and me, John, Dave and Lina, Scott . . . and his sister Billie. She was between men at that point and he'd asked if he could invite her, to make him feel less of a spare, I guessed, although he said that it was because he felt sorry for her. She tried to pull John, of course; they were next to each other at the table, facing me, and I could see right from the gazpacho that she was on the move. I could see that he wasn't embarrassed, or taken aback, either; as the evening went on he paid more and more attention to her and less and less to everyone else. But that was all right; it was Christmas . . . I'd given Grace a gold Star of David on a chain; she'd given me a sweater that was too small and that I'd eventually have to replace through a special order from Jenners, without ever letting her know . . . and it was the biggest dinner party I'd ever been part of in my life. It occurred to me there and then that I'd never sat at a table with more than three other people.

It's not something I've revisited very often since, but the memory of that evening, that shining evening, still has the power, thirtyish years on, to stir feelings within me, however much I try to suppress them.

It makes me wish that I could have frozen the moment.

It makes me wish that I had taken Grace by the hand, when dinner was at an end, led her from the room, from the flat, to the airport, and slept there until we could board the first flight that would have taken us eventually to Spain, and never returned.

It makes me wish for things that never were, but could have been, yet never will be now.

And still sometimes, when it's returned in the dark of night as I've lain alone, it's made me cry, sent great salt tears running down my great lugubrious face, as I've contemplated the inevitability of the sorrows that lie in wait for us all, and confront us, sooner or later.

I had that table burned, years ago, but it did no good. It was as if its ashes still sat in a pile, beneath its successor in the dining room, and I knew that however wide I opened the window, even in the strongest of gales, they would never blow away.

The evening did end, of course. A taxi arrived, for Lina and Grace to share. John insisted on seeing Billie home to Bruntsfield. (He didn't return until the following evening.) That left Dave, Scott and me to wash up and bin the wreckage, but we weren't complaining; we were three well fed and happy lads.

By the time Christmas Day became Boxing Day, we were finished, and back in the living room, gazing out at the street lights, betting a pound a head in a sweep on when John would return . . . Scott won, of course; he knew his sister, and Dave didn't really know his dad all that much better than I did mine. The boys were killing tins of Tartan Special, but I was restricting myself to Irn Bru, since I had a reserve league game in the afternoon, three o'clock kick-off at fucking Merrytown. Yes, fucking Merrytown, arch-enemies of the Jam Tarts, but I was too contented to care. I can still recall my last thought, as I went to bed. It was of how little I'd known until then about what life had to offer. And yet, even then, I hardly knew a damn thing.

'He's a nice lad, is your son.'

'I'm glad you said that. I think so myself, but it's nice to have an objective opinion. I'm carrying a lot of guilt about that boy; if he'd turned out the other way it would have been down to me.'

'How old was he when his mother died?'

'Nine.'

'What happened to her?'

'A brain tumour. It took her in six months.'

'Shit, that's too bad. You were left on your own with him, were you?'

'Yes. My mother was still alive then, and Deirdre's dad, but neither of them were in a position to take him on. I could have resigned my commission, but I decided not to.'

'It was your career, John.'

'My career could have been raising my son; maybe it should have been. But I chose to stay on in the army. My excuse was that it would have been difficult for me to leave.'

'Why?'

'Because of the work I was doing at the time. I was part of a team, and if I'd pulled out, it might have put the others at risk.'

'Does that mean you've been in action?'

'Sort of.'

'What does that mean?'

'It means "don't ask". It's not something I can talk about.'

'Careless talk cost lives?'

'Not really; it gives me nightmares.'

'Poor baby.'

'The army's been good to me, though. It's taken care of David's education and that'll go on till he's finished university, even if something were to happen to me.'

'Could it?'

'Of course. Just as something could happen to you, crossing the road, or getting on the wrong plane. As a serving soldier, my chances are a bit higher, that's all. Enough about me and mine though; I felt a bit sorry for Scott, the way it turned out. He was on his own at the end.'

'My kid brother gets his share, with those big, wide, challenging eyes, and those looks; don't you worry about that. From what he says he's boned half the girls at his school.'

'Not including Grace, I hope.'

'He told me she'd had her sights on the Aislado boy since they were in primary. And she's the sort of girl who always gets what she wants. And yet . . .'

'And yet what?'

'Nothing, it's just that sometimes . . . No, no; forget it.'

'What's her background?'

'Jewish, although you wouldn't think so from the blonde hair. Her dad has his own business, out near Bathgate; he's a pharmacist, but in a hell of a big way. He's a manufacturer; his factory supplies the NHS, from what Scott told me. Minted, but not as much as Joe Aislado.'

'You're on first name terms with Xavi's dad?'

'Yes, I know Joe. I met him in the Royal Terrace Casino a few years back, before he sold his pub chain and moved to Spain.'

'Why do I imagine that you're on more than first-name terms?'

'I'm that transparent, am I? We were for a while.'

'So you could have been Xavi's stepmother?'

'Not a chance. Joe was generous . . . with gifts; I don't mean he paid me . . . but he made it clear from the off that the one thing he'd never give me would be a marriage certificate.'

'How did it end? With him going to Spain?'

'No; I chucked him. I found out that he'd shagged my mother as well, a few years before, when she was still married to my dad.'

'Did he know about the connection?'

'Sure. It didn't bother him. It was too much for me to handle, though.'

'Does Xavi know about the two of you?'

'The three of us, you mean? No, no chance. Nobody knew. Joe kept a wee flat in William Street, above one of his pubs, that only he knew about. We used to go there. He told me that it was the one place he could truly get away from his mother.'

'So he's a secretive bugger, eh. What do you think of his son?'

'Mmmm. If I hadn't screwed the father I might have fancied him myself. Have you seen the size of his hands? If the rest of him's in proportion, it's no wonder the Starshine girl had that well pleased look in her eye tonight.'

'I didn't quite mean it in that way.'

'I know you didn't, man. Xavi's a nice lad. I've met him a couple of times before, with Scott, when they were younger. But he's deep, very, very deep. I've never even seen the granny, but from what Scott's told me, she's left her mark on him. Joe's not a man you would cross, but Xavi . . . even less so, I'd say.'

'No, no, you've got that wrong. Xavi's a big lad and he might not take shit, but a slap's as far as it would go. There's no real violence in him. I can tell you that, and I'm a judge you can rely on. I know about his dad too; friends of mine checked out the family background before I let David move in with him.'

'Friends? What sort of friends?'

'Let's just call them intelligent; I have to be a bit careful.'

'Is that something else you can't talk about?'

'You got it.'

'My name didn't come up in these checks, did it?'

'No, they just looked into his business, and his connections. It was clean, and he wasn't in the grip of any local gangsters. Far from it: he had an ex-cop as his group security adviser, so nobody ever went near him looking for protection money or any crap like that.'

'Hell, I could have told you all that. My mum's bidey-in might have a different view from yours about Xavi, but that's not what I meant. I suppose I don't really know what I mean. There's something in him, something big and dark and very serious, and if it's ever . . . Ah hell, John, enough of that. Thanks to my wee brother, I've turned out to be the fairy on your Christmas tree; make me feel like that again.'

Six

Looking back, either I'd put the fear of God in wee Dave and Scott, or we were boring young farts, for in the two years that the three of us lived together we had no more neighbour trouble after that first incident. There was no serious boozing, there were no cigarettes smoked, never mind dope, and Grace and Lina were the only regular female callers. In fact we were so proper, that Grace complained that our sex life was as contrived as it was at her folks' place, restricted to the odd occasion when there was no one else in.

We began to address that situation after a year, once we'd both turned eighteen. I'd saved enough of my football money to afford the ring that Grace wanted. I did the proper thing by calling formally on her mother and father, on the day after she finished her last exam at Watson's, and a week after I'd finished my football season with another shut-out.

Magda . . . we were all on first name terms by then . . . was genuinely pleased; she beamed all over her face when I told them why I was there. Rod was a bit less sure, but when I said that we didn't plan to be paying Watson's primary fees until we were at least thirty-five, he grinned, said, 'Okay,' and shook my hand. When we went to Spain, a few days later, we thought that it would be as a couple, but, after admiring the ring, Grandma Paloma showed each of us to the same rooms we had the year before, without a flicker of a smile.

I spent more time with my dad that summer than ever I had before. It wasn't because I felt drawn to him, but because I wanted to know more about the business. As he'd anticipated, Ramon Hernandez was gone by then, having resigned in frustration, and so there were no constraints on my being seen at the paper. I was also a free agent as far as travel was concerned. I'd managed to pass my driving test the previous March, at the second attempt, and was given the use of the old Land Rover. There was a new one on the premises, parked beside what Grace once called 'the servants' quarters'. (Only the once, though: Grandma Paloma overheard her and told her sharply that she had never had a servant in her life and that the Mali family were staff, just as much as the people in 'the fine building in Girona'.) The new vehicle was much posher, a Range Rover, indeed. Pablo looked slightly nervous whenever I saw him drive it, but his daughter looked as if she had been born for it.

Esme and I renewed our sparring sessions on my first day back in Girona, but there was no malice on either side. I was a year older, but I'd probably gained a lot more than that in maturity. I'd also come to realise that she was an important part of my dad's life; she represented continuity, a link between the world he'd grown up in and that to which he'd returned.

A flashier guy might have seen himself as a conquering hero in Spain, but that's one thing I'll say about Josep-Maria Aislado. He's always been simple in his personal tastes. For example, while he's always been a Mercedes driver, he's never owned anything more lavish than a mid-range saloon. His grander personal purchases were usually inspired by his mother. He told me that he'd bought the Range Rover after she'd complained that the old four-by-four was a rattletrap. (Actually there was more to it than that, but I didn't twig at that time.) If it had been down to him, without Grandma Paloma laying down her requirements, he probably would have bought an unpretentious apartment in Girona when they went back to Spain, rather than the masia, and been quite happy there as long as it was handy for the office, just as I was always content to live in the flat he bought thirty years ago . . . and in which, incidentally, he has never set foot.

Pilar Roca gave me the run of the editorial department whenever I was there. I suppose she expected me to hang around the sports writers, but I only did that once or twice, out of politeness to Angel Esposito, who was still trying to sell me on the idea of Barcelona B. On the rest of my visits I attached myself to Simon Sureda, running errands, taking copy to the typesetters . . . new technology was planned but it hadn't arrived in Girona at that point . . . and eventually doing small reporting jobs, the sort of research that could be done on the phone then passed on to a real staff reporter who would write the finished story.

Pilar did something else for me too; she gave me a name, that of a man she'd met in Madrid when he'd been a correspondent for the *Daily Telegraph*, until he'd been called back home and put in charge of the foreign desk. 'Once you're finished at university,' she told me, 'you might give him a call, that's if you're still crazy enough to want to get into this business.'

'What if I want to come here?' I asked her. I meant it as a joke, but throughout my life, people have always assumed that everything I say is serious . . . as, almost invariably, it is.

Like the rest of them, Pilar didn't get it. Her expression turned frostier than I'd ever seen it. 'Then there will be a place for you,' she replied. 'You're the owner's son and if it's his wish that you join the staff, it must be so, even if I have to fire someone else to make a place for you.'

At the time I was taken aback by her coldness, but now I understand her. Pilar was looking not at me, but at the future, imagining an ambitious Aislado Junior arriving in her office like a two-metre cuckoo, and wondering how long it would take for her own position to be under threat. Not that it would have been; she's one of the finest journalists I've ever known. Pilar Roca is sixty-four years old now. She is managing editor of all of InterMedia's Spanish titles, a member of the corporate board and she has no plans to retire.

I said something similar to her then. 'Pilar, I don't expect special treatment. More than that, I'll never accept it. I'll make my own way in my own world, and for all the name I carry like a burden, that's Scotland.'

Actually, if she hadn't made the offer of the man at the *Telegraph*, that exchange would never have taken place. My first year at Edinburgh had gone well, but I still wasn't sure about my future after I'd finished my degree, or how big a part football, my only profession at that time, remember, was going to play in it. It wasn't something that my dad and I had discussed for a while, but one night . . . maybe Pilar had told him of our talk . . . he raised the subject over dinner. 'How's the goalkeeping career developing?' he asked me. 'Polished any good benches lately?'

'None,' I told him with more than a little pride. 'I'm the number one reserve keeper; I played every game last season. But the first team got back into the top league, and their goalie's in his prime, so I don't expect to be stepping up any time soon.'

'They won their league,' he agreed, 'but will they stay up next season? My spy at Tynecastle has serious doubts about that. He reckons they'll struggle. Your chance might come sooner than you think.'

'Your spy?' I laughed. 'Who would that be? You don't know anyone there.'

'Ah, but I do. Your future father-in-law.'

'You've been speaking to Rod?'

He beamed at Grace across the table. 'You think he didn't call me after you'd asked for his daughter's hand?' He paused. 'It would have been nice to hear it from you, by the way.'

He hasn't made me feel guilt very often in my life, but that was one of those times. In fact, I'd called Grandma Paloma to tell her that Grace and I were engaged. I was surprised she hadn't told him, but I supposed that she'd expected me to do it myself. 'Sorry,' I said.

'Accepted, as long as you invite me to the wedding. Rod's not my only source, though. One of your directors approached Willie Lascelles and asked him if I'd be interested in buying a controlling stake in the club.'

I sat bolt upright, staring down at him. 'You what? And are you going to? I'll have to get a transfer if you do. The other players would give me hell.'

He laughed. 'Then you can relax, kid. There's as much chance of me investing in a football club as there is of you becoming a ballet dancer.'

Grace giggled, and Grandma Paloma almost smiled; I had a quick mental flash of myself in tights, and relaxed. 'But you are saying that the club's for sale, though?'

'Sure, but it's a mess, as a business. It'll need to be restructured before anyone in his right mind would think of putting money into it, and the present board aren't sold on that idea.'

I filed that information away, then forgot about it for the rest of our brief holiday. We had fallen into a pattern of heading for Spain once our exams were over, and staying there until I was due back for training in early July. That summer, though, we had another deadline to meet. Grace had finished with Watson's and had a theoretically free summer until October, when she was due to start her accountancy degree at Edinburgh University. But Rod Starshine had decided that she should pass the time, and gain some experience, by working in his office. She had been sniffy about the idea, but for once her father had been firm and had told her that it wasn't optional. She'd gone along with it, but only after cajoling him into giving Scott Livingstone a job as well, a smart move as far as I was concerned, as it meant that even during vacation time he'd be able to pay the modest rent that I charged him, for his dad kept him pretty tight for cash, and his mother was no help in making up the shortfall, with the useless boyfriend showing no signs of moving on. If it hadn't been for Billie, Scott would have struggled; she was a regional manager with a fashion chain, and was a reliable source in times of cash-flow difficulty. We had seen quite a bit of Scott's sister around the flat since the Christmas dinner. Her visits would be casual, but she seemed to pay special attention to wee Dave. He read nothing into it, but Scott and I suspected that either she was still in touch with John, who had disappeared back into the mystery that was his life, or she wanted to be.

Every year our time in Spain seemed to pass more quickly, as our responsibilities grew back home. On the day before we were due to leave I didn't go to Girona, staying around the house with Grace instead. I'd left her alone for much of the fortnight, but she didn't mind; she had a summer in her dad's factory ahead of her and she was happy to spend her time sunbathing by the pool. I didn't realise it at that stage of my life but I am constitutionally incapable of being 'on holiday'. I can't remember the last time I took a proper break. I suspect others would tell you that I never did.

Even on that last day, I couldn't settle on my sunbed. I swam a few lengths and tried lying there to let the sun dry me off, but soon I was on my feet again, on the pretext of fetching a couple of beers from the fridge in what my dad called 'the summer kitchen', in which occasionally Grandma Paloma would allow him to cook barbecues. I popped the caps, went back to the pool and laid one beside Grace, who had turned over to lie face down. 'Oil me,' she murmured. I obliged, spreading the high-factor stuff that she needed for her fair skin all over her back, her legs and a few other places that weren't quite exposed to the sun. 'Want me to do you?' she asked, as I finished.

'I'm fine,' I replied, but she knew that anyway. I have olive skin that just goes darker in the sun, and all I've ever done with it is keep it moist. Risky, with all the skin cancer scares? As if I care.

She murmured, sleepily; I took my Cruz Campo and strolled into the garden, heading for the orchard to check on the ripeness of the apples. The cultivated areas were fenced off from the grounds nearest the house but with gaps instead of gates, so I stepped through . . . and stopped in my tracks. Carmen, the gardener's daughter, was stretched out on a towel between two stands of trees. She was wearing even less than Grace. I was about to back off, but she seemed to sense my presence for her eyes opened. 'Sorry,' I said, in Spanish, as she sat up and reached for the black bra that lay on the ground beside her. 'I didn't realise.'

She smiled as she made herself half-decent. 'You weren't to know,' she replied. 'Anyway, this is your garden; you can go where you like.'

'It's my father's, not mine,' I pointed out.

'It's the same thing.'

'No, really, that's not the way it is. I'm just a visitor here. Whatever, you're entitled to your privacy. I shouldn't have disturbed you. I'm sorry; I'll leave you alone.'

'It's okay, really. Do you always apologise as much?' She smiled; when Carmen did that, there was something about it that made you smile back.

So I did. 'Hardly ever,' I told her. 'It's not in my family's nature.'

'I wouldn't know about that,' she said. 'Nobody in your family has ever had any cause to apologise to me, or to my parents. Far from it; my father says that when they bought this estate it was the best thing that ever happened to my mother and him. They've always treated us perfectly.'

'Even Grandma Paloma?' I exclaimed.

'Is that what you call her? Senora Puig is a very great lady.' She screwed her eyes up and peered at me. 'I'm trying to see if you look like her, but you don't, not really; not like your father either, I don't think.'

'I'm twenty-five centimetres taller than him, so that might be hard to judge.'

'That's true.'

'Look,' I ventured, 'why do you sunbathe here? Why don't you come up to the pool with Grace and me?'

'I'm fine here, honestly. I'd have to go to the cottage for a proper costume, and mine are all well worn. Besides, your father wouldn't like it.'

'It's got nothing to do with him. If you come it's at my invitation.'

'Still, I won't, thank you.'

'Well,' I persisted, 'can I bring you a beer?'

She laughed. 'If you like you can pick me an apple.'

I reached up and plucked one from the nearest tree, from the top, where they were at their most red. She nodded her thanks as I handed it to her, then polished it on her towel. 'What are you doing here, Carmen, out in the country like this?' I asked her, boldly.

'Living,' she replied, with no hesitation, 'as I choose, and who's to fault me for that?'

'Not me,' I told her, 'for I do the same thing.'

'But you're rich, so your choices are greater.'

I shook my head. 'I'm not rich; I'm a badly paid professional football goalkeeper. It's my dad that's wealthy. I don't want to be. I want to look after Grace on my own, by my own efforts.'

She smiled again. 'That really is how you think, isn't it? And it's . . . it's noble. But you can't hide from it, Xavi. You're a wealthy guy. Get used to it.'

But I couldn't then, and the truth is, sometimes I still can't. I shook my head. 'No, I'm my own man.'

'Not any more,' she countered, 'not in every sense. I saw that ring on Grace's finger; that means that you're her man, as well as your own. You might deny your own background to yourself, but is it right that you deny it to her?'

'Grace is in the same situation as me. Her father's well off, but she doesn't care about that. She and I, we're a team and what we have we'll make for ourselves.'

'Are you going to be a football star? Will we see you at Camp Nou?'

'If a man called Angel Esposito had his way you might, but no, I'll stay in Scotland with my club there. I'm good; I'll make the grade.'

She wrinkled her very attractive nose, managing, with the gesture, to make it even more attractive. 'I don't know,' she said. 'You're a goal-keeper, you said. I went out with a footballer once, one of the Espanyol team. I got to know his crowd, the goalkeepers among them. They were all a little crazy, a little wild. You're not at all crazy, and you're not at all wild.'

'Thanks for the vote of confidence. But Bob Wilson isn't crazy,' I told her.

She stared at me, puzzled. 'Who's Bob Wilson?' Maybe she had made her point there, without knowing it. 'When I was your age,' she continued, 'and a student like you, I was an idealist too. I studied art; I was going to be a famous painter. Now I know better. I'm good, but I don't think I'll ever be famous. You have to be two things for that, in Spain at any rate; you have to be very, very old, or better still, dead, and you have to be a man.'

'So you chucked it? You gave up?'

'No, I still paint.' She pointed behind her at the old cottage, that had become a store, as my dad had told me. 'I use a room there as a studio, and I turn out impressionist landscapes that I sell for a few thousand pesetas, maybe ten or twelve on a good day. And I live with my parents and help them.'

'I'll buy one,' I said at once.

'Don't patronise me.'

'I'm not. I'll buy one.'

'You haven't even seen them.'

'I've seen you. Anything you paint will have some of you in it, so it'll be good. Really, I'm serious.'

'Okay, but you won't buy it: I'll give it to you.'

'No, you can't do that. I'll pay you.'

'It's the only way you'll have it. Call it an engagement gift to you and Grace.'

She was as good as her word. Next morning, after we'd said goodbye to Grandma for another year . . . and that was all, 'Goodbye', no hugs, or any other public display of affection . . . and as I was loading our two small cases into the boot of his Merc, my dad handed me a rectangular parcel, wrapped in cardboard and tied securely with string. 'From Carmen,' he said. 'Don't let them make you put it in the hold.' I headed towards the cottage, to thank her, but he stopped me. 'No time,' he insisted. 'You can drop her a line, or wait till you see her next year.'

Grace wanted to open the package during our stopover in London, but I didn't fancy retying it, so I made her wait until after our taxi had dropped us back at the flat. (The boys were out when we got back; a note from Dave on the kitchen table told us that they were in a pub in Stockbridge called the Bailie, if we cared to join them. We didn't.) When eventually we saw it, we were taken by surprise, and not only by the fact that it was damn good. Impressionist it may have been but it wasn't a landscape. It was a painting of the masia and garden, with two significant additions, a blonde girl on a sunbed by the pool, and a tall, brown figure crouched beside her, with his hand resting between her shoulder blades.

As I thought back to that garden conversation with Carmen, the more remarkable it seemed to me that such a talented, intelligent, not to mention attractive woman should hide herself away as she had done. No, I couldn't see her waiting on tables in a fast-food restaurant in Tossa del Mar, but there had to be other opportunities open to her, even if the dice were loaded against her as a female artist in a part of the world that was still up itself over the icons that were Salvador Dali and the ancient Miro. And then another oddity occurred to me; she had given me a fair grilling about my life, my plans, my philosophy, and yet unlike any other stranger I had met at that point in my life, she had asked me nothing at all about my mother. They all got round to it, in time, but not her. I wondered whether, and how, she knew that even in Spain, the subject was not to be broached with me.

Grace loved the painting . . . not least because she was in it . . . so much that I told her she could hang it in her folks' house, since it was half hers anyway. But she wouldn't have that. 'It's our picture,' she insisted, 'so it should hang in our house.'

'But we don't have a house,' I pointed out.

She looked around the living room. 'Oh no?' she murmured.

'Grace, this is my dad's place.'

'It's your home, and it's going to be our home . . . or don't you want me to move in?'

'Of course I do, but I can't chuck Scott and Dave into the street.'

'I'm not asking you to.'

'You want us to share a flat as a couple with two single guys?'

'Why not? We're engaged.'

'Privacy?'

'We've got an en suite bathroom.'

'They don't.'

'Then the house rule will be no willie-waving in the living room.'

'What are Magda and Rod going to say?'

'They've already said it. I told them before we went away that I was moving out. Mum was fine, so was Dad.'

'He agreed just like that?'

'Sure. I told him that since he was regarding me as an adult by making me work for him all summer, then I'd make my own adult choices. I also said that if he made up a fuss about me moving in with my fiancé, then I'd take a room in a flat with a bunch of pot-smoking, whoring female students. Or would you prefer that too?' she challenged.

'Are you going to pay rent?' I asked. She stared at me and for a second I thought I was in another Pilar Roca situation, then she smiled, pulled me close and rubbed herself against me.

'Are you?' she countered. I took her into the bedroom and we called it quits. She stayed with me that night, and almost every other night from then on, until . . .

It's funny, but being with Grace didn't banish altogether my feeling of isolation. In my mind, I was still outside the world, looking in, but as of that moment, our first real night together, she was standing beside me. There was still that sense of loss within me, the loss of the normal childhood that I had been denied, but I had learned to live with it, and as I learned to live with her, I came to feel that nothing was beyond us. Together I saw us as one entity, one being; together I saw us as special. That was my belief. We were charmed, that year and in those that followed.

But it didn't rub off on those around us, or keep all the demons at bay.

*

90

Our new situation established, we drifted into a quiet domesticity, four teenagers, each of us older than our years, each for a different reason. We had the luxury of Willie Lascelles' hired cleaners to keep the place spotless . . . that really impressed Grace . . . and we even ate well. Dave had learned to cook out of necessity, I had picked up quite a bit from Grandma Paloma, when she'd let me help her in the kitchen, a privilege that would have been granted only to a child, and Grace had learned the basics from her mother. She didn't eat pork, her one concession to her heritage, but nobody ever complained about its absence when she was over the hob. Only Scott was totally useless, as he proved by a succession of disasters, the messiest of which was when he insisted on cooking a large lemon sole whole in the microwave. It would have been fine, but that specimen had a particularly large roe; after it exploded it took him an hour to scrape the wreckage off the inside. We operated a catering rota, but it was agreed that when Scott's turn came up, that would be takeaway night. There was the odd variation when Lina was around. We never asked, but whenever she volunteered to cook Chinese, we never tried to talk her out of it. Her relationship with Dave was as stable and proper as it had been from the start, with no public displays of intimacy between them, and no sleepovers, although I had dropped a gentle hint to him that I would have no problem.

The closest we ever came to a fight was over Lina. Scott, Dave and I were in the kitchen one evening, washing up after a great Chinese dinner, with Bobby Hannah, who had dropped in on a visit from Aberdeen, while Grace studied in our room for an imminent class exam, and Lina watched *The Bill* in the living room. We were absorbed in our individual tasks, when Scott dug the by-then-not-so-wee chap in the ribs. 'Okay,' he said, 'time to spill the beans. Have you given her one yet? Is it true what they say about Chinese girls?' I guessed at the time this was for Bobby's benefit, and I'm still sure that it was. Those two had always sparked off each other at school, each one always looking to be one up on the other. Scott's put-down of his flatmate was his unsubtle attempt to show that he was still the big man on campus, although in truth, he never had been. I suppose that was always me, not that I ever sought the role.

Dave reacted very slowly. He dried his hands on the tea towel he was using, and laid it down. Then he turned to Scott, and replied, very quietly, 'If you ever ask me that again, or say anything about Lina, I will tie you to a kitchen chair, and soak your tackle in a pan of boiling water.'

Scott was still slightly taller than him, more heavily built on the face of it, and he could handle himself, as his mother's bloke, and a few others, had found out. His immediate reaction was to laugh. 'You?' he challenged, his voice suddenly loaded with the contempt that I'd hoped he'd left behind him with his schooldays.

Dave nodded. 'Me,' he whispered.

Bobby and I stood there, looking at the two of them nose to nose, taken aback by the speed with which the teenage pissing contest had developed. Only it wasn't a pissing contest. Dave was completely calm; as I looked at him I knew that he wasn't going to back down an inch, but not only that, I knew that if he was pushed to it he was capable of living up to his promise. I looked in his eyes and I saw his father there, Major John, courteous, considerate and for sure absolutely fucking lethal, wherever his mysterious postings took him.

I was ready to put my bulk between them, but I didn't have to. Scott did something I'd never seen him do before in such circumstances; he let his brain take over. He backed off. He wouldn't have admitted it, but that's what he did. He saw the same thing I did, and he recognised what I did. So, regardless of Bobby's presence, he relaxed, laid his hand on Dave's shoulder, and said, 'Hey, pal, cool it. I'm sorry, I wouldn't disrespect anyone who can cook like Lina.'

'You shouldn't disrespect anyone at all, Scott,' Dave replied.

'I know. You're right, sorry.'

We never talked about the kitchen incident again, but we didn't see Lina as often either. A couple of months later Grace noticed this and asked me whether she and Dave were on the skids. I told her it was work, that was all, that she was busy studying.

She understood that, for she and Scott were busy themselves. Their jobs with Starshine Pharmaceuticals plc may have been casual, but they weren't sinecures. Grace started in her dad's office, assisting his secretary, then was moved to sales and marketing, to see what went on there. Rod didn't say as much, but I realised that he was beginning the process of teaching her all about the business. He had no partners, or even minority shareholders, and he was firmly in control of everything. There were never any prizes for guessing who his designated successor was. I know now that there were people in Spain who were saying the same about me after my introduction to the newspaper, but at the time that thought did not cross my mind, far less lodge there.

Scott? On his first day there, Rod had him kitted out in a white sterile tunic, stuck a brush in his hands, and set him to sweeping the floors. 'Best place to find out what goes on in any factory,' he told him. He might have chucked it, but after a couple of weeks, he was transferred to packing and dispatch, where life was more interesting and varied, and where there were several young female employees.

They had the factory, Dave had a summer job in the Edinburgh Book Shop and I had my football. None of us had a lot of time on our hands, that was for sure. Dave's college term started earlier than ours, but it was pretty intensive, with the Oxford entrance exam on the horizon, so he was even busier, if anything.

University did start though, eventually. Grace joined me at Edinburgh, and Scott headed for Heriot Watt, to begin a maths course that he hoped would lead him to a career in surveying, which he assured me was going to be a licence to print money.

And money was something he would need. It's a hell of a thing to be brought up with expectations then to have them ripped away. I never met Scott's father. All I knew was that he was a heart surgeon, eminent in that fast-developing area, and I had been told that he worked twelve to fourteen hours a day. Scott's mother maintained that his absence had placed a fatal strain on their marriage, a view she never managed to sell to him or to Billie, especially after the divorce, which left her with the house, car and personal maintenance, as well as the sum that the court ordered him to contribute to his son's education. While it was only meant to be a contribution, Scott never saw an additional penny from his mother. Father and son saw little of each other, but that didn't strike me as odd at the time. Hell, it struck me as the norm.

And so, when Daniel Livingstone added credence to the old Scots saying about cobblers' bairns always being the worst shod, by collapsing and dying one Friday afternoon in November, in his own operating theatre, from a previously undetected heart condition, I was probably more shocked and upset than his son was.

I expected that Scott would move back in with his mother in the period leading up to the funeral, but that idea didn't seem to occur to him. Instead he stayed in the flat, grim-faced and silent, brushing off all offers of condolence or sympathy. The other four of us, Grace and I, Dave and Lina, went to the funeral . . . the first I'd ever attended . . . on the following Thursday afternoon at Mortonhall Crematorium. We stood as the family entered, Scott in the lead, escorting a very old man who turned out to be a grandfather he'd never mentioned, followed by two uncles and aunts, then by Caro, his dry-eyed mother and her 'mistake', as her son always called him, and finally, Billie Livingstone, escorted by . . . Major John Colquhoun, out of uniform in a dark suit.

'Did you know?' I whispered to Dave.

He nodded. 'He called me at college this morning. He only got cleared to come yesterday.'

The service was short, as they are in crematoria, where the next funeral is usually ready to go in even before the previous mourners are out of sight. It occurred to me that the celebrant, a dog-collared Presbyterian, was speaking about a man he barely knew, but since I didn't know him at all, that didn't bother me. I contented myself with watching the front rows. Scott sat motionless through it all, staring straight ahead, as did his grandfather, although from time to time a tremor ran through him. Once or twice, his mother put a white handkerchief to her eyes, but I doubt that there was a single person there who didn't know that it was purely for effect. Of all of them, Billie was the only one who seemed to be grieving genuinely; she sobbed her heart out during the service, and John seemed to be supporting her when we all stood for the committal, as the coffin sank into the plinth, under its velvet covering.

Afterwards, we accepted the invitation from 'the family', conveyed by the minister, to a reception in the Braid Hills Hotel. When it was over we wished we hadn't. I knew not a soul there, save for Scott and the rest of our crew, Billie, John, and Mrs Livingstone's appalling stud, who treated the event as a party, helping himself to as much of the free booze as he could corral. As we spoke with Billie and John, his braying in the background grew so loud that I felt the slow fuse of my rarely roused anger begin to ignite, and began to look seriously in his direction. But just as I was entertaining the idea of taking him to Tynecastle for a training session, or maybe no further than outside, Scott seemed to read my mind, for he put a hand on my arm. 'Leave it, Xavi,' he whispered. 'Billie and I have told our mother that we'll never speak to her again for as long as that guy's there. Maybe she'll get the message, before he bleeds her dry.'

'And if she doesn't?'

He smiled up at me, sharp-eyed, with a look there I hadn't seen before. 'Then he's all yours, my big pal, if you want the job.' (As it turned out, the guy . . . I still struggle to remember his name, but as I recall it was Blake something: yes, Blake Seven, Scott called him . . . hung around for a few more weeks, and then he was gone. Scott never mentioned it, but Billie told me that her mother had come back from Brian Drumm's one afternoon, to find that he had left. She was minus a couple of Louis Vuitton suitcases, but she was shot of him.)

Scott and Billie had to leave themselves at that point, for a meeting with their father's solicitor: the reading of the will. She insisted that

John go with her, and Grace, Dave, Lina and I took that as our cue to leave. We went straight back to the flat. John had said that he'd catch up with his son there, but when he arrived he wasn't alone. Billie was with him, still in her funeral suit, looking agitated, but in a different way. 'Is my brother here?' she asked, speaking to Grace, woman to woman.

'No,' I replied for her. 'Should he be?'

'Oh shit! I was hoping.'

John took her by the arm. 'Billie, calm down,' he told her, gently. 'He'll be all right. He needed to blow off some steam, that's all.'

'What's wrong?' Grace asked her, anxiety showing.

'It's the will,' she replied. 'It's upset him. I can't believe the bastard did that.'

'Which bastard?'

'Our father!' she snapped.

She really was spitting feathers. It was down to John to explain. 'It was pretty brutal,' he said. 'The lawyer just read it out. He might have prepared them for what was coming but he didn't; he just launched into it. As near as I can recall, it said, "Since I have been raped of most of my assets by the ludicrously biased divorce law of Scotland, it is my belief that my children, Wilhelmina Gertrude Livingstone and Scott Armour Livingstone, should look to their mother for any inheritance they might hope to receive. The only exception I make to this is the following provision: that should I die before my son has completed his formal education, he should be paid the sum of two thousand four hundred pounds per annum from the date of my death until that of his graduation, pro rata. The balance of my estate I bequeath in its entirety to the . . ." ' He paused. 'What was the charity?'

'The British fucking Heart Foundation.' She glared at me. 'Do you know how much he had left after being "raped" as he put it? Add up insurance, investments, pension pot, his house, etc., and the estate's estimated at nine hundred and thirteen thousand. Yet that bloody lawyer had the nerve to hand Scottie a cheque for a hundred and sixty pounds, and told him that he'd be getting two hundred pounds monthly from now on.'

'What did Scott say?' I asked.

'Nothing,' John told me. 'He tossed it back on the desk and stomped off, out of the room.'

I looked at Dave. 'Mather's?' He nodded.

And that's where we, Dave, John and I, found him, in that dirty smoke-filled pub at the West End, two weeks short of nineteen years old, full of hell and doing his best to drown himself in beer, but on the point of being chucked out, at best, by an aggressive, angry bartender because he couldn't pay for the pint he'd just ordered and half-consumed. John sorted the row with a pound note, and a word in the man's ear that had an instantly calming effect.

We didn't take him straight home. Instead we found a coffee shop that was still open, poured some of its finest Kenyan into him and waited with him until he was more sober, if no less angry.

'What did I do to him, Xavi?' he asked me. 'Your dad gave you a flat, mine gave me the fucking elbow.'

'My dad gave me nothing,' I pointed out. 'It's his place, not mine, and I doubt that I'd be there if it wasn't for my grandma. I don't expect anything from him. We're not that different, you and I. What we get from now on, we'll have to make for ourselves.'

'Or take,' he mumbled. He looked at John. 'Could you get me into the army?'

Dave's father grinned. 'Not at this moment in time,' he replied. 'Come on. We'd better get you back to your sister. Maybe young Grace will have calmed her down by now.'

She had. Billie was so relieved to see her brother in one piece, even if that piece was slightly bedraggled, that she hugged him to her and cried. He did too, and the rest of us thought it best to allow them to get on with it in private. Grace and I went for takeaways, leaving Lina, Dave and his dad in the kitchen, ready to provide more coffee should Scott need it. When we returned from the Stockbridge Pizza Hut, he seemed to have recovered some of his bounce. Billie was calmer too, as we gathered in the living room, with plates on our laps and mugs by our sides.

'Don't worry,' she told her brother. 'You will be all right, you know. When that guy read the will, as coldly as he did, I was as mad as you. But I'm thinking straight now, and I see things differently. Dad might have left you a bit skimped, but . . .' she paused, 'if you think about it, he was never any good with money. He made it, Mum spent it; that's how it was. When he made his will he probably thought that two hundred a month would be plenty.'

Scott frowned, his eyes dark and sunken in his pale face. 'Don't make excuses for him, Billie. He knew what fuck all is worth, and that's what he left you. And he knew what the divorce cost him.'

'It cost him pride,' John told him, quietly. 'From what Billie's told me, the split was more your mother's doing than his . . .'

'He was never there,' he shot back, 'always bloody working. Mum was lonely.'

'Working at saving lives,' Billie pointed out. 'As for our mother . . . Scottie, I'm twelve years older than you. I'm here to tell you that she has less experience of loneliness of anyone I've ever known. I remember, before you were born and after it, Dad getting home from the hospital, absolutely knackered, to find a plate of sandwiches on the kitchen table and her in his ear because she was going out with a friend and he'd made her late. And yes, the friend was always male.'

'How do you know that for sure?' he challenged. 'They could have been women friends.'

'What's she been like since the divorce? Do you think she only started collecting blokes then?'

'Possibly.'

The rest of us sat there, the cheese on our pizzas gelling as the brother-sister debate developed.

'Not a chance,' Billie scoffed, pausing to take a bite of hers.

'But how do you know?'

'Because I followed her! When I was about fourteen or fifteen. I'd heard whispers about her at school, so one night when Dad came home and she went out, I told him I was going to visit a pal and slipped out after her. He was too frazzled to object. The first time . . .'

'You did it more than once?'

'I did it for years. The first time she went down to the Canny Man pub. I couldn't go in there so I waited across the road. Not for long, though, before she came out with a bloke, and got in a taxi. I knew him; his daughter was in my year at school and I'd been to her house. He was the first of many. She used to meet them in hotels up in Bruntsfield. Chic Murray's place was a favourite; she must have made them take a room, for when she went in there, it was for the evening. Sometimes, though, she'd take a taxi. That scuppered me, but only till I learned to drive. One time, when Dad was working really late and Grandpa was looking after you, I followed her cab . . . literally . . . to the Royal Terrace Casino. That happened a few times, but she always stayed in there longer than I was able to wait. If she hadn't I might have followed her to a flat in William Street and made the connection before it was too late.'

'What connection?' Scott asked.

I've been told that in the right circumstances everybody blushes; in some people it's barely noticeable, others turn into a red traffic light. Billie Livingstone's face would have stopped a bus. 'Forget it,' she murmured. 'It's not important.'

'Maybe not,' said Dave, 'but it sounds interesting.' Out of the corner of my eye I saw John nudge him, and I was sure he glanced at me as he did.

'Yes, Billie,' I chipped in, 'tell us. Who was the mystery man?'

'I never saw him,' she replied.

'But you knew who he was.' She looked down at her plate. 'Yes, you did, didn't you? So what's the se . . .' She turned her face towards me and met my gaze; that was all she had to do. 'Jesus Christ,' I exclaimed. 'My old man. Your mother was having it off with my old man.'

She nodded. 'He met her at a parents' night, when you and Scott were in primary.'

Funny, but for all my bizarre imaginings of him and Esme, I'd never really considered the possibility that my dad might have had the same sexual appetite as I had. Indeed, I'd never considered the possibility that he and I had anything in common other than genes. I haven't researched the question but I suspect that many people share the notion that sex was invented for them, and for their own special pleasure.

'I don't remember him ever going to a parents' night,' I said. 'He never said anything to me about it. He hardly ever said anything to me about anything, come to that.'

'Your grandma made him go.'

'That would figure.' I felt myself frown. 'Did your mother tell you that? Did she tell you about my dad?'

Billie nodded; but she didn't meet my gaze. I jumped on that. 'Are you saying that you told her you'd been following her around for years, and she confessed everything?' I quizzed.

'No, but I told my father, after she'd sued for divorce. I told him he could counter-sue, but he refused. He said it would make him look like a fool.'

'So how did you know about the parents' night?'

'I can't remember now.'

'And what's this about a flat in William Street? Are you saying that they went there?'

She nodded.

'Whose was it? Hers? How could she have kept that secret from your father?'

We were all staring at her now, even Scott. Or rather, I thought we were. John was looking at me. 'Leave it, Xavi,' he said, gently, 'please.'

I did. I let it drop. Not because he'd asked me to, but because by intervening to protect Billie from my questions, he'd set out the truth for me, as clear as the brightest day. The flat wasn't Caro Livingstone's,

100

it was my dad's, and Billie knew about it because she'd been there herself.

I don't believe that anyone else who was in the room ever made the connection. Dave and Lina were innocents, in their own peaceful world, and had been bewildered by the whole exchange. I know that Scott didn't, for he never as much as hinted at it afterwards. As for Grace, later that night, when we were alone, she teased me over Caro and my dad, but didn't mention Billie, so I guess it must have passed her by as well.

'It doesn't matter,' I told Billie in the moment, back in the living room. 'I understand what you're saying. You're trying to tell Scott that your dad was a victim and that although he was angry about the way the divorce went, and about the way he was treated, he didn't actually set out to punish the two of you in his will. Isn't that it?'

She nodded again, then reached out to squeeze my hand. 'Yes. Thanks, Xavi.' I knew why she was really thanking me. 'Sorry about dropping that on you.'

'I should be apologising to you and Scott,' I pointed out, 'for my father, immoral old bastard that he is.'

'No,' she countered. 'He's just a man, and an okay man at that, not the only one to have been fooled, nay, pulled, by Mum's neglected love-starved woman act.' She turned to her brother. 'It's going to be all right, Scott. After you'd gone, John asked the solicitor whether the will was legal. He told us that we should consult someone else about that, but that in theory we could challenge it.'

He looked at her. 'Do you want to?'

'This isn't about me,' she replied.

'Of course it is. It's about both of us. Do you?'

'If you do.'

'Fuck's sake, Billie,' he snapped, 'answer me!'

'Dad's will is what he wanted,' she said, slowly, 'and it will benefit God knows how many people in the future. If it was me alone, I wouldn't challenge it.'

'Then neither will I,' he declared.

She looked doubtful. 'It's a lot of money, Scott.'

'I don't give a shit. Xavi's right; we have to make our own way in this world. We have to play the cards we're dealt.'

'Hey,' I exclaimed, 'don't quote me. I'm a privileged bastard with a dad who's set me up in this place; even if it was under duress.'

'Don't be so sure that it was,' said Billie, so quietly that only I, sitting next to her, could hear. 'If that's what you really think, Scott,' she continued, louder, 'I'll go along with it. You know who's going to be hurt worst by this, of course,' she added. 'Mum. Dad's left you very little, but at least it's something. She loses her maintenance allowance, and her lawyer wasn't smart enough to get her pension rights in the divorce settlement. Christ, she might need to get a job to support that fucking toy boy!'

'Tough shit,' Scott growled, and with these two words he did something I had never thought possible. He made me imagine that I belonged to a relatively normal and balanced family . . . which undoubtedly I did as a de facto Starshine, although that didn't occur to me at the time, or indeed until this very moment of self-confession. That status was all too brief, but there is no forever, just as, within the great mortality of us all there are no happy endings.

'You'll be fine,' I told my flatmate. On that day, Scott and I were closer than on any other in our lives. 'Your student grant will go up, maybe to the maximum. I'll see you all right here too; we'll get you through it, mate.'

He shot me one of those unfathomable looks of his. 'Thanks, Xavi,' he replied. 'I appreciate that. But I'll get me through it.'

'What do you think of him?'

'I think he's all right. He's big enough, that's for sure, must be, what, six foot six, he's got safe hands, and he gets down well for someone that tall. For my money, potentially, he's the best they've got at Tynecastle, but the trouble is, footballers don't always live up to their potential and especially not goalies. My Uncle Bob played centre-half for Stirling Albion, and he always swore that he never saw a keeper under thirty years old who really knew the game. That boy there, he's impressive, but he's got flaws: he doesn't use his height to dominate and he doesn't impose himself on the opposition like he should.'

'He's only eighteen.'

'That doesn't matter. He's the size of a bloody house. Everything in the six-yard box should be his, but it's not. When he decides to go for the ball he should clear everything out of his way, but he doesn't. He thinks too much.'

'He'll get better.'

'Maybe not here though. He's got a good goalie holding down the first team jersey, and another in the queue ahead of him. Those guys are pals, so neither will be rushing to correct his faults, for if they did, if they took the caution out of him, at least one of them would be out of a job.'

'Then he should ask for a transfer.'

'To where? Who'd buy him? Nobody's ever heard of him. If he'd a couple of caps for the Under-nineteens maybe, but from what I heard, he was passed over because the guy who picks the squad looked at his name and assumed that he wasn't qualified for Scotland.'

'You see? That was good, Tommy. That was braw.'

'Yes, but the striker shat himself. They don't do that in the top division. If somebody pauses there, it's most likely to draw the goalie in so he can do him.'

'They don't do that, do they? Hurt someone deliberate.'

'Mary, do you see anybody out there with a handbag? This is not a game for poofs. There's a guy in England called Chopper; he didn't get that nickname because of the size of his whang. The lad's a goalie.

103

If he's going to be any good, he's going to wind up with a few stitches in his head.'

'In that case, I'm not coming back.'

'But I thought you wanted . . .'

'It was you who wanted; it was you who talked me into this. Come on, let's go. It's nearly time up anyway, and he'll come past here when he goes off.'

Seven

Scott did settle down. He applied for an increased student grant on the ground of changed circumstances, and got it. That, with his two hundred quid a month, would have seen him through the term times at least, but he supplemented his income by finding a weekend job in the Pear Tree pub.

He and Billie were as good as their word to each other. Neither of them contested their father's will, not even when their mother found a new lawyer, who sued her former lawyer for negligence and went to court to claim the pension rights that he had failed to secure in the original settlement. Once again, the law was proved to be an ass: she won, and the British Heart Foundation lost around a quarter of a million pounds. When Caro died five years later, of a rare cardiac complaint like her ex-husband, ironically, the unspoken view was that justice had been served in the end.

Crisis over, our lives went on as before. But no, perhaps not quite as they had been. That upright Steinway in the living room had been little used since we had moved in. With Scott out of the way at weekends, and Dave spending more and more time at Lina's uncle's place or occasionally with Billie, at hers, I found myself drawn back to it when Grace and I were alone. She had heard me play in Spain, and she encouraged me in Scotland. I was out of practice, but it didn't take long for the feel to come back. I played a bit of Chopin, out of homage to Grandma Paloma, but mostly I stuck to Monk, and to a repertoire that I nicked from Chet Baker and adapted to my own developing technique. Grace loved it; she said I had a lazy style, that would have made her stretch out along the top of the piano, if only it had been a grand.

Fifteen years down the road, I caught up, belatedly, on a movie called *The Fabulous Baker Boys*, in which Michelle Pfeiffer does just that. She looked so like Grace, that it chilled me to the marrow.

Christmas was a repeat of the previous year's, with Major John pulling leave once again, but there were only six of us at the table, since Scott was being paid triple time to pull pints in the Pear Tree. We kept him some dinner but he missed out on a sing-song round the piano. It started with Christmas carols, but soon degenerated into, into . . . whatever I felt like playing, which turned out to be mostly the slower Stevie Wonder stuff. The trouble was that while everyone . . . even Grace . . . could remember the words to 'Oh Little Town of Bethlehem', only I knew the lyric of the likes of 'Knocks Me Off My Feet', so pretty soon I'd lost my backing chorus. I gave up on Stevie after a while, when I realised that everyone had stopped to listen to me sing, and got the choir back in shape with 'Can't Take My Eyes Off You', a chorus that everyone knew off by heart, if they had no clue about the rest after the first verse, and nobody could resist.

We were belting it out 'Oh baby, baby!' so loud that when the phone rang I almost failed to hear it. As I walked to the table on which it lay, I wondered who could be calling. I'd made my duty call to Grandma and Dad, Grace and I had been to see Rod and Magda . . . Why, them being Jewish? Because they'd visited us three weeks earlier to wish us Happy Hanukkah, and we insisted on returning the gesture, with gifts . . . so there were no obvious candidates, other than the downstairs neighbour asking us to cut back on the volume, or maybe to switch back to Stevie.

The last person I expected to hear was Chic McAveety, the Hearts' assistant manager. 'Aislado,' he barked. 'Are you sober?'

'Of course I am, Chic,' I insisted. 'I've got a reserve game tomorrow, remember; fucking Merrytown again, away.'

'No you don't, son. Ian's cut his hand carving the fucking turkey, so we need you on the bench against Airdrie. Report to the ground at midday. Party's over, kid; have yourself an early night, and don't be giving the girlfriend her Christmas bonus.'

I must have been smiling as I hung up. 'What's brightened up your life?' Billie asked. 'Good news from Spain? Is your dad getting married?'.

I almost told her she should know better than that, but cut that one off before it slipped out. 'No,' I replied instead, 'good news from Tynecastle. I'm in the first team squad tomorrow.'

'Xavi!' Grace squealed. 'That's great.'

'Not that great, I'm only the substitute.'

'It's a start, though, and you never know, you might get on. God knows, they need you.'

They needed someone, that was for sure, but an eighteen-year-old goalie was unlikely to be their saviour. For Rod's gloomy prophecy to my dad was in the process of fulfilment. While my reserve side was seeing most opponents off, the first team was doing a fair imitation of Atlas, supporting the rest of the Scottish Premier Division on its shoulders. Tynecastle was not a happy place on match days, or on any other day for that matter.

I went back to the piano . . . Chic McAveety wasn't going to put an end to my party . . . but after I'd played 'Tonight's the Night', the other four decided that it was indeed . . . at least John and Billie did, Dave and Lina still being very circumspect . . . and left Grace and me alone to ignore another of the assistant manager's instructions.

In the morning, she told me that she was coming to the game. In fact she insisted on it, so I arranged for Rod to take her there, and for a ticket to be left for her at the players' entrance. Grace didn't like football, and reserve games weren't to be inflicted on anyone you cared about, but she told me that there was no way she was going to miss my potential debut, even if the odds against it happening were around fifty to one. Goalies are never subbed tactically, and since they tend to be involved in the game less than outfield players, they aren't injured as often. That was what I told her, and it was true; but every now and again a long shot does come up. I suppose that if it didn't, there would be no bookmakers.

I had never been in the first team dressing room before. Ronnie

Crown, the manager, welcomed me, courteously, then left me to get changed into my strip, green jersey, number thirteen, white shorts, maroon socks, while he delivered a tactics talk to the eleven starters that seemed to be based more on faith than anything else, since there was no obvious evidence to support any belief that Hearts could come close to handling mid-table Airdrie.

Looking back on that day, the first thing that I recall is that I wasn't nervous. I could see that most of the players were, and that a couple were on the point of being physically sick, but all of that washed over me. In truth, I don't know what the feeling that people call nerves is like, because I've never experienced it. I'm an analytical person; I always have been, and always will be. Things are as they are, and the future is always uncertain, so why worry about it? In my life I've known the grief of loss, and I've known the shock of the unimaginable. In my younger days, I knew love and I knew elation, although it came to pass that my best hope, and the thing I wished for most, was contentment. But I've never known what it's like to be apprehensive, and I've never known fear for myself. What's the point of either? When it happens, deal with it.

I was last out of the tunnel on to the playing field. In those days, before the entrepreneurial chairman who transformed it, Tynecastle was nothing like it is now. The original grandstand is still there, but the terracing that I saw all around as I stepped into the fading daylight of Boxing Day, 1980, a Friday, as it happened, has been replaced compulsorily by seating, for all that the facility is ignored by many of the modern fans who insist on standing through games, even though many of them have never known anything but all-seater stadia.

I looked around. I hadn't expected a full house, not for Airdrie, but what I saw was a reflection of the pall of gloom that hung over Gorgie. A few thousand people stood on the damp concrete terraces, the loyalists cheering our arrival, some clapping, and the rest concentrating on drawing maximum value from their cigarettes. I didn't look for Grace in the stand: that would have been bad form. There was no pre-match warm-up in those days: we went out five minutes before the scheduled kick-off, the strikers took shots at the first choice keeper, while the fullbacks gave me catching practice. Then the referee, a fat little man with slicked down hair, whose name was given in the match programme as Mr E. Nurse, Kilbirnie, came out with his linesmen, tossed a coin with the two captains and the game was under way.

The miracle happened after seven minutes. One of our midfielders . . . I can't tell you who it was, since I was looking away at the time . . . thumped a long hopeless ball into the Airdrie penalty area at the Gorgie Road end, more to get himself out of trouble than with any attacking intention. It dropped around the penalty spot. As it bounced, everyone stared at it. 'Black Pudding' Gibson, our number nine, with six goals fewer than that to his name for the season, reacted as he would have to a hand grenade lobbed into a foxhole. He hid behind the nearest person, the Airdrie centre half, and took a good grip of his shirt. Anchored to the ground, the defender swung an elbow at Pudding and a foot at the ball, but missed with both. Fascinated by the exchange, the visiting goalkeeper, who was on the short side, it has to be said, was suicidally late in going for the save and could only claw helplessly as the bounce took it arcing into the top left-hand corner.

An eerie silence fell over Tynecastle, as everyone in the ground waited for Mr E. Nurse, Kilbirnie, to award the obvious foul. But when finally he blew, he was pointing to the centre circle, giving the goal. The stand behind me and the home fans to my right erupted, in a mix of delight and disbelief, as Mr Nurse ran back towards the centre circle and my teammates mobbed Pudding. The Airdrie team chased the ref to a man, the red diamonds on their white shirts hiding him from view as they screamed imprecations that we could hear in the dug-out. The wronged defender's protest was so obscene that a red card was brandished and he was sent straight to the dressing room. As the banished Airdrieonian walked past us, still cursing, Chic McAveety leaned close to me on the bench and whispered in my ear. 'Learn from that, son. Everyone else in the ground might know that the ref's a blind, useless cunt, but he disnae, and if ye've got a number on your back, it's always a mistake tae tell him.'

So there we were, league stragglers but a goal and a man to the good. The boss was smiling; there was an air of optimism in the dug-out, for the first time since the start of the season, I guessed. It took half an hour for it to vanish. As the game developed, it became obvious, to me at least, as I was probably the only guy in our squad with any degree of objectivity, that it had dawned on the ref that he had made a howler. There was a hard core in the travelling support, in a knot behind our goal, and every time play took them near him, they seemed to grow more and more threatening. Football referees are advised to have ex-directory phone numbers, but it was known that Mr Nurse was a teacher in his home town secondary school, so he wasn't exactly untraceable. Given that truth, it was understandable that the longer the game went on, the more decisions seemed to be going in Airdrie's favour. The inevitable happened five minutes from half-time. 'Big Mental' McIntyre, our goalie, went to gather a ball in the box that was at least sixty-forty in his favour. He had it in his grasp and was actually beginning to stand up when the lone Airdrie striker ran into him, then fell over. The Pringle-clad Airdrie Casuals roared, 'Penalty!' with one furious voice, and Mr Nurse caved in. He pointed to the spot. Chic had to restrain the boss, physically, from running on to the field, but it would have been pointless anyway, for no ref in the history of the game has ever changed his decision in circumstances like that.

That wasn't the worst of it. The collision had left Big Mental the worse for wear; even from the touchline I could see that his wrist wasn't meant to be at that angle. 'Warm up, son, while the trainer's on,' Chic told me, as our physio ran on to inspect an injury that we all knew was beyond his skills. That fifty-to-one shot had come up. I did a quick sprint up the track and back again, then I was on. My first team debut, and my first job was to face a penalty kick.

I took a look at the striker as he placed the ball on the spot, and realised . . . he hadn't been in the game till then . . . that I knew him. I had been up against him in a reserve match at Airdrie a few weeks before. He hadn't been very good, and I guessed that Airdrie must have encountered injury, or too-much-turkey, problems for him to be in the top team. Late in that game we'd had a one on one, which he'd messed up, made me look good, and in the process cost his team at least one point. He'd had a kick at me as I cleared the ball, but it hadn't bothered me.

Daylight was fading as he placed the ball on the spot, and the floodlights were taking over, but the look he gave me as he straightened up was plain enough, and it told me that he remembered me too. 'Nae fuckin' chance,' he called to me, as he stepped back to begin his run up.

He was wrong. He'd obviously been taught that the keeper always dived, for he drilled his shot straight down the middle, with not much power behind it. I knelt to gather it in, and stood up as his follow-up brought him towards me. 'Thanks very much,' I told him, but in Spanish. He glared, and shoulder-charged me, but bounced off and landed on his rump. 'Don't you be doing that again,' Charlie 'Burger' Bull, our centre half and captain, warned him, as he sat there. The Casuals behind me were embarrassed into silence.

We were on the attack for the rest of the first half, and so I didn't have another touch before half-time. As I walked into the tunnel behind Burger, I looked up. The season ticket-holders were on their feet, cheering; I looked for Grace, but didn't see her.

I'd expected the boss to be beaming when we got into the dressing room; that's how little I knew of the real game at that time. But he was grim-faced as he went through every one of the ten outfield players, pointing out everything each of them had done wrong during the half. I thought I'd get off, having saved a penalty, but I didn't. He turned to me last. 'And you, Iceland,' he bellowed. (His attempt at my surname was my nickname at Tynecastle from that moment on.) 'You do not talk to that fucking nark of a centre Mulligan. That's what he wants you to do.'

He drew a finger across his mouth. 'Keep it zipped and leave Burger to sort him out. It's his job to look after you.' I hadn't even known the striker's name until then, far less been bothered about him.

Where our boss should have sent us out for the second half full of positivity, he managed somehow to make us feel that while we were a goal and a man up (if you don't count the ref), we were still second favourites. He was a fatalist, that man. The trouble was he was spot on.

The Airdrie manager must have got his team talk right, for in the second half his team came for us like ferrets after rabbits. We were pinned in our own half for over fifteen minutes and I was as busy in that time as I'd grown used to being for the whole ninety in the reserves. We held out, though, and began to force them back as they tired. One man short out of eleven might not seem like much, but if you're in the ten it goes for your legs.

We didn't look like scoring a second, but with fifteen minutes to go we had the game in the bag. Airdrie were done and they knew it. They were reduced to the tactic that had brought us our seeming winner, punt and run. I wasn't worried when one of those hopeful thumps sent Mulligan and me on another collision course, a one on one, as Burger slipped while turning on the cut-up surface. On the face of it, it was a fifty-fifty, but it was well inside the box and I had everything on my side. I went down for the ball, but just as I did, Mulligan slowed down just a fraction, then dived in, right foot raised, studs up. I collected the ball, and him, at the same time.

Thankfully, he missed what he was aiming at, but I felt six plastic bullets rip through my shorts and into the inside of my left thigh. He flew over the top of me, yelling 'Penalty!' even in mid-air, but Mr E. Nurse, Kilbirnie, was within reach of our supporters now, and he was no braver than he had been at the other end. He didn't give us a foul, though; instead he ran away backwards, as refs do. My thigh was burning, and bleeding, as I got to my feet. I doubted if I could punt the ball so I tossed it to Burger. As I did so, Mulligan kicked me behind the right knee, shouldered me on his way past and growled, 'Away, ya big Tally cunt.'

Maybe it was him calling me Italian that did it, or maybe I'd just had enough. I honestly don't know why I hit him, but I did. I pulled him round to face me and tossed the only punch I've ever thrown at another human being in my life. I'd had no coaching, and I didn't even watch boxing on television, far less had I been to a live fight, but it was a beauty. It was an uppercut, of a sort, it caught him mightily under the chin, and lifted all twelve and a half stone of Mr Mulligan at least six inches off his feet . . . I know, because I saw the video afterwards, and the stills . . . and dumped him on his back.

Mr Nurse stopped running backwards, and headed for me. His red card was in the air before he reached me. 'Violent conduct,' he shouted, 'violent conduct. Off! Off!'

I pointed to my torn shorts and my bleeding thigh. 'And what the fuck does that constitute?' I asked him. He didn't even look at my injuries. Instead he shouted, 'Off!' even louder.

'Their guy was right,' I told him. 'You are indeed a blind, useless arsehole.' My only mistake . . . but a big one . . . was speaking English, rather than Catalan, which he'd never have understood in a lifetime. He brandished the red card again. 'Foul and abusive language!' he screamed.

Burger got hold of me then; he took me by the arms and pulled me away. I let him, or he wouldn't have managed. 'Off you go, son,' he murmured. 'I'll take care of what's left of that cunt on the ground.' As it turned out, he didn't have to. They took Mulligan off on a stretcher and straight to the Royal Infirmary to have his twice broken, upper and lower, jaw wired, and to be detained for observation overnight, suffering from severe concussion. His season was over, but mine was pretty much ruined as well. My two red cards earned me an automatic six-match ban, and the Scottish Football Association's disciplinary panel showed its sympathetic attitude to a provoked eighteen-year-old by adding on a further four for good luck. Big Mental was back from his broken wrist before I'd finished my suspension and when I had, I found that my place in the reserves had been usurped by a new kid who'd been playing too well to be dropped.

That was all to come, though. The boss and Chic didn't even glance in my direction when I walked past them on my way to the dressing room, and I sure as hell didn't look at the stand, for all that they gave me a round of applause. The last thing I wanted at that moment was to make eye contact with Grace or her dad.

I was left to look after myself, to clean the grass and mud out of the six bleeding holes in my thigh, and to listen alone to the moans from above as Airdrie slotted two goals in quick succession, past Pudding, the stand-in keeper, the first of them being the penalty that I'd conceded by nearly beheading Mulligan. I was standing there naked, pressing a wet towel against my leg, when I heard the door open behind me. I didn't turn round, just waited for the blast that was to come from the boss, or Chic, or Burger, or whoever it was.

'Excuse me,' came a voice. 'Do you think I could have a word?'

'This is not the best time,' I replied as I looked over my shoulder. I felt my eyebrows rise as I looked at the newcomer. He was a uniformed policeman, an inspector, if I read the pips on his shoulder correctly. 'Oh shit,' I sighed, 'you're not going to charge me with assault, are you?'

'If I was, I'd be doing the other guy as well as you, so don't you worry about that. No, I just want to talk to you, that's all. Not here, not now necessarily, but before you leave the ground.'

'About what? Is there a problem at the flat?'

'No, nothing like that. It's a family matter.'

'What?' I snapped, suddenly alarmed. 'Has something happened to my grandma, or my dad.'

'Not that I know of. This is nearer home. My name's Tommy Partridge, Xavi. I'm your stepfather.'

I turned to face him, laying down my pressure pad and wrapping a towel around my waist. 'And what do you want?' I asked him, quietly.

'As I said, I'd like to speak to you.' I said nothing, just staring at him, until he continued. 'It's about your mother,' he added, eventually.

'Is she ill?'

'No, she's fine.'

'Then what's to talk about? She left me ten years ago and I've got on fine since.'

'Maybe you have,' he murmured, 'but . . .'

From outside I heard the clattering of studs, and knew that our privacy was almost at an end. 'Wait for me,' I told him, as the door opened. 'Wait in the tunnel. I could be a while, though.'

Chic McAveety barely looked at him as they passed each other; he was focused on me. I waited for the tirade, but his frown wasn't anger; it was concern. 'Are you all right, son?' he asked. 'Let's see your leg.' I parted the towel and showed him my thigh. He gasped as he saw it. 'Fuck's sake!' He turned to the boss. 'Ronnie, get the referees' supervisor out of the fuckin' boardroom. He's got tae see this.'

The manager nodded agreement, and dispatched the kit man to fetch the SFA guy. 'Sorry, boss,' I told him. 'I let you down there.'

'What are ye sorry for?' Chic barked, in his rough, kind way. 'There isnae a boy in here that wouldnae have flattened that shite for what he did tae you.' The one thing I knew about Chic's playing career was that he had set a record for the time he spent under suspension.

'I didn't take your advice, though, about keeping my mouth shut. That's what the second red card was about.'

He shrugged his shoulders. 'Sometimes guys like him need tellin' regardless,' he growled.

'Too right,' Burger agreed. He held out his hand and I shook it. 'Let's hear it for Iceland!' he called out to the dressing room. A chorus of muted cheers responded. 'Don't feel bad, kid. You'd never have stopped that second penalty, and their winner was a pure fluke.' I might have pointed out that I'd conceded the second penalty, but I didn't.

Ronnie Crown sat beside me on the bench. 'I should tell you that you cost us the game,' he said.

I was beyond diplomacy. 'I could argue that you did, by sending us out to sit back when we should have been piling on goals and making it safe.'

He frowned up at me; then his lips formed a thin smile. 'You could at that,' he conceded. 'But you didn't really cost us: Ian did, when he couldn't tell the difference between a turkey drumstick and his thumb. He should have been in the sub's jersey, not you. He'd just have put a boot through that ball, and whacked it into the stand, instead of doing it like it says in the coaching manuals. You're only a kid; you don't have the experience to take that option. What worries me is that you didn't have the instinct either, goalkeeping being at least seventy-five per cent instinct. You should address that.' He stood, and patted me on the shoulder. 'And the bottom line is this, Iceland,' he added, loudly enough for those around to hear. 'If you hadn't flattened that animal Mulligan, Burger would have, and I'd rather have you suspended than him.'

That made me feel a little better, but to be honest, I didn't feel all that bad about what had happened. Mulligan had earned his broken jaw. I had saved a penalty, and if I'd contributed to the loss of three points, they weren't going to make any difference at the end of the season, for the team was crap, the manager didn't have the dynamism or the resources to make it better, the club was moribund and all Scotland knew that it was going down.

As the physio patched up my leg, after the SFA's referee overseer had looked at it and made a couple of notes that I hoped wouldn't be good news for Mr Nurse (in fact, all that happened was that Mulligan was given a three-match ban, to be served after he'd recovered from his injury), I asked Chic to find Grace and Rod . . . I'd arranged to meet them at the players' entrance . . . and tell them that I'd be a while and would make my own way home. Once I was fixed and dressed, I passed on tea with my teammates, disappointing no one, other than any football reporters who might have wanted a word with me, and headed for the tunnel.

Partridge stood in the entrance with his back to me, framed against the light cast by the single bank of floodlights that had been left on so that the ground staff could see to repair the winter-worn pitch. A cloud of cigarette smoke billowed out beyond him.

'Should you be doing that in uniform, Inspector?' I asked.

He turned. 'There's nobody left here to object,' he chuckled, 'unless you do. And it's Tommy, by the way. You're not a smoker?'

'No. I suppose that's something of a miracle, given that I'm half Spanish and half Scottish.'

'Good lad. Keep it that way.'

'I'm not going to start now; my fiancée doesn't like it.'

'You're engaged?'

'For almost a year now. We live together.'

'You're young for that. Known her long?'

'I've known her for longer than I knew my mother. As for being young, you're an officer of the law. What does the law say?'

'Actually it doesn't say anything about betrothal,' he responded to my challenge. 'The law's only concerned with the minimum ages for marriage, and consent to sex; in Scotland that's sixteen for both.'

'Not even Scots law's silly enough to allow you to marry but not consummate it,' I pointed out. 'Marriage is something that Grace and I will get round to when we're ready, once we've got our career plans sorted. We're fine as we are for now.'

'That's good. Does that mean that you don't see your career in football? You'll get your name in the papers tomorrow, that's for sure, and that's never a bad thing, long term.'

'Fine, I saved a penalty, put a thug in hospital and got two red cards, all in the same game. That's not fame, it's notoriety, and it's bad news in football. This is a part-time job as far as I'm concerned. It's putting me through university; once I'm done with that I want to be a journalist.'

'What?' he exclaimed. 'Like those pissheads in the press box here?'

'That's a stereotype,' I snapped at him. 'But no, not sports journalism.

News. Where? That's another question, but it'll be in Britain.' I'd had enough of the small talk. 'Tommy,' I demanded, 'what's this about?'

'Like I said, it's about your mother. I'd like you to meet her.'

I looked him in the eye. 'And why would I want to do that?' I murmured.

'Jeez,' he sighed, 'she was right about you. She says you were about thirty when you were born. You're a serious lad, aren't you?'

'I am what I am. Can't change, won't change. I don't do stand-up comedy, and I never will.' I held his gaze again. 'How long have you been married to my mother?'

'Almost seven years.'

'Big wedding?'

'It was in the registry office, but there was a reception afterwards. Friends of both families.'

'But not me?'

'Eh?'

'My mother got married, but she didn't invite her son. Didn't that strike you as a wee bit odd?'

He shook his head. 'It struck me as sad, but she told me that she didn't have rights of access under the terms of her divorce.'

'You knew I existed, though?'

'Yes. She told me that she had a wee boy by her previous marriage, but that it had ended badly.'

'It ended when she left. She walked out, and didn't even leave me a note.'

'She's never gone into detail about the split and I've never pressed her. We're happy, and that's all I care about.'

'You got any kids?'

'Twin girls, June and Nannette. They're four now: your half-sisters.'

The revelation stirred nothing in me; if anything it deepened my annoyance at his invasion of my life. 'Congratulations,' I said, drily. 'Do you know anything about my family? My real family, that is.'

'Very little. I know your father was in the pub business and that he sold up and moved to Spain. I'd heard of him before I knew who he was, so to speak. When I was a young cop, one of our big bosses retired and went to work for him.'

'When did you find out about me . . . as in, who I was?'

'Just over a year ago,' he replied. 'There was a report in the *Evening News* of a Hearts reserve game. The headline was "Spanish Eyes" and it was all about this new young goalie having a blinder. Mary read it; her hands started shaking and I saw all the colour drain out of her face. I asked her what was the matter. At first she said that nothing was, but I didn't let it go. Eventually she told me that the young goalie in the paper was her son.'

'So you checked up on me?'

'Only to confirm that Joe Aislado was your dad. She didn't even tell me that. I was able to get a copy of your birth certificate.'

'So what have you been doing for the last year?' I asked.

'Watching your progress, from a distance. Like I said, I am your stepfather.'

'Please!'

'Take it at face value, Xavi. I love your mother, and you're her boy, so I take an interest in you.'

'But does she?'

He nodded. 'She follows your career, and she's seen you play. I've taken her to a few reserve games, home and away.'

'She wasn't here today, was she?'

'No. Son, nobody knew you were in the squad till the team sheet was handed in.'

'Don't call me that, please, Tommy.' At the football club, I was called 'Son', on a daily basis, but that was different.

'Sorry,' he replied mildly. 'I happened to be on ground duty today.'

I felt my face screw up. 'Did you like what you saw?' I growled.

'Yes, I did as it happens. You were very cool with that penalty, and for the rest of the game. You didn't put a foot wrong.' He grinned. 'You've got a hell of a punch on you, too. I've seen some scraps in my time, but

I've never seen anybody get hit like that. We could use you in the force if you change your mind about a career.'

'I'll pass on that, I believe.'

'Maybe just as well; we'd need to buy bigger panda cars.'

I looked at my watch. 'Bottom line, Tommy; I've got to go. Grace'll be back at the flat by now. You want me to meet my mother. But does she want to meet me? Whose idea is this, yours or hers?'

'It's mine,' he confessed. 'She's never asked, or suggested it, but I've seen her pride when she's watched you play. I feel there's something that's not complete inside her. She's a mother, isolated from her son, and I just don't believe that's right. I'd like you two to have some sort of communication. Will you do it? Meet her and see how it goes?'

I took a long look at him. He seemed like a good guy, and he was sincere. 'All right,' I conceded. 'I'll meet her. But I don't want her to come to my house and I don't want to go to yours. Neutral ground, and nobody else there, no kids, just her, just the two of us.'

'Not even me?'

'Not even you, Tommy. We'll be talking about a part of her life that you had nothing to do with. Maybe you don't want to know.'

'Okay. I'll set something up, and give you a call.'

The flat number was ex-directory; I recited it and he noted it in his book. 'Thanks.' He smiled at me. Suddenly we were thrown into darkness as the last floodlights were switched off. 'Sorry to have kept you back.'

'That's all right,' I told him. 'You can make up for it by giving me a lift home . . . unless you're driving a panda.'

Rod was waiting with Grace when I got home. I misinterpreted his presence. 'Are you here to tear a strip off me?' I asked, as soon as I saw him. I wasn't smiling.

'No, son.' He could call me that any time. 'I'm here to make sure that you're all right, that's all.'

Instantly, I was contrite. 'Sorry, Rod,' I said. 'And I'm sorry about what happened at the game too.'

'Don't be. That referee was a damn disgrace; worst I've ever seen. He'll never be back at Tynecastle, I'll tell you that. There was a crowd waiting outside for him; they were chanting your name, "Xavi! Xavi!" all the time. I think you're a hero. The police had to escort him to his car, and see him safely out of the park.'

'They won't be seeing any more of me for a while. I've got myself six games off.'

He gasped. 'The club will appeal surely.'

He looked so outraged that I had to laugh. 'I broke the guy's jaw, Rod. He's in the Royal right now. Plus, I can't deny calling the ref an arsehole.'

'Well he is,' Grace snapped, angrily. 'I'd have told him so too if I could have got at him.'

'How's your leg?' her father asked. 'It was all bloody when you went off.'

'It's a mess, but it probably looks worse than it is. Mulligan's got a lot worse; so has Big Mental for that matter.'

'If you're sure . . . Grace made me wait so I could take you to hospital if you needed it.'

'I'm fine, really. I'm sorry I was grumpy just now. It's been a weird afternoon.'

He smiled. 'You've survived it, that's the main thing. I'll leave you two alone; Magda will be wondering where I am.'

I saw him to the door. When I returned to the living room, Grace was frowning. 'It is just your leg, isn't it?' she murmured. 'I didn't like to ask in front of Dad.'

I nodded. 'It's just my leg.'

'You sure?'

I headed for the bedroom. 'Come and see for yourself.' She proceeded to do so; with caution.

I did indeed find my name in the press next day, with a vengeance. A very lucky freelance photographer had taken a strip of still pictures with his motor-drive that showed my punch landing, Mulligan on his toes, then hitting the ground, and he had sold them to every paper in the land. One broadsheet used them on the front page. Most of the writers called it the way it had happened, accusing Mulligan of trying to maim me, but one Glasgow tabloid called me a mindless hooligan. It was probably a fair description, given what I'd done, but I couldn't stop Grace from phoning its editor and offering him the chance to photograph my leg, which, by that time, was all the colours of the rainbow.

I didn't tell her about my visit from Tommy Partridge, or about the meeting we'd agreed. But she found out. At first she thought that my sombre mood flowed entirely from the incident, and from the pain in my thigh, which didn't really kick in until the next morning. My suspension wasn't due to start until after our next game, and I retained a fleeting hope that I might be given the starting jersey for that one, but by ten o'clock, when I called in at Tynecastle as instructed, for treatment, I was limping heavily. The club doctor took a look at me, muttered something about 'incipient infection', gave me a massive shot of antibiotic, and said that I wouldn't be fit to train, let alone play, for ten days.

While I was on the treatment table, Tommy Partridge called the flat; I hadn't expected him to move so fast. Dave answered and took his message, which he left on a note on the kitchen table, for Grace to read.

'Who's Inspector Partridge?' she asked, as soon as I'd dragged my stiffening leg indoors. 'And why does he want you to meet him at eleven tomorrow morning. Is it to do with you hitting Mulligan?'

'In a way,' I reply.

'Do the police usually interview criminals in the Palm Court of the North British Hotel, on a Sunday?' she persisted.

'I'm not a criminal; I'm a folk hero.'

She wouldn't be deflected, and I couldn't lie to her. I can't lie, period. God knows why not, given my heritage. I've only ever done it once, and even then it was more a case of . . .

'After ten years, your mother wants to meet you?' she exclaimed, when I'd finished. 'Then mine was right, as usual. She told me that she'd get in touch with you one day. I told her no chance; I should have known better than disagree with her.'

'Maybe she should start telling fortunes.'

'Maybe she should. A couple of months before his dad died, Scott's name came up, and she said, "That boy's got hard times coming." Prophetic, eh.'

I smiled. 'Madame Magda, gipsy fortune teller. We should get her a crystal ball next Hanukkah.'

'Can I come with you?' Grace murmured, in the tone that always produced 'Yes' as the answer.

'No.'

'Aw, Xavi, why not?'

'Because I don't really want to meet her myself. I'm only doing it as a favour for Tommy.'

'Not for yourself? Not even a wee bit?'

'Maybe,' I conceded. 'But it's still something I've got to do on my own, love. If it goes well, she'll insist on meeting you.'

'Are you going to tell your father? Or Grandma Paloma?'

I had asked myself that question. 'It's got nothing to do with my dad, or Grandma for that matter. She won't have my mother's name spoken in her presence, so what's the point of telling her?'

'You never keep secrets from her, Xavi,' she said.

I looked at her, surprised. 'What do you mean?'

'It's true. You tell your grandma everything that's happening in your life.'

When I considered what she had said, I couldn't deny it. I rarely spoke to my dad when I wasn't in Spain, but I called Grandma at least three times a week. I'd even phoned her that morning, in case those photographs had found their way to the sports desk of *GironaDia*, and beyond. I hoped that if they had, Angel would have binned them, but I couldn't be sure. She hadn't been angry, or even upset by what I'd told her. 'Sometimes you have to mark out your ground,' she declared. 'Your grandfather did a similar thing once, when he and I were young, and Josep-Maria was a toddler. We were having a picnic in the country, the three of us, when a Francoista who knew us happened upon us. He was an evil man, ugly in all ways, and he was jealous of us. He insulted me, and he threatened to harm us; your grandfather did what he did, what you did, and he wasn't an aggressive man by nature, any more than you are.'

'He hit him?'

'No. He took the man's gun from him and shot him. There was no other option. That was why we left when we did. Fortunately we had already made our preparations, and all our money was out of the country. We hid the body where it wouldn't be found for a while, packed our suitcases, took your father and crossed into France.'

'He shot him dead?' I exclaimed. She had to be joking, hadn't she?

'A shotgun isn't a subtle weapon, Xavi. At close range, it's . . . how should I say it . . . definitive.'

That put Mulligan's smashed jaw in perspective. 'Was the body ever found?' I asked her.

'I suppose so,' she replied, calmly. 'But in the years that followed, bodies were found all over Spain, so I don't imagine it caused much of a stir.'

Yes, Grace was right for sure. Apart from . . . and maybe even including . . . her, Grandma Paloma was my closest confidante. But one thing about what Grace said puzzled me. 'When I'm on the phone with Grandma,' I pointed out, 'most of the time we're speaking Catalan. How do you know what I say to her?'

'I've picked enough up over the last couple of years to understand some of it. And I've been studying it; there's a learning group at university, and I'm a member.'

'I've never heard of it.' That wasn't improbable. Grace and I were doing different courses, and I was a year ahead of her. Very little of our class time overlapped, so we didn't see much of each other on campus.

I thought that was no bad thing at the time; now I wish that I'd spent every minute of every day beside her.

'When we have kids,' she continued, 'they'll learn it from you, and I want to be able to understand them all the time.'

I couldn't argue with that, although I still thought of kids as something that would happen way in the future. 'Now you've told me,' I said, 'I can help you.' From then on, we made a point of using Catalan around the house, when Scott and Dave weren't there. By the time that summer came, and we returned to Spain, she was speaking the language pretty well, and her Castellano was coming on too.

She didn't say any more about me meeting my mother alone. In fact, next morning she made sure that I was up and ready in plenty of time. I was planning to take the bus to the North British, but sleet was falling thick and wet outside, driven on a flesh-slicing wind from the north, so I didn't protest when Grace insisted on calling a taxi. My leg was worse than the day before, and my right knee had flared up where Mulligan had kicked me; walking was an all round painful experience, and sitting wasn't too comfortable either.

I must have cut a pitiful figure as I hobbled into the Palm Court of the great grey hotel, for when she saw me, my mother almost jumped from her seat. Her eyes widened and her hand went to her mouth, in a gesture that was more than the shock of seeing her son for the first time in ten years.

'My God, Xavi,' she said, as I approached, 'you've been in the wars. Now I see why you hurt that man so badly.'

That was her opening gambit. Not, 'Hello, son, it's been a long time. I've missed you.' But I couldn't say that to her either, so I didn't hold it against her.

Mary Inglis, who had given birth to me, wasn't a bit like the woman I remembered. For a start she didn't look at all out of place in the posh surroundings. She was better dressed than I had ever known her to be, in a dark green, square-shouldered dress, and her hair was expertly cut and arranged. She was attractive, still short of forty, a woman in her prime. It seemed that she hadn't looked back since the day she had abandoned me to the care of my dark grandmother and my indifferent father.

'He was lucky he didn't meet my grandfather,' I retorted, in answer to her remark, and at once her expression changed, her face grew pinched, and lost its confident, fetching look. I suppose that was pretty brutal, that it pulled her back to a place that she might not have wanted to revisit, but I didn't care, not at all.

'Well?' I continued. 'What the fuck are we doing here?' I didn't swear often, not outside the football club, at any rate, but I felt I had to emphasise that she hadn't come to meet a kid, rather a man, on his own terms, a man who stood his ground . . . even if it was damned painful at that time.

'I'm not sure,' she replied. 'I'm really doing this for Tommy.'

'So am I,' I told her. 'Now that we've done it, we could just go away again, and leave it at that.'

'If you want.'

'Right now,' I confessed, 'I want to sit down. If you want to leave, that's fine with me.'

She shook her head and stepped to one side, to allow me to arrange myself as best I could on a straight-backed chair at her table. A waitress . . . I was sure I recognised her; eventually I realised that she was a fellow student . . . approached us, pad in hand. My mother looked at me. 'Coffee and biscuits?'

'Americano.' The girl looked at me, helplessly. 'Double espresso?' I tried. She smiled, gratefully, scribbled the order and left us, facing each other, sizing each other up, like two dogs who didn't know whether to fight or start sniffing and licking.

We chose a neutral option; polite conversation. 'That seems to be a nice guy you've married,' I said.

'He is,' she agreed. 'Now go on, say it.'

'What?'

'For a copper. That's what people usually add.'

'Not me. I see plenty of cops on match days. And I've met a couple in Spain. They're just people doing a job as far as I'm concerned. Aren't we all?'

'And football's your job?'

'It is for now; even if the pay's pathetic for a young pro. At least it won't stop while I'm suspended. I'm not going to be able to play for a few weeks.'

'And afterwards?'

'We'll see.' I fobbed her off. I wasn't there to be interrogated.

'How's your father?'

That took me aback. I didn't have a ready answer for that one; I had to wait for one to come to me. When it did it surprised me almost as much as the question. 'He's happy,' I told her.

'Still spending his time in the casinos and with his women?'

'Not as far as I know. In Catalunya my dad's become what we'd call a media baron. He bought a clapped-out business and he's making it sing. That takes up all of his time.'

'Joe Aislado?' She whistled. 'The first respotted leopard in history.' She paused; I knew what was coming next. 'And . . .'

'Grandma's fit and well and where she wants to be. She's blooming. If she walked in here, you wouldn't recognise her.'

'Oh, I would,' she murmured. 'I'd know that old . . .'

I started to push myself off my chair, to head for the door, then thought, *Why the hell should I?* Instead I pointed a finger at her. 'Not a word,' I warned her. 'You don't have the right to badmouth Grandma Paloma, not to me. She brought me up, not you.'

'I can see that,' she said, stiffly. 'She's stamped all over you.'

Our meeting might have ended there and then, had it not been for the arrival of the student waitress, with our coffee. We suspended hostilities while she set it out for us.

'If that's so,' I said when she had gone, 'I'm proud of it.'

'Do you want to know about your other grandparents?'

'I don't give a shit about them. I don't ever recall getting a smile from either of them, any time you took me to see them. The only word I ever recall being addressed to me was "Don't!" whenever I touched anything of theirs. The only gesture I ever had from my grandfather was a slap round the ear when I was seven and spilled a drink on his moth-eaten hearthrug.' A truth occurred to me. 'Do you know, that's the only time in my life that anyone's ever lifted a hand to me, other than you, of course. If he were to walk in here, this minute, I'd know him for sure. I doubt if he'd fancy hitting me now.'

'He won't be doing that,' she whispered. 'He died five years ago.'

'I'm grief-stricken,' I retorted. I smiled, but with no humour. 'Let me get that right. My grandfather died, I was in my teens at the time, and you never bothered to get word to me. That says it all.'

'Your grandma's still alive,' she ventured.

'I know she is. I spoke to her yesterday; twice. The woman you're talking about is nothing to me.' I cast my mind back, trying to interpret as an adult what I had seen as a child. 'I was never anything to them, either, other than an embarrassment. And not just me, I reckon. When we went to see them, they didn't greet you with open arms either, as I recall. Is it still the same, or is it okay now that you're married to a nice Scots bloke, a pillar of our society, rather than a randy Spanish publican? You were a fucking embarrassment too, weren't you?'

'Xavi, please,' she snapped. 'I'll go if you don't stop that.'

I shrugged. 'I don't give a bugger whether you go or not. It won't stop me being right.'

'Change the subject,' she said. 'Tommy said you're engaged, and living with her already. Is that not awful young?'

I chuckled. 'That's ironic. Did you not tell Tommy that I was thirty when I was born?'

She allowed herself half a smile. 'Maybe I did at that,' she conceded. 'How long have you known each other? Did you meet her through football?'

'I've known her for more years than I've known you. We started school on the same day . . . the school that you didn't want me to go to, as I remember . . . and there's never been anyone else for either of us. Her name's Grace, Grace Starshine, her parents' names are Rod and Magda, they're Jewish, and the only time I've ever come close to falling out with either of them was when Magda tried to persuade me to get in touch with you. Grandma and Dad have met her, and approve. We go to Spain every summer and Grandma lets her help in the kitchen from time to time.'

'Then she must like her. I was never allowed in there in Merchiston; I got to clean and do the laundry, but that was that. That was the Aislados; that's how they treated me.'

Her bitterness had returned. 'And I'm one,' I said. 'I'm an Aislado. You hate them, that's very clear, so by extension, you must hate me.'

She shook her head, vigorously. 'No, son, I don't hate you. You're an Inglis as well, remember.'

'Didn't you hear what I just said about my Inglis grandparents? I was never accepted by them, so don't try and put their family brand on me. You, on the other hand, were accepted by the Aislados, as you call them; you were married to my dad for eight years and then you did a runner on him, and on me.'

'You know nothing about that.' She tried to make it a declaration, but her voice wasn't quite firm enough.

'Oh no? Then enlighten me, I'm an adult. What happened with you and my dad? How did you meet, how long were you engaged? Why did you move in with Grandma after you were married?'

She shifted in her seat and pressed down the plunger of her cafetière. I killed half of my double espresso and watched her. 'What has he told you?' she asked as she poured.

'Nothing.'

She added milk. 'Your grandma?'

'Are you kidding? She wouldn't even tell me if you died. As far as she's concerned you did, ten years ago.'

She took a sip and picked up a piece of shortbread from the plate.

'Your father and I just met as young people do, on a night out. We fell in love, or I thought he had. We got married and I fell pregnant with you. We moved into Merchiston because your Grandpa Aislado had just died and the house would have been far too big for your grandma on her own.'

Buckingham Palace wouldn't have been too big for Paloma Puig on her own, but I let that pass without comment. Because my mother had just lied to me, comprehensively, and by doing so she had told me why she had agreed to meet me. It had nothing to do with pleasing Tommy. She wanted to find out whether I knew anything that I could use to hurt her, and even to damage her second marriage.

I could have let her story pass, chatted inconsequentially for the rest of our meeting and left, for each of us to get on with our lives. But I couldn't. The instinct, the involuntary reflex, if you prefer, that for all its personal cost has made me what I am as a journalist, kicked in. I cannot leave a falsehood unchallenged or uncovered. 'That doesn't quite square with what Esme told me,' I said quietly.

She was raising her cup to her lips as I spoke. Her hand shook, and a little coffee spilled on to the serviette on her lap. 'Esme?' she murmured, as she replaced the cup in its saucer.

I gave her a couple of seconds. 'Come on now. Nobody could forget Esme; mid-fifties now, on the porky side and not well blessed with looks . . . although that's not quite how my dad describes her.'

'Where did you meet her?'

'In Girona. Dad's moved her out there to work for him; he got her residency. She's his secretary, his confidante, his friend. I like Esme.'

Her eyes narrowed. 'They're not . . .'

I laughed again, not mocking her, although she probably took it that way. 'No chance. Like I said, they're pals, that's all. If they were anything else, he'd be breaking his number one rule.'

'And what's that?'

'It's the one he broke with you, when you worked in Grandpa Xavi's office. When you got knocked up, when Grandma Paloma came roaring into the office like a thunderstorm and you and he were marched off to the altar. I know what happened, so please, no more bullshit.'

She pursed her lips and took a deep breath. 'Okay, so you think you know,' she murmured. 'Maybe now you'll understand why the old witch had a down on me.'

'I've told you,' I snapped, 'don't call her that. If she had a down on you, it was because you caught my dad. You trapped him; you had an eye for the main chance, just like Esme says.'

'That's an ugly thing for a son to say to his mother,' she hissed.

'It's an ugly truth, and don't you deny it.'

'Okay, I won't. I admit it; I saw it as a way out of my parents' clutches. It wasn't just you that my father knocked about, Xavi. And you're right; your grandma knew it from the start. She made my life hell from the day I moved in there, right up until I left.'

When I'd agreed to meet my mother, I'd carried the hope that spontaneous warmth might flow between us, and that perhaps, in spite of everything, she might have found a place in my life. But there was none; even after her small confession, the atmosphere remained icy cold. I was looking at a stranger. 'Yet you stuck it for nearly nine years,' I pointed out.

'She gave me an allowance.'

The implications of that revelation took a few seconds to sink in. 'She gave you an allowance,' I repeated. 'How much?'

'More than I'd ever have earned in any job I was qualified for.'

'So for the first part of my life, I didn't have a mother, I had a paid nanny.'

She shrugged her shoulders. 'If that's how you want to look at it, yes. I wasn't welcome there, I was tolerated and compensated, that's all. I was even less welcome out at Falkirk. My sisters were the idols there; they were both teachers, respectable.'

I gasped. 'You mean I have aunts that you've been hiding as well?'

'And four cousins, two of them older than you are.'

'Jesus! So why did you leave?'

'I'd had enough, that was all. I wanted my own life.'

'Without me?'

She nodded. 'If you like.' She paused. 'This hasn't worked, Xavi,' she said, briskly. 'We've both kept our promise to Tommy. Let's leave it at that.'

I finished my espresso. It complemented the bitter taste in my mouth. 'Fine by me,' I agreed. 'But there's one thing I don't get. My flatmate Scott: his mother divorced his father, and although he was really the innocent party, the court gave her the keys to his fucking treasure chest. He died an angry man because of it. Why the hell didn't you sue for divorce, and get something out of it?'

She slumped back in her chair. 'If only,' she murmured. 'There would have been a problem with that, son. We may have lived as man and wife after a fashion, but your father and I were never actually married.'

My mouth opened, in shock, in anger; maybe both. 'Don't lie to me!' I growled. 'I've heard him describe himself as a divorced man.'

'Then it was him that was lying, putting on a show for whoever it was he was talking to.' She was right there, although she didn't realise it. When he'd said it, he'd been making a point to crush Ramon Hernandez.

'Married or not, that wouldn't have stopped you taking me with you, if you'd wanted.'

'There were reasons.'

No, there was one reason, and I guessed what it was. 'What did you do for a living, after you left?' I asked. 'I'm curious. What do you do now?'

'Nothing. I'm a housewife.'

'With a husband who earns a decent salary but not a huge one, and has a mortgage and two young, high-maintenance kids to support, as well as a homebody wife. Yet you're sat there dressed up to the nines, in a designer outfit that Magda Starshine would envy, and we're meeting in the best hotel in town, which you chose. Most people would expect someone with your socio-economic background . . .' big phrase for an eighteen-year-old, but I was studying economics in my second-year syllabus '. . . to be waiting here, rather than being waited on. How can that be? Hah! It stands out like me in a bus queue of pygmies. You were paid off, and you're still on the fucking payroll.' Her eyes dropped to the tabletop. 'No more deception,' I warned. 'I can find out with one phone call.'

'Yes,' she whispered. 'I still receive an allowance from your family, more than when I lived with you, and I have done since I left. The agreement is that it will continue for as long as your father or your grandma are alive. It goes into a bank account that Tommy doesn't know about, so please, please don't mention it to him.'

'And why the hell would I do that?' I asked her. 'The one positive that's come out of the last couple of days is that I've discovered a stepfather, and I like him. He's a decent, honest man, and why the fuck would I want to hurt him by telling him that he's married to a woman who sold her own child?'

She looked me in the eye. 'Do you promise that you never will?' Her voice was emotionless.

'That's what I've just said.'

'And that this stays between us? Entirely?'

'Do you mean will I also promise not to go running to Grandma Paloma, or my dad?'

'Yes.'

'What would be the point? They know that you mean nothing to me. Go back to your nice life and enjoy it, if you think you've earned it. Tell Tommy what you like, I don't want to see you again.'

'Do you want to meet your sisters?'

'Never. Goodbye.' I pushed myself stiffly to my feet and limped out of the hotel in search of a taxi. I left her to pay the bill. She could afford it.

'How did it go?' Grace asked, before the door had closed behind me. I put a finger to my lips because Scott and Dave, who'd both been well under when I left, were up and about, and I didn't want to get into it in their presence. I hung my dripping raincoat on the hallstand and went into the bedroom, to change out of the suit that I had worn. She followed me. 'Well?'

I looked at her. 'Read my face,' I suggested. It didn't take her long.

'Not well, then?'

I laughed. 'That, my love, would be overstating the success of the mission. Try "disastrous" and you'd be close. Tommy Partridge is an idealist; he believes that mothers and their children should all live happily ever after. I don't know how he'd handle the discovery that some of us just can't stand each other.'

I sat on the bed and let her help me out of my trousers, then into a pair of shorts. I noticed that my right knee was badly swollen. As for my left thigh, the bruising had spread, and there was a pink tinge around the edge of the bandage that I didn't like. I didn't feel like Sunday morning boys' talk at that moment, so I lay back, my feet hanging off the end of the bed as always.

Grace settled beside me, and stroked my hair. It was in need of a trim; I've always kept it short in the summer, and let it grow longer in winter. 'Was it bad?' she whispered.

'I don't know how to describe it.' I gazed at the ceiling. '*Chica*,' Pablo Mali had called Grace that the first time she and I had gone to Spain and it had stuck, 'would you say that I'm a proper bastard?'

'What a silly question. Of course I wouldn't; nobody would ever say that about you.'

'Well you, and they, are all too kind, because that's exactly what I am. My mother and father were never married.'

'And you never knew? Wouldn't it show on your birth certificate?'

'I've never seen my birth certificate. Grandma applied for a passport for me when we went on that school cruise. She filled in the form; all I had to do was have my picture taken and sign things. I'm going to get a certified copy now, for sure.' I sighed. 'But that's not all, love. She didn't just walk out on me. My dad paid her to go away and leave me behind, and he's still paying her.'

'Even though she's remarried?'

'Yup, and for the rest of his life.'

'That's pretty generous of him.'

'Too bloody generous; she's a whore.'

She sat up, abruptly, and frowned at me. 'Xavi, don't say that. She's your mother.'

'And whores don't have kids?'

'Then look at it this way. You think that you and your dad have never been close, that he's always been too busy to bother with you, but if he's been paying your mother for all these years so that you can stay with him . . . that proves that he really does care about you, doesn't it?'

I hadn't thought about it from that angle until then. Grace was good at that; she was my positive side. At that time in her life, I'm certain she'd never seen a half-empty glass. She really did believe in me. I have no doubt of that; without her constant encouragement, it might have been a different Xavi Aislado who emerged from childhood and adolescence.

I drew her back down beside me, not with any sexual intention, but simply because I loved her and I was at my happiest when I was looking into her eyes, letting her smile wash over me, cleansing me, warming me, making the sun rise within me.

'You know, my girl,' I told her, 'you are right yet again. It's been different since my dad's been in Spain. He spends more time with me in the couple of weeks we're over there every summer than he spent with me in all the years he lived here.'

'You know why that is, don't you?' she ventured. 'It's because you're an adult now. Some men just aren't good at communicating with kids, and your dad's one of them. I reckon that if you asked Scott, he'd tell you that his was the same. It's not that they don't love you and such, it's just that they don't know how to say it, or show it.'

'Maybe it came from his own childhood. Grandma's . . .' I smiled, as the face she had shown me in my early years came back to me. 'You know what she is.'

She chuckled. 'You said it. Then there's your grandpa; maybe he was the same. How much do you know about him?'

'Very little. But from what I've heard, he was a big, outgoing man; he didn't have any communication hang-ups with anyone.'

'You'll learn from your dad's bad example, will you? You won't make the same mistake with our kids?'

'I haven't got off to a very good start. I didn't tell you this earlier, but I have twin half-sisters, four years old. I told my mother that I didn't want to meet them. Since she's out of my life, and by God she is, they can't be in it.'

'Are you sure?'

'Can you see how?' I asked.

'No,' she admitted with no hesitation. 'But I'm selfish. I don't want you pulled in all directions, I want you focused on me.'

'You'd better mean that, *chica*, for you've got a lifetime of it ahead,' I promised. 'I am one hundred per cent for you, and whoever comes out of your womb.'

She laughed. 'My womb will stay the way it is for a while yet; unoccupied.'

The vow of separation from my mother and her offspring held good, but it didn't extend to Tommy Partridge. He called me next morning. 'What happened, Xavi?' he asked. 'Mary won't talk about it. All she says is that you won't be seeing each other again.'

'And that's true,' I confirmed. 'She took a decision ten years ago, and it's worked out all right, for both of us. I'm not blaming you for trying to find out whether we could rebuild the bridge, but neither of us wants to. We don't fit in each other's lives, we never did, and neither of us is grieving about it; so neither should you.'

'Fair enough,' he conceded. 'I've done my bit; I'll let it lie. I'll still see you around, though, if that's okay. I am your stepfather, and although it might not make us blood, it's a tie as far as I'm concerned.'

'Fine by me,' I told him. 'Nobody has so many pals that they can afford to reject even one.' I sensed a response, and beat him to the punch. 'Mothers, though, they're different.'

And so Tommy Partridge and I became friends. At that time he worked out of the division that included Tynecastle, so I saw him often on match days. During my suspension I helped around the ground in any way I could, with the kit, putting up the nets, repairing the pitch after the game and even stewarding, when Rangers visited and the regulars were hard pressed. Thanks to some careless talk to an *Evening News* reporter, my nickname had spread out of the dressing room, and since I was easy to spot, a chant of 'Iceland, Iceland' became a regular occurrence at our end.

Tommy and I met for coffee too, from time to time, although not at the North British, usually in a café near his nick. He said no more about my mother, or their children. His interest was entirely in me, and soon I found that I was just as interested in him and in the progress of his career. He wasn't without prospects, but as it turned out he never made it right to the top. When he retired, it was as a superintendent, with a pension tidy enough to keep his wife in comfort; by that time she was more in need of it.

Once the post-Mulligan frenzy had calmed down, and Edinburgh anger over my bonus SFA suspension had subsided, I returned to a state of happy obscurity, just another part-time player who'd had his five minutes on the big stage ... if Hearts versus Airdrie merited that description. The bruising on my thigh took weeks to fade, but eventually it disappeared, as did that niggling pain in my knee, after a few weeks of physio. I didn't like idleness, indeed I felt guilty about it, as I still drew my wages, but on the other hand, it was a relief not to be directly involved as the club's relegation grew nearer and nearer, until the day that it became an arithmetical certainty. It was clear that the boss was heading for the exit, but the disintegrating board kept him on until the end of the season. There was little option; if they had sacked him, nobody else would have wanted the job. I had three more games that season, that was all, in the reserves, after the new kid had a crisis of confidence. My old teammates welcomed me back, and I paid them back with three shut-outs to cement another good season, but we all knew that an era was coming to an end, for us as players, and maybe for the club also.

The same was happening at home. The university term was drawing to a close, and with it, our unit would break up. Wee Dave was bound for Oxford, assuming that he passed his last set of Higher examinations, and with Dave that was pretty much a certainty. We didn't know how it would be with Lina and him, for nothing was volunteered and no questions were asked, but Grace had a hunch that she wouldn't be rushing back to Hong Kong.

None of us expected to be resitting exams in the autumn, but I would have a decision to make, whether to carry on for a further two years in pursuit of an honours degree, or settle for an ordinary, and only one more year. Grace wanted me to take the longer view, but I had my career plan in my head by that time, and I was keen to start. I had never been offered a full-time football contract, and as third choice goalie at Tynecastle, that wasn't going to happen.

On the day, a Wednesday, that the last of the five of us . . . Lina was a member of the group even though she didn't live with us . . . sat our last exam, we had a party in the flat. There were no guests . . . we invited Billie but she couldn't come . . . and there was no catering, only a delivery from the reliable Pizza Hut, some of the Spanish cava that Grace had come to like, and a variety of beers. We sat around, we shot the breeze and talked over our good times, until once again, as at Christmas, it turned into a sing-song.

'Kick it off, Iceland,' Scott insisted, and so I did. I'd just heard Frank Sinatra sing 'Lonesome Road', and I couldn't get it out of my head, so that was what I chose. I'm not sure I was word perfect on the lyric, but I got pretty close as I put my heart and soul into it. Looking back, was that prophetic, or what?

Grace wasn't allowed to sing anything but 'Hava Nageela', wee Dave murdered 'Flower of Scotland', and Lina floored us all with 'Two Little

Boys', quite unique as sung by a Chinese. Then it was Scott's turn. 'You don't know me,' he said.

'Sometimes I wonder,' I laughed, but I knew what he meant and started to play the Walker-Arnold song. None of us had ever heard Scott sing solo before; he'd always been one of those guys who just mumbled in the background. Maybe it was the booze, or maybe he was just feeling sentimental, but he laid his head back and sang his heart out. He wasn't Ray Charles, but he was pretty good. It occurred to me as he finished that he'd been the most open I'd ever seen him, revealing more of himself than he ever had before. He'd always been intense, and the business with his father had left him more so. It was emphasised by his eyes; they weren't piercing, but they had something that drew you to them, something unique to him. It was as if they were slightly more open than anyone else's, and were taking more in.

It was all due to end three days later, on the following Saturday. Dave was moving out, heading south to live with his father before finding digs in Oxford. He never did tell us where John was based, but by that time I'd come to assume that he was in the SAS, and so it would have been Hereford. However he did promise to keep in touch. Grace and I were going south too, for what had become our annual June trip to Spain. I was pretty sure that I'd be able to keep my new knowledge about my mother to myself, even face to face with Grandma and my dad. But I wasn't quite so sure about Grace. It wasn't likely that either of them would mention her, but if they did . . . might she let slip that I had met her? I had a chat with her about it, to impress the sensitivity of it upon her. Not the best move I ever made; she bit my head off. 'Do you think I can't keep a confidence?' she asked, frostily. Of course she was right; of the two of us, I was the security risk, bound for a career that was dedicated to uncovering secrets, not keeping them hidden.

Scott? He was staying on at the flat, going straight back to work at Starshine Pharmaceuticals plc, and keeping on his pub job. 'To build up a war chest for the winter,' was how he put it. Grace had taken me by surprise by floating the idea that we might invite him to come to

Spain with us, but I had vetoed that. My time with the woman who had brought me up, for better or worse, had become very important to me and I couldn't bring myself to share it with anyone other than my fiancée.

The last day came: rain fell steadily for most of the morning, but when the weather turned fair after midday, Grace and I walked down to a coffee shop we knew in Stockbridge. I picked up an *Evening News* on the way, and was surprised to see Heart of Midlothian Football Club on the front page, rather than the back. The board had resigned, after approving a share restructuring, and a new investor was being sought. Change, long needed, seemed to be on the way. By that time the boss had resigned, departing gracefully and taking Chic McAveety with him to a new job somewhere in England . . . that's how it is in football, they travel in pairs. In an off-guard moment, during my suspension, Chic explained why this is. 'Every good manager, son,' he said, 'and Ronnie is good, given decent players tae work with, needs a guy under him tae bowf at the team when they need it, so that he can keep his dignity. I'm Ronnie's bowfer.' I'll let you work out what 'bowf' means, but trust me, Chic was good at it.

It was my turn to cook that evening, although we had to wait until the boys were back in, and that was pretty late. It didn't bother me, though, I was mellow. We sat in the living room afterwards. 'They've been a good couple of years, Dave,' I said to him. 'Even if this one has been a bit eventful, one way or another.'

Scott grinned. 'Iceland, Iceland,' he started to chant, softly. Dave joined in, then Grace, and finally so did I.

We were still chanting when the phone rang. 'Five to eleven! Bloody late,' I swore softly as I stepped across to pick it up. 'Yes?' I said.

'Is that Mr David Colquhoun?' a male voice asked.

'No, it's his flatmate. How can I help you?'

'Is Mr Colquhoun there?'

'Yes.'

'Then put him on.'

'As soon as I can tell him who wants him.' The chant had faded to nothing. I felt eyes on my back.

'It's the police.'

John, I thought immediately. *Something's happened to John; this is the bad news call.* Then I realised that couldn't be. The military always does its own dirty work.

'Okay,' I said, then turned and looked at Dave, putting my hand over the mouthpiece. 'It's the boys in blue, for you.'

He looked puzzled as he took the phone from me, but not apprehensive. Then as I watched him, his expression changed. I'd never seen such fury in his eyes before. He frowned, so hard that the muscles in his forehead formed a ridge. 'Just before ten,' I heard him say, then, 'Tollcross,' and finally, after a long pause, 'Okay. No, I'm five minutes from it.' He put the phone down and headed straight for the door. I reached out and caught him by the shoulder; he tried to shake himself free, but I wasn't letting go.

'Dave,' I said, 'take a breath and calm down. What's happened?'

He took my advice, and inhaled, deeply. I felt him relax, and so I released him, knowing that I could reach the door before him if he bolted. But he didn't, he became Dave again, albeit a cold, scared version of our friend. 'It's Lina,' he told me, when he was ready. 'She's been attacked.'

Suddenly I felt as cold as he looked. Scott and Grace had come to stand behind me. 'Is she all right?'

'Yes, thank Christ. She's safe, but she's in the Western. She's asking for me, Xavi. I've got to get there, now.'

'I'm coming with you,' I declared.

'And me,' said Scott.

'Don't think you're leaving me behind either,' Grace added.

He didn't have time to argue.

As Dave had told the cop, when you're young and in a hurry, the Western Infirmary is only five minutes' brisk walk from the flat, down one hill and up another. 'What did they tell you?' I asked as we crossed the road at the roundabout, dodging between two slowing taxis and drawing a horn blast from the second. Its driver pulled up beside us as we headed up Crewe Road. I thought we were in for trouble, as he pulled down his window, but instead he called out, 'Is that you, big Iceland?' and I saw the Hearts sticker on the cab. He took us, off meter, the rest of the distance to the door of Accident and Emergency. None of us had known where it was, so he saved us even more time. I offered him money, but he refused. 'That's no good wi' me, son,' he said. 'I hope to see you back next season. We need the likes of you, lads that are prepared to put it about for the club.' If only more people had felt like him at Tynecastle, my football career might have worked out differently.

There were four uniformed police officers, all constables, at the admissions desk as we walked in. There were a few people waiting for treatment, seated on benches. One of them held a pad to his bleeding forehead; two of the cops stood close to him, watching him, but his glassy eyes signalled that he wasn't going anywhere in a hurry unless they took him. Dave walked up to the other two. 'Do you know where Lina Chan is?' he asked. 'I'm her boyfriend.'

'Ah,' said the older of the pair. 'We were told to expect you.'

'Okay, but where's Lina?'

'In due course,' the uniform declared, with the expression of a man with a clear understanding of his own authority. I realised at once that to him, my friend was a suspect until he decided otherwise. I had a good view of Dave's face. It was too calm; I was reminded of the confrontation in the kitchen, and I could see trouble approaching at a rate much faster than the cop could think.

'Excuse me,' I intervened, 'but my pal was told that his fiancée had been attacked and is asking for him. He's concerned about her.'

The younger PC looked me up and down, then up again. 'And who would you be, big boy?'

'I would be the guy who's taking a note of your badge numbers so that I can pass them on to my stepfather.' I can make excuses for those cops' attitude now; I came to realise very quickly through my experience as a working journalist, that no A&E department, in any city, offers a good working environment on a Friday or Saturday night. But there and then, I was annoyed.

The senior man turned to me, an eyebrow slightly raised. 'Who would that be?' he murmured.

'Inspector Partridge. Tommy. Works out of the Torphichen office.'

'We know Mr Partridge,' he replied. 'I've never heard of him having a stepson.'

I looked down at him, hard. 'My name is Xavi Aislado,' I said. 'Put it to the test. Phone him.'

He shook his head. 'No, that'll be all right. The lassie's back there.' He glanced at his colleague. 'Jim, take the lad back.' He looked up at me again. 'The CID'll want tae speak to him, mind.'

'I'm sure he'll want to speak to them too.' As the junior man took Dave behind the counter, I caught Scott staring at me. I didn't need him to say what he was thinking. *You never told me you had a stepfather, let alone a cop.* I nodded to him, almost imperceptibly, but he caught it and stayed silent.

'What happened to Lina?' I asked the constable.

'She was jumped on the canal bank up behind Tollcross. She said she was taking a short cut home to her uncle's. A guy came running up behind her and knocked her down, then he blindfolded her and ripped half her clothes off. It was a rape . . . or it would have been, if some good soul hadna' been walking his dog a bit later than usual, and disturbed the bastard.'

'In time?' Scott whispered, sounding shocked.

'It seems so, according to the quick look the paramedics gave her. They couldnae tell for sure though. The swine tried to shove the poor lassie into the canal before he ran off. He'd have done it too, if the dog-walker hadna' started to run at him.'

'Has he been caught?' I was behaving like a journalist, even then.

'No. And no chance, to be honest. The light was poor and the dog fella wasnae near enough to give us any sort of a description. The girl never saw him either. He was always behind her, even before he put the blindfold on her.'

We waited for a few more minutes, then Dave reappeared. He looked at me, red-eyed, and said solemnly, 'Xavi, I'm going to find the guy who did this and . . .'

I guessed what he was about to say, and hushed him before he came out with it in the presence of two cops. 'You won't be here to find him,' I reminded him. 'You're leaving, if I have to put you on the train myself and tie you to the luggage rack. The police will find him, and he'll go to jail for a long time. Now, how's Lina? That's what we all want to hear.'

'She's all right. The doctor's given her a full examination and there's no damage done.'

'Are they going to keep her in?' Grace asked.

'They want to, but she's asked me to take her home to her uncle's.'

I turned to the cops. 'The CID can catch up with him later, yes?'

The older one, whose name I didn't discover until over a year later, nodded. 'They should have been here by now, so bugger them. I heard what you said about him catching a train. He and the lass can make statements at Torphichen before he does. If not, we'll be after you, stepfather or not. It's turned out a lot better than it might have, but we still need to catch this tosser.'

'That's a deal,' I said. They nodded, and left.

Grace went through to the treatment area to find Lina and help her get ready, leaving Dave, Scott and me together. 'Thank God for the guy with the dog, eh,' Scott sighed.

'Too right,' Dave agreed.

'What was she doing on the canal path?' I asked him.

'It's a short cut to her uncle's place. She takes it quite a lot. Most of Edinburgh doesn't know about it.' He clenched a fist and slammed it into the palm of his other hand. 'It's down to me,' he exclaimed. 'We'd been at the Film House. I was going to walk her home, but she knew I'd be late back for our wee party, so she made me go. She told me it would be fine. If I hadn't been so fucking selfish . . .'

'Nothing has changed,' I told him. 'Your lives go on as usual, apart from an extra visit tomorrow morning.'

'Our last night,' he chuckled, but grimly. 'What a damper on it. Sums up the whole fucking year.' He looked up at me. 'Now, what's this about you having a stepfather in the police? Or was that the famous Aislado deadpan bullshit?'

'I never bullshit, chum. Tommy exists.'

'And your mother?'

'Not in my world.' I said it with feeling.

'That boy of yours. What are you going to do with him?'

'You're asking the wrong person, Esme. The only one who's ever been able to do anything with him is my mother, and even she's only got him on a light rein now. Xavi might be only nineteen, but he's his own man; they tell me he's a bit of a hero in Edinburgh among the Hearts supporters.'

'For getting sent off and costing them a game?'

'For standing up for himself when the rest of the team spent the season bending over for the opposition.'

'Who tells you?'

'What d'you mean?'

'What you said. "They", these sources of yours.'

'Rod Starshine, for a start. He and I talk quite a bit. Then there's Tommy Partridge, of course.'

'Does Xavi know that you and he have spoken, that he asked you to approve that meeting with his mother?'

'No, and he never will. He'd probably blank Tommy for good if he knew it, and I don't want that to happen. He's a big lad, Xavi, and he's mature for his age, but he's still innocent in a lot of ways. He's naive, still. It's good to have someone watching over him, other than the Starshine clan.'

'Hey! Don't you go anti-Semitic on me.'

'Their faith's got nothing to do with it. Or maybe it has; maybe it's the lack of it. Rod's not seen in synagogue very often, and he never seems to observe his Sabbath when the Hearts have a home game. The women, Grace and her mother, are so blonde that you'd never take them for Jewish.'

'What are you saying?'

'That consciously or not they're denying their culture. To me, that's a character flaw.'

'What's Xavi doing then, by insisting on being educated in Scotland? Is he not denying his?'

'Only half of it; if he's denying it at all. Xavi's roots and half his genes

are in Scotland. It's natural for him to think of Edinburgh as his home.
But that might change.'

'Are you hopeful of that? Do you want to retire?'

'And stay at home with my mother? Are you fucking joking?'

'I could see other reasons why you might want to.'

'You know me too well to be serious about that. Esme, I'm fifty, that's
all. I'm not winding down in this business, I'm winding up. In twenty
years' time, I might be looking to back off, and then maybe Xavi will take
over . . . but I'm not banking on that, far less planning for it.'

'Won't you even encourage him to come here?'

'No. He's got to find his own career path, not have it imposed
upon him. Sure it would be nice to have him here, but it'll be his choice.
There's this too; since it's clear as day he is going to be a journalist,
it's better for him to gather some experience outside this tiny wee universe
of ours, so that if he ever does decide to join us, he brings new skills
in with him and passes them on. He'll make it wherever he goes; I've
no doubt about that. I still don't really know reporters as a breed, but
I can tell that he's going to be a star. So can Pilar and Simon. They've
told me as much.'

'You love that boy, Joe, don't you?'

'Of course I do. We're blood.'

'Then why don't you tell him?'

'Because I don't need to, any more than he needs to tell me his
feelings, and don't you go fucking schmaltzy on me. Esme, for many a
year I've wished you were the boy's mother, but we both know there's
no . . . conceivable . . . way that would have happened. Let's just leave
him to find his feet.'

'With Tommy Partridge keeping an eye on him?'

'Yeah.'

'How long have you known the man?'

'Oh, must be fifteen years now. I met him when he was in CID.
Remember when the pub in St John's Road was broken into?'

'Yes, nineteen sixty-six, the night after England won the World Cup.'

'That's right. He was one of the guys who investigated. I bumped into him a couple of times after that, then I heard he'd married Mary.'

'There's no way Xavi's going to see her again, is there?'

'From what Tommy says, not a chance. The lad's much better off without her anyway.'

'I won't argue about that. Here, there's something else I was going to mention to you. I should have done it before now, sorry. That guy Mulligan, the Airdrie player that Xavi banjoed; my cousin Doris lives near him. I was on the phone to her the other night; she says his family's a right rough crew.'

'I know that, but it's been taken care of. They've been warned not even to think of doing anything daft.'

'Will folk like that take any notice of Tommy Partridge?'

'It wasn't Tommy that gave them the warning. It was someone else, an old casino acquaintance of mine, by the name of Perry Holmes. They sure as hell will take him seriously.'

'Joe!'

'Would you rather I'd called him after something had happened to Xavi?'

Eight

When we left for Spain two days later, Grace and I were still shaken up by what had happened to Lina. I went with Dave and her to the Torphichen Place police station on the Saturday morning and waited while they gave their statements to the duty CID officers, knowing that in all probability they would be futile, since the attacker was unlikely to be caught, unless he reoffended. Even then, attempted rape wasn't like housebreaking, where a burglar might cough to previously unsolved break-ins, to get them out of the way; nobody was going to volunteer for an extra ten years inside.

Once they and the police had finished their business, we went back to the flat, where Dave picked up his gear. The two of them caught a taxi to the station, and that was the last I ever saw of either of them. They promised to keep in touch, but they didn't; it was only through Billie Livingstone, who married John in 1984, after he'd retired from the army, that I learned that they'd completed their degrees as fast as they could, then she'd taken him home to Hong Kong. As far as I know, they're still there, but I've never tried to contact them. If Dave wants to look me up, all he needs to do is pick up the phone; the number hasn't changed in thirty years, apart from picking up an extra '1' somewhere along the line, although these days it's always on divert.

For the first time ever, I felt relieved to be back in Spain. I don't mean that I'd been indifferent before about seeing Grandma Paloma, or even my dad. No, I actually needed a break from everything that had been going on. I'm sure that Grace did too. The first thing she did after we'd arrived was to look for Carmen . . . yes, she was still there . . . and to thank her properly for our picture. She seemed as contented as ever; her painting was beginning to gain some recognition, thanks in part to an exhibition in a gallery on the Ramblas in Barcelona that had been sponsored by *CatVi*, a new monthly celebrity-based magazine that my dad had launched over the winter. She had sold twenty pictures and been given six commissions, and as a result was spending less time helping her parents around the estate and much more in the old cottage studio.

I went back to the paper as soon as I could. It had grown in the year since I'd been there, in circulation and in advertising. On my first day there I asked Pilar whether they'd considered changing the name from *GironaDia* to *CatalunyaDia* and selling throughout the region. 'Too risky,' she told me, 'and too big an investment. But there's another way of spreading our coverage; four months ago your father took over a company that owns titles in Tarragona, Lleida and Olot. Much easier, yes?' I had to agree.

I went back happily to being Simon Sureda's news desk assistant, but only on every second day, so that I could spend some time with Grandma, and with Grace, of course. Our status as a couple had been accepted that year. Or maybe asserted would be a better word. I had simply dumped our cases in what had always been my room, and nothing had been said about it; not at the time.

For all her protestations of age, Grandma still looked as youthful as she had appeared since returning home. At dinner that first night . . . there were just the three of us at the table; my dad was working late . . . after we'd given her a full account of our year, she said, 'Edinburgh is changing, it seems. And so is Spain. We're becoming a modern country, more prosperous and more youthful. My generation belongs with the dinosaurs. It's yours that has the power now. Values are changing.' The briefest glance towards the ceiling was the only comment she ever made about Grace and me sleeping together, unmarried, under her roof. 'And we have to accept them. It doesn't matter whether we like them or not; the biggest dam can only hold back so much water, and once it spills over the top you can't make it flow back uphill.'

'You can't put the genie back in the bottle,' I murmured.

'A different analogy,' she replied, 'but just as true. And speaking of genies, how is your mother?'

The question came out of the blue. I stared at her, then at Grace. I must have been frowning at her, for she shook her head and said, 'No, not me.'

The rarity among rarities: Grandma laughed. 'I told you, boy, you can't keep secrets from me. I am supernatural.' I'd have believed her, but she went on. 'The girl who waited on your table in the hotel is the granddaughter of one of my old Italian acquaintances in Edinburgh, the only one who isn't too senile to keep in touch with me. The child told her that she had seen you with a woman in her late thirties, and my friend could guess who that was.'

'Jesus,' I whispered, astounded. 'Nothing's beyond you, right enough. I didn't ask to meet her, and she didn't ask to see me. It was set up by her new husband, and as your friend probably told you, it wasn't a success. I won't be seeing her again.'

'She did,' Grandma confirmed. 'What did she have to say for herself, the woman?'

'Nothing that I wanted to hear. I'm surprised you have to ask that; it's a wonder that wee waitress didn't take notes.' I looked her in the eye. 'I want my birth certificate,' I told her.

'Of course. I'm sorry, Xavi, I should have given it to you before now.'

'There's no reference to any marriage on it, is there?'

'No. After your name it says, "Father, Josep-Maria Aislado, mother, Mary Inglis," then their address and that's all. You will know by now that your father is no fool; he can tell the future.'

'Maybe,' I conceded, 'but I know that often he's had help. Does he know we've met?'

'Of course not. There was no reason for me to tell him, any more than there was for you to tell me.'

'Fine. There won't be any more reason in the future; there will be no return fixture, I promise you.'

She smiled, deprecatingly. 'Football,' she exclaimed. 'I see in the *Scotsman* that your club is not in a pretty state.'

'It's a total shambles,' I admitted. 'We don't have a manager, and at this moment we don't even have any directors. The club secretary is running things for now, but he doesn't have the authority to appoint a new boss. When we go back to training, I suppose the second team coach will be in charge.'

'And will you still be there?'

'I signed a new part-time contract last summer; it has another two years to run, till I finish university . . . and maybe beyond.'

She looked at Grace. 'Are you happy with this, my dear?' she asked.

My fiancée grinned. 'It keeps him off the street corner. It's ideal for me; it means I know where he is all the time.'

'Which is more than he knows of you.' For just a second I imagined that I could see sparks fly between them.

'I suppose,' Grace replied, 'but he knows that I'll always be there when he gets home.'

I cut across them. 'University, Grandma,' I said. 'I've got a decision to make; honours or ordinary degree. What do you think?'

'Do you hear that?' Her gasp was just a little exaggerated. 'He's asking me for an opinion.'

'He values it,' Grace told her.

'But in this I can't offer one. All I can do is ask, will that extra year and a fancier degree make you a better journalist?'

'No,' I replied, with barely a thought.

'Then how would it be better spent?'

She didn't give me her opinion; instead she made my mind up for me. That's how it usually worked out.

My dad had bought a new Jeep since our last visit; he still commuted in his Merc, so Grace and I used it to do some exploring. We headed for Figueras, where the Salvador Dali museum was beginning to attract visitors from all over Europe and beyond, although nothing like the numbers that go there today. Both Dali and Gala, his fairly notorious wife, were still alive in those days, but in poor health and little seen, most certainly not by us. We found it as amusing as it was artistic, maybe even more so. The place has evolved over the years, but much of what Grace and I saw in 1981 stands unchanged. From there we drove towards the coast and discovered the ruins of Empuries, the site of the first Greco-Roman footfall in Iberia. I took photographs all the way, with the Nikon that Rod and Magda had given me for my nineteenth birthday. As we walked the narrow streets of the ancient Greek town, I wondered whether tourists will still be visiting Dali's edifice in two and a half thousand years. Perhaps not, but I'd like to think so.

Much of what I have done as a journalist is for the preservation of an accurate record of our times. Most of our history has been written by the winners; people like me, objective reporters of events as they happen, are there to change that. I said as much next day, to Pilar in the office. Her response was to invite me to write a feature describing our tour, contrasting our two visits and setting down those observations. It took me a couple of days, for I had to do some detailed research on the history of Empuries, but when I handed it in, she was impressed. 'I'll use it,' she told me. 'You can have a by-line, too, but not Xavi Aislado. I don't want anyone saying that the boss is ordering me to publish his son's stuff.' Neither did I, so we came up with the name Francisco Gracia. That stuck with me for a while.

It was a good piece. I know this, for it impressed my dad. I was at the news desk on the day it was published when he came wandering by, reading it. 'I like that,' he declared, shoving it before Simon. 'Who wrote it?' he asked the news editor. I thought that the first name of San Francisco Xavier allied to the Spanish translation of 'Grace' might have made my father twig, but it didn't.

Simon shrugged his shoulders. 'Some freelance Pilar found.' He knew quite well that it was me, but he decided that if the editor hadn't told him, then he was not about to spill the beans.

'Then he should get paid top dollar. We want to hang on to this guy.' He picked the paper up again and turned to me. 'Xavi, find the original copy and send it to all the other papers in the group. I'm going to invite all my editors to use this.' I nodded, and headed for the features desk. I had a copy in my drawer, of course, but I couldn't let him see that.

Under Aislado ownership, the InterMedia group of Girona has always been at the head of the game when it comes to new technology; my dad had installed some of the earliest fax machines in every office in the group, making the old telex machines almost redundant. The other editors didn't receive too many 'invitations' from the boss, so they knew that when one arrived, it should be taken seriously. My piece was published throughout northern Catalunya, and drew quite a few letters of agreement from readers. I believe that there may still be a copy in the archives of the Empuries museum curators, but I'm not certain.

It would not be honest of me to downplay the buzz this first journalistic success gave me; I was pumped up with excitement. The downside was that Grace was the only person who could know about it, other than Pilar, Simon and me. In my pride I'd have liked to have told Grandma, but she might have said something to my dad, and I didn't want him to know he'd been duped.

I spent more time at home after that. My 'success' had made me unnaturally excited, and I didn't like the feeling, so I went into the office only every third day. It was on the Wednesday of our second week that I broke the pattern. The night before had been hotter than usual and we had used the air con; the problem with that was the steady hum of the fan, which meant that we each slept fitfully. When I finally awakened, it was half past eight, and Grace was gone. I listened for her in the shower, but the bathroom was empty. I went downstairs, out to the pool and swam for fifteen minutes, then dried, put on my back-up swimming shorts, and stuck my feet into a pair of espadrilles. I expected to find Grace in the kitchen, when I went in for breakfast . . . tomato bread, fruit, and coffee, always . . . but she wasn't there either.

'She went outside earlier,' said Grandma Paloma, reading my mind.

'You might find her in the orchard.' She seemed to peer at me. 'You've looked different for the last day or two, my boy,' she murmured. 'You and the young lady haven't been . . . careless, have you?'

'Hell no!' I didn't want to discuss contraception with my grandmother, so I left it at that.

'That's good, but I didn't think so anyway. This journalism, it means a lot to you, doesn't it, Francisco?'

She'd done me again. 'My mother was right,' I told her. 'Four hundred years ago you'd have been ashes.'

She chuckled . . . or did she cackle? 'Of course she was right,' she replied, 'if recognising the obvious can count as witchcraft. I saw your mother for the gold-digger she is, and I gave her what she wanted, but as little of it as I could. And when you and Grace go visiting museums and ruins then three days later a very erudite article on the subject appears in your father's newspaper, written by somebody I've never heard of, even though I read *GironaDia* every day, then it's a simple matter to realise who he is. Especially when he's sitting in my kitchen with a well-fucked look on his face that he didn't get between the sheets.'

My jaw almost dislocated itself.

She laughed. 'You're shocked by my language? My lad, you may think that I'm a recluse, but I've lived in the same world as you, but for over seventy years, so I know a hell of a lot more about it than you do, and I know even more than that about people. Your father, he doesn't, because he has his head up his arse most of the time.'

At the time, that was the least expected moment in my life, and it remains among the most joyous; a short list, I admit. I felt such a wave of happiness that my eyes flooded with tears. I picked the old lady up, and I hugged her for the first time ever, years late, but thank God not too late. And she hugged me back. Neither of us said a word; we didn't need to.

I set her down, back on her feet. 'Go on with you now,' she murmured. 'Go find your Grace, in every way.'

I was still slightly stunned when I went outside, so I didn't go to the orchard right away. Instead, I put on my RayBans, lay on a sunbed and looked up at the blue, cloudless morning sky, considering what had just happened. The last barrier that separated me from adulthood had been breached. I had faced what had always been the truth. To hell with biology; I had acknowledged my real mother.

It was half past ten before I was ready to move on. Still Grace hadn't returned. I swam again and dried myself thoroughly before going to look for her . . . few things smell worse than wet rope-soled shoes. I headed for the orchard, calling out her name, expecting her to appear from behind a fruit tree, but she didn't. I walked between the rows, up and down; if she was playing a game, she was winning.

The last stand of apple trees led me to the old cottage. I looked at it and saw that the door was open. As I stepped inside, I heard the sound of voices, and a light laugh that I'd have known in the darkest place on earth. I opened the door to the room that had become Carmen's studio. Grace was standing there, leaning back against a stepladder; she was naked. The windows were open, but it was still baking hot; there was a fine sheen of sweat on her body and her hair, above and below, was slightly damp.

'What the f . . .' I exclaimed.

I looked to my right, and there was Carmen, at an easel, palette in her left hand, brush in her right. 'She's posing for me,' she said, in Catalan. 'I have a commission, for a female nude. I need a model, and Grace agreed to do it.'

'Who's the commission for?'

'The gallery in Barcelona where I had my exhibition.'

'You mean it's . . . she's going to hang there?'

Carmen shook her head, and a few other things, involuntarily; she was wearing a T-shirt and what might just have been shorts. They were sticking to her. 'Not for long. They have a buyer.'

'Fuck that!' I declared. 'I'll buy it. Fifty thousand pesetas.' That was around two hundred pounds, decent money in those days.

She laughed. 'Keep going.'

'A hundred.'

'Keep going. When you get to three hundred you'll have my attention.' She paused. 'Only you won't. It's a contract, Xavi; I have to deliver.' She grew serious. 'Look, if you really object, then I'll stop right now, destroy everything and find another model. But I'll never find one like Grace. Look at her, for Christ's sake, she's fantastic.'

'I know that,' I pointed out. 'I look at her every day; every morning, every night. But only I do: that's my point.'

'Then don't be selfish.'

'Xavi,' said Grace, quietly, 'I want to do this. Please let me. The painting is going to a private buyer. We'll never know who he is, and he'll never know who I am. Carmen's promised me that.'

She always had the combination that opened me up; maybe I should have changed it from time to time. 'Let me see it,' I said, stepping towards the easel.

'There's nothing to see yet,' Carmen told me. 'I've only just started the oil. All I've done so far are studies in charcoal and in watercolour. You can look at them; they'll give you an idea of what it will be like.' She opened a folder and showed me a series of sketches, rough and ready, but very impressive, even more so after I made myself think of the subject as a stranger. 'The deal is that all these go to the gallery as well, but you can choose one if you like. They'll never know.'

'Well?' Grace made it sound as if I had a choice.

'Okay,' I sighed, knowing that I didn't really, for put to the test I would never have considered imposing my will on hers. 'Go ahead. Will it be finished before we leave?'

'With luck,' Carmen replied. 'If not, it'll be close enough for me not to need Grace any more.' She smiled. 'There's a commission for a male nude as well,' she added. 'I don't suppose . . .'

I did consider it, for around five seconds; during that time I took a good look at Carmen, weighed up the potential for embarrassment and decided that it was too great. 'No, I don't think so,' I told her. 'You could always ask my dad, though.' The smile vanished; she winced.

Grace didn't have to stand there for all the time that Carmen was painting; that was what the studies were about. But she did have to be handy, so she stayed around the house for the rest of our visit. I found myself wanting to spend as much time with Grandma as I could, and so I only spent one more day in the office. When it was over, and I was ready to leave, I went into Pilar's office to bid her farewell for another year. She wasn't alone; Simon and Angel were with her.

'Join us for a moment, Xavi,' she said. I took the seat that she offered me.

There was no preamble. 'We want to offer you a job,' she told me. The two guys nodded, in harmony.

'That's very nice of you,' I replied, 'but I'm going back to Edinburgh. I've got another year to do for my degree. Once I've got that, my intention is to look for a start there. On top of all that, there's the small matter of my contract with the Hearts.' I looked at Angel. 'Or are Barcelona B going to make me an offer as well?'

'We could probably secure you a transfer to the Girona team,' Pilar went on, 'but the job we're talking about isn't here. We'd like you to be our representative in Scotland, covering news and sport, and we'd also like you to send us regular feature articles, on, on . . . on whatever you like, really, anything that's topical, and likely to be of interest to our readership. Since you're a reader through your subscription, you'll have an appreciation of their tastes. What do you say?'

I considered it, looking at them, from one to the other, as I judged my time constraints. I was still a part-time footballer, and having taken the decision to go for an ordinary degree, my final year was going to verge on being a formality. From what Pilar had said, I'd be able to do what I could and no more, and still leave time for what I had come to consider my family life.

'Does my dad know about this?' I asked.

Pilar nodded. 'He approves, as long as you continue to be Francisco

Gracia when we give you a by-line. I told him this morning that was your article. He didn't say so, but he was very pleased.'

'In that case it's a deal.' I stood.

'Don't you want to discuss money?' she asked.

I looked at Simon and smiled. 'You heard my dad the other day, didn't you? He said you should pay Senor Gracia top dollar.'

'What you've got to understand, Michael, is that my arrival doesn't mean that the company is suddenly awash with money. The fact is that the opposite is true. This business has never been subjected to proper financial controls but all that's going to change. My associates and I, although it's mostly me, are investing a lot of money through the new share issue, but much of that's going to be grabbed by the bank to reduce the debt level. They'll leave us a certain amount of working capital, and we'll have an overdraft facility, but any spend on top of that we'll have to raise ourselves. Do you understand what I'm saying?'

'You're telling me that we'll still be broke.'

'Not quite, but we'll still have to run things on a tight budget. So we have to look at what we have, at the value of each item on our asset list. Some will be positive, others will be worth nothing . . . indeed less than nothing, for their costs will be much greater than the return we get from them. You and I must decide how to manage each one. Still with me?'

'I'm not sure.'

'Okay, let me try to explain. The underlying strength of a business is in its asset base, that's a universal truth. But not all businesses are the same, and the sector that we're in, or that I'm about to be in, seems to have evolved its own unique rules. In this specific case, there are no real tangible assets. Okay, the company owns some buildings, but that means nothing. One, they're of no value because they're unsellable and two, the company doesn't own the ground they stand on, or on which it conducts the rest of its business. The acquisition of that land from its current owners will be my top priority. It's a must, and it'll happen before any other major investment is made. We'll have bank support, but it'll be secured borrowing and it'll need to be serviced. Hence the need for the rationalisation of the rest of the assets, unique and largely intangible as they are. Clear?'

'No, but please go on.'

'Did you bring those lists as I asked you to? Thank you. Are they annotated?'

'Pardon?'

'Are they marked?'

'Yes. Ticks and crosses.'

'As many as this? My God, no wonder this company is in trouble. What the hell have I let myself be talked into? No wonder the Spanish guy turned it down. I thought the overhead was on the high side when I saw the due diligence report, but I didn't realise it covered all this. Do we need two of those?'

'Not all the time.'

'Then one will have to be more productive. Three of those? No way. But these aren't the real assets, are they? They're not your business; I shouldn't waste your time, Michael.'

'Last two pages.'

'Michael, relax. You're not under review here. Ah, here we are. I see what you've done. So, the ones with the crosses . . . ?'

'No future, no value.'

'What would be the cost of disposal?'

'In most cases, nothing.'

'Then dispose. The ones with the ticks?'

'Worth keeping.'

'These numbers, are they values?'

'The first ones are, in thousands. The second are the wages costs.'

'And the ones with no marks against them?'

'I'm not sure about them.'

'Okay. I appreciate your honesty. Let's look at them sector by sector, starting at the top. We have three here, two ticks and one with nothing. Clearly we don't want them all; which of the three would have the greatest disposal value? The two you're sure of are low value, low cost. Do you have a feel for the potential of the third? That's what I'm trying to get at here, raising as much cash as we can through strategic disposals.'

'Well, no guarantees, but I reckon that, potentially, that's your biggest . . . asset. The situation would have to be carefully handled, and it might take time, but with a bit of luck . . .'

Nine

The painting wasn't close to being finished when we left on the Thursday of the following week, but there was enough on canvas for Carmen to show us, and it was clear that the buyer wasn't going to be disappointed. I was still ambivalent about a naked likeness of my beloved hanging on a stranger's wall, but I confess that some flaw in my character, maybe it was pride, drew a bit of a furtive thrill from the idea. We were allowed to choose one of the studies, and we agreed on a charcoal version that bore the closest resemblance to the intended oil. We took it back with us, had it framed, and presented it to Rod and Magda. That was my idea, and Grace jumped at it, although I don't believe she ever suspected the reason for the gesture; no way was I going to have it hanging in our place for anyone else to see.

I came back from that two and a half week holiday with a firm career plan in mind, for the first time. I talked it over with Grace during the journey home, telling her what I had decided about my university course, and about the occasional job that I'd be doing for the paper. She asked about my future in football, and I told her the truth. 'That's out of my hands. I have a contract for another two seasons at Tynecastle, and I will see it out. The club's in the mire, and I'm not going to desert it. I'm young for a keeper; maybe I won't make the cut. But I have to give it a try.'

We talked about ourselves too. Grace was on a high; she had an air of excitement about her, an aura that I could almost touch. She had never been short of self-belief, but I could tell that the business of the portrait had given her an independent endorsement that would raise her confidence levels even higher. I told her as much as we sat in the

162

departure lounge at Heathrow, waiting for the Edinburgh connection. Her eyes sparkled, full of mischief, as she looked back at me. 'I know,' she agreed. 'I was nervous to begin with. When Carmen asked me at first I said no, but she said to me she'd be struggling otherwise, and after she gave us our picture last year, well, I felt I had to help her out. When we started, I wanted to keep my bikini on, but she said it had to be natural, that a nude had to be . . . ' she grinned '. . . well, naked. Then she said, "If it helps you we'll both do it," and she stripped off herself, right to the buff. I was fine after that.'

'She didn't fancy you, did she?' I asked, more in earnest than not, although I kept my tone light-hearted. Lesbianism was not something I'd encountered at that time, but I'd heard of it.

'Are you kidding? Carmen? She really did want to paint you in the nude, you know. She asked me if you were as well hung as you look. I told her that's why you never wear tight-fitting swimming trunks.'

'What did she say to that?'

She shook her head. 'No, that was real girl talk.'

'Go on.'

'Well . . . she said that if I had any left over, any I couldn't accommodate, could she have it, because she could certainly use a bit more. I told her no, that I can handle what's there, thanks. I'm glad you turned her down when she asked you to pose.'

'Sure, because she'd have known you were exaggerating.'

'Who says?'

'How much comparing have you done?' I murmured, smiling.

'A bit,' she confessed. I sat up straight and stared at her. 'Compared to Michelangelo's statue of David, you win by a mile.'

'I might not be as hard, though.'

She exploded with laughter, drawing a look from a suit, a youngish, thirty-something, stocky guy, who was seated facing us, his study of the *Daily Telegraph* interrupted. 'That's something I'm never going to test,' she said. She leaned in against me. 'Would you mind if I did some more?' she asked, more quietly.

'More what?'

'Modelling.'

'I thought that models had to be . . .' I paused, trying to find my tact button '. . . on the skeletal side, thirty-two A maximum. You're slim, *chica*, but you fill a size thirty-six bra.'

'Thirty-six C, my love,' she corrected. 'But I wasn't talking about the catwalk.'

I frowned. 'Not photographic? You're not meaning that?'

Her face expressed distaste. 'What? Flashing my minge in girlie magazines? Certainly not. No, I'm talking about the sort of modelling I did for Carmen. I'm sorry, Xavi, but I enjoyed it. You know I did; you just said as much. What do you think?'

'I think it sounds bloody dangerous. How would you find clients? A classified ad in the papers? You'd attract all sorts of geeks.'

'I know that! No, I was thinking of approaching Edinburgh Art College and asking them if they needed anybody.'

'Mmm. So you do that, the two of us are in Bert's Bar one night, and some student with a drink in him comes up to us, digs you in the ribs and says, "Hey, Grace, great tits." I give him a Mulligan and where do we go from there?' I must have raised my voice, for the suit peered across again.

'Art students don't do that. Anyway, it would be no more than the truth; I have got great tits.' The suit shot a look at them, and blinked. I nodded affirmation in his direction and he dived back into his broadsheet.

'Not disputed,' I said, 'and I wasn't maligning art students as a species. I was talking about the one clown in every circus.'

'But people come up to you in pubs,' she protested.

'Yes they do,' I conceded, 'but Grace, I'm six feet seven inches tall, broad with it, and I have an accidental reputation as a slugger, so they're invariably polite.'

She pouted. 'It's not fair. You're being a chauvinist.'

'No, I'm being a realist. And a pragmatist,' I added. 'Look, if you want to do that, and it makes you happy, I'm not going to argue, but why don't you approach Glasgow Art School, or try to find an organised group of artists where you'll be sure of discretion.'

She looked up at me. 'You won't mind if I do that?'

'No, not at all. Just don't tell Scott, that's all.'

She frowned, and stared at me. 'Why?' she asked.

'I don't want him joining the bloody group, that's why.'

She squeezed my arm. 'Oh, you're a love.'

'I know,' I agreed. Was I ever. She could do anything she liked with me; if she had wanted to be a Page Three girl . . . and she could have been . . . I'd have gone along with that too, in the end.

Rod and Magda were waiting for us at Edinburgh Airport, just after six. Rather than drive us straight home, they insisted on stopping for a meal on the way, in the Barnton Hotel. Magda simply wanted to catch up on her daughter's news . . . Grace kept the modelling to herself at that point . . . but I could tell that Rod was bursting to talk with me, football stuff, I guessed.

Correctly. 'Have you been keeping up with the local news while you've been away?' he asked. I shook my head; Grandma's mail-order copies of the *Scotsman* had been around, but I had made a point of ignoring them. 'Then you won't know,' he continued, eagerly. 'The takeover's gone through at Tynecastle. There's been all sorts of stuff going on, but I'm told that there's a new majority shareholder. I don't know who he is yet as all the legals have still to be tied up, but I'm assured it's for real.'

'That's good,' I told him, 'but have we got a manager yet? Every day that goes past without one, we're in more trouble.'

'Yes. Mike Dean's been given the job, apparently with the approval of the new guy. Quite a few of the fans aren't happy; they want a big name.'

'Mike's okay,' I said. Dean was the reserve team coach, the guy who had spotted me when I joined from the Boys' Club. He was indeed okay, but that was as enthusiastic as anyone could ever be about him when it came to managing a supposedly top side. He was sound, and his second team had been successful, but he was the gentle persuader type. Thinking back to Chic McAveety's managerial philosophy, he would need a 'bowfer' and I couldn't see who that was going to be. Burger could have done it, but he'd just been sold back to Rangers, where his heart lay.

'Any new signings?' I asked, thinking of the big hole that his departure had created in the centre of an already dodgy defence.

Rod snorted. 'No chance. I was talking to one of the club's bankers the other day; he said that the emphasis will have to be on getting the overhead down, not putting it up with expensive new players. Not the way to protect an investment, by starving it of cash, but bankers have never known anything about football.' He was still excited; there was something he was holding back. When it came, it was a question. 'It's not your dad, is it? Is he the new majority shareholder? I've heard it rumoured. It would be great if he was.'

I chuckled; it became a laugh. Grace and her mother broke off from their discussion to look at me. 'Rod,' I replied, 'take a look under the table, at my feet. If I am wearing ballet shoes, then my dad is the new owner of the Jam Tarts. If not, then your rumour-monger is way off the mark.'

I was intrigued, though, wondering inwardly all the way home, and for the rest of the evening who the new owner might be. I called a couple of my teammates, whose phone numbers I had in my Filofax, but they were no wiser than I was. I even called Burger, but he had scraped the literal and allegorical mud of Tynecastle from his boots and had no interest, or, as he put it, didn't give a fuck. I was so wrapped up in it that I dug out my typewriter and banged out a philosophical piece, in Catalan, about half a city on tenterhooks waiting for its football Messiah, the man who would lead them to the promised land, contrasting the secrecy of the process with the openness of Barcelona, where the president is elected by the registered supporters themselves. I was happy with the way it looked, so, having no access to either a fax machine or telex, I phoned the paper and dictated it to the late duty copy-taker, who yawned his way through the process. I had to tell him twice when I was finished that the story was to be marked for the personal attention of Angel Esposito. The sports editor called me back next morning, early; he told me that he liked it and would use it, although I suspected that he might be simply encouraging the new guy.

A couple of hours later, I was distracted from football, for a time at least. The street level door buzzer sounded. I picked up the receiver in the kitchen, wondering who it might be. 'Xavi,' I answered.

'Hey,' came a familiar, if metallic, voice, 'it's Bobby. Can I come up?'

Bobby and I had kept in regular touch, through his occasional visit to what he called the 'gang hut', but mainly by telephone, during the two years he had been at Aberdeen, and we had met once or twice during university vacations. 'Sure,' I told him. 'We're decent.' I pushed the button that would let him in.

'Just the two of you?' he asked as I showed him into the living room, where Grace was waiting. 'You told me that wee Dave was leaving, so have you moved Scott out as well? Natural enough, I suppose. When are you getting married?' That was Bobby; why ask one question when you've got breath for two.

'Not until we're both fully qualified,' Grace told him. 'And Scott's at work. Xavi and I don't start till Monday.'

He grinned at me from the sofa as I handed him a cup of coffee; percolated, not instant, revealing my Spanish side. 'Do you call catching balls work?' he chuckled.

'Hey,' Grace exclaimed, 'you should have seen the mess he was in after the Airdrie game.'

'And the other guy,' Bobby reminded her. 'I got into a fight over that; one of the guys in my year's an Airdrie supporter. He wanted you suspended for life, and done for serious assault. When I told him that his man was an animal, he had a go at me.'

I frowned. 'They let Airdrie supporters into Robert Gordon's? Bad enough they let them into fucking Tynecastle. I hope you didn't hurt him, though,' I added. Bobby had been a chunky kid at school, and he had filled out since he left. He'd been playing rugby, and had made his college's first fifteen in his first term there.

'Nah, I just shoved him. He was as drunk as he was stupid; his mates took him away before any damage could be done.'

Grace looked at him, disapproving. 'This RGIT place sounds like a bear pit.'

'Every university is a bear pit, love,' I pointed out. 'When you release hundreds of young people from the discipline of their school and, in most cases, their home, and give them the run of places with their own bars, snooker rooms, weekend discos and the like, you've created lab conditions for boozing, brawling and bonking.'

She smiled. 'Have we been missing something?'

'I don't drink much,' I replied. 'I brawl even less. As for the other . . .'

She finished my sentence. '. . . quality not quantity.'

'Perfectly put. As for Robert Gordon's Institute of Technology, with all the offshore stuff up in the north-east, it's become a centre of excellence.'

'And I hate it,' said Bobby quietly.

I looked at him, surprised. 'Since when?'

'From the beginning, really. The college itself is fine; it's the city I don't like. It's grey and it's cold; sometimes when we're playing the rain actually hurts.'

'You're a softie at heart, Hannah.'

He held up his hands. 'Absolutely. I am a complete pussy. And speaking of those, how's Scott getting on? Has he got over his dad dying?'

'He got over it on day one. Scott's fine. He's had the same girlfriend for four months now; that's got to be a record.'

'Jesus yes,' Bobby agreed. 'Anyone I'd know?'

Grace stared at him. 'You mean you don't? It's Jilly.'

Bobby's older sister had been two years ahead of us at Watson's. She'd done a course in textiles after she'd left, and had found herself a

job with Billie Livingstone's store chain. She and Scott had met up
again the previous February when he'd called in at Billie's office. They'd
been going out ever since; we'd met up as a foursome a couple of times.
He'd never brought her to our flat, but he'd stayed over a few times in
the one she shared with another girl.

'She hasn't mentioned it,' he said, quietly.

'Why should she?' said Grace. 'Do you discuss your girlfriends with
her?'

'I don't have girlfriends,' he replied, 'but if I was going out with Billie
Livingstone, don't you think she would tell Scott?'

I laughed. 'No she wouldn't, in case he told wee Dave, and then
you'd be in real trouble. She's got serious with Dave's old man, the
secret soldier.'

'Aw Jeez,' Bobby moaned. 'That goes to show you how far out of the
loop I've got.'

'Never mind,' Grace told him. 'Only another two years and you'll be
back where you belong, out of that awful rain.'

'Ah well,' he said, 'that's just it. I've had enough. I'm not staying up
there any longer.'

'Come on, man,' I protested. 'You can't quit halfway through your
course.'

'I'm not,' he replied. 'I've managed to wangle a transfer to Heriot
Watt. They're going to accept all my credits from RGIT and let me
carry on there, in the honours stream if I choose.'

That explained the morning visit. 'Okay,' I said.

'Okay what?' he asked cautiously.

'We weren't going to replace Dave in the flat, but if you want to
move in with us his room's yours, providing you agree to the same
house rules as the rest of us . . . and providing that Grace approves, of
course.'

She smiled. 'The house rules mainly involve smelly feet, trainers and
the like. Banned, that is.' She jerked a thumb in my direction. 'That
includes his.'

'What about Scott? Doesn't he have a say?'

'No he doesn't,' I decreed, then added, deadpan, 'Best that way, if he's shagging your sister. She might not fancy you around; she might make him say no.'

We told him what the deal was, monthly rent with bills included, kitty for food, share the cooking, and we told him what wasn't allowed, apart from noxious trainers. He was fine with all of that, so we told him that he could move in any time he liked, and stay for two years. Grace was due to graduate then; while we were students we were happy to live like students, but after that we would want to be on our own.

He had barely left, before the phone rang again. I thought it might be Angel, with a query about my piece, but no, it was Shirley, one of the backroom staff at the football club, calling on behalf of Mike Dean, the new manager. 'Players' meeting, Xavi,' she said. 'Two o'clock in the supporters' club. I'm glad you're there. Not all the boys are back from their holidays yet, and the boss wants as many of you there as we can round up.'

'Fine. What's it about?'

'He'll tell you that.'

I didn't spend too much time pondering over the reason for the call. I'd thought, from the time the date was announced, that we were a week too late in restarting training, and that might have dawned on Mike Dean. On the other hand, if Rod's banker friend was right, perhaps some of us were going to be told that we were surplus to requirements. If that happened to me, I would ask Willie Lascelles to direct the club to the signatures on my contract and to tell them how much termination was going to cost them. In any dispute over money and the value of a contract, there is no more formidable opponent than someone who is half Scottish and half Catalan.

I took my training gear with me when I headed for Tynecastle. I had done nothing for a month, apart from swimming, chins, press-ups and some stretching exercises while we were in Spain, and I thought it might be wise to have a warm-up session before full training started on the following Monday. One look around the supporters' club bar, which was located in the grandstand, with its own entrance well away from the players' door, was enough to convince me of this. Professional footballers are a different breed these days, or most of them are. The seasons are longer, and the top guys have very little summer break, so their fitness levels are always high. My day came towards the end of the dark ages, when players weren't paid all that much, and their attitudes often reflected the fact. I hadn't seen my teammates for almost two months; some were red from days on the beach without sun protection, others had the pallor of men who had spent much of their break in the betting shop, and one or two, more, maybe half a dozen, had the bloated, glassy-eyed look of men who were just coming off a bender, or were still on one.

'Hey, Iceland,' Big Mental greeted me, waving me over to sit beside him in the goalies' corner. Just the pair of us; Ian, his number two, was still on holiday.

'Hi, Walter,' I replied. (Big Mental did not like being addressed by his nickname, and because that was his nickname, his wishes were usually respected.) 'What the fuck's all this about?' I asked him. I've rarely used and never really approved of industrial language in any other workplace, but in the world of football, it's compulsory.

'Fuck knows. Maybe the gaffer just wants tae give us all a pep talk.' As reserve coach, the manager had been plain 'Mike' to all of us, but his new office brought him a title and automatic respect, even before he'd earned it.

The buzz around the room continued as the stragglers drifted in; the last three had the flush, and slightly raised voices, of men who had lunched in the Diggers' or another pub close by. It stopped as the door opened, and Mike Dean stepped into the bar.

'Fuck me,' Big Mental whispered. 'Look at that.' Since we had last seen him, our new manager had acquired a designer haircut, a Mexican moustache and, most surprising of all, a suit. None of us had ever seen him in anything other than training gear.

He looked around his squad, showing no sign of being impressed. Nobody spoke. It was his call after all, he was the boss. Eventually, he took the plunge. 'Welcome back, boys,' he began. 'You all know that training starts on Monday, so those of you that have been on the piss had better back off now. You'll know too that I'm in the manager's office now. I'm still the same bloke though; I'm not goin' to be remote all of a sudden. Any problems, don't be afraid to tell me about them. I want to run a happy squad; that's the first step to gettin' us back into the Premier Division, where the fans expect us to be.'

Heads nodded around the room, and one young sycophant called out, 'You're the man, Mike.'

Big Mental reached out and cuffed him round the ear. 'That's "Boss" tae you, son,' he growled.

'That brings me to the one team announcement I have to make. Since Burger's gone back to the 'Gers, we're without a captain.' He looked to our corner. 'Walter, you've got the loudest voice in the squad, you're the senior player, and you'll take shite off nobody, so you've got the job. In the dressing room, when I'm not there, you're the boss. I'd like you to take first team training as well when I'm busy, starting on Monday. You'll find squad lists for the new season in the dressing room.' Without warning, his eyes fixed on me. 'Iceland,' he said, 'you're the new reserve team captain, and I want you to supervise second squad training till I find a replacement for myself as their coach.' As I took in this bombshell, he looked at a couple of grim faces in the group, older guys who rarely got near the first team. 'I know he's only nineteen,' he added, 'but he's a natural leader. You'll either follow him or you'll fuck off. If he tells me he wants any of you out, then out you'll be.'

He stopped, and drew a deep breath. 'And now,' he announced when he was ready, 'to the real business of this meeting. You're all aware that things have been going on in the boardroom.' That may not have been true; a couple of the young guys had reading difficulties. If it wasn't in the *Dandy* or the *Beano* it was beyond them. 'Well, I'm pleased to tell you that everything's been sorted, and the club's got a new majority shareholder and chairman.'

I was still absorbing my unexpected promotion, and the implication that came with it that, barring injuries, I had been consigned to the reserves for a season, so I wasn't hanging on his every word. A new chairman? Fine, but no big deal; I'd never met the old one, or any of the directors for that matter. Thus when the boss continued, he did get my attention. 'He's new to football,' he said, 'and he wants to learn about the business as quickly as he can. As a first step, he wants to meet the team. You lot stay there, while I go and get him.'

Interest level rose in the room as we waited, but not by all that much. Some of the team were true Hearts supporters, but the majority, myself included, were there for the game itself or for the money. We didn't care who paid our wages as long as we got to play. Some of the boys didn't even look round as the door opened. Big Mental and I were deep in discussion of training supervision . . . I was a student, so he assumed that I would know how to go about it . . . but we were facing that way. I stopped in mid-sentence as the new chairman came into the bar, followed by the manager. He was wearing a maroon blazer with the club crest embroidered on the breast pocket, and a Heart of Midlothian tie, different garb from the last time I had seen him. He was the suit from the departure lounge in Heathrow, the guy who'd shot a look at Grace's tits. For an instant, our eyes met; his widened, I smiled.

His composure wasn't dented, though. As he took his place in front of the bar, where Dean had stood earlier, I sized him up properly for the first time. His youthful face made it hard to nail down his age, but he could have been no older than thirty-five, making him at least three years younger than dour Dan Doughty, the departed Burger's partner in central defence. He was no more than five feet eight tall and his build was that of a rugby player rather than a footballer. His manner seemed assured, but I sensed an inner tension behind the confidence.

'Gentlemen,' he began, his voice strong and assertive, pitched to hide any nerves he might have felt. 'My name is Alexander Draper, and I'm proud to be the new chairman of this great club. I won't go into detail about the financial restructuring that's taken place, but my colleagues and I have invested a considerable amount to assume control. This doesn't mean that there will be a flood of big money signings, not in the short term at any rate, so the burden of securing promotion will remain largely with you. I don't know football yet, but I do know business, and I can tell you that companies stand or fall on the strength of their assets. You are the assets of Heart of Midlothian, and I'm confident that as a group you have strength that we can build on. You'll be seeing a lot of me for I intend to be a hands-on chairman, in executive control of the club. My first task will be to sit down with the manager and look at the squad individually, to determine where it might need to be augmented or refreshed. I have to go now to meet the press, but any of you who have any questions or any problems will find that I'm accessible to you at any time. Just make an appointment through the manager. Thank you.' He nodded, gave a brief bow to his audience, and then he was gone.

'Fuck was that about?' Big Mental murmured.

'That was a new broom,' I told him. 'What he said was that he's bought the club, but that he doesn't have enough dough left to go shopping for new players.'

'What was that crap about "argumented"? What did he mean by that?' asked Black Pudding Gibson, who had joined us.

'Maybe not what he said,' I ventured. 'My guess is that he's going to look at the so-called "assets" one by one, and decide which of them are really liabilities.' As it turned out, I was correct, but only partially.

The new club captain stood up. 'Okay,' he shouted, stilling the chat. 'All you guys get round to the dressing room and check which squad you're in, then meet Iceland and me out on the pitch. No trainin' today but let's get ready for Monday.'

For all my misgivings, the arrival of Alexander Draper had an immediately positive effect on the club. The press corps loved him from the start, since he proved to be an absolute diamond mine for quotes, every one a gem. They described him as a tycoon, a magnate, and the humble *Saltire*, poor relation among the broadsheets, even called him 'an entrepreneurial genius with plans to revolutionise football in Scotland by introducing sound business practices to a hitherto ill-disciplined industry'. For years I kept that cutting in my desk and showed it to young journalists when I felt that they needed to understand that it is possible to use hyperbole and understatement in the same sentence.

I didn't have to take training for very long. The new chairman allowed the manager to re-sign Gary Whyte, an old club favourite, and install him as reserve team coach. I was happy about that; for all that the boss had given me authority, I didn't have the motivation to use it. Big Mental was one of nature's sergeant majors; I am not. In addition to that, in Draper's second week in charge, six reserves were axed, and I felt that some of the survivors were blaming me.

At the end of July we played a couple of warm-up games, pre-season friendlies, one against Falkirk and the other at fucking Merrytown. We won the first easily, but fucking Merrytown were a sharp outfit with a battery of talented young strikers. We came through that one, thanks to a ridiculous free kick from forty yards by a kid from the youth squad, but only after I'd played what I still rate as the game of my life. Too bad that it took place behind closed doors, with only the coaching staff of the two teams as witnesses, and the managers, Mike Dean and the 'Town boss, Lex McCuish, who had been something of a legend in his playing career.

My good form carried into the start of the season. We won our first four games hands down, almost literally as I conceded only one goal. I had entertained no hopes of first team football that season, but on the first Saturday in September, the top team managed to lose to East Stirlingshire, and in the process Big Mental dislocated a finger. The next match was on the following Wednesday, at home to the formidable Kilmarnock. I expected to be on the bench, but to my surprise and to the undisguised anger of Ian, the back-up keeper, I went straight into the side. I had a quiet word with the boss after the team sheet went up. 'You're in form, Iceland,' he told me. 'Ian hasn't been playing.' Logically, that meant that the club was prepared to pay a guy first team wages and bonuses for doing nothing at all. I didn't buy that, but I didn't question it either.

The team was better under Mike Dean than it had been the year before, but the Saturday loss had been a shocker: East Stirling were cannon fodder, and everyone knew it, especially Killie, who were on us like a wolf pack from the kick-off. My luck held, though. They hit the bar a couple of times in the first half, I made a few saves and we kept them out until they ran out of legs and Pudding Gibson, captain for the day, nicked a late winner. The sponsors made me their man of the match. The prize was a bottle of champagne; I gave it to Ian.

Big Mental was waiting for me in the dressing room. 'Give me a rundown on the reserves,' he said, quietly. 'I'm sitting on no fuckin' bench.'

'You'll be back on Saturday, Walter,' I told him.

He shook his head. 'The punters love you, son. You're no' the best, but they cannae see past the sheer size of you in the goal. You enjoy it while it's goin'.'

I did: for two days. I'd trained the night before, but on Friday of that week, I had a call from the manager, asking me to come to his office for eleven thirty. I went along, expecting to be told that, shut-out win or not, the club captain had to be in the team. I'd have been happy with that, but it wasn't what happened.

When I got there, Dean told me that the chairman wanted to see me. I headed for the boardroom; he was waiting for me at the door, but instead of inviting me inside he asked me to take a walk with him on the field. We strolled out to the centre circle. 'This is my real meeting room,' Draper told me, with a grin. 'Nobody can overhear me here.'

'What do you want to say?' I asked him, bluntly.

'I want to talk to you about opportunity,' he began. 'As I told everyone at our first squad meeting, the manager and I have been looking at the asset base. We've made some necessary cuts already, sad but unavoidable, but now we're looking at the positive.' I reckon he'd have put a conspiratorial arm around my shoulders at that point, had I not been a foot taller than him. 'Xavi, we've identified you as the club's brightest asset. You're an outstanding young keeper and we're very proud that you're a product of our youth academy.' I'd never heard that grandiose term before; it may have been that Alexander Draper coined it, right there and then.

'As I'm sure you'll realise, given your family background . . .' he winked up at me '. . . yes, I've done some research on you; asset management is one of the key elements of business success, and the most vital decision that a chief executive can make is knowing when to realise so that he can reinvest.'

I had to laugh. He was telling me how bright I was, and yet he was trying to bullshit me.

He frowned. 'Yes?' he said, a little querulously.

'You're going to put me on the transfer list, chairman,' I told him, 'so cut the crap and come out with it.'

He nodded. 'You're almost right,' he admitted. 'We've got three goalkeepers on our books and we only need two. Walter and Ian have very limited value, whereas you . . .'

'So that's why you played me on Wednesday rather than Ian. I was in the shop window, yes?'

'That's absolutely right.' He laughed, and to my surprise I began to like him. 'I wish I'd been able to persuade your father to invest; you'd be very useful on my board.'

'How are you going to play it?' I asked. 'Circulate my availability?'

'It's gone further than that. We've had an offer for you, and we've accepted. Seventy thousand, Xavi. I believe that's a record for a keeper in Scotland. Your new boss is in the boardroom. Let's go and meet him.'

I said nothing. I fell into step beside him and walked back into the stand. We reached the boardroom, and Draper threw open the door. I stepped inside, where a smiling figure stood beside the trophy cabinet, hand outstretched. 'Welcome, son,' he exclaimed. It was Lex McCuish; Draper had sold me to fucking Merrytown, our greatest enemy.

But he hadn't, not quite. The contracts lay on the boardroom table with a pen beside them. 'If you'd like to read them and sign, Xavi,' said Draper. 'All your personal terms are set out there.'

'I'll read, sure,' I replied. 'But not alone. I'll sign nothing that Willie Lascelles, my lawyer, hasn't approved. I'm sure you know him.'

McCuish's cheesy grin melted a little at that, but the chairman kept things on the move. 'Fair enough,' he declared. 'Yes, I know Mr Lascelles. I'll call him right now.'

In those days, very few Scottish players had agents. If they were lucky they had a father who looked out for them but that was as far as it went. I suppose I was a groundbreaker. Willie arrived at the ground in less than half an hour, and he laced into the chairman and the manager. 'You do realise that this lad is under twenty-one,' he said icily, 'and that he's entitled to a certain degree of legal protection in a situation like this? Yes?' He picked up the contract and read through it, then sat down at the table and took a pen from his pocket. 'Right,' he began, 'let's see.'

An hour later, the length of the contract had been cut from seven years to four, my university requirements were acknowledged and guaranteed, my wages had been increased and included a built-in annual increment, and performance bonuses, and I was down for ten per cent of the transfer fee, since I hadn't asked for a move. Oh yes; my new club would give me a car, as well. It would carry the logo of the local Ford dealer, but that didn't bother me one iota. Alexander Draper was fine about the ten per cent. Sixty-three thousand was still great money to him. McCuish wasn't so pleased though. 'You'd better be fuckin' worth it, son,' he muttered after I'd signed.

I smiled. '*Caveat emptor*,' I replied.

'Aye and that's another thing,' he retorted. 'There'll be no fuckin' Spanish in the dressing room.'

Draper, as he was to do many times in the future, called an immediate press conference. It was my first, and as it turned out, my last . . . on that side of the table. He and McCuish made all of the running. I was asked if I was pleased to be joining such a progressive club. My reply, 'Actually, I'm sorry to be leaving one,' wasn't premeditated, but it ensured that I kept a few friends among the Hearts support. Only one of my teammates was at the ground when I left, Big Mental, in for treatment on his finger. 'Lucky bastard,' he grinned as we shook hands . . . carefully. 'Me, not you,' he added. 'You'll get no quarter when we play fuckin' Merrytown, mind.'

Grace had a day off work, so I rushed home to tell her, before she heard the news on local radio. When I arrived she had just opened the morning mail. Her eyes were gleaming, with pride and satisfaction. A cardboard-backed envelope lay on the work surface and I recognised a Spanish stamp. Before I could open my mouth, she handed me a photograph. It was a full-colour, ten by eight shot of Carmen's finished portrait, framed and hanging in the Barcelona gallery; utterly naked, utterly provocative and utterly Grace. Utterly, the sexiest thing I'd ever seen. 'Wow!' I whispered.

'And there's this,' she added, taking something else from the envelope. It was a press cutting, taken from the weekend colour section of *La Vanguardia*, the Barcelona daily, and it was headed, 'The Mystery Woman'. The gallery had done some PR; there was the portrait again, front and centre, alongside an interview with the artist. 'I could be famous,' Grace murmured. 'Carmen's letter says that she's had dozens of people asking her who the model is, including a couple of movie directors, but she's not letting on.'

'And she'd better not,' I growled.

She smiled. 'I don't know,' she countered. 'I could put my modelling fees up if she did. Glasgow Art School have offered me work.'

After her news, mine seemed like flat beer; she probably had more press coverage in Spain than I did in Scotland. She was pleased for me, though. 'You'll be valued in Merrytown, more than you were at

Tynecastle. And you'll be in the first team every week.'

'I expect to be,' I conceded, 'for that sort of money. My first game's tomorrow, at home to Queen's Park.'

By the time they came in that evening, Scott and Bobby had caught up with my transfer in the late edition of the *Evening News*. They were more elated than I was. I should have been consumed by it, excited and nervous over my Oak Street debut, but I could think of nothing but that portrait. The image was burned into my mind, even though the photograph and cutting were back in the envelope and buried at the foot of my shirt drawer. Every time I closed my eyes, I saw it. Even now, I still do; sometimes I don't even have to close them.

I was so engrossed that I forgot to send Angel a 'Francisco Gracia' piece about my own transfer. Naturally, I'd sent him copy on my first team debut. I was wakened up to the omission when he called me, after a news agency telex landed on his desk. 'I'm sorry,' I told him. 'I've had a busy day, but I'll do something for you now.'

'That's all right,' he replied. 'We'll go with the agency story tonight. It says you're playing tomorrow, yes?'

'Yes.'

'In that case, send me a report on that game. Do it Sunday, we'll use it Monday.'

Apart from me (even Grandma was quietly pleased when I called to tell her), the only person who wasn't pumped up about my transfer was Rod Starshine. 'Why are you going to that mob?' he asked me, when he called that evening. Rod was old school; fucking Merrytown was his second least favourite club, after Hibs, the implacable city rivals.

'A car, seven grand in my hand and three times the wages,' I replied.

'That's short-term thinking, Xavi. Fucking Merrytown's a step down for a boy like you. I don't know what this new chairman's thinking about. We should be holding on to our best players, not selling them.'

That was a view that many of the supporters shared, according to next day's sports pages; forty-eight hours later, those same people thought that Alexander Draper was a genius.

Let's face it; I was only a team man as a journalist, never as a footballer. I didn't grow up as a Hearts supporter. I only joined the Boys' Club because Rod suggested it, and I'm pretty damn certain that when he did he wasn't thinking only about the good of the club. I wasn't wearing a violet and grey scarf either when I walked into Oak Street that Saturday, to be introduced to my new colleagues by a tense, unsmiling Lex McCuish. Some legend he turned out to be; he didn't even have the brains to insist that I have a medical before he put pen to paper on a seventy grand contract. No, he went down in history as the man who orchestrated the shortest playing career in the three centuries of fucking Merrytown Football Club.

I didn't even have a chance to memorise the names of the guys in front of me, that's how long it lasted. The jersey was tight, the shorts were too small, and the team socks only just stretched over my feet. It was as well I'd brought my own boots. Not that they ever picked up any of the notorious Oak Street mud.

There were four minutes on the clock, and we were a goal up, when Queens Park, looking like fat zebras in their black and white hoops, crossed the halfway line for the first time. Not that they did anything offensive. Their right-side midfielder didn't even look up before whacking a long cross in the general direction of my back post, but clearly off target. I could have let it go out, but I wanted to show my stuff to my new fans, so I moved out to catch it. I pushed myself off on my right foot, and as I did, I heard a loud 'Crack!' from inside my right knee and felt something snap. I didn't make it off the ground; instead I went down in a heap, in screaming pain, as the ball floated harmlessly past.

Our trainer . . . he wasn't close to being a physio . . . ran on, and crouched beside me. 'What's up, son?' he asked. The question did not fill me with confidence in him.

'My knee's fucked.' That was the best diagnosis I could give him. He waved for the ambulance volunteers. I was too big for them to lift comfortably, and their stretcher was too small for me, but they heaved me on to it as best they could. Nobody attempted to treat me, or immobilise the joint; they simply carted me off as if they were dragging a slain bull from the ring. Grace was in the stand with Scott and Bobby. As I disappeared into the darkness of the tunnel, and the stand, I heard her scream my name.

The club had a doctor on duty. He was a local GP, with no training in sports injuries; he squeezed my knee until I yelled loud enough to be heard by the crowd outside, and until I seized his hand, crushing it as I tore it off me. 'Ambulance,' he said.

Grace came with me; the boys wanted to join her, but I wouldn't allow it. 'Go tell the Spartans,' I ordered them. The doctor had given me a strong pain-killing injection and I was well woozy from it.

'Eh?' said Bobby.

'I think he means to let my father know,' Grace translated.

I'd expected to be taken to Glasgow, to one of the big infirmaries there, with all the best facilities on hand. Instead, the ambulance drove to something called Cameron Hill Hospital, out in the country. I thought it was an army camp, and in a way it had been. It had been opened forty years before as a temporary measure, and had survived to well beyond its planned lifetime. They left Grace outside in a waiting area while they took me into X-ray. Once that was done I was wheeled into a curtained cubicle, where I lay for half an hour, until a man appeared, in a green coat, with a stethoscope hung round his neck like a badge of rank. He told me that his name was Mr Clapper and that he was an orthopaedic surgeon.

'You've ruptured the cruciate ligaments,' he announced. 'Both of them, anterior and posterior. Very unusual. I would say that you had an existing weakness in the posterior ligament, a tiny fault initially, but worsening every time you jumped for a ball. Today it tore all the way through, and when that went, it took the other one with it. Your size contributed to it, undoubtedly.'

The drug had worn off; I understood what he was saying better than he did. That bastard Mulligan had done me after all. That little kick behind the knee; the small, niggling, undiagnosed injury that had eased during my suspension.

'I'm going to operate,' the surgeon went on, 'right now. You have to sign this consent form.'

The calls we make. The choices we take that we'd give half a lifetime to reverse, but never can. I could have called for a second opinion; no, undoubtedly I should have done so. But I was nineteen, I was in pain, I was on my own, I had no experience of doctors and I assumed that Mr Clapper was a top man who knew exactly what he was doing. So I signed, and asked him to let Grace in to see me.

He didn't though. The next person I saw was a nurse who shot me full of pre-med, sending me back to the land of the deeply confused. In fact, I didn't see Grace until I swam slowly back up to the surface in a hospital bed, thinking that she was a mermaid until I broke through and realised that yes, it was her, white-faced, with her dad by her side.

'Where the fuck am I?' I croaked, realising that my leg was encased in plaster and lying outside the covers.

'In hospital,' Rod told me. 'You've just had reconstructive surgery on your right knee.'

'Why?'

'You injured it, playing for fucking Merrytown.'

'Me?' I shouted. 'Playing for fucking Merrytown?'

It all came back to me, though, over the next few hours, through a sleepless night, for I refused to let them knock me out again. Out of it all, one single memory was the most vivid, even though it hadn't registered properly at the time: the smile on the face of the goalkeeper I'd displaced, as he'd looked down at me, being carried past the dug-out on my stretcher.

I had several visitors next morning. The first, at nine forty-five, was my surgeon, Mr Clapper. He didn't look pleased to be at work on a Sunday, and he didn't pull any punches. By the time he was finished I wouldn't have been pulling any either, if I'd been mobile. Mulligan had been pure reflex; for the first time in my life, I found that I actually wanted to hit someone. It wasn't what he told me, it was his total indifference that shocked me.

'How's the knee feeling?' he began sternly.

'Sore.' Prescription strength codeine wasn't doing the job.

'That's an occupational hazard for you guys,' he retorted. 'If you can't take the pain, you shouldn't take the pay. That's what I always say to footballers when they moan to me after surgery.'

'I'll remember that next time. No moaning allowed.'

He shrugged. 'There probably won't be a next time.'

I sighed with relief. 'So I'll be as good as new?'

'You misunderstand me,' said Clapper, coldly. He'd flunked the bedside manner course. 'I've patched you up, repaired both ligaments as best I could, but you're going to have to spend at least three months in plaster, or in a leg brace, to keep the joint immobilised; after that you can start physio, and see how that goes.'

I sighed again, but with disappointment. 'Are you saying that's me finished for the season?'

'I'm not saying anything definitive, boy. I'm certainly not going to give you a positive prognosis. I don't want you or your football club coming back in six months and trying to sue me. I'll give you the worst case scenario if you like. Your knee may never be up to professional sport again. Think along those lines, and anything better will be a bonus.'

I could feel my expression darken; Mr Clapper could see it. 'Don't glare at me, okay!' he snapped. 'I spend too much of my career patching up kids like you who think that what they do is actually important. I've done my best for you and that's it. Now get on with your life. You can leave here on Monday.'

I can look back at it now and make allowances for the man, if I try really hard. If he'd ever drawn up a career plan, it wouldn't have included a stopover in a shabby, under-equipped hospital in the back of beyond. He was stuck in the surgical equivalent of East Stirlingshire, when he'd probably wanted desperately to play for Celtic, or Rangers, or even fucking Merrytown. But even at the Shire, the players have ambition. I suspect that Mr Clapper had lost all of his. Lying in that bed, though, I didn't think or care about any of that. The blood seemed to boil in my veins.

I held up my right hand. 'Is that still working?' I asked him.

'Yes. Why, are you thinking about playing wheelchair basketball?'

'No,' I growled. 'I'm thinking about wrapping it around your head and squeezing it like a pineapple. See how you feel about patching yourself up.'

He opened his mouth for a second, then snapped it shut, turned and walked away. I never saw him again.

A pretty nurse came to my bedside, after the rubber doors of the ward had slammed together behind him. She was dark-haired, wore an upside-down watch on her tunic, and a badge that said her name was Student Nurse Craig. 'What did you say to him?' she asked, smiling.

I put on my Spanish accent and replied, 'I made him an offer he could'n' refuse.'

She giggled. 'Good for you. He's a bully, that man. We hate him. He's awful to the patients, especially the young ones. Are you ready for some breakfast now?'

I'd been feeling nauseous earlier . . . from the anaesthetic, another nurse had told me . . . but since then I'd seen what the other patients had been offered, and so I declined.

'The tea's okay,' she suggested. 'My name's Sheila, by the way.'

'If you recommend it, I'll give it a go.'

It came in a white mug that looked as if it had seen wartime service, but it was okay. 'That didn't come out of an urn, did it?' I ventured.

'No,' Sheila admitted. 'I made that one myself.'

'Is any of the food edible?'

'Not much. The mince is poisonous; don't go near that.' She looked at the clipboard on the end of the bed. 'How do you pronounce your name, by the way? And what does "X" stand for?' I told her. 'Nice names,' she said. 'They say you're a footballer.'

'That nice Mr Clapper has his doubts about that. I'm not worried, though; I have other career plans.' And then I thought of Angel Esposito, sitting in Girona, waiting for Francisco Gracia's copy. 'Sheila,' I asked her, 'is there a phone in here? One that the patients can use?'

'There's one on a trolley, that plugs into the wall, but it's coin in the slot.'

'That doesn't matter. I'll transfer the charges.'

She patted me on the arm. 'I'll see if I can get it.' She bustled off, returning a couple of minutes later wheeling the unit. She connected it to a jack, then rolled it to my bedside. I dialled the operator, asked for international, and gave her the number. It took a few minutes; I thought I'd been lost in translation, but eventually, Angel came on line. 'I know where you are, Xavi,' he said, before I could get a word out. 'Your father told me last night, and we had some agency copy too. Tough luck. How are you doing?'

'My knee's pretty much wrecked,' I replied. 'It's a long-term injury. I can't do you that piece just now, but I will when I get out of here.'

'Whenever you can.'

'But one thing. It'll be a Xavi Aislado by-line: I'll be writing first person about my own experiences, so it can be no other way. And that's how it will be from now on. No more Francisco Gracia. I don't care what the readers think about me being the owner's son, and everything. I'm not hiding away from my name any longer: believe it or not I'm proud of it. You can tell Pilar and Simon that as well.'

Angel laughed. 'With pleasure, kid, with pleasure. But you can tell your father yourself.'

I hung up, and Sheila came across to unplug the phone and take it away. 'Was that Spanish you were speaking?' she asked.

'Catalan,' I replied. 'It's a language in its own right.'

'A bit like Scottish?'

'Same idea.'

I'd have enjoyed talking to her for longer; her happy nature was lifting my spirits. But she had the rest of the ward to look after, and before long I had my next callers of the morning. I recognised Lex McCuish, but the guy with him, grim-faced, fifty-ish, with his hair slicked back, was new to me. I wondered how they'd got in, since the visiting hour wasn't until the afternoon. They hadn't charmed their way past the ward sister, that was for sure.

'We need to talk to you, son,' the manager began.

'I'm fine, thanks,' I replied. 'Nice flowers you've brought too.' For some unfathomed reason I thought of Big Mental, and lapsed into football-speak. 'Who's this cunt?' I asked, nodding towards the other man.

McCuish's face took on a look of outrage. 'This is the chairman, Mr Soutar. He's as upset as I am about this.'

I'd taken a dislike to the manager at our first meeting, but his attitude shocked me. I tapped the plaster on my leg. 'Upset? Do you reckon you're one-tenth as upset as me?'

'What happened is too bad,' said Soutar in a clipped, worked-on, accent. 'But we've been speaking with your surgeon and he tells us you had a pre-existing condition when you signed that contract. You didn't disclose it, young man. Now why would that have been?'

I stared at him, this guy I'd never met, who was accusing me of fraud. And then I had the strangest feeling. I imagined that Grandma Paloma was standing on the other side of the bed, beside me, and that her voice had become mine.

'The first thing I'm going to tell you,' I began, 'is that I'm going to ask my surgeon to confirm that he's been discussing my case and condition without my permission. When he admits that, I'm going to have his professional balls off. Second, I had no idea that I had any sort of weakness. When I played my last game for Hearts, against Killie last Wednesday, there was no sign of it then. There couldn't have been, for McCuish here was so impressed that he signed me two days later. Third, your such a hotshot manager had the opportunity to ask me to take a medical before I put my name on your contract, but he didn't. I wish he had; a full examination might have showed the fault in my ligament, and it could have been corrected before this,' I tapped the pot again, 'fucking disaster happened. Maybe I should be looking at suing him for negligence.' McCuish tried to interrupt me, but I froze him solid with a look that came from Grandma for sure. 'There's a fourth item,' I said, calmly, not wanting to disturb the ward. 'What sort of a cowboy outfit lets a badly injured nineteen-year-old go to hospital on his own, or rather accompanied only by his frightened girlfriend, to be operated on by the first arsehole with a hacksaw who happens on the scene?'

'You're not helping yourself, young man,' Soutar spluttered.

'I haven't even started helping myself, pal. When I get home, I've got a piece to write for my dad's newspaper in Spain.' At the mention of his name, the family pride that I'd displayed to Angel came flooding back. 'My dad could buy your fucking football club, incidentally. He turned down the Hearts before Mr Draper bought them. The story I give to his sports editor will run all over the north of Spain. I might even do an English-language version. Now suck on that and fuck off.'

Soutar looked stunned but McCuish's expression turned even uglier. I had spoken his language, but I had also broken one of the first principles of 1980s football. The hired help rarely met the chairman, and when they did they were always obsequious. McCuish leaned over me. 'You're not gettin' away with this,' he hissed, 'and neither's Mr Draper. For a start, the cheque's going to be stopped, for your transfer fee. You'll get ten per cent of fuck all. We'll cancel your registration tomorrow morning, and the Hearts can have you back. As for wages . . .' he sneered, 'we'll give ye four minutes' worth.'

I put my hand, the great big hand that I'd wanted to use on my surgeon, in the centre of his chest, and pushed him away from me. He was quite a large guy, and he hadn't been in the dug-out long enough to have lost all of his fitness, but still he staggered backwards. My bed was at the end of the ward, close to the wall. He hit it, hard.

Sheila was over in a flash, her blue-grey eyes on fire. 'What are you people doing?' she demanded. 'Upsetting one of my patients! You leave

Mr Aislado alone and get out of here now, or I'll call the porters.'

They left, with McCuish jabbing a finger in my direction. 'You can forget your fuckin' car as well,' he said.

As it turned out, the car was all they got away with. They did try to stop the cheque, but the combined might of Hearts' lawyers and Willie Lascelles put paid to that very quickly. They did try to cancel my registration, but the Scottish Football Association pointed out that I had already played for them, so I was theirs. I received my signing-on fee, and more besides, although I never set foot in Oak Street again.

I didn't spend another night in that hospital either. Sheila tried to talk me out of it, but I signed myself out. Clapper's registrar saw to the formalities. I suspect that he didn't like his boss any more than I did, for he gave me my case notes, even though I hadn't shown the presence of mind to ask for them. 'You'll need these,' he told me. 'If I were you I'd go to the Princess Margaret Rose Hospital in Edinburgh, and ask to see a Mr Jacobs. Top man; too bad this didn't happen at Tynecastle, for that's where you'd have been taken.'

When Rod arrived with Grace that afternoon, they found me dressed for the road, although the right leg of the jeans I'd worn the day before had been cut open from thigh to ankle. The hospital gave me crutches, on indefinite loan, and I hobbled out to the car, which, thank God, had a wide back seat. After I'd eased myself in, my nurse gave me a parting gift, and a kiss on the cheek, through the window that I'd wound down to receive it. That drew a frown from Grace, but she said nothing. 'These are the painkillers that were prescribed for you,' Sheila told me, handing me a small bottle. 'They're called DF 118. Your own doctor will give you a line for more when you need them.'

I needed one by the time I'd made it back to the flat, just after six that evening; Rod had driven very carefully, and very slowly, taking the A71 to Edinburgh, rather than joining the high-speed M8. I hadn't been troubled before by the lack of a lift in our block, but climbing the stairs to the fourth floor on one leg and crutches was nothing approaching a joke. The boys were there to help me, but there wasn't much that they could do, not even if Rod had joined in. Not counting the plaster or anything else, I weighed a hundred and eight kilos at that time.

It took a while, but by the time I'd made it and lowered myself on to the sofa, I was actually on something of a high. I popped one of Sheila's pills, and looked around the room. The first thing that caught my eye was a large bouquet, in a vase, on the table by the window. It hadn't been there when I'd left. 'What's that?' I asked Grace, but it was as new to her as it was to me.

'Your old chairman dropped it off,' Scott volunteered. 'Alexander Draper. He called in about an hour ago, asking after you. The flowers are for Grace. Yours was a bottle of champagne; we drank that.'

I raised an eyebrow. 'You better not have.'

'What are you going to do?' Bobby chuckled. 'Chase us round the room?' Since he'd moved in, the two guys had seemed to bond better than they ever did at school. 'Relax,' he said. 'It's in the fridge. Nice of him, though.'

'Nice?' I laughed. 'That man has just made sixty-three grand out of me, saved himself a few months' worth of useless wages, and made a couple of guys in fucking Merrytown very unhappy.' During the drive home, I had said nothing to Rod or Grace about my morning in the hospital. I kept it that way; it would only have upset them.

'How long will you be in that thing?' Scott asked.

'I don't know,' I replied. 'The surgeon said three months, but I'll need to see someone else now I'm through here. I've been given a name, but I don't know how to contact him.'

'You may leave that to me,' said a familiar voice. It came from behind me. I twisted round and there was Grandma Paloma, standing in the kitchen door.

I almost cried, right there in front of my two flatmates, who wouldn't have let me forget it, but I managed to keep it in check. I stared at her, my eyes following her as she came round to stand in front of me. She reached out and patted the top of my head, an unprecedented gesture for her. 'You look fine,' she said to me in Catalan. 'Have I come all this way for nothing?' She was back in her Edinburgh mode of dress, entirely black, with her silver hair tied in a bun.

'No,' I told her in the same language, told her exactly what I was feeling at that moment, even as it came to me. 'You have no idea how relieved I am to see you. It's as if a weight's been lifted off me.'

'You're still young,' she said. 'Both you and Grace. You can't be expected to deal with everything yourselves. Josep-Maria would have come with me, but I forbade it. He'd only have got in the way, and after a couple of days he'd have been fretting about his newspapers and his radio stations. So I said no.'

It didn't occur to me, then or for a couple of days, to wonder how she had got there so quickly. When I got round to asking, she simply shrugged her shoulders and said, 'I flew.'

'Broomstick?' I asked, and she laughed . . . still a rare event. I didn't find out until some time later that my dad had chartered a Learjet for her, from Girona to Edinburgh, and had her picked up by limo.

She'd been cooking, of course, while she waited for us to arrive. She'd sent the boys to the local Safeway with a shopping list and had put together, casually, escalivada, chicken with langoustines, and a few potatoes, then cream cheese with honey, all of it Catalan food that Scott and Bobby had never experienced.

When we were finished eating I said to Grace that she should move our stuff into the spare room. That was the proviso my dad had laid down for himself when he'd bought the place. But Grandma wouldn't hear of it.

'I would find it a little crowded,' she said. 'And it would deny Grace the privacy that a woman needs.' She threw her a quick, expressive look. 'Even a woman who is a talking point all over Catalunya. I have taken a suite in the Caledonian Hotel,' she announced. 'I have always wanted to stay there.'

Before she left, she asked me about the name I had been given, that of the surgeon at the Princess Margaret Rose Hospital. By the time she arrived at the flat next morning, she had everything in hand. I had an appointment with Mr Jacobs that afternoon, not at the PMR, but in his private consulting room at the Murrayfield Hospital. 'Grandma,' I protested, 'my signing-on fee from Merrytown wasn't that much. I can't afford this.'

'You couldn't afford George Watson's College either,' she retorted, 'not personally, but you went there. Do you have any idea how long you would have had to wait for an appointment with this man through the health service?' I hadn't, so I let it go.

By that time, I'd had a call from Dave Nelson, a guy I knew on the *Evening News*, the only sportswriter I trusted with my number. He was tipping me off that Lex McCuish and his chairman were out to make trouble, and asking for a quote from me at the same time. I didn't hold back. I told him that I had no idea that I was carrying any injury, that they'd signed me without a medical, and filled him in on my morning visit in the hospital, including the threats that McCuish had made. As soon as we were finished, I called Willie Lascelles to turn him loose on them, but by that time he had gone into action, unbidden.

I had a few more calls during the morning, from journalists with access to unlisted numbers . . . a well-placed bung will get you many things . . . but they wasted both their time and their money, for Grandma fielded them all, dismissing them in tones that ranged from derisive to ferocious. As it happened I was busy, writing my feature for Angel, describing my surprise transfer, and my brief debut. But it was more than that; it became an angry denunciation on the continuing exploitation of young men by an unfair and oppressive system, and by people whose interest in them was based on pure greed, for success and for gold, and looking forward to the day when all of them had the kind of professional representation that I'd been fortunate enough to enjoy. It was a damn good piece, powerful, unlike anything a footballer had ever written before, not because others lacked articulacy, but because they had lived with a fear of the consequences that I did not have. I put a heading on it, one that would be understood in Catalunya. For longer than anyone can remember, supporters of Barcelona have been proud to call themselves '*Els culés*'; in English, roughly, 'The arses'. Only they really know why. My story was titled, 'In Scotland the arses are in charge'. Grandma listened as I dictated it to the copy-taker. When I was finished, she nodded; I took that as approval.

The only call that she let me take that day was from Tommy Partridge. She knew who he was, but she said nothing, simply handing the receiver to me and withdrawing to the kitchen on the pretext of making lunch. 'Was that who I think it was?' he asked.

'Absolutely.'

'I never thought I'd speak to her,' he murmured. 'How's the knee?' he continued.

'It's either the right side of fucked, or it's the other,' I told him, graphically.

'Not so good, son. You know what the papers are saying, don't you?'

'Yes. Is it true? No. Do I care? No.'

'That's the spirit. Anything I can do to help?'

'Nothing, Tommy, but thanks for asking.'

'Okay,' he said. 'I'll keep in touch.' I was on the point of hanging up, but he continued 'Oh, by the way, I haven't forgotten about your friend.'

With everything that had happened I had. 'Eh?'

'The girl that was attacked, the Chinese girl. I've been keeping an eye on the investigation, and not just because she's a friend of yours. Guys like that don't usually stop at one, and they're not usually scared off for good. They learn from their mistakes. If we don't catch him, the next poor kid won't be as lucky as she was.'

'So you haven't?'

'Caught him? No, not yet. CID have been doing their best. They've been stopping and interviewing regular users of that path, asking if they've seen anyone behaving oddly. The only thing they've turned up so far is some bastard drowning a litter of kittens. We're not going to give up, though, and I'll be able to push it a bit harder myself soon.'

'How's that?' I asked.

'I'm going back to CID; detective inspector, still working out of Torphichen.'

'Congratulations.'

'Thanks,' he murmured, sounding perhaps slightly under the moon.

'Isn't that good?'

'It's a career move, for sure, but it's back to the dirty end of policing. There's something to be said for striding round Tynecastle in a uniform, keeping the crowd in order. It gets a bit exciting there from time to time, at the derby games and when the Glasgow teams come through, but most of the time it's like an office job and you never get your hands dirty. There are times in CID when you go home to your family and you feel like you're polluting them with some of the things you've seen.'

'In Edinburgh?' I exclaimed.

'Christ, son, you've had a sheltered upbringing right enough. There's an underbelly in this city. You ask your dad if you don't believe me.'

'You're not saying he was part of it, are you?'

'Of course not, but you don't operate in the business he was in, at his level, without knowing about it. It's always been there, preying on the weak, but your class knows nothing about it.'

'Don't quote class to me, Tommy,' I protested. 'I don't believe in that stuff.'

'Maybe you don't, kid, but it's real. Half of Edinburgh envies the other half; the other half neither knows nor cares. Your class lives in blissful ignorance of the drug dealers and the loan sharks and the pimps and . . . It does because there's a rule, an unseen, unspoken rule that says to the lowlife that if they ever cross the line that divides the comfortably off from the rest, then my lot will visit the wrath of God upon them. So they leave you alone, other than selling cannabis to silly students, and cocaine to flash young professionals who think it's the thing to do.'

'So why don't you visit the wrath of God regardless?' I countered. 'You're underpinning the class system if you don't.'

He laughed; I could sense the resignation in it. 'Last time I was in

CID, I was a DS out in the west of the city. One night we got a call to one of those places that are no-go areas for the likes of you. There was this guy, working man, a fitter in a car service place. He'd got behind in his payments to a loan shark, so you know what they did to him? There was a fence in front of the building he lived in and they nailed his fucking foot to it, in front of his wife and kids, with neighbours watching and everything. Just the one foot, mind, so he could limp to work, and they never touched his hands. It was just a wee warning, to him and to the whole community.'

'What happened?'

'Do you need me to tell you? Nobody saw a fucking thing, nobody would name, or even describe, the guys who did it, not even the victim's wife, even though every one of them knew who they were, even though we bloody knew who they were! That's how it was, Xavi, and that's how it still is.'

'Can't these people help themselves?'

'Every so often someone tries, and we have to clean up the mess.' He paused. 'You say you want to become a journalist, son. If you ever do, I hope you have the balls to write about this sort of stuff, because nobody else seems to want to. The guy I told you about merited a two-inch story in the *Evening News*. A footballer does his knee, and he gets half a page.'

'I am a journalist,' I told him. 'I've been writing for my dad's papers for the last few weeks.'

'I bet they wouldn't print the story I just told you.'

I had been imagining the opposite. 'You're on,' I declared. 'I show you the cutting, you double my money.'

'Deal. I win, you pay me what you didn't get.'

'Fine. How are your girls?' I don't know what made me ask that; I'd always avoided the subject before.

'They're fine, thanks; turned five now. Do you want to meet them?' I sensed caution.

'Thanks, but no thanks, Tommy.'

'Yeah,' he murmured. 'Probably just as well, the way things are. It would just confuse the wee souls.'

As soon as we had said 'so long', Grandma appeared with lunch, mine on a tray, hers on a plate on her lap. I don't know where she found a decent baguette in Edinburgh in 1981, but she did; she'd stuffed it with tomato and mozzarella, and soaked a little olive oil and balsamic into the bread rather than buttering it. Hers was a salad, same ingredients: she said that her teeth were too old for crusty bread. That wasn't true; I suspected that there had been only one baguette left and she'd given the lot to me.

I spent the afternoon on my second story of the day. I was still full of anger, so it was easy for me to put real passion into a tale of the dark heart of a picture postcard city, and to extrapolate the situation into surroundings that would be familiar to Catalans, including a quarter of Barcelona of which I had heard, but never visited. I called it 'An alternative tourist guide'. When I was finished I called Pilar, sold her the concept and dictated it.

When that was done, it was time to leave for the Murrayfield Hospital. I hadn't been looking forward to going downstairs on crutches . . . with even less margin for error than going up, and without the boys, who were both at work, Bobby having been taken on at Starshine Pharmaceuticals as well, as catchers . . . but Mr Jacobs had sent a private ambulance to collect me, with two chunky paramedics who looked as if they'd been hand-picked for the task. They sat me in a chair and carried me down, no problem, then secured me in their vehicle.

Mr Jacobs looked as if he could have done the same job on his own. He was a great bear of a man in his mid-forties, an inch or two over six feet tall, with paws that, while not as big as mine, looked just as powerful. His greeting was as hearty as he looked. He shook Grandma's hand, formally and delicately, then mine, a little more firmly, almost as if he was testing my grip, and got straight down to business. His time was money. He settled me down on a long leather-topped bench, raised at one end, and began to read the case notes I'd handed him. When he was finished, he put my X-ray on a light box and examined it, carefully. 'It's a rare one, right enough. Both ligaments do appear to have been ruptured.'

'Appear to be?' I interjected.

'That's as far as I can go from this image. I have to tell you, Mr Aislado, that we don't see too many injuries like this in young men, not in footballers at any rate, or other field sportsmen. Are you in much pain?' he asked.

'I've been taking the medication that they gave me,' I replied, 'but it's still pretty uncomfortable.'

'I'm not surprised. The first thing I'm going to do with you is take that plaster off. That alone will relieve the discomfort. It should never have been put on in the first place, not post-operative like that. You should have been put in a brace; it would have done the same job, immobilisation, while allowing for swelling. However, in my opinion the surgeon at the other hospital shouldn't have operated in the first place. Did he discuss options with you when you were admitted?'

I looked up at him. 'Does "sign here" qualify as a discussion?'

'I see.' He frowned. 'Bloody disgraceful,' he muttered.

'What should this man have done?' Grandma asked.

'Nothing at all, until the swelling had gone, and he . . . or preferably someone else . . . could examine the injury properly. X-ray's the crudest of tools. I need to find out what he's done in there, the sooner the better.'

I frowned. 'How will you do that? Another X-ray?'

'No. I'll subject your knee to a CT scan. Fortunately, we have the equipment here to do that. Much better than a simple X-ray; it builds an image that'll let me see your knee as it is now and get a better feel for the original damage.' He handed me my crutches. 'Let's get on with it.'

Grandma Paloma would have come with us to the scanning room, but Mr Jacobs persuaded her to wait in the visitor's lounge instead. It was as well, for the sight of my knee when a technician took the plaster off would have upset even her. It was a hell of a mess, even after he'd cleaned it up, as gently as he could. It was puffed up like the ball I'd failed to catch, and several shades of purple, with long stitched wounds front and back, but it felt much easier with the constraint of the horrible pot removed. 'There's a new technique called magnetic resonance,' Mr Jacobs told me as I was helped on to the flat couch that would take me through the imaging tunnel, 'but it's not widely available yet. This should be good enough, though.'

I sat as patiently as I could as the machine did its work. I had left a note for Grace, telling her where we were, but I knew she'd be worried and I wanted to get in touch with her as soon as I could. There was more to be done, though, after the image had been taken. As Mr Jacobs waited for it to be processed, another specialist fitted me with a removable brace which, as he had said, did the same job as the plaster, with an added benefit, in that I didn't want to tear it off with my bare hands.

When he was satisfied with his work, Grandma and I were shown back into the consulting room, where my career as a footballer was effectively put to bed. I could tell as soon as Mr Jacobs came in that he wasn't going to make my day. He was almost spitting with anger and couldn't hide it. 'I'm told that I'm one of the top surgeons in my field,' he said, 'but not in a million years would I have risked operating on your injury at that time and in that condition. There are various techniques that could have been used here. I believe that there's a young man in America who's building a reputation for using grafts in this type of situation, but it's high risk. You should have been referred at once to a specialist, which this man Clapper clearly is not. Having seen the CT scan, it's my opinion that the anterior ligament was not completely ruptured, and that it might have been possible to treat you without resort to such rudimentary but radical surgery. It would have taken a long time, and a positive result could not have been guaranteed, but it would have been worth a try. What this man, this . . .' the surgeon's nostrils flared, 'he's simply stitched both ligaments together, and botched it.'

'What does that mean?' I asked him, as quietly as I could.

'It means that he has rejoined the anterior ligament, but that he's shortened the posterior. Did you notice, when we took the plaster off, that your knee was slightly bent?'

'Yes, I did.'

'You'll never be able to straighten it fully again. You'll walk more or less normally, and you'll probably be able to jog, but for a young man in your profession, and particularly in your position, a goalkeeper, it will still be an insuperable handicap. You won't have any spring in the joint, and turning rapidly will be impossible.'

'Is there nothing to be done?' Grandma asked. 'Could you not operate and repair this?'

Mr Jacobs shook his head. 'No. It may be that at some time in the future a graft might be possible, but in all honesty, I wouldn't recommend it.' He looked at me. 'Your grandmother tells me you're a university student,' he said. 'Do you have a career in mind other than football?'

I told him what it was.

'Then I would advise you to focus on that from now on. It's normal practice these days for professional football teams to insure their players. I suggest that you take that up with your employer. I'll certify that what I've just told you is the case.'

There was nothing more that he could say. He made a series of appointments for me to come back to see him so that he could monitor my recovery, and he wrote me a prescription for more DF 118, then he wished us a sincerely sad 'Good evening'.

The same two guys took me back upstairs. Grandma didn't come with me. She told me that her fury was best not shared, and went back to the hotel.

I wish I could say that I was as angry as she was, but part of me was relieved. I had never been in love with football, not in the way that I was with journalism. It had been a means of paying my own way through university, or asserting my independence from my dad, and as such it had served its purpose. As I told Grace when we were alone, I could live without it. I had her, and I had my real career to look forward to. Against that, not being able to dive to my right wasn't such a big deal.

'Football wasn't the love of your life, then,' she whispered, in the dark.

'No, *chica*,' I replied. 'You are, unchallenged.'

'What can you tell me about the lad?'

'He's just turned twenty, and he wants to break into journalism.'

'And you've sent him to me? Barry, are you losing your grip on reality? To equate a job on the Saltire with breaking into journalism is like saying that a lump of coal's an acceptable substitute for a diamond. Do you know what they think of this paper in Scotland? The best they call us is a poor relation of the Scotsman and the Glasgow Herald, but that's generous. We're a pauper, man, compared to them. We sell fifty-four thousand a day on average: half the Scotsman's circulation, and much less than half of the Herald's.'

'If it's that bad, John, why did you leave the Telegraph to take the chief reporter job? You were number two on the House of Commons team; the next political editor for sure, before you were thirty-five.'

'You know damn well why I left. Sheena hates London; she couldn't bear the thought of sending wee Danny to school there. This job was going so I took it. But believe me, the first chance I get to move up to North Bridge, or even through to Glasgow, I'll be taking it. I'll say the same to your boy protégé as well if he comes to see me.'

'I'll bet you don't.'

'I wouldn't take your money.'

'What's the problem with your paper, John?'

'Which one will I begin with? Alongside the other two, we're an upstart. They're two hundred years old, we're thirty-four years old. The Saltire was founded by Charles McCandlish, a millionaire supporter of the Scottish Nationalists, who wanted to make it the standard bearer of the independence movement. That hasn't quite worked out, has it? The SNP got its arse kicked at the last election, Thatcher has the country by the throat and the dream is dead. The founder's dead as well; his family trust own the paper now and it's an open secret that it's for sale. There was some thought that the Glasgow Herald might buy us to get a foothold in Edinburgh and annoy the Scotsman, but that's not going to happen, because they can see what I'm telling you, that there's nothing here to buy. The position's getting worse too. The other two are planning *to introduce new technology, and we don't have the resources to keep pace with them. That's the marketplace problem. The other one's practical. The whole place is depressed; most of the staff are poorly paid, and with no other motivation. Barry, I'd sack half the reporters, but the editor crapped himself when I suggested it. He's terrified of any possibility of a strike.'*

'Who is your editor?'

'His name's Torcuil Bannerman. He was a Nationalist MP until he lost his seat in nineteen seventy-nine. McCandlish, the founder, took him on, then promptly died. The family trust has no interest in replacing him; the view is that he's a useful figurehead who'll help the sale of the paper. He's got no journalistic background; he was a surveyor, believe it or not, before he got into parliament.'

'Do you have any strengths . . . apart from you?'

'Our lead sports writer's good. He operates across the board; does football, but his best contacts are in golf, and that's a positive in this part of the world. That's where our sales are. We haven't broken a big story in the news pages since . . . since I've been here, to tell you the truth.'

'How does Sheena feel about London now? They'd take you back here in a flash.'

'That's not going to change. I'll see how it goes here; I've got a notion to try broadcast journalism if nothing opens up on a decent paper.'

'Have I called the right number? I can't believe I'm listening to John Fisher.'

'Well you are. The truth is, I'm as demotivated as anyone in this place. The editor's a tube, the proprietors don't give a monkey's, and if I didn't have a family to feed I'd probably take my coat off its peg right now and walk out the fucking door. And you're sending a bright-eyed young man to talk to me. Christ! What else can you tell me about the lad, anyway? For a start, what's his name?'

'Xavier Aislado, Xavi for short.'

'That name's familiar.'

'He was a professional footballer, until he was forced to give up the game through injury.'

'Ah yes. He's the kid that lasted four minutes at Merrytown, after Alexander Draper sold him for seventy grand on the basis of one good game. "Iceland", they called him at Tynecastle. He's a man-mountain. How did you meet him?'

'I've never met him. He called me a couple of days ago. He said he'd been given my number by a woman called Pilar Roca, the editor of a paper he writes for in Spain. His father owns it, and a few others. I knew Pilar when I was on the Telegraph foreign desk and based out there. She's a damn good journalist, and hard to please. That's why I gave the kid a hearing. I called Pilar to check him out. She says that he's a natural. He's been doing freelance stuff for her since last summer and some of it's bloody brilliant. She sent me a couple of items by facsimile transmission. One of them describes what happened to him when he was injured; it's great, full of anger.'

'That's fine, but he's Spanish, isn't he?'

'Only half. His mother is Scottish, and English is his first language. He doesn't sound quite as Jockish as you do, but it's there. He was educated in Edinburgh, and he's due to graduate from the university there in a couple of months.'

'What about his father? Why can't he help him?'

'His father's a businessman. He has no contacts outside of his own business and the kid doesn't want to work in Spain.'

'So why didn't you offer him a job?'

'If I had a suitable vacancy in Edinburgh I would. That's where he wants to be. Pilar sent him to me as a doorway to the profession, not as a potential employer, but she doesn't really understand our infrastructure. Listen, John, I'm doing you a favour here, although after what you've told me about your paper, I'm beginning to regret it.'

'Okay, Barry, I'll see the kid. As it happens one of my reporters is working his notice, so you never know.'

'You won't take advantage of him, will you, John? I wouldn't want to *fall out with Pilar. You never know, I might wind up asking her for a job myself one day. Things are going to change in our industry in the next few years.'*

'You're lucky you can look that far ahead. I wish I could see any sort of a future.'

Ten

I could have kept drawing wages from fucking Merrytown for another few months. My consultation with Mr Jacobs was private, and had nothing to do with them. I could have sat tight and let them wait to find out that my career was over. But I didn't; Soutar and McCuish might have been strangers to honour, but the concept had been instilled into me by a good teacher. She stayed in Edinburgh for a week, until she decided that there was no more she could do, and went back to Spain . . . by scheduled flight.

With Grandma gone, as soon as I received the surgeon's written report, I forwarded a copy to the chairman and asked him what arrangements his club had in place for compensating injured players. I should have known; they had none. The only thing they were insured against was their own loss. In other words, they would get my transfer fee back, while I would get nothing.

That didn't strike me as fair, and it struck Willie Lascelles as grounds for legal action. So Xavier Aislado raised an action against Merrytown Football Club Limited, alleging a failure in its duty of care to an employee, and negligence in its treatment of me at the time of my injury. It didn't get even close to court; their lawyers advised them to settle and they did, agreeing to pay me eighty per cent of my potential income for the duration of my contract, a nice deal, since the award was tax free. Willie was prepared to sue Mr Clapper at the same time, but we didn't have to. The mere sight of a copy of Mr Jacobs' report sent the Health Board that ran Cameron Hill Hospital scurrying to its insurers, who made us an offer of compensation by return of post. I didn't keep all the money, though: I donated half of my payment from Merrytown to a benevolent fund run by the players' union. I was lucky; in those days too many guys limped away from the game with less than nothing. Today, many of them become pundits for satellite television.

I had to wear my leg brace until the middle of November, when Mr Jacobs allowed me to go on to elbow crutches. Going up and down stairs was still an absolute bugger, but it did leave me massively strong in my upper body. It took six months before the surgeon decreed that he had done as much as he could for me; he took his time, secure in the knowledge that his fees had been taken over by the Health Board's insurers. When he was finished, I had a knee that he declared serviceable for non-sporting purposes, even though his prediction was correct in that I've never been able to straighten it since, and that I'll never be a ballroom dancer. One good thing did come out of that disability. Mr Jacobs advised me to buy a bike; he said that cycling would be good exercise for me. He was right. In the years that followed I came to spend more time on my mountain bike than I do in my car.

My rehabilitation didn't get in the way of my studies. I was reasonably mobile by the time the university term started, so I missed nothing. With football out of my life, I had become a full-time student, apart from the stories that I sent to Girona from time to time. My class marks had always been comfortable, but as my final year progressed they reached distinction level. For all that, I stayed determined to graduate as soon as I could. Grace tried to talk me into doing an honours year, so that she and I, and Scott and Bobby, could all finish together, but for probably the only time in her life she didn't have her way with me. We had a small argument, but I told her that I wasn't changing my mind, and that she'd have to live with it. I told her that I'd humoured her in her modelling, and she should do the same for me. She seemed to be landing a fair amount of her posing work. Barely a week passed without her being off on an assignment, from Glasgow Art School, or from a private art group. I lived with it, but one thing I did insist on: she said nothing to the boys.

That Christmas we broke the pattern of the previous two years. With Dave and Lina no longer on the scene, there was no glue to hold us together. Billie was heading south to see John, and Bobby's sister invited Scott to their parents' place. Grace and I could have cooked for ourselves, gone to a restaurant, or even tried a combined Christian-Judaic thing with Rod and Magda, but we did none of those. Instead, free of football commitments for the first time since I was sixteen, I bought us a couple of seats on a charter flight from Edinburgh to Girona Airport. I felt I owed it to Grandma. She'd been there for me, and I wanted to repay her as best I could. Grace needed a little persuasion, before she agreed. She'd been hoping for an invitation to the Hannah party, but my view was that we saw enough of Scott and Bobby through the rest of the year. In truth, since my life had become more focused, my thinking had changed. I'd have preferred Grace and me to be living on our own. Even after the donation to the PFA fund, I'd been left with a tidy chunk of money, which, carefully handled for me by Willie the lawyer, who chaired an investment trust in his spare time, produced an income that was a lot more than the boys paid in rent, so I didn't actually need them there, but I'd made a commitment and was honour bound to stick to it.

I decided to make our visit a surprise. We flew into Girona on a Sunday afternoon, five days before Christmas, and the plan was to take a taxi from the airport to the masia. We had a shock as soon as we stepped out of the plane. Despite the fact that most of our fellow passengers were skiers bound for Andorra and the other Pyrenean resorts, I hadn't appreciated how cold it would be. Grace and I only knew Spain in June and early July, when the sun is high overhead and the rain falls mainly on the mountains, well away from the plain. On that December day, the sky was grey, a steady drizzle was falling and the temperature could only have been a few degrees above freezing. It had been warmer in Edinburgh. Everyone else ran across the tarmac, apart from us; I was still using one elbow crutch. There were plenty of taxis, though. Very few flights used Girona in the winter in those days, so when one was due, the local licensed cabbies mobbed the place. For all that, it was very orderly, with all of them lined up at the rank. Our turn came fairly quickly. Our driver didn't know much outside Girona, and I had to give him directions all the way there, but he didn't waste any time, or try any detours. The fifteen-kilometre trip took twenty minutes.

The taxi pulled up in front of the house. The front door was closed and most of the windows were shuttered. I paid the cabby and he climbed out to retrieve our case from the boot. Even after he'd driven off, we were still on our own, and there were no signs of life within. The doorbell was as old-fashioned as they come, a brass handle on a bar that disappeared into a hole in the lintel. I pulled it, and heard a chime inside. We stood there in the gentle rain, waiting for the great oak door to swing open, but it didn't. Instead, there was a faint creaking noise to our right, then a voice called out, 'Hello?' in Castellano, not Catalan, and a figure stepped into view. It was Carmen, the gardener's daughter, the artist; she wore a white blouse, a dark close-fitting skirt, and black, high-heeled shoes.

'Xavi! Grace!' she called out loudly in her surprise. 'This is wonderful.' She held out a hand, beckoning. 'Come in this way.'

I left the case against the door and we followed her, round to the side entrance that only my dad ever used, the one that led into his private apartments. 'I was doing some dusting for him,' she explained. 'He's only ever home during the day on a Sunday and he doesn't like anyone in his rooms when he's not there.'

'Paranoid old bastard,' I said, cheerfully, as I stepped inside, after the girls.

'Maybe so,' his voice came from within his study, 'but you can't be too careful.' He stepped into the corridor to greet us. He wore a long-sleeved blue sweatshirt, jeans and tan moccasins. I hadn't even known that he possessed such clothing. My expression told him so. He smiled, and shrugged his shoulders. 'I like to go native at weekends in the winter.'

'Where's Grandma?' I asked him. You may not believe this, but I swear it's true; although we were in another part of the old mansion, I knew that she was nowhere within it, for the house took on a sense of her presence, and it was missing. The house itself told me that she was gone. Anxiety gripped me; I was holding Grace's hand and I squeezed it, a little too tight, because she yelped.

'She's in Barcelona,' he replied, 'in a clinic. She's being treated for breast cancer.' A surge of dread passed through me. 'But,' he added, quickly, 'she's going to be all right. The place is a world leader. They say they've caught it early and there's been no spread to the lymphatics or anywhere else. She had a wee operation on Friday. They removed a lump from her left breast, and they're certain they've got it all. She doesn't even have to have chemotherapy. They're putting her on a new drug called tamoxifen, and as long as she keeps taking that they say she'll be fine. Her age is in her favour too; she's seventy-seven, and they say that the older you are, the slower these things go.'

'I want to see her,' I declared. 'Can I take the Jeep?'

'If you wait till tomorrow, you can go and get her. They're letting her out.' He looked at Grace, for the first time. 'Hello, dear. It's nice to see you. Now tell me, what the hell are the two of you doing here?'

'Surprise, surprise?' she offered. 'We just thought it would be nice to spend Christmas with you for a change.'

'Ah, of course. It's Christmas; I should have remembered. All that stuff goes right over my head. Always has done. That Cratchit family had it far too easy if you ask me.' He looked up at me and he laughed. 'I suppose you'll be Tiny Tim, on that bloody crutch.' Even I had to smile at that one. 'Where's your luggage?' he asked.

'I left it at the front door.'

'Ah.' He went into his study, and returned with a key ring, one key selected. 'That's what you need.'

Grace took it from him. 'I'll get it,' she insisted. 'Xavi, you need to get your weight off that knee.'

'The bed won't be made up,' Carmen told her. 'I'll do that for you.'

'Not at all; just tell me where the sheets are.'

'I'll help you; I insist.' I had a feeling that she wanted to be out of there.

They left me alone with my dad. 'Come on,' he said. 'Do as Grace told you.' He led me into the study, where I collapsed into a big leather armchair. As I sat, I noticed a framed photograph on his desk. This was unusual, as I'd grown up in a house where images from the past were not displayed. Grandma Paloma kept one in her room, of her own parents, but that was all. There was no family album. Grandma told me that when they left Spain they took only essentials with them. Possibly there never had been an album. I'm not kidding when I say that the first-ever photograph of me, solo, other than a few class pictures at school, was taken for my passport, when I was fifteen years old. I reached across, picked it up and looked at it. My grandparents stared severely back at me; standing alongside them was a boy who might have been seven years old, but no more. The mount within the frame was embossed with the words, 'Edward Naughton, photographer, Edinburgh'. I looked closely at Grandpa Xavi; I'd never seen his image before. He was standing awkwardly, crouching slightly, but I could see that he'd been a tall man. Mr Naughton couldn't have been all that skilled, for his features weren't all that distinct, but I fancied that I looked more like Grandma. I stared at his face closely, looking for something, anything, in his eyes that told me he had once killed a man, but I saw nothing of the sort, only the slight insecurity of a person out of his element. Grandma, on the other hand, glared, not merely at the lens, but through it, impelling the photographer to get on with his business. I smiled as I replaced the study, taking care not to leave finger marks on the glass.

My dad pointed at my knee. 'Does that still hurt?' he asked.

'Not much. It gets tired more than anything. It's stiff from the flight, but I've got an exercise programme. My consultant was fine about me flying.' I glanced out of the window. 'Looking at the weather, I'm beginning to wish he'd vetoed it.'

He shook his head. 'Don't worry; it'll improve. You check your watch and you'll see that it's getting dark around now in Edinburgh. Tomorrow's the shortest day, but it'll still be light here until going on six. That's the great difference, much more than the weather.' There was something new in the room; a twin-control, glass-fronted, wine cooler stood in the corner. He went across to it, produced a bottle of Torres Esmeralda, uncorked it then poured some into two glasses that sat on a tray beside it. 'Welcome to Spain, again,' he said as he handed one to me. 'That's you done with football, then?' he continued.

'For good.'

'Blessing in disguise, son. Draper used you, to make a quick buck; he sold you and he bought three reasonable outfield players with the money. Good business, and you can't condemn him for it, but you're out of that now, and you won't miss it.'

'I've worked that one out for myself; I've got a bum knee but a pile of money to make up for it. That's a good deal as far as I'm concerned. Now stop trying to divert me.'

He looked at me, all innocence. 'From what?'

'You know damn well what. How long have you been banging Carmen?'

'What the hell makes you think that?' he chuckled.

'Several things. First, she's got a flourishing career as an artist, which you helped launch by sponsoring an exhibition, yet she's still here, living with her parents. Second, you don't dress the way she is to dust the fucking bookshelves. Third, even if you do, you need a duster and there isn't one in sight. Fourth, there's lipstick on this glass. And fifth, your fly's open.'

I caught him with the last one; he looked down at his jeans and fumbled for the zipper, only to find that it was in place. He raised an eyebrow and smiled as close to sheepishly as he could manage. 'Pilar's right,' he murmured. 'You are going to be a great journalist.'

'Not really. It's probably taken me a couple of years to work it out. Am I right?'

He nodded. 'Carmen and I have an arrangement. It suits us both, and nothing will come of it, so if you're worried about any half-brothers and -sisters diluting your inheritance, don't.'

'Why should I worry about that?' I retorted, for the idea had never entered my head. 'I'm going to make my own way.'

'I'm sure you are, but nevertheless . . . Carmen and I aren't heading for the altar.'

'What happened to not shagging the hired help?'

'She's not,' he snapped, suddenly flustered. 'I don't pay her. I might buy her a few things, but she earns her own money from her painting.'

'Dad, I don't care,' I told him. 'I like Carmen, and if you and she are good for each other, I'm on your side. Does Grandma know?'

His good humour returned in an instant. He smiled, broadly. 'I take it that was rhetorical. We've never discussed it, but she knows for sure, and she treats Carmen with respect. All I ask is that you do the same.'

'That goes without saying. Believe it or not, you blinkered old bugger, if it makes you happy, it makes me happy.'

We had finished the Esmeralda by the time Grace came to collect me; Carmen was with her but hanging back, in the doorway. 'Will that be all, senor?' she asked, tentatively.

'You can cut the pretence,' I told her. 'He and I have had a man-to-man chat. You're a brave and generous woman.'

After I'd changed out of my travel clothes, I went into Grandma's kitchen and took a look in the fridge. I'd assumed that we'd eat in that night, but my dad vetoed that; instead he took us, and Carmen, to a very nice, very traditional restaurant, not far from the airport at which we had arrived. It was a lifetime first; I had never imagined ever being out in a foursome with my old man.

Next day, he was as good as his word, and let me go to collect Grandma Paloma from the clinic, alone since he went to the office as usual. I was going to take Grace with me, but Carmen grabbed her to do some more modelling: clothed for a change; it was too cold for any stripping off in the cottage. I found the place without any difficulty. It was on Avinguda Diagonal, and there was a big green sign on top. She was waiting in her room when I arrived, sitting on the side of her bed, dressed in a long dark skirt, and a loose top, to keep her wound comfortable. There was a small suitcase at her feet, and she was clutching a paper bag.

I was sure that for once in my life, I would surprise her. In a sense I was looking forward to it, given her miraculous arrival in Edinburgh after my accident. Instead, she simply nodded as I ducked under the door frame: it was a new building but the architect hadn't caught up with the fact that Catalans were growing taller as a people. 'At last,' she said, 'you're here. I can't wait to get out of this place.'

'How did you . . .' I began.

'I phoned you last night, to tell you about my . . . little difficulty. One of your young friends told me that you and Grace had left for Spain.'

'You're amazing. Now,' I continued, picking up the suitcase with my free hand, 'do you need help, or can you walk out of here?'

She looked at my crutch. 'Better than you, it seems.' She eased herself off the bed.

'What's in the bag?' I asked her.

'The pills they say I must take for the rest of my life.'

'You'll be taking a hell of a lot of them, then.'

She shrugged as I stood aside to let her take the lead. 'Maybe yes, maybe no. When you get to my age, you never know.'

'Seventy-two?' I asked. Casually.

'Exactly,' she agreed. Oh yes, she was human, beneath her supernatural cloak.

Her departure was like a procession. Every nurse in the place seemed to line the spotless corridor to wish her well, as if she had been there for a month rather than a long weekend. I couldn't help contrasting her hospital experience with my own. As we reached the lift a man in a suit stepped out of the office opposite. 'Madam, my good wishes,' he said as they shook hands. 'I'll see you again in a month, as we agreed.' He looked at me and smiled. 'This is your grandson, yes? The footballer who is now a journalist.'

She nodded. 'This is he.' She patted my arm. 'But it was not our football, so it does not really count.' I realised that she had been talking about me, with some pride, it seemed.

The weather had changed overnight; the clouds and rain had moved north, the skies were blue and there was hope that the afternoon temperatures might edge into the sixties. My dad had insisted that I take the Range Rover rather than the Jeep, as it was a softer ride, and easier to drive. (The Merc had been out of the question, since the seat didn't go back far enough to allow for the limited flexibility of my knee.) Grandma smiled when she saw it; she must have read some meaning into its presence, but I didn't inquire.

She guided me out of Barcelona by another route, then north towards Girona by a road I didn't know. It was much quieter and less frantic than the one I'd taken earlier, but even so I drove very gently, not wanting to cause her any discomfort. She tolerated it for a while, but finally she told me that she didn't expect to be travelling in a hearse for quite some time, and that if I was trying to get her used to the experience it was kind, but premature.

Grace was waiting for us when we returned. She tried to make a fuss of Grandma, but the old lady wasn't having any. She marched straight into the laundry room where she dumped the suitcase, then into the kitchen to see what damage had been done in her short absence. Grace and Carmen had found time for shopping, as well as posing and painting. They had thrown together, as Grace put it, a salad of lettuce, tomatoes, capers, olives, hard-boiled eggs and anchovies, but Carmen hadn't hung around to share it.

I asked Grace where she was. 'She's gone back to work,' she replied.

'Bloody nonsense,' I said. 'Grandma, we know all about Dad and her. Have you been giving her a hard time about it?'

'Of course not,' she retorted severely. 'They're both adults, like you, and no harm is going to come of the relationship. My son needs a companion; God knows he had enough of them in Edinburgh, in that little flat of his. In Spain he has his secretary, the Scottish woman in the office, and Carmen at home. But I don't know if her parents know about it, that's the thing. Her mother works here most days, and she has never mentioned it. So how can I mention it to her? It could well be that she doesn't know. Then, if I talk to the daughter and not the mother, I'm involved in deception, and I wouldn't want that. It's a big burden.'

'Well, it's all bollocks,' I declared. 'So here's what we're going to do about it.' For the first time in my life, I laid down the law to her. When I was done, she nodded, almost meekly, in agreement.

And so, four days later, for the first time in our family's ownership, there was a Christmas lunch in the dining room of the great house. Grandma would allow nobody else to touch the turkey, but Grace and I did most of the rest, a Scottish fish soup called Cullen Skink that Magda Starshine had taught her daughter to prepare, and Crema Catalana, a dessert that I've always regarded as an insult to crème brulée. It had to be on the menu, though, for the Mali family, parents and daughter, were all invited. Pablo and Carmen senior were a little out of their comfort zone at first, but once I had poured some beer into him, and Grandma had topped up her champagne glass a few times, they both relaxed. When they saw how their daughter was treated by the rest of us, especially my dad, it became clear that they had known all along, and had regarded the situation not as an affront but as something of an honour. I came to realise that the feudal mentality was still alive and well in the twentieth century in the Spanish countryside.

I kept a close eye on Grandma for the rest of our stay. She seemed to recover very quickly from her operation. I'm sure that was true, physically, but nonetheless, I could see a difference in her. Or was it that the change was in me, not her, in the way that I looked at her? For all that she was robust for her age, the true one, without the five years she was happy to knock off, to me she seemed diminished. I suppose that it was natural; I had grown up imagining her to be immortal, and it was disturbing to have been presented with clear evidence that she was not. I had never contemplated a life without her, but from that time forward I was forced to confront the fact that only my own early demise would prevent that from coming to pass, one day.

I believe that she sensed that feeling within me. The day before we were due to leave, at the start of the new year, she made me sit with her in the garden. I had been walking there as much as I could, to exercise my knee, taking what warmth the sun had to offer. A gentle wind was blowing from the south and the clouds were few and high, seasonal conditions that often precede rainfall laden with red dust from the Sahara. 'You'll be twenty soon,' she began.

We were sitting side by side, but I glanced at her and caught her eye. 'Fifteen,' I countered, quietly.

She took my point, and laughed. By that time in my life every one of those was worth a small fortune to me. 'Allow me my little vanities, Xavi,' she said. 'Whatever, they've been the longest twenty years of my life, watching you grow from a sad little boy into a serious man. But you're there; you're ready to do what you are meant to do. Sometimes I wish I could talk you out of this passion of yours, this thing you have for journalism.'

'Why?' I asked her, puzzled. 'It's become the family business.'

'Yes, I know. I take an interest, as I always have in the things we've been involved in, since I was young, since they were Puig enterprises, before the Aislado era, before my husband and my son came along to manage them. Because I do I know that journalism has many branches. There are those who have a great time following football, basketball and all those other trivial games. There are those who report on politics, and who are made self-important, and often corrupted, by that world. But there are those like Senora Roca and Senor Sureda, who are at the heart of the profession. They report on the things that matter, and no newspaper that isn't built by, and on, people like them is worth the trees they kill to print it. I've read the things you've written for them. I've even watched you as you write, remember. There's a passion . . . yes, I use that word again because it's fitting . . . in you that exceeds even theirs, and the sooner you put it to work the sooner you'll be fulfilled.' She reached out and patted my arm; another of those rare gestures that I cherished. 'I would like it if you could do it here,' she continued, 'but I recognise why you can't. You have Scottish blood in with your Catalan, a double dose of independence of spirit and of stubborn determination. So you go back to Scotland and begin, my boy. Don't wait for the ink to dry on your degree. Finish it, sure, but get out there as soon as you can, find yourself a job on a newspaper that's worthy of my respect, and build your career. As you do, remember that you're an Aislado. You may find your own path, but everything in which you succeed will be to our credit as well. You are part of what you call "the family business", Xavi, whether you like it or not. You can't walk away from it, because your blood won't let you, because I won't let you, not even after this thing . . .' she tapped her left breast, lightly . . . 'has finally got me, as I know it will in the still distant future; you'll always be close.'

'We'll see,' I mused, unsettled by her prophecy. 'But I'll do what you say. Pilar's given me a name, a man to contact. I'll call him as soon as I can and ask him for advice, and maybe for some introductions.'

'Do that, boy, and take it from there.' She paused. 'One thing more, though. Don't give all your passion to your career. Keep some for your . . . Hah! I was going to say for your girl . . . for your woman. We all need a passion, all of my kind; you make sure that you're always hers.'

'And what's yours, Grandma Paloma?' I asked her.

She looked up at the sky. 'I've had a couple,' she said, 'but the greatest came late in my life, almost twenty years ago, in fact, and you'll be with me for as long as that life lasts.'

The weather had turned when we caught the flight next day. The red rain had fallen, then stopped, leaving a covering of desert dust everywhere. Carmen drove us to the airport: I wasn't sure how to think of her in her acknowledged status. 'Acting' stepmother? I found it hard to think that way about a woman only ten years older than me. I wasn't blind to the attractions of women other than Grace, and she had those in abundance. But even if my dad confounded me, and himself, by marrying her one day, I knew that I'd never think of her on the same plane on which I had placed Tommy Partridge.

I didn't call Pilar's friend's number as soon as I got back. Instead I waited until my knee rehabilitation had run its course, and until my twentieth birthday. Both events happened around the same time. When I did ring the man, it was at a time when I was alone in the flat; I didn't seek privacy, that's just the way it happened, but I wouldn't have wanted Scott or Bobby overhearing my first serious career move.

The man's name was Barry Race. Pilar had described him as a 'news desk executive'; whatever that meant, it must have carried seniority, for it took quite a while before the second person in his phalanx of guardians decided that I was worthy of being put through to him. 'Yes?' he said, brusquely, as he took my call. He had the air of a man who was professionally busy, a type of journalist I came to know well later, short on patience, short on time.

'My name's Xavi Aislado,' I began.

'They told me that much,' he replied. 'Now you tell me why the fuck I'm talking to you, son.'

'Because I'm a fucking good journalist,' I retorted, 'and because an even better one thought that you might be able to give me some career advice. If she's wrong, I won't waste any more of our time.'

'Our time?' he grunted.

'Yes. I've already invested about fifteen minutes of mine just getting through to you. If I've wasted it, I'm going to cut my losses.'

I expected to hear a dial tone; instead Race laughed. 'Who told you that you were good?'

'Pilar Roca, Simon Sureda and Angel Esposito, for starters.'

'The last of those means nothing to me,' he said, 'but Pilar and Simon I rate. Tell me about yourself.'

I did: my education, my ambition and where it came from, how it had been inspired by my first conversation with Simon Sureda, my published work, and my curtailed football career. When I finished, I waited for a reaction, but none came. He simply asked for my phone number, and said that he would call me back. No time frame was specified; indeed, I wasn't convinced that I'd ever hear from him again. But I did, just over half an hour later.

'You left out an important piece of information,' Race snapped, as soon as I had put the receiver to my ear. 'You didn't tell me that your father owns the paper you've been writing for.'

'That's got nothing to do with it,' I retorted. 'I didn't pull any strings to get published.'

'I know that . . . now. I asked Pilar whether she'd given you my number just to keep her boss happy, and she nearly took my head off. But that's not the point. It's a fact and you withheld it from the story you gave me. That's a habit you will have to lose if you want to have any sort of a future in this business.'

'Point taken,' I conceded.

'It begs a question. Pilar's sent me a selection of your work, which she says hasn't been sub-edited to any great extent, and I'm impressed.'

'You speak Catalan?'

'Not fluently, but I can read it. What I must ask you is the obvious: your dad's a newspaper proprietor, so why are you coming to me for help?'

'Because I don't want to work in Spain, and I don't want to work for him. I'm not above asking him for help, but the fact is that the family was in the pub trade here; he's in media now because it attracted him as a business. He doesn't know any journalists in Scotland.'

'And why should Pilar have thought that I do?' said Race. 'She's bright, but she's got the foreign mentality; she thinks that everywhere else is a village.'

219

'I see.'

'Yeah. Look, if you want to move to London after you graduate, I could give you a start here.'

'Thanks, but I don't.'

'No, I suppose I realise that. However I do have one good friend in your neck of the woods. His name's John Fisher. He used to be in our parliamentary team; currently he's chief reporter of a broadsheet called the *Saltire*. I know little or nothing about it, but I know him. I'm prepared to call him and ask him if he'll see you, if you'd like me to.'

I was familiar with the *Saltire*, as an occasional reader, and from a couple of contacts with its sports staff during my playing days. To be honest, I had been hoping that Race would know someone on the *Scotsman*, but I reasoned that if I saw the man Fisher, even if nothing came of it, he might be able to direct me there. 'Yes please,' I said to Race. 'That would be kind of you.'

It took only fifteen minutes for him to call me back for a second time. 'Okay,' he told me. 'You're on. John's expecting you to get in touch.' He gave me his number, and I thanked him. Eventually I met Barry Race, face to face, years later when I went to London for some trivial awards ceremony. I thanked him again, but he was in the grip of Alzheimer's by then, and looked back at me, bewildered.

I rang the *Saltire* straight away. Fisher was busy, but the news desk secretary fielded my call. She had been told to make an appointment for me; ten o'clock next morning, take it or leave it. I had to cut a politics class, but I was well in credit there, so I accepted.

If I suggested that Charles Dickens might have begun his journalistic career in the office to which I reported next day, only geography would make a liar of me. The *Saltire* was based in a building that had stood in Old Assembly Close, off the Royal Mile, since before the French Revolution, since before the foundation of the United States of America. I won't say that it hadn't been redecorated since that time, for it had, but not often. The editorial staff were on two floors, news on the ground floor, sport above, in open-plan offices that I learned later had once housed looms. A receptionist showed me into the newsroom, where half a dozen reporters, five male, one female, sat slumped over desks, some of them reading the stories to which they had been beaten by the opposition, others pecking at typewriters. A pall of blue smoke hung in the air, drifting on the draught from the newly opened door. Only the woman looked up as I entered; she was blonde, and probably ten years younger, but she reminded me of Esme, without her sharpness of eye.

The man who was seated in the centre of a raised area at the furthest end of the long chamber was the youngest person there, in his early or mid thirties. He waved me towards him and my escort withdrew. 'You'll be Xavi, then,' he greeted me, standing as he did so. 'Come on through here; the editor doesn't come in till lunchtime, so we can use his room.'

I had assumed that every editor had a desk, but that one didn't. There was a coffee table in the centre of the office, with four chairs around it, one leather, the others covered in various worn fabrics. 'I'm John Fisher,' my interviewer began. 'Welcome to the cutting edge of journalism. Impressed, eh?'

I couldn't come up with a response that would have been safe, so I eased myself into a chair that was too small for me and said nothing.

'What's wrong with this paper, Xavi?' he asked. I wondered how many more trick questions he was going to put to me, but he wasn't joking. 'Come on, tell me.'

'I'm not sure I'm qualified to say.'

He grinned and I began to like him; twenty-seven years later, I still do. 'I've checked you out. I spoke to the news editor in Girona. Torcuil Bannerman'll have a fit when he sees the phone bill, by the way. From what he told me about you, including a story about you crucifying his political editor on your first visit there, I'd say you're well qualified. Go on; don't be shy.'

'If you insist,' I sighed, foreseeing a very short interview. 'It's not very good. When you set it alongside the papers it's supposed to be competing with, it's drab and dispiriting. You will hardly ever see the word "exclusive" anywhere apart from the sports pages, now and again, but even there you seem to concentrate on football far too much in a big rugby city. There is no dynamism in that room out there and one or two of the people I saw in it seem to be asleep, at ten in the morning.' I thought about it. 'We're in the editor's office, but he isn't. Pilar Roca spends twelve hours a day in her office, six days a week; Simon Sureda spends at least ten. My dad spends at least eight, usually more. Where's the proprietor's office here?'

'There isn't one; there used to be, when the founder was alive, but it's a storeroom now.'

'So, effectively you're in charge, and you're what? Chief reporter?'

'On another paper I'd probably be called the news editor, but that doesn't necessarily mean I'm in charge. Yes, I fill in for Mr Bannerman when he's on holiday, but there's a chief sports reporter and there's a features department run by the leader writer. That's her out there.'

'And she is, with great respect, crap. Her leaders have no consistency and carry no conviction. The party you were set up to support was decimated at the last election, and you don't show any sort of belief that it can ever bounce back. Mr Fisher . . .'

He held up a hand. 'John, the name's John. Who knows, one day you might get to call me Jock.'

'John it is. You asked me what's wrong with the *Saltire*? Summed up, as far as I'm concerned as a reader, and now on the basis of a very brief look inside the place, comparing it with the Girona paper, this is not the sleeping giant of Scottish journalism. It's the sleeping midget.'

'So why the hell do you want to work here?'

'Who says that I do?' I countered. 'I phoned a mate of Pilar Roca to ask for some contacts; yours was the only name he gave me.'

'Touché. You're a young man with ambition, that's clear. Plus your name's known in a certain section of the city through your football . . . even if it's laughed at in the part that supports Hibs. Look, Xavi, let me be honest with you; I could send you down to North Bridge to my opposite number in the *Scotsman*, and you could probably talk yourself into a job there. Or you could finish your degree at Edinburgh, go on up to Stirling and do a masters in journalism that would get you an even better number. The world's your oyster, lad. Like I said, why would you ever want to start in this antiquated shithole, with printing presses out the back that were bought second hand and are nearly as old as the century?'

I could have agreed with him right there and then, thanked him for his time and taken up his offer of an intro to the *Jockstrap*, as Scott and more than a few others called it. Yes, I could have, and I almost did. Yes, I would have . . . if the answer to his question hadn't come to me, clearly and logically, and given itself voice.

'My dad and I are poles apart,' I began, 'but we've got something in common. When he sold up and took my grandma back to Spain, as he'd promised, he could have sat on his big fat one and enjoyed his multimillions for the rest of his life. But he didn't. He's a businessman, instinctively, and he saw a challenge so he took it on. He bought a newspaper that was just as fucked as this one, and although he knew nothing about the industry . . . truth is, he doesn't know much more than that today . . . in less than five years he's turned it into one of the most progressive and successful in the country. I don't think the way that he does, but I'm like him in that one respect. It's precisely because this place is a shithole, because it could go out of business if a strong wind got up, that I'd want to work here. I don't think I'm God's gift, and I'm not a man on a suicide mission, but I see a challenge here, and believe I could make a difference, even if it's only a small one, and even if it does no good in the long term. I'll tell you something else for nothing,' I added. 'You might run this place down, and you might do your best to save me from myself, but you didn't come here from where you came from without wanting to, and without feeling the same as me.'

John smiled. 'Don't tell anyone else, okay?' he said. 'The money's crap,' he added abruptly.

'I don't come free,' I told him, 'but it's not such an issue with me. That doesn't mean I live off my family, other than my girlfriend and I staying in my dad's flat. I was weighed in quite well financially when I had to quit football, so I have other means.'

'Okay. When do you finish uni?'

'Four months: June.'

'Then I'll offer you a job when you do, with the title of graduate trainee. I have hiring powers, so I can do that. You'll be under my direct control, but you'll work across the board initially.'

'What does that mean?'

'It means you'll do whatever I tell you.' He took a pen from the pocket of his shirt, scrawled a number on a newspaper that lay on the table and shoved it towards me. 'That's the starting money.' It wasn't much, but I nodded. 'Fine,' he said. 'Expenses receipted where possible, but not exclusively. If you buy somebody a pint, claim it. But you do not pay for information, not without clearing it with me first. Deal?'

He held out his hand and I shook it. 'Deal,' I repeated. 'But I've got one condition.'

His eyes widened. 'You have?'

'Yes. I live in a non-smoking flat, and I'm not coming to work to be polluted, or to go home with my clothes stinking. Smoking's banned in my dad's paper. I want the same here.'

John gasped. 'You want me to ban journalists from smoking?'

'In the office, yes. And in the toilets,' I added. 'You want me to sweat blood for this paper, I will, but that's what you do for me in return.'

'I'll need to discuss it with the editor.'

I looked around the room. 'I don't see an ashtray in here,' I pointed out.

He shook his head. 'You don't get it. I hate smoking as much as you do. I mean that I'll need to fix it so that Bannerman gets the blame when it's banned. Won't be a problem.'

'Good,' I said. 'See you in June then.'

'You'll see me before then,' he said. 'You were right in what you said about our rugby coverage. It's pathetic, and it costs us sales. Your weekends must be clear now that your football's done for. Go and cover some for us. I'll tell Sandy Jeffrey, the sports editor; we'll pay you as a freelance till you start with us.'

'I don't want to do sport, John.'

'As I said earlier, as a trainee you'll work across the board. I've bought your condition, now you buy mine; rugby's the payback. Don't worry, it won't be long-term.'

'Fair enough.'

The offer was formalised a few days later in a letter signed 'Torcuil Bannerman, Editor'. When I showed it to Grace, she was less than ecstatic.

'Is that all they're paying you?' she asked. 'I'm sure you'd have got more on the *Scotsman*.'

'For sure,' I agreed, 'but I've got a good feel about this.'

'I won't see as much of you at the weekend if you do this rugby stuff.'

'You can come to games with me,' I pointed out.

'Ugh, I hate rugby. Fat sweaty trolls rolling about in the mud and knocking lumps off each other.'

'There's more to it than that.'

Actually, in quite a few of the games I covered, there wasn't a great deal more. The professional era didn't begin until 1995, so the players were all part-time, and doing it for love. At the lower level some of them were doing it for love of a brawl, and occasionally that would permeate the first team games.

I took my first proper assignment seriously. I reasoned that if I was to build up the *Saltire*'s rugby coverage, that meant more than simply turning up at weekends and describing play in print, so I began to build relationships with the city's top teams, most of which had grown from schools rugby: Edinburgh Academicals, Heriot's, Stewart's-Melville, Boroughmuir and, of course, Watson's, all essentially, although not exclusively, former pupil clubs. I had a flying start with Watson's, since Bobby Hannah had rejoined and was in the first team squad, alongside a few other guys from our era. Modern coaching was in its infancy, but I was able to build relationships with the key men in each of those clubs, and with some of their adherents. Once I'd won their trust, by fair and balanced reports and analyses of their games, which began to command more space on the sports pages of the Monday *Saltire*, they began to see me as a conduit, and learned to feed me stories of what was going on within the clubs, and even inside the game itself. I began to pick up exclusives, and realised that in sales terms there was more to be gained by stories of what was happening off the pitch, spread through the week, than from match coverage that was common to everyone, and where the Sundays had a built-in advantage. The rumblings of discontent that would lead to the end of the purely amateur game were beginning, and I tuned into them early. It made me a few enemies in the Scottish Rugby Union, the ruling body, but far more friends within the clubs and that made me happy.

It made John Fisher and Sandy Jeffrey happy too; when the rugby season ended at the beginning of May, with the seven-a-side circuit, they took me aside in the office and showed me the latest circulation figures, which showed a small but consistent rise, from early March, the time when my 'exclusive' sports tags began to appear. It gave me a buzz, and I knew for sure that I had made the right career choice in joining a paper for which the only way . . . other than oblivion . . . was up. There was an obvious corollary, of course; like it or not, I had landed myself a job within a job. I couldn't leave the rugby beat after the progress I'd made in such a short time, and so I bowed to the inevitable and accepted the designation as the Rugby Correspondent of the *Saltire*, and the few extra pounds that would be added to my starting salary when I joined full-time. John had promised me that it wouldn't be long-term, but, although I was freed from some of the match coverage as the sports staff expanded, it took a few years before I was able to hand over the role completely to a successor, a former player.

I sat my final university examinations at the end of May, spent a couple of relaxing and uneventful weeks with Grace in Spain, where

Grandma assured me that she had no recurrence of her cancer and even showed me her most recent consultant's report to prove it. I spent much of our holiday swimming, and did some cycling in the countryside on a bike that I'd bought to keep there, as I continued the long process of rehabilitation on my knee. I had abandoned the crutch months before, and although there was still some stiffness and restriction of movement, week by week, I could feel it strengthen, day by day.

I didn't tell Grandma or my dad that my formal graduation would be on the last Saturday in June. It was a silly ceremony, and it wouldn't change me. I would be able to call myself 'Master of Arts', but I would never choose to do that, any more than I would ever wear the hired gown again, so I didn't want to wake up on the day to find that either of them had travelled a thousand miles to witness thirty seconds of nonsense. Grace was in the audience, with Magda and Rod, and that was fine by me. The 'acting parents-in-law', as their daughter had christened them, took us to Vito's afterwards for lunch, but that was the extent of the celebration.

My life didn't change on that day, but it did two days later, when I became a full-time employee of 'Saltire Publications plc', an appointment that I still hold, officially, as I write this, even if my status has altered. When I stepped into the newsroom, a couple of minutes before nine, there were two significant differences from what I had seen on my interview visit. The first was that I could see clearly across the room; the blue fog had gone. This was not news to me, as I had been back a few times as a freelance, but what I had not seen before was an extra desk and chair, bigger than the rest and close to John Fisher's position on what everyone on the staff called the 'headmaster's platform'.

'Welcome,' said the chief reporter as I entered; there was only one other person there, a veteran called Chick Harvey, an insomniac who did the early shift because it suited him. 'That's your spot,' John told me, pointing to the new furniture. 'I didn't think you'd fit behind one of the old desks, so I got the editor to sign for it. Your phone's not ready yet, but there's supposed to be an engineer coming in today to do it. Lots of treats in store for you today.'

I had dressed for the occasion; I was wearing a single-breasted two-piece, tailor made, of necessity, since High and Mighty didn't always cater for upwards of six feet four in those days. As the other reporters filed in, gradually, I began to feel, more and more, like an oddity. Sports jacket and slacks seemed to be the unofficial uniform among the older guys; only Doug McGrane, the crime reporter, and Mary Hackett, the features editor, broke the mould, he in a brown leather jacket and blue denims, she in a white, flared trouser suit that I guessed dated back five years, to when *Saturday Night Fever* was the hot movie ticket.

The men were affable as we were introduced. A couple knew what I'd been doing on the sports pages, but to the majority, I was a total stranger. 'You the new copy-boy then?' McGrane asked as we shook hands. There was no malice in it, but as I smiled, I squeezed a little harder than my norm, just to make a point.

'Chuck it, Dougie,' John warned him, loud enough for the others to hear. 'I'll have none of that from any of you. It might say "trainee" in Xavi's job description, but he's here on an equal footing to all of you. He's done some bloody good work already for this paper, and for others, so you'll all respect him. He's got my permission to clout the first person to ask him to go and get them a coffee. If you remember what happened to that Airdrie player last year, you won't be doing that.'

The only hostility I faced was from Mary Hackett. She greeted me with a grunt and turned her back on me. It didn't take me long to discover that the day after my first visit, the editor had relieved her of the leader-writing job, and that she had put two and two together and blamed me. I was able to live with that; our paths didn't cross, professionally or otherwise, and I could sense that she wasn't going to be there for the long haul.

'Come on,' the chief reporter said, 'and I'll take you for a proper tour. They say that Noah built this place, you know.' He led me back out of the newsroom and down a flight of stairs to a level where I'd never been before. It was full of machines, with fans overhead. The area was superheated, but I knew why. Linotype wasn't quite as old as printing itself, but its principle was, molten lead moulded into lines of words in negative. All but one of the operators wore oil-smeared brown overalls; the odd one out sported a pullover that might once have been green. He was bald and I could see spots of dried lead on his head, relics of the splashes to which the contraptions were prone. 'See Archie's jumper?' John whispered. 'See those seams on the outside? He came in one day with what everybody thought was a new jersey, but he'd just turned the old one inside out.' He introduced me to each of the operators in turn; they seemed pleased to meet me, but I guess they could simply have been glad of the break. I noticed that smoking was allowed in the production areas; it would have been pointless to ban it, given that the atmosphere was polluted by something just as bad as cigarette fumes.

'We have one advantage here,' John told me as we walked through to the case room, where the pages were set out on long metal worktops; in the time of newspaper pre-history they had been made from stone, and had kept the name. It was early in the day, so the only work going on involved clearing away the debris of the previous day's edition. 'There's only one print union in this place, the Scottish Typographical Association. All the other dailies have unions for different specialties and they are a nightmare, believe me, arguing among themselves, chalk lines drawn on the case-room floor, all that shit. Nationally it costs millions every year in lost sales through strikes. If we had that here it'd finish us. Mind you,' he added, prophetically, 'it'll finish the rest too, in their present form. Computer layout, photographic plates, sent by facsimile for printing hundreds of miles away, web offset presses, they're all coming; some of it's already here. It'll take huge investment, on new sites, and the big proprietors won't commit to it without sorting out the unions for good. Thatcher's preparing the ground already.' He glanced around. 'Even we'll have to change, although God knows where the money'll come from. All the guys here will have to retrain for their own industry. The linotype operators, they're dinosaurs, and they'll go the same way.' He pointed across the stone; I followed the finger and saw a young man, maybe twenty-five years old. 'That boy, Ricky Thomas, he's doing freelance photography already. Sandy uses him. He wants to join the NUJ, and we'll fix it for him as soon as he's ready.'

The printing presses were located in a massive annexe that had been tagged on the back of the original building when Charles McCandlish had bought it in the forties. There were three of them, huge multi-level machines, so old and susceptible to breakdown that it was unusual for them all to be running simultaneously. Beyond them were loading bays, with huge doors that opened directly on to the Cowgate. 'That's a listed building upstairs, surely,' I said. My escort nodded. 'So how was the proprietor allowed to do this to it?'

'Back then? You got away with a hell of a lot more. Crazier things than this have happened in Edinburgh, and I dare say that a few more will in the future. They'll probably re-lay the tram lines one day.'

He took me back upstairs, back to the mere hinterland of hell, where the advertising department worked, 'pissing against a hurricane of indifference', as he put it, then spent as much of his time as he could for the rest of the morning briefing me on the history and structure of the paper. I'd done my own research, of course, so I'd heard of Charles McCandlish. I also had a fair idea of how Torcuil Bannerman had come to be appointed editor, but the chief reporter didn't mention that, so neither did I. He looked around the big room. 'We've got a news reporting staff of fourteen, not counting you and me, to run this mighty enterprise; that's way fewer than any of our rivals. There are seven general reporters, including Chick there, on early, the late shift being rotated, plus specialists in court, council, crime and politics. Then there's Mary and two others on features. You've done some time on sport, so you know what they've got.' I did; they didn't have enough. Without Mick Norman, easily their best guy, they'd have been a laughing stock, but he kept them above the respectability threshold. 'There are three sub-editors. Their job is to process copy, mark it up and pass it through to the typesetters. The chief sub does most of the layout, after the editor's decided what the story priorities will be.'

'What time's the morning news conference?' I asked. Doug McGrane heard me and smiled.

'What's the point in having one,' the chief reporter murmured, 'when the editor never shows up before lunch? Sandy and I decide where we're going to major and I tell Torcuil. That's how it works.'

'What about Westminster?' I asked. 'What staff do we have there?'

'None. We use the Press Association.'

'So that by-line, "By our Political Editor", that's a lie?'

He grinned. 'Yes and no. I decide what we use, so technically, that's me; but I don't write it.'

'What about Europe?'

'Agence France Press.'

'International?'

'Reuters. And before you ask who "Our Foreign Editor" is, that's me too.'

'I see,' I said, keeping my tone neutral. 'Photographers?' When I'd covered rugby, I'd had no input on that side.

'We have three staffers; they spend most of their time up at the High Court waiting for people to come out, so they can press their motor drives for half a minute. The rest of their time they spend in the Black Swan or the Halfway House, in the finest traditions of Scottish newspaper photography. They're known in the business as "The gang that can't shoot straight", and they don't have a driving licence among them, since they're all disqualified at the moment. Our taxi bill is horrendous.'

'Why do you tolerate them?'

'The union would call a strike if we didn't. Then we'd have picket lines outside and placards, saying "Save the Black Swan Three". Still glad you came to work here?' he asked, quickly.

'More than ever.'

In the silence that followed, a course of action suggested itself to me. Today I'm sure that if I had followed it up with sufficient vigour, even then, when I was only twenty years old, it would have been pursued, and taken to a conclusion. If I had done that, many things would have changed. For example, Jock Fisher would now be some time into a comfortable retirement. But I didn't, not then and not for another eighteen years, when circumstances forced my hand. Why not? Because I was young, because I was stubborn, because my pride overcame my logic, and because I was still hugely ignorant.

And so, instead, I added, 'Tell me how to do it.'

'Well,' said John. 'You were a good feature writer before you came here, as your Spanish work showed me, and Sandy's started to teach you how to write news, even if it is for the sports pages. I'm going to teach you the rest. I'm going to pair you with the guys I have in here, starting with Doug McGrane. He might be a right wee smart-arse,' he raised his voice for a few seconds, 'but he knows what he's doing, and it's only the general distrust of this paper that's holding him back. You'll spend some time shadowing him, then I'll move you on to council, then court.'

'For how long?'

'For as long as it takes.'

'And after that?'

'We'll see. I've got an idea, but I'll keep it to myself for now, in case you don't measure up after all.' He leaned forward, and put his elbows on his desk. 'Before I turn you loose, Xavi, there's one thing I have to say to you. Journalists have a range of different skills, and we come in all shapes and sizes, but there is one thing that defines the career of every one of us, and differentiates the good from the mediocre and the best from all the rest. That is the quality of our sources, the people who give us the facts that we report, and even those slippery bastards in PR and politics who try to use us for their own purposes. It's not always bad for someone to have his own agenda, but the reporter has to spot it when it's there and handle it accordingly, so that he never becomes just an accomplice. That's how political journalism has always worked. Sources are the heart of journalism; I can't stress that enough. There's an old guy through in the west, a football man. He's an annoying wee bastard, and he can't write a bloody line, the subs do that for him, but he's an absolute legend, one of the truly great reporters. Why? Because people trust him enough to tell him about things that matter, even when they're a wee bit scared to do it, because they know he'll deliver and won't let them down. Nobody trusts this paper any more, lad, not that very many ever did. Go out and change that, and you'll be great for us, and for yourself.'

I expected him to hand me over to Doug after that speech, but instead he picked up his phone and dialled an internal number. Not far away I heard ringing; as it stopped, John turned away from me and muttered something. 'Okay,' he said, finally, and hung up. 'The greatest of those treats I mentioned; this is when you get to meet the editor.'

Although I had been freelancing for the paper for four months, and had called into the office several times during that period, I had never seen, far less met, the man who was supposed to run it. I followed the chief reporter as he rose and opened the door to the office behind him. 'Torcuil,' I heard him say, to a figure still unseen, 'this is Xavi Aislado, our new graduate trainee.' He stepped aside and I moved past him.

The editor jumped, very slightly, in his leather seat as I entered his presence. Nervous people often do that when they're confronted by my bulk for the first time. He was small, and looked even fatter than he really was, in a shapeless dark tweed jacket. He was forty-four years old at that time, but his puffy eyes, beneath a dome head and white fly-away wispy hair, made him look at least fifty. He recovered himself. 'By God,' he said, 'you're a big fellow. Be seated, please.' He glanced behind me. 'John, leave us please, but have the copy-boy bring us coffee.' I could hear Fisher's low growl, as the door closed.

Bannerman didn't say anything more as we waited; not a word. Instead, he looked me up and down, as if he was making lifetime decisions about the cut of my jib, and whether he took to it or not. He

233

didn't make eye contact, though, not once, even though after a while I began to pursue him with mine. At first I had wondered how he had made it into his room without being seen, but there was a second door, in the far corner. I'd had my back to it during my first meeting with John. Eventually, there was a knock. 'Come,' called Bannerman and it opened, for a pretty, pale-faced, white-bloused girl to enter, carrying a tray with two mugs and a plate of chocolate digestive biscuits. It turned out that the copy-boy was a girl. Her name was Juliet Coats, and she was the niece of the editor's brother-in-law. Against all expectations, Juliet stayed the course, became a reporter, and is now a respected columnist on a Sunday title in London. She is most fondly remembered in the *Saltire* in connection with the discreet resignation of Mary Hackett following an alleged proposition made in the ladies' toilet. Yes, she blossomed, but she was a quiet little mouse then; she laid her tray on the table and scampered out, saying no more to me than had her patron, at that point.

He picked up his coffee and took a biscuit, indicating to me, with a nod, that I should help myself. He waited until I was taking my first bite of a McVitie's, before launching himself. 'What are your politics, Mr Aislado?' he asked, in a reedy, but powerful voice, spraying crumbs over the plate.

He'd made me wait, so I did the same to him. I put away all of the digestive, sipped some of the Maxwell House . . . I detest all instants, apart from Nescafé Alta Rica . . . and finally, taking him unawares, looked him in the eye. 'My politics,' I repeated, then paused again. 'Well, thanks to the inefficiency of the registration system, I'm still waiting to be enfranchised.'

'Hmmph,' he grunted. 'If you were,' he persisted, 'how would you cast your ballot?'

'In secret,' I told him, politely.

'I see.' The library research I had done on the man had uncovered an article that suggested that he had acquired a reputation as a sharp-witted intellectual within the Scottish National Party. If that was the case, his contemporaries must have been spectacularly slow thinkers. 'Let me put it another way,' he ventured, after a second biscuit. 'How do you lean?'

I came within a couple of seconds of telling him that after my football injury I had a tendency to lean to the right, but I had a premonition that he would misinterpret that completely, so I stopped myself. Instead, I nailed his slippery gaze again, and replied, 'By birth, I'm half Spanish, on my father's side, and half British, on my mother's. By the latter, I mean that I carry a United Kingdom passport, and that my nationality of record is British. However, the Catalan nationalism that's been instilled into me by my grandmother has had the effect of making my Scottish nationalism equally strong.' He began to beam, but I stopped its spread quickly. 'But that doesn't mean that I'm a supporter by definition of the party whose standard you carried in Parliament for a while. I'm in favour of the good governance of my country. By that I mean I want it run on practical and effective economic policies, with a recognition of human rights that include social justice, high-quality education and health care, protection for the weak against the abuses of the strong, and of the state for that matter, sound policing and a judicial system that's firm enough to let the people sleep peacefully, without ever becoming repressive. I want it to be respected abroad, but not feared. Those are the beliefs I was brought up with. I don't care whether they are secured within the context of a United Kingdom or by a separate Scottish nation state, be that monarchist or republican, as long as they are secured. I will add one more principle: as a working journalist, even on my first day on the job, I prize my integrity and my objectivity. That will bar me from ever carrying the card of any political party, anywhere.'

The editor's ever-moving eyes glazed over. I hoped that he wasn't going to ask me to repeat what I'd just said, but he didn't. Instead, he murmured, 'Ah, so you're one of those floating voters, are you?'

'That's still to be seen,' I told him, 'although by me alone, and I promise you this. Until I'm sat in your office, or another like it, determining the editorial policy of a newspaper, you will never know whether I am or not. I've just finished three years of specialist education, and one of the things they taught me is . . . that's how democracy's supposed to work. And you won't be surprised to learn that as the grandson and son of refugees from fascism, I'm pretty strongly pro-democratic.' *Even if my grandfather was a murderer, and I've just argued for his imprisonment, even execution, under such a system,* I thought as I finished, but I wasn't sharing that with Bannerman.

He took refuge in some more deep thought, or the appearance of it. 'Hard to nail down, aren't you,' he declared as he emerged. 'What's your belief system?'

In days in the west of Scotland that I hope are dead or dying, when people asked, 'What school did you go to?' what they were trying to establish was whether the subject was a Protestant or a Roman Catholic. Effectively, that's what Bannerman asked me; the file on him that I'd found in the university politics department library included a quote that he was 'an elder of the established Church and proud of it'. In a Scottish context that was a strangely pro-unionist remark for a nationalist to make, but I knew that it was a signal to diehard Orange Order voters grown disenchanted with the modern Tories.

'My father was baptised and confirmed as a Catholic,' I said. He'd never practised as an adult, but I was damned if I was going to admit that. 'My mother comes from a Church of Scotland house-hold.' And a nasty shower of bastards they were, but I kept that to myself also. 'I'm engaged to a girl from a pretty unorthodox Jewish family, and the only Christian churches I've ever set foot in are Girona Cathedral and the Sagrada Familia in Barcelona, and St Peter's Basilica in Rome, as a tourist. That's the foundation of my belief system and I reckon it's pretty sound.' I added a question. 'But what do I believe in? Different thing. I believe in the truth, Mr Bannerman, and that's why I'm here.'

'I see.' I doubted that he did; after all, he was a failed politician put in place by a zealot. He pushed himself up from his chair, signalling the end of my audience. He really was very small, more than a foot shorter than me; that's probably why he didn't look up as he offered a limp handshake. 'Welcome to the *Saltire*,' he murmured. 'Serve it well.' I've tried; I believe that I did.

I stepped into the newsroom, heading for my desk, but John stopped me before I reached it. 'Well?' he murmured.

'Well what?' I stalled, cautiously.

'What do you think of him? Full and frank now; that's the way it's got to be between you and me.'

I sat on the edge of his desk, my back to the room, so I couldn't be overheard or lip-read, journalists being cunning folk. 'He's an idiot. How did he ever qualify as a surveyor, let alone get to be editor of this paper?'

'Spot on, Xavi; chromium plated. And he didn't qualify: his father owned the practice. The guy surveyed a building once, passed it sound, and it fell down two weeks later . . . when it was empty, luckily. He's just a bloody wee demagogue; that, and his obedience, was what made him useful to old McCandlish. The heirs and successors don't give a shit. The business does have a general manager, Nick Newis, lurking in an office up in the attic, but he reports to Bannerman, so even if he wanted to do something about him he's powerless.' He looked me in the eye, emphasising the contrast between him and his titular leader. 'But all that said, Xavi,' he told me, 'he's what he is, and we have to live with it and give him the respect that the office demands, if not the man. Understood?'

I didn't agree with him; respect has to be merited or it's worthless. But John had earned mine, so I nodded. 'Understood.'

'Do you ever worry about the consequences of your actions?'

'Never. Even if I knew what they were.'

'Not at all? Not even when you're taking a risk with someone who's completely unpredictable?'

'Nobody's unpredictable. I can read people; get inside their heads.'

'From what I saw, you didn't read wee Dave too well.'

'Oh yes I did: just in time, I'll grant you. I recognised that I'd underestimated him, and I took appropriate action.'

'What do you mean, "appropriate action"?'

'I got on my horse and got out of Dodge, as gracefully as I could.'

'Sure, you mean you crapped it when you realised that his old man had taught him the tricks of his trade.'

'No, I made a tactical withdrawal to fight the battle on another front. Anyway, wee Dave and I will be family soon. My sister's going to be his stepmother, when she and John get round to it. That'll make me . . . what the fuck will it make me? . . . his step-uncle, I suppose, and Lina, she'll be my step-niece.'

'Was he in the Falklands, Dave's dad?'

'You never know with him, but Billie told me that when it was all happening, he was completely off the radar, even hers. He's finished with that now, she told me. He's been promoted and he's got a desk job in the MoD.'

'What's he like? I've never met him, remember.'

'He's a very quiet chap, sociable, buys his round; you meet him in the pub and you'd never suspect that he is what he is, a trained killer.'

'Reminds me of somebody.'

'Who? Him? You're kidding. Shit, man, you've been smoking too much of that stuff. Come on, pass it along, I want a hit. Don't Bogart that joint, my friend, don't Bogart on me. Bollocks. Him? Trained killer? I know you've got the hots for him, you big poof, but come on . . .'

'That's crap.'

'No it's not; Jilly told me one night, when she was in a mood to give away secrets. What team you bat for; well, that wasn't a surprise. We've *both known what we know since the time I caught you being rogered up the bum by that prefect when we were in the third year . . . so don't say I can't keep a secret, by the way. Fuck, if your rugby mates knew . . . How do you keep it down in the bath after the game?'*

'Sod off.'

'Sure, but you fancying him: I should have twigged. He probably has done himself. Here, you haven't had the monster up you, have you?'

'No chance. You're just fucking jealous anyway.'

'Jealous of what?'

'The monster, what did you think I meant?'

'Ah, man, I'm just taking the piss. In vino veritas, maybe, but hash doesn't count. But honest to Christ, him a trained killer? Get the stars out of your eyes.'

'That's not what I said, you idiot. We were talking about unpredictability. You think you're a fucking genius at reading people, but you have no idea about him.'

'What makes you think so?'

'Because he has no idea himself. Who knows what he would do if . . . He's a great friend to have, but he has one enemy, his own mother, and look at how he's treated her. He's cut her out of his life, completely. He never mentions her, and if you ever ask about her, you draw a look from him that you'd never see otherwise. If that's how he reacts to his own old dear, then what the hell would he do if he found out that . . . I don't know, but I would not want to see it, or be anywhere near it.'

'Mince. He's a wuss at heart.'

'You know, your problem, the one that's going to get you done in one day, is that you think everyone's a wuss alongside you. You were wrong about wee Dave, but my God, you are so much more wrong about him. You take him for granted, and that's the worst mistake you could ever make. If he found out what was happening, in his own house . . .'

'You reckon?'

'I reckon. You know who brought him up, yes?'

'Sure. We both do.'

'Well, consider this. You've met her, recently and when we were kids. She's the only influence he's known, all the time he was growing up. A lot of what he is, his languages, his de . . . de . . . demeanour, that's the fucking word . . . Christ, I'm tonked . . . comes from her. So ask yourself this: how much time do you think she spent teaching him forgiveness?'

'I hear what you're saying.'

'So maybe you'll go carefully in the future.'

'I might, if it was up to me. But to be frank with you, I don't know if I'm in control any more. That's if I ever was!'

Eleven

John Fisher finished my brief induction by taking me for lunch in Gordon's Trattoria, across the High Street. 'Useful place, this,' he murmured as he attacked a plate of seafood linguine. 'That grey-haired bloke in the corner, he's the Dean of the Faculty of Advocates, Scotland's top QC. The guy he's with is a civil servant, the head of the Courts Service. Maybe they're just comparing pizzas, but . . . the Dean's overdue a move to the bench. Watch this space; we might have a new judge soon.'

Before we'd finished he had pointed out another half-dozen people to me, with comments about each one, and also made me appreciate a problem that I would have throughout my career. 'You'll never be able to do discreet, Xavi. There are people who can meet privately in a public place, where they might not be known, but you'll never be one of them. Even sat at a table, you stick out like a lighthouse. What height are you? Six six?'

'Six sevenish, last time I was checked.'

'There you are then. The more that folk around the city get to know who you are and what you do, the more you'll be a marked man.'

'Are you saying that might give me a problem finding the sources you were talking about?'

'No, but it might give you a problem managing them. You will never grow fat eating working lunches.'

Actually, I will never grow very fat, period, but that's the way I'm made.

When we went back to the office, it was Doug McGrane who introduced me to the world of the jobbing journalist. 'Let's pay some visits,' he said, then led me on a tour of some of the police offices in the centre of the city. We began in the High Street, then moved on to Gayfield Square. At once, I felt even more of an oddity; my new mentor's leather jacket and jeans blended in with the surroundings and with the civilians who gathered there, for whatever reason, while, in my suit, I looked like a floor walker in Jenners. Doug seemed to know every cop behind the counters as he introduced me around, and they seemed to be on good terms with him, but I didn't notice any of them taking him aside for whispered conversations. They were free enough with the latest events, incidents entered into the log book, a shop-lifting arrest in John Menzies that would wind up in court, a disagreement in a Rose Street pub that had led to handbags at five paces and a couple of cooling-off arrests that would not result in charges, a sudden death . . . 'Unremarkable,' remarked the constable who told us about it . . . another . . . 'Suicide; hung herself; that one's not for reporting' . . . but it was all routine stuff that would be available to anyone with an NUJ membership card. (I had joined the union myself, a requirement of employment, a couple of months earlier, courtesy of my freelance work for the paper.) The most senior of Doug's police contacts seemed to be sergeants, and in uniform at that; not the most likely sources of front-page exclusives, I suspected.

Our round ended at Torphichen Place. I knew it well enough from meeting Tommy there, but I wasn't expecting to see him in the public office any more. In truth, I didn't expect to see anyone there that I knew, but I did. He was a PC and his name was Jim, Jim McCracken, by his badge, and he was one of the guys I'd met a year before at the Western Infirmary, on the night Lina was attacked. He was behind the counter, and he spotted me as soon as I came through the door. 'Hey,' he called out, 'it's big Iceland.' We shook hands across the counter. 'Sorry, I didn't know who you were that night at the hospital. Sorry about the knee too; a great career cut short, eh.'

I shrugged. 'One door closes, and all that stuff. It's my first day on my new job.' I nodded towards my escort, who had moved on to talk to a sergeant. 'I'm a graduate trainee on the *Saltire*. Doug's showing me the ropes.'

'Between you and me,' Jim said, quietly, 'any ropes that Dougie holds aren't attached to anything. He's a nice guy, but if we're tipping anybody off about something, he's last in the queue.'

'Why? Because we sell fewer papers than the rest?'

'Partly; but mostly because they look after us better. I'm not saying they bung us. It would cost us our pension if any of us got caught taking cash, but there's no harm in a case or two of lager for the office Christmas party, or a pint when we're off duty.'

'And we never do that?'

'No.'

And yet we could, I thought, remembering John's expenses briefing. I found myself wondering what Doug's claims covered, and whether the supposed recipients of the casual hospitality we were allowed to provide ever saw any of it.

'I can't see why not,' I told him. 'I'll be moving around the departments, and it'll be a while before I have any influence, but I'll remember that. Thanks for the tip, Jim.'

'Would you like another?' His voice was no more than a whisper. I nodded. 'Not here,' he said. 'Give me your home phone number.'

I took out my pristine notebook, scribbled seven digits, ripped off the page, and handed it to him. Doug was so wrapped up in his pointless conversation with the desk sergeant that he didn't notice.

I'd been home for half an hour from my first full day at work, being grilled by Grace over every detail, when Jim called. 'You free to go out?'

It was quarter to seven. I looked at my fiancée, mouthed the word 'Work' and said, 'Yes.'

'Where's handy for you? Pub, like.'

I remembered John's warning. 'If this is sensitive,' I told him, 'you don't want to be seen with me in a pub. People don't forget me.'

'That's true enough. Where can I pick you up?'

'West End?'

'That'll do. Coates Crescent, half seven.'

'Is it going to be like this every night?' Grace complained, when I told her that my evening meal was going to be a corned beef sandwich.

'No, but I've got to follow this up.'

She squeezed my crotch, not as gently as she might have. 'Okay,' she allowed, 'but don't make a habit of it.'

I reached the corner of Coates Crescent and Walker Street just as Jim McCracken pulled up there in a red Ford Granada with a black vinyl roof. I had changed out of my suit, into Doug's uniform of jeans and leather jacket. I eased myself into the passenger seat and reached beneath it for the bar that would give me more leg room. There was a child seat in the back, and a harness for a second.

'What's this about?' I asked as we headed off, wheels roaring on the cobbles.

'You'll find out.'

'Where are we going?'

'You'll find that out too.' He glanced at me. 'I can trust you, Iceland, can't I? My name stays out of this. I hope to make sergeant one day, but if this came out I'd be fucked.'

'Jim, I'd go to jail before I'd spill your name. That's a promise I hope I never have to keep, but if I have to, I will.'

'Fair enough.' He moved out into Shandwick Place, then turned right into Stafford Street. A couple of minutes later we passed my building. I glanced up and caught a brief glimpse of Grace and Scott, standing by the window, each with a glass in hand and smiling, then we took a right at the traffic lights and headed down the hill towards Comely Bank, and I focused on the road ahead.

Our destination turned out to be a semi-detached house in a street in Granton, council by the look of it, although three years of the right to buy were having an effect. The door to which Jim led me was new, as were the windows, double-glazed UPVC units, unmistakable signs of private ownership. He reached out for the bell button, but before his finger found it, the door swung open. It took me a few seconds before I remembered the face of the man who stood there; I struggled for his name until I realised that I'd never known it. He was Jim's mate, the senior cop at the Western.

'How you doin', son?' he greeted me.

'Fine, thanks,' I replied, lamely, wondering what I had walked into.

'I hear your stepfather's back in a suit.'

'True. Same office, though.' I glanced at the nameplate by the door. It read, 'H. Bracewell.'

He had followed my eyes. 'That's Hughie,' he said, extending his hand. As we shook, I saw that his right forearm was bandaged from wrist to elbow. He looked a little older than he had in uniform. 'Come on in,' he said. I followed him into the hall; Jim McCracken closed the door behind us, as he led us into a room with a three-piece suite set around a fireplace and a gateleg dining table in the bay window.

A woman stood as we entered; she wore an anxious expression as she glanced at Jim and me, then looked back at Hughie. 'Are you sure about this?' she asked him.

'It's got to be done,' he replied.

'If you say so,' she muttered. 'I'll be in the kitchen.'

'What happened to your arm?' I asked, as I sat on the sofa of the suite. The springing was old, and I sank into it. 'Injured on the job?'

'Aye,' Hughie Bracewell said, 'but no' the one you're thinking. I did my thirty years, so I retired three months ago, still under fifty, just. The pension's a' right, but there's a lot we need to do to the house, so I took another job, as a jannie at Maxwell Academy, on the other side of the city.'

I'd heard of that place; everyone in Edinburgh knew about it. 'The Academy of Mayhem' was one of its milder nicknames. A forty-nine-year-old ex-constable was just the sort of man you'd expect to find as its janitor. 'What happened?' I asked him, quietly.

'Let's just say that it didn't live down to my expectations.' He chuckled, as if surprised by his own turn of phrase. 'It was worse than that. Ah'd been there less than a week before I realised that a lot of the kids were really no' focused at all, from the first years, the twelve-year-olds, right up. They were like fuckin' wee zombies, and I guessed that they were just fillin' in time till they could get out of there, start signing on and drawin' benefit.' He frowned. 'But after a while, I began to think that there was more to it than that. I took a closer look at some of them, and I got it. They were on drugs. They were at school and they were fuckin' stoned. And not just that, it happened all through the fuckin' day. I reckoned they were bringin' the stuff in wi' them.'

'What sort of stuff are we talking about? Hash?'

Hughie glowered. 'I wish. More than that.'

'What did you do about it?'

'The wrong thing. Christ, I had options; I could have gone to the guidance teacher, but she's away wi' the fairies, and stuck with a job that a nun couldnae handle. I could have gone tae the head janitor, but I thought, naw, Hughie. This thing's developed under his fuckin' nose. Sort it out, then take it to him. I ticked the wrong box, big time. I decided to investigate myself.' He rolled his eyes. 'Thirty years in the polis, never get a fuckin' sniff o' CID and all of a sudden Ah think I'm a detective. So I went on the prowl, Xavi. I spent less time in my room; I went on patrol, as if I was back on the beat. I was watching them, watching the kids, looking for behaviour patterns, but changing my routine as much as I could, changing my patrol times, so that they didn't clock on tae me. Eventually, Ah worked it out. There was this one wee bastard, Watson his name is, Ryan Watson, fourteen-year-old, third year. He was a real time-server, made a complete fucking nuisance of himself all the time, but there was nothing the teachers could do about him or to him, since he never put himself into expulsion territory. He always went to the toilet twice a day, regular, morning and afternoon, but out of different classes so it wasn't obvious to the teachers. He'd go into the bogs area on the ground floor, and he'd be in there for fifteen minutes, a long time, ye'd think, but his classes were better off without him there, so nobody went lookin' for him. I watched him and I saw a pattern. While he was in the toilets there was an increase, a big increase, in the number of kids using them, and the unusual thing was, they were all girls. I asked Trudy, the wife, about that; she was a teaching assistant for a while. She explained that if girls ask to go to the toilet, chances are the teacher's going to let them every time, just in case they're on their periods. You can't ask a kid to announce that to the whole class, can you? Anyway, I watched, and one day I made my move. I waited until Watson had been in the bog for ten minutes and until half a dozen lassies had gone in, and I marched into the boys' toilet. It was empty; all the cubicle doors were open, there was nobody there.' He sighed and shook his head. 'What I should have done, by rights, Ah should have locked the door of the girls . . . I had my keys on me . . . and got the guidance teacher then, so that she could go in first. But I didn't. I went barging straight in there myself. Wee Watson was there right enough; he was selling baggies of heroin to the girls, a few at a time. They'd gather in the money and go and buy, and then they would take them back and distribute them to their mates.'

'What did you do?' I asked.

'I shut the door behind me, and I said to him, "Watson, you little shite, you're nicked!" and then I went to grab him. Wee bastard had a razor, hadn't he, taped to the inside of his left blazer sleeve. He whipped it out and cut me, right through my overalls, right into the muscle. I was expecting more, so I went back against the wall, but they all made a run for it, leavin' me like a big eedjit, blood all over the place. I ripped off my overall and I grabbed some paper towels to try and stop the bleeding. I was still doing that when Geordie Ramsay, the head jannie came in. I told him what had happened.'

'How did he react?'

'There's a health centre right opposite the school. He told me to get straight over there and get attention and he'd deal with things.'

I stared at him, and at Jim. 'This is amazing,' I said. 'I've never read a thing about this, anywhere.'

'No,' McCracken agreed. 'You haven't. Tell him why, Hughie.'

His mate nodded. 'I did what he said, rushed across the road. They stopped the bleedin' and fixed me up. The cut was about four inches long; it took twenty stitches. Then I went back tae the school, to see what had happened to wee Watson. But when I asked Ramsay he wouldn't speak to me. Instead he told me to go and see Mr Mulholland, the head teacher, straight away. When I got there his secretary looked at me like I was shite or something and told me to go in. Mulholland was sitting behind his desk. He looked up at me and said, "Don't even think about asking for a second chance, you're sacked." Ah just stared at him, like I was dumb, until finally I said, "What?" bewildered, like, and he said, "You heard. I'm not having people like you in my school." I showed him my arm and asked him what the fuck he was talking about, said that I'd been attacked by one of his pupils, that wee cunt Watson. Mulholland said, "Yes, George Ramsay warned me you might say something like that to deflect attention from yourself." Then he picked up a folder on his desk and waved it in ma face. "In here," he rants on, "Ah've got statements from three female pupils, one aged fourteen, two aged fifteen, all saying the same thing, that they were in the girls' toilet when you came bursting in, carrying a bucket, even though you'd seen them enter and knew they were in there, and even though cleaning's not one of your duties. They're good girls; Miss Favor, the guidance teacher, vouches for every one of them." Then he said that one of them was bare from the waist up; she'd taken her bra off tae adjust it because it was uncomfortable, and he said that I'd just stood and leered at her even though the lassies were screaming at me tae get out, and then I'd reached out and squeezed her tit. Ah held my arm up again, and Ah said, "What about this then?" And he said that I'd cut it when it went through the window. Ah said, "What fucking window?" and he said the window in the toilet . . . there is one; it's obscured glass, ken . . . that one of the kids had pushed me, I'd slipped and my arm had gone through it. He even showed me my overall. It was on the floor beside him, all bloody and it had bits of glass in it. Ah said tae him, "That's bollocks, Ramsay knows that's bollocks; Ah told him it was wee Watson cut me when I caught him selling drugs." Mulholland said that was nonsense, that Ramsay had told him Watson was with him when the thing had happened, and that the girls had come screaming to him. Then he said, "As for this preposterous . . ." that was the word he used, ". . . drugs allegation, if you repeat it, I'll change my mind and call the police." Then he said that the only reason he wasn't calling the paedo squad was because the school needed more bad publicity like a hole in the head, and because the girls were embarrassed. He told me to get out of his sight, and not to expect any pay.'

Bracewell slumped back into his chair, exhausted, just as I realised that I should have been taking notes in the lousy shorthand that I'd picked up over the previous few months. I whistled. 'So this guy Ramsay, he's covered up for the kid Watson?'

'Bastard,' said Jim McCracken. 'Yes.'

'What are you going to do about it?' I asked him.

'We're doing it, talking to you. Hughie's sure that if he does go to the police, even to a pal, Mulholland will lay a complaint against him. By now you won't find a single fleck of smack in that school, the place breaks up tomorrow for the holidays, and even if they were all there, no court will ever grant a warrant to drug test a school full of kids on the word of a man charged with sexual assault. He's fucked, Iceland.'

'What about you?'

'I'm a serving police officer. The minute Hughie told me this story I should either have reported it to my bosses, or I should have arrested him. I didn't do either, and now it's too late, I can't. That's why my name can't ever come out in connection with this.'

'But if I report this, if the *Saltire* runs this, you're both screwed anyway, and so will the paper be, for Ramsay will sue us for defamation. Christ, he won't have any choice. My first day in the job and I land us in the Court of Session.'

The former PC Bracewell nodded. 'I can see that, son.' He paused. 'Could you go to your stepfather?'

'What? And compromise his career too? No, there's only one thing I can do.'

'What's that?' McCracken retorted.

'My job, Jim, my job. You've given me a story, Hugh, but you're only one source. I need more, so I have to investigate. This man George Ramsay; I need his address.'

'Christ, you're not going to knock on his door, are you?' He looked at me and grinned. 'Mind you, you'd scare the shite out of him if you did.'

'Of course not, he's minding young Watson's operation, but I can't believe that the kid's paying him to do it. The boy Ryan's dealing, so he has a supplier; I have to find out who that is, and link him to Ramsay. Once I've done that . . .' I frowned. 'Guys, what's Ryan likely to do? Will he think himself lucky and stop?'

'He has to anyway, for the holidays, but after that no chance,' Jim replied, vehemently. 'What he's doing, he's building a market for the future. They won't be selling huge amounts to the schoolies, just a taste, and they might be smoking it rather than injecting, but enough to give them a habit that'll make them big-time customers when they're older. He'll stop for a bit, till he's sure he's got away with it, and then he'll start up again.'

'Okay,' I told him. 'Get me Ramsay's address and I'll take it from there. Don't call me at the paper, though; safer still, you give me your home number and I'll call you.' I looked at Bracewell. 'Hughie, if this works out at some point, you might have to be a witness.'

'That won't be a problem, as long as I'm not in the dock. There's people selling heroin tae kids and they need stoppin'. Good luck, son; but watch yourself.'

He gave me a description of Ramsay, and told me everything he knew about the man. We left him possibly even more nervous than he'd been when we arrived. I made Jim drive me back to the West End rather than straight home. I figured it was best if nobody at all saw us together. Naturally, Grace, Scott and Bobby were all over me when I got home, asking me about my mystery trip. I told them that was how it would stay, and I didn't say it in a way that invited any argument. Then

I sat down at the piano and started to play Elvis Costello's song 'Alison'; I could rely on that to stop any discussion that I didn't want to continue. That night Scott sang the lyric, really leaning on the punchline, 'My aim is true', with an arm round my shoulder, and Grace's as well. I guessed he'd had a couple while I was out.

The next morning I had a choice to make. Did I let Doug McGrane in on the story? He was a skilled, experienced reporter and I was a novice, and I was only supposed to be tailing him when I'd picked it up. Then I thought of what Jim had said about him, and took a big decision; if he didn't trust him enough to have asked for his help, then neither could I.

So I took it to John Fisher, first thing next morning, in the editor's ever-available office. He listened, without a word, to what I had to tell him . . . I didn't mention either Jim or Hugh by name . . . until I was finished. Then he looked up at me. 'Are you saying to me that you want to investigate this thing on your own?' he asked. 'After one day in the job?'

'No,' I replied. 'Unless you want to work on it with me, personally, I'm insisting on it.'

His eyes narrowed. 'Do you have any idea of the meaning of the phrase, "pushing your fucking luck", Xavi?'

I stood my ground. 'I've got sources to protect. They came to me alone.'

He nodded. 'Point taken. Do you think you're up to it?'

'If I feel I'm in over my head, I'll come to you, I promise.'

'Okay, what do you need?'

'I need a car, and I need a good photographer, who can be trusted.'

'Mmm. Car's no problem, but the other? The Black Swan Three are ruled out, on both counts.' He scratched his head. 'Tell you what,' he murmured, 'you leave that with me. I'll need to do some negotiating.'

It didn't take long. Half an hour later, while Doug McGrane was on a coffee break, he called me over to his desk. 'Sorted,' he said. 'I've had a word with the printers' union man. He's a reasonable guy who can see the future, so he cooperated. That young compositor I told you about yesterday, Ricky Thomas; he's been seconded to me on a freelance photographic assignment.'

'Is he good enough?'

'He's what you've got, Xavi, and he'll do what you ask him to do . . . not what you tell him, mind. A point to remember, lad. Asking usually works better than telling, especially with photographers.'

'What about the staff guys? Won't they object?'

'They're not going to know. Ricky's been told it's a highly confidential project. And if they did find out . . . let's just say they'd be ill-advised to cross me. I control their work schedule; if I chose I could send them across to Denny to spend all day and night looking for the UFOs they claim to see out there. Those boys would die if they were separated from their pubs.' He smiled at the thought, then turned serious again. 'What's your plan?'

'I'm going to follow this man Ramsay. I want to find out where he goes off duty, who he sees, where he sees them, how frequently, et cetera. If he has any contact with the kid Watson outside school I want to know that as well. All of it will be photographed; I plan to build an album of the guy's life.'

'You're not going to do an Eamonn Andrews are you: step out with the red book and say "So-and-so Ramsay, This Is Your Life!"?'

'Hell no.'

'So what are you going to do?'

'I'll know that when I get there, but you're the boss. The paper's paying for this; once I get the information, it'll be you who decides what happens to it.'

John grinned. 'That was the right answer to my next question. When do you start?'

'I'm expecting some information from my source tonight; when I have it, I'll be ready to go.'

'Fine. But don't come back to the office till it's done; if you're seen to be operating on your own already, even this lot will ask questions. I'll tell them I've sent you on an induction course. None of them will have a fucking clue what that is, but they won't want to admit it by asking. It'll be the same with Ricky; we'll come up with a cover story for his absence. Car,' he said brusquely. 'We have a couple of staff vehicles. You know that, of course; you and Dougie used one yesterday. But they have drivers, so they're out. So use a hire car. We've got an account with Avis; I'll tell the local office that you're okay to use it. But you should change the vehicle every two or three days, to cut down the chances of you being spotted. This operation involves drugs. Those people are watched by the polis all the time, so they're used to being on the lookout. They are also bloody ruthless, so watch yourself . . . and do not go near that wee boy Watson. Fourteen or not, he's a proven psycho, and I don't want you getting hurt.'

'I won't get hurt, John. And I'll keep Ricky safe too.'

There's something I should explain here. I knew some of it even then, at twenty, but not all. I have never regarded myself as a hard man, not even as an adolescent, when lads often start flexing their fledgling muscles. I've said already that I've only ever hit one bloke in my life, and that was football, so in a way it doesn't count. Neither does pushing Lex McCuish. If I'd been standing rather than recumbent he'd never have invaded my personal space in the way he did. I have never acted tough, and I have never been tough, but I know that there is something about me that says, 'Don't.'

I am very large, and I exercise, even more now that I'm in middle age, but I've known plenty of big men who have found that bulk can make you a magnet for trouble. The bar bouncers who have least bother tend to be the smaller ones, people like, well, the Colquhouns, father and son, because you know that if they're doing that job and they're that size, it's best not to mess with them, but when they're six three or six four, every noisy drunk seems to want to make a name for himself. Not with me, though; I've seen people look at me and I've read their eyes as they thought about it, then seen them lose whatever notion they might have had. I didn't know why, not then, but I did realise, even at twenty, that there was something forbidding about me, and that it showed in a way I didn't understand, and couldn't suppress. Today I know for sure from whom it came, for I've been told.

John had arranged for Ricky and me to meet 'accidentally', at lunchtime in the Ensign Ewart pub, near Edinburgh Castle, chosen because none of our colleagues drank there. He was a nice guy, twenty-six years old, naturally intrigued by his unexpected assignment, but full of enthusiasm, seeing it as a big step to the career change that he wanted. I didn't tell him the whole story at that first meeting, only that it involved watching an individual, and photographing him, discreetly and from no closer than was necessary for him and anyone he met to be recognisable.

'How will we know him? Have you seen him?' Reasonable questions.

'No, I haven't, but the description I have is that he's five foot nine, slim built. He's bald on top, the hair he has is black and he wears a beard to match. Age around forty.'

Ricky chuckled. 'So we're fine as long as he doesn't shave or wear a hat, and he's not on holiday.'

'He won't be. That much I do know.' Hugh Bracewell had been able to tell me that Ramsay was due to spend the whole of July carrying out minor maintenance jobs around the school and supervising the painting and the renovation of the staffrooms, once the Edinburgh Trades Fortnight was over. His own break was booked in for the first fortnight in August. 'He won't be hard to spot anyway. He's a school janitor, and as of tomorrow, he'll be the only person there for a while.'

'That's a start. One thing we need to get sorted though, Xavi,' the new boy photographer continued. 'Where do we work from? We can't go to the office, Fisher says, but we need a base.'

He was right, but I hadn't even begun to consider that. The one thing I knew immediately was that my flat wouldn't do. Grace and the guys would want to know why Ricky was there, and I wouldn't be able to tell them. 'Mind your own business' wouldn't cut it either; they lived there, and that made his presence their business.

But the problem vanished as he continued. 'It would suit me best if we based ourselves at my place. I guess a lot of this is going to be evening work, yes?'

I nodded. 'Yes, no time sheets on this job.'

'I didn't think so, and that's okay with me. Thing is, I've got a darkroom in my house, and my wife works for Standard Life, so she's out all day. If we used that, I could process the stuff I've shot the night before, and you can do . . . whatever you've got to do.'

'Deal.'

We went back to work, to our respective departments, having agreed that I would call Ricky at home later, to sort out the first day's agenda. I spent the afternoon touring more police stations with Doug McGrane. It occurred to me that a crime correspondent must do a little more than that; nice enough guy he may have been, but I suspected that he had spent so long being secretive that he couldn't behave any other way. I'm not going to criticise him for it; I may have become worse than he was.

Jim McCracken phoned me at six thirty with George Ramsay's home address, a flat in a block in a street I'd never heard of. He sighed as he spoke.

'So?' I said. I'd taken the call in the bedroom, for privacy.

'What are you going to be driving?'

'Avis hire car.'

'Christ, no, not there. You'll have the wheels stolen from under you while you're parked. Worse, they'll take you for the DHSS and set it on fire with you in it.'

He may have been exaggerating, but I took his point. I called John Fisher, on the home number he'd given me, and told him about the glitch. He came up with a solution in ten seconds. I liked him even more. 'Take mine,' he said. 'It's a mound of rust held together by paint, I need to replace it, and anyone who trashes it will be doing me a favour. I'll drop by your place just before eight thirty tomorrow morning; you can drive me to the office and go on from there.'

When he arrived next morning, I saw that he had been talking it down a little, but not too much. It was an Austin Allegro, navy blue, one of the cars that played its part in wiping British mass market manufacturers from the face of the earth. The engine sounded like a bag of hammers, and the gear change required quite a bit of guesswork, but my head didn't bump against the roof, and that was all I cared about.

Ricky Thomas's house was in an area called Forrester Park, to the west of the city. It was a small mid-terrace; he and his wife weren't ready to start a family, and so the second bedroom was available to serve as his darkroom. He let me take a look inside; I didn't know a lot about photo processing, but he seemed to, if the amount of equipment jammed in there was an indicator.

Once we were on the road, I told him where we were going. His brow knitted into a frown, so hard that it pulled his ears back. 'Maxwell Academy?' he exclaimed. 'The Insane Asylum?'

'You've heard of it?'

He threw me a sidelong look. 'Who hasn't? You must have led a sheltered life, mate.'

I had a city street-finder map, but I didn't need it; Ricky was able to direct me straight there. The school stood in the heart of a post-war estate that was as dark and depressing as Hugh Bracewell's was bright and upwardly mobile. I couldn't imagine that Mrs Thatcher had sold, or would sell, too many houses there. Maxwell Academy was a series of buildings that seemed to have been constructed without the services of an architect, a three-storey system-built monstrosity made up of two great rectangular blocks with a one-floor, flat-roofed services unit between them, but set back a little. As I looked at it, I saw that one of the windows on the right was boarded up. I couldn't see what was written on the green door beside it, but I was pretty sure it was 'Girls'. There were plenty of cars in the street where the entrance stood, and none of them was less than five years old. Jim McCracken had been right; an Avis car might as well have had a target painted on the roof. Within the school perimeter itself, I could see only two vehicles. One didn't really merit the description, as it was a blackened, burned-out shell, but neither did the other in a way; it was a green Hillman Imp.

'Do you think that's his?' Ricky asked.

I stared at him. 'I don't see the teaching staff volunteering to come in here on their holidays, do you?'

We sat there for around twenty minutes, looking at ugly concrete and nothing else; then just as Ricky yawned, the first of many to come, a man in blue overall work clothes walked out of one block, carrying a toolbox, and crossed the quadrangle. He looked to his right as he walked, in our direction but not at us. George Ramsay, beyond a doubt, from Hughie's description. My photographer was able to snatch a couple of quick shots through a long lens, before he disappeared into the second building. We were in business.

I checked my watch; eleven fifteen. I decided to take a chance. The health facility was twenty yards further along, on our right, its functional ugliness mirroring that of the school. I started John's pile of rust and drove into its car park, picking a spot from which Ricky could keep the school in view. 'I'll be back,' I told him, then stepped out and into the building.

I was dressed for the occasion, jeans and a Sex Pistols T-shirt . . . mostly I had to take what I could find in XXX size . . . and I hadn't bothered to shave. The receptionist looked up at me. 'Yes, officer,' she began. 'You're new around here.'

I almost corrected her mistake, until I saw that it could work for me. 'A couple of weeks ago,' I began, 'one of your doctors treated a janitor from the school. I'd like to speak to him, please.'

Her interest level rose. 'Oh yes,' she exclaimed, 'that poor man. It was Dr Cairns that saw him; him and the practice nurse. I'll see if he's free.' She left her post, went through a door behind her, then reappeared half a minute later from another. 'Along here,' she called.

The consulting room into which I stepped was in contrast to the rest of the place. Several art prints hung on the walls. I glanced at them as I entered, and recognised a Picasso and a Miro, the latter because it was on the cover of a Dave Brubeck LP in my collection. Their owner caught my look. 'I try,' he said, wearily. For his part, Dr Cairns looked as if he might have been painted by Dali, he was a small man with sharp eyes, black hair and a strange thin moustache that dropped at the end. 'You took your time getting here,' he continued as he offered me a seat. 'No disrespect, but are you the most senior man they had available?'

I couldn't go along with the mistake beyond that point, or I'd have been impersonating a cop, never a good idea, so instead I showed him my NUJ card. 'The police won't be along,' I told him as he studied it. 'The injury to Mr Bracewell was never reported.'

For a second I thought Dr Cairns was going to explode, but he subsided. 'I shouldn't be surprised, I suppose, at anything that happens in that place. Did you notice the burned-out car in the grounds? It's been there for three months.'

'You saw Mr Bracewell,' I went on.

'Mr Ahzlado,' he mispronounced, 'I saw the inside of Mr Bracewell. He was opened up good and proper, almost bone deep at one point. I'd have called an ambulance, but he could have wound up waiting for a couple of hours at the Royal and I decided that he needed treatment there and then, so we attended to it. He's all right, is he?'

'He's fine; you did a good job on him. Doctor,' I asked, notebook in hand, 'would you say that there was any chance that his injury was caused by him putting his arm through a window?'

The sharp eyes almost popped out on to his cheeks. He laughed. 'Is that what's being claimed? If so, it's preposterous. If it had happened, there would have been glass residue in the wound, and it would have been jagged. There was none at all, the only residue were fibres from clothing, and it was absolutely straight. It was caused by a bladed instrument, unquestionably, and very sharp, a surgical scalpel possibly.'

'Did Hughie . . . Mr Bracewell . . . tell you what had happened?'

The doctor shook his head. 'Not really. He said that he'd been cut, but I could see that. He did mutter something about a wee cunt but I didn't pursue that, with Sister Faulds present.' He fixed the gimlet eyes on me. 'Where are you going with this, Mr Ahzlado?'

'To its conclusion,' was the only reply I could come up with.

'I had assumed that the matter had been reported to the police. Now that I know it hasn't . . . I really ought to. Is there any reason why I shouldn't?'

'Yes,' I replied, 'but I can't tell you what it is. All I can say is that it wouldn't help Mr Bracewell, more likely the opposite. In time, I'll be reporting it to the police myself, and to the readers of my paper.'

'And which one is that?'

'The *Saltire*.'

He sighed, loudly. 'I was hoping you'd say *Daily Record*, or even the *Evening News*. As many people as possible need to know about that place.'

'They will,' I promised. 'Trust me.'

Dr Cairns raised his eyebrows. 'That's a big thing for a journalist to be asking,' he said. 'But I will.'

When I stepped out of the centre, Ricky was looking in my direction, slightly anxiously, I thought. He beckoned to me; I rejoined him as quickly as I could. 'Where you been?' he asked.

'Seeing the doctor. Why?'

'A bloke went in; to the school.'

'Yes? Did you get a shot of him?'

'Only the back. Camouflage trousers and a Hearts top. He walked in the gate, about five minutes ago, then straight into the building on the right, the one Ramsay went into.'

'Let's hope there isn't a back gate. I'd better move, though. If we stay here he'll be looking straight at us when he comes out. Which side did he come from?'

'From the right.'

I pulled out of the centre car park into the street and eased into a space just along the road, to the left. As I stopped, Ricky rolled out of the passenger seat and into the back, to give himself a clear shot of the building. 'This guy,' I asked him. 'Could he be a workman?'

'If he is he was carrying his tools in a Safeway bag.'

As he answered, I was looking at the school, at the door Ramsay had used earlier, when it swung open, and the man in the football shirt, tall, lanky, skinhead, stepped out, followed by the janitor. Ricky focused on them and fired off several quick shots, manually rather than using his motor drive. As I looked over his shoulder, I saw Ramsay pat the man on the back, then retreat into the school. The photographer kept taking pictures through the rear window, until the visitor stepped out into the street and headed away from us. 'He must have left his tools behind,' I pointed out. 'The Safeway bag's gone.'

'Wonder who he was,' Ricky mused.

'Let's find out.' I started the car, did a leisurely three-point then cruised after him, fingers mentally crossed that Ramsay wasn't looking out of the window, spotting what I'd done. As we watched him, Jambo, as I christened him, swung right at the end of our street. I eased my pace, made the same turn, noting the name 'Vanburgh Drive' on a sign then stopped, keeping him in our vision. A hundred yards ahead, he crossed the road and walked up a path that led to a mid-terraced house, with a grey roughcast exterior, similar in design to Ricky's but vastly different in appearance. I drove on, checked the number, thirty-three, then made our way quietly back to the school.

If we'd been a minute later we'd have blown the whole operation. We had only been back in position for a few seconds when Ramsay came out of the school building. His overalls had been left behind him; instead he was wearing denim, from head to foot, jeans of an unidentified make, and a Wrangler jacket that to my eye seemed slightly bulkier than it should have.

'Where's the bag?' my companion asked.

'More important, what was in it?'

The janitor headed in the opposite direction to Jambo, towards another T junction, a couple of hundred yards further away. I let him reach it before I started and moved out, then caught up after he turned left. We kept him in sight through two more turns until he reached

Blackheath Street, the main road that was the de facto boundary of the scheme in which Maxwell Academy stood. My assumption had been that he was going home for lunch, but he walked past his own address and kept going, into Blackheath Street, past the post office, past a pub, past a bookmaker's, past another pub, past a newsagent's, then pausing beneath a sign that read 'The Bluebell Café', peering through the window, then stepping inside.

I swore quietly. There was a pedestrian crossing five yards past the café, with no parking zones on either side. Ricky read the situation too. 'Go in there,' he said, pointing to the entrance to a big DIY warehouse that was set back off the street, with a car park in front. I did as he asked, finding a space with a view across the road, but not good enough to let us see into the Bluebell. 'I'm going to chance it,' Ricky decided. 'You stay in the car though. You'd be as invisible as the Forth Bridge.'

I couldn't, and didn't, argue with that, so I was forced to sit and watch him as he walked across to the line of saplings that was set just inside the perimeter fence of the warehouse, looking for a suitable vantage point, taking up position when he found one, at least partially hidden from view. He was there for only a few minutes, certainly less than five, before he stepped back, and returned to the car. Before he had reached it, Ramsay stepped out of the café, and headed back in the direction from which he had come.

'Not there for a coffee and a bacon roll then,' I murmured, as the photographer rejoined me.

'Indeed not. He never bought a thing. I had a good view, though. There are tables in there; he was sat at one of them, with three kids, all girls. They all had drinks in front of them, but he had nothing.'

'Ages?'

'Mid-teens. Hair piled up, make-up, one of them with big bangle earrings; jailbait, I'd say.'

'Three of them?'

'Yup. Now to the interesting bit. I'd only just got focused on them when he went into his jacket and took out three envelopes, business letter size. He passed one to each girl, across the table. Two of them put them away, quick, but the third opened hers. She looked in, took something out, a wee package, just a couple of inches across, then put it back. Ramsay said something to them after that; whatever it was they all got very serious, and nodded. Then he left.'

'How about pictures?' I asked him.

He smiled. 'That's what I'm here for. What do we do next?'

I pondered that, posing the same question to myself about Ramsay. I checked my watch again; ten past twelve. Chances were that he would head home for lunch, for real, then go back to work. We could either sit and watch nothing, or . . . 'Let's go back to your place, and process your pics, to see how good a photographer you are.'

'The best, scribbler, the best. Let's do it.'

I was on the point of starting the engine when I took another glance across the road. As I looked, a boy walked up to the Bluebell . . . no, 'walked' doesn't describe it properly; this kid swaggered in a way that only a certain type of kid does. In Glasgow they christened them 'neds'. Today he'd be wearing a hoodie; then, he wore yet another ubiquitous Hearts top, long-sleeved on a hot day. He wasn't a big lad, and he never would be, but he was full of himself, even at fourteen, or maybe fifteen at the most. I had a feeling about him.

'I'll go and get the lunch,' I said.

'Those girls are still in there,' Ricky pointed out.

'So? I'm not going to interview them. I'm going to buy some corned beef rolls.'

He shrugged. 'You're the boss. Make mine cheese and tomato.'

I left the car park, and used the road crossing, waiting for the green man, then walked straight into the café. I didn't even glance to my left, but I was aware that the girls were still there, and that they had been joined by someone else, someone wearing maroon.

'What rolls have you got?' I asked the girl behind the counter. 'Corned beef? Cheese and tomato?'

She nodded. 'Pickle wi' the corned beef?'

'Perfect. Two of each; no, three of the corned beef.'

I was paying for them when a young voice called out from behind me. 'Hey!' I looked in the mirror behind the counter, which I had been deliberately avoiding, and saw Junior Jambo gazing at my back from his table. I looked over my shoulder, but otherwise ignored him.

'Hey,' he repeated. 'Big man!'

I took my change, turned and looked down at him. 'Yes?' I said, quietly. I saw a small attitude adjustment take place, even if the three girls missed it.

'Are you big Iceland, that used tae play for the Jam Tarts?'

'That's what they called me,' I confirmed.

'Gie's yer autograph.'

I frowned at him. 'Say that again?'

'Can I have your autograph, please?'

'Certainly.' The kid stood and offered me a menu card. I had a pen in my back pocket.

'Who's it for? You?'

'Aye. Make it to Ryan, Ryan Watson.'

'Sure.' I leaned on the table and wrote, *'For Ryan Watson, a true Hearts man, Big Iceland, aka Xavi Aislado'*, then handed it to him.

He studied it, then looked up. 'Cheers mate. What does "aka" mean?'

'Almost known as,' I told him, picked up my rolls and left.

'Christ,' Ricky exclaimed when I slid into the Allegro, 'you took your time. I was nearly coming to get you.'

'Everything freshly made. She'd to open a new packet of Stork.'

'What did you get?'

'Three things. Our lunch, a new friend, and the makings of a case of conspiracy to pervert the course of justice. Let's go. I'm hungry, plus I want to see what you've got on that film.'

What he had was a string of images, some unusable, some okay, and some excellent. Those of most interest to me were a rear-view shot of Jambo arriving with his Safeway bag, a full face shot of him and Ramsay with the school in the background and no bag to be seen, and several good, identifiable prints of the janitor with the three girls, in two of which he was placing envelopes on the table. A third showed one of the trio holding a small flat packet, with an open envelope lying in front of her, with a few items protruding that on greater enlargement proved to be banknotes.

'What's all this about, Xavi?' Ricky asked, as I inspected them all on his dining-room table. He still didn't know the full story, but it was time for him to find out.

'Let's go see someone, then I'll know for sure.' The photographs were barely dry, so Ricky put each in a separate folder, then we headed out to the car. I drove us straight to Granton, to Hughie Bracewell's house, taking the chance that he'd be in.

He was, and at first alarmed when he saw Ricky, until I explained who he was. 'I need you to look at some pictures,' I said. He took us into the kitchen, where he poured us tea from a pot he'd just made, then sat down with us at the table. I began with Ramsay.

'That's him,' he confirmed. 'Bastard.'

I moved on to the shot of the janitor with Jambo. 'Do you know the other guy?'

He studied it at length, but shook his head. 'Never seen him in my life before.'

'Sure?'

'Son, I was a polis for thirty years. Ah would know if Ah had.'

'Sorry.' I found the best image of Ramsay with the three girls and slid it in front of him.

His eyes widened as he saw it, then a low growl sounded in his throat. 'Those three! Those three wee slags! They were in the toilets wi' wee Watson when I caught him.'

'Swear to it? On oath?'

'All day, Xavi, all fucking day.'

'That's great, because they're still in touch with Ryan. I saw them all together at that same table after Ramsay had gone. The little shite even asked for my autograph. I gave it to him on a café menu, so he can't deny having been there, even if we haven't got him on film.'

'So this other cunt: who's he?'

'I don't know yet but he gave Ramsay the money, and maybe a bit of something else, to pay the kids for setting you up. Do you know if Jim's at work?' I continued.

'Aye, he's on days.'

'Then give him a call. I daren't, but the switchboard will put you through without asking questions.'

We went to the phone in the hall. I stood beside Hughie until Jim came on line. 'Xavi needs to speak to you,' he grunted, then passed the receiver.

'Jim,' I said. 'A quick one; I need to know who lives at number thirty-three, Vanburgh Drive.' I spelled the name for him. 'Male occupants will be enough.'

'Council house?'

'For sure. Nobody would buy that place.'

'No problem. You stay there till I call back.' We did. It took less than ten minutes, but long enough for me to tell Hughie about my conversation with Dr Cairns, and for Ricky to come to understand the whole story. When the phone did ring, I picked it up. 'Only one male occupant,' Jim told me. 'His name's Gavin Spreckley. Couple of convictions for breach of the peace, and one for assault that got him sixty days. A few other arrests, no proceedings taken.'

'Cheers.'

'How's it going?' he asked.

'Very quickly. Next thing we do will be to take a look at Mr Spreckley, then we've got a nice pretty picture.'

'You could run this now, Xavi,' Ricky murmured as we walked down Hugh's path, back to the car.

'That's John Fisher's decision,' I told him, 'but I want to give him more. If Spreckley's paying off kids to cover up for Watson, and paying

Ramsay too, I guess, then it stands to reason Spreckley's the supplier, but where does he go? Who's above him? If we can find that out, we've got an exclusive that'll wipe the floor with every other paper in Scotland.'

We had the janitor by the balls already, so I decided that we would leave him and concentrate on Jambo. We weren't going to be ringing his doorbell, though. More hours of stake-out loomed. I headed back to Vanburgh Drive, stopping off en route at my place to change, and to leave a note for Grace saying that I'd be working late. The cars in Spreckley's street were even cruder than those outside the school, but the Allegro still blended in. By that time it was late afternoon, and there were few people about. I was glad about that; with houses on both sides, I felt hemmed in, and sure we were going to be rumbled sooner rather than later.

I'd decided that we were going to stay there for no longer than an hour at a time, move on and then find a new spot. We didn't need to do that, though. Half an hour later, Spreckley's front door opened and he stepped out, still wearing that Hearts replica shirt. If he'd walked down the street, he'd have gone straight past us, and that could have been trouble, two guys sitting in a car in jungle land doing fuck all. But instead, he took a quick and slightly furtive look left then right, opened the door of an old bottle-shaped Ford Escort and eased himself inside.

Ricky slid out of sight as he drove past. That option wasn't open to me, so I concentrated on my copy of the *Saltire*, and glanced at my watch as he drove past, in the hope that if he did notice me he would think I was waiting to pick someone up. When he was behind us I watched him in my rear-view, and saw him turn left to go past the school. As soon as he was out of sight I did a quick three-point turn, scaring the life out of a telephone repair man when I came close to clipping the ladder away from the pole on which he was working.

Gavin Spreckley was a lousy driver. He hugged the middle of the road and went so slowly that I feared we might get too close, but it worked to my advantage when we were stopped by a red light after he had gone through. I caught up without difficulty. He led us towards the centre of the city; indeed I thought we were going all the way there, until he took a right turn halfway along Nicholson Street. I was a few cars behind, but he was still in sight when I followed suit, parking a hundred yards ahead. I closed half the distance then eased into a space myself, just as he emerged from the Escort, and after another furtive look, crossed the street and opened the door of a shop opposite; only it wasn't a shop, more of an office, with a sign above that read 'Sherlock Private Hire'.

'He's a taxi driver,' Ricky exclaimed. 'He's going to pick up a car. We'll be chasing him all over fucking Edinburgh at this rate.'

I probably would have, but for the tap on the window. It took me by surprise, as I hadn't seen anyone approach. I looked around, at the figure who was kneeling beside the car, and into the eyes of Tommy Partridge. He mimed, 'Wind down the window,' but I was already doing it.

'Xavi,' he said, quietly. 'I don't know what the hell you're doing here, but get on your way, now. Go home and wait, for as long as it takes for me to get there.'

'I'm on a job, Tommy,' I told him. 'I started full-time with the *Saltire* on Monday.'

'I don't care if you started with the fucking *Times*. I'm on a job too and you're getting in the way of it. Now do what I told you, wait for me, and do not speak to anyone about this, especially not to the owner of this tank you're driving.'

There was no scope for further discussion. I restarted the car and drove off. 'Who was that?' my photographer asked once we were well out of sight.

'My stepfather. Name of Partridge; Detective Inspector Partridge.'

'Oh shit.'

'Not necessarily. Let's wait and see what he's got to say.'

'Probably "You're under arrest", or something along those lines.'

'Have faith, man, have faith.'

It was gone six thirty by the time we got to my place, and gone nine by the time Tommy buzzed from downstairs. I'd fed Ricky, and everyone else by then. I described him as a work colleague and left it at that. As I let Tommy in I told everyone else to make themselves scarce, even Grace, who was intrigued but starting to get just a little impatient with my secrecy. She huffed off into our room, while Scott and Bobby took the chance to head for Mather's. Even so I took my stepfather into the kitchen, just to be sure we weren't overheard. 'Okay,' he said as soon as the door closed, 'why were you following Spreckley?'

I wasn't being interrogated in my own kitchen, not even by him. 'Who's Spreckley?' I replied.

'The guy you tailed all the way from Vanburgh Drive, in a car registered to Mr John Fisher, chief reporter of your newspaper. The guy up the telephone pole was one of ours. I'm not at Torphichen any more; I'm drugs squad, out of headquarters. What's up here, Xavi?'

'You share, I share,' I told him. 'I'll rephrase my question. What's Spreckley?'

He shrugged his shoulders. 'Off the record?'

'For now.'

'Okay. He's a minor league drug dealer. He connects up to a very big player called Perry Holmes, a man with interests all over the city and well beyond, some legal, some very criminal indeed. We've got a continuing operation against him, and Spreckley's one of the surveillance targets. We think he uses the hire firm to make drops, but we can't nail that one. Now it's my turn. Why did a PC called Jim McCracken pull his name from the council housing department this afternoon, and his sheet from the records office? And a supplementary. Why is McCracken refusing to tell us himself?'

'Spreckley's involved in something we're investigating. It's a story that involves the supply of hard drugs to kids within Maxwell Academy. We believe that he's the supplier, through a nasty little bastard called Ryan Watson.'

'What's that name?' asked Tommy sharply. I repeated it. 'You sure?'

'He gave me it himself, this afternoon, when he asked for my autograph.'

Finally, he sat in the chair I'd offered him. 'Ryan Watson is Spreckley's sister's son. He's spent half his life sitting in children's hearings. Are you telling me that Spreckley has got his nephew selling smack to children at his school?'

I nodded. 'Girls, Tommy, not ten years older than yours.' I could see that he was shaken. I bounced his question back at him. 'Off the record? And no comeback on Jim McCracken? He's a good guy, I promise you.'

He nodded. 'I know Jim. I know he's straight. Let's have it, then.'

I took him through the whole story, from start to finish, showing him Ricky's photographic evidence as I went along.

'They set Hughie Bracewell up as a beast?' he exclaimed, when I was finished.

'Stitched him up as tight as the doctor did. Ramsay and the three girls we saw him pay off.'

'Then this overrides everything. To be frank, and very off the record, we'll never pin Holmes down, but I'm having this bastard Ramsay, for sure, and Spreckley too.' He looked at me. 'Boys, I need you to back off from this and let me take it on.'

'Two conditions.'

'It's not conditional, Xavi.'

'Two requests then. One, I want to interview the headmaster, Mulholland, before you do, and I want to run the story, as an exclusive, at the same time as you pick up Ramsay, Spreckley and wee Watson, before they're charged and it all goes sub judice. How about it?'

He smiled. 'You've got that. The Crown Office will hate it, but as long as you run it before they're in court, they'll be stuck with it. Now I've got a condition.'

'Shoot.'

'In your story, you write up Hughie Bracewell as a hero.'

'That's already done. But not a word about Jim McCracken, outside this room, okay?'

'Sure. I want to keep him out of the papers. I'm going to get him a job on my team after this.' He picked up Ricky's folders. 'Can I take these?'

'Of course,' the photographer told him. 'You can have more if you like.'

And that's how it played out . . . eventually.

I took Ricky home, and told him to do nothing till he heard from me. Then I went home where I had to placate Grace. 'When have we ever had secrets, Xavi?' she complained when I refused to tell her what was going on. We were in bed, her back was to me, and she wasn't on her period, a flag signal that read, 'You are in the shit, boy.'

'These aren't secrets, *chica*. You'll get to know everything when the time's right. It's the job I've signed up to do, and you'll make it easier for me if you don't push me about the few things that I might have to keep to myself.'

'But I'm your . . .'

She was going to say 'wife', I'm sure, so I said it for her. 'Yes, you are, even if we haven't made it official yet. And there might be times when I feel I have to protect you. Look, this thing I'm doing, I didn't go looking for it, it came to me, but I can't walk away. It involves some rough people; I don't want to bring even the thought of them in here.' I slid an arm around her waist and she didn't pull away; a positive development.

'Is it dangerous?' she whispered.

'Not for me,' I said, and I believed it, so young and innocent was I.

'Who was that man? The one you didn't want us to meet.'

'He's a cop. What Ricky and I were doing bumped into something he was doing. But we're together on it now.' She turned to face me, and I could have left it there, but after what I'd said about secrets, I felt that I couldn't. 'There's something else about him. He's my stepfather, Tommy. He's my mother's second husband.'

Her eyes lost their pre-coital mist and widened. 'That's him? Does that mean you're still . . .'

'Seeing her? No, she's dead to me and she always will be. But Tommy, he's a nice guy, he likes me and he seems to love her. He's on some sort of a guilt trip about our relationship. Thinks he should be able to fix it, but he can't. It doesn't mean I have to blank him, though.'

'Can I meet him?'

'There's no reason why you shouldn't, love, but I'm not going to invite him for tea.'

'No, but if he comes back here . . .'

'Sure, promise.'

She kissed me, and it was okay again. 'Xavi,' she whispered, 'we're never going to be a normal family, are we?' I couldn't tell whether she was smiling or not.

I called John Fisher next morning, after everyone had left, and briefed him on our rapid-fire day.

'Are you okay with it still?' he asked.

'I'm fine; so's Ricky.'

'Do you trust this detective?' I hadn't named Tommy, far less tell John of our relationship.

'Completely. He'll come through. I didn't have any choice but to cooperate with him, John.'

'I know you didn't; you'd have been breaking the law otherwise. Technically we did, in not going to the police as soon as Bracewell told you his story, but with his circumstances and all . . .'

'That's working in our favour. Bracewell's a thirty-year polis. He's one of them, and we've done him a turn.'

'Hey, kid,' the chief reporter chuckled, 'you're good, right enough. Have you had my car stolen yet?'

'Sorry, John.'

'Ah, what the hell, nobody's perfect.' He paused for a few seconds. 'Okay. You stay where you are for now. You're still on that induction course anyway, aren't you? Sit tight and wait for your cop to get back to you. From what you've told me, I don't think it's going to take long.'

I wasn't so sure. I called Ricky to update him. He was keeping himself busy turning out prints from the previous day's haul. I decided to follow his example, work being the best antidote for boredom. I set up my typewriter on the kitchen table and began to write my story. It took all morning and most of the afternoon; I had to invent names for the girls, but other than that, the first draft seemed not too bad. I was pondering picking up Ricky and taking a shot of Sherlock Private Hire, which we hadn't been able to do at the time, when the phone rang. 'You free?' Tommy asked.

'Ready and waiting.'

'Then come up to my office, now. Ask for me at reception.'

Lothian and Borders Police headquarters was even closer to my flat than the Western Infirmary. I could have walked, but I took the car. In no more than five minutes I was sitting at a table across from Tommy, and another detective, a sergeant named Bruce Wallace, whose father must have been a true Scottish patriot. The DS pushed one of Ricky's prints under my nose, the one of Ramsay with the three girls. 'We've identified them,' he said, then pointed to each in turn. 'Sherry Alexander, aged fifteen. Lana McAlpine, aged fifteen. Sandra Macbeth, aged fourteen. They've each been interviewed in the presence of their parents, and a social worker. Lana and Sandra have both admitted to buying heroin from Ryan Watson. They both say that it was for older boys at the school, and that they aren't users; blood tests will show that one way or another. They also both handed over the packages that you saw Ramsay give them. They contained twenty pounds each and a small sachet of heroin that's been adulterated so much that it's nearly all paracetamol. The girls have also told us that they saw Ryan Watson cut Hugh Bracewell with a straight razor that he keeps hidden in his sleeve. The wee shite calls himself "Blade" apparently. They say that afterwards, when Hughie had gone to have his wound treated, they were cornered by Ramsay and told they'd be going to jail unless they told the story his way. He told them that there would be money in it and a wee taste.'

'What about the third girl?' I asked.

'Sherry's saying nothing. According to the other two, she's Watson's girlfriend. Her father's in jail for house-breaking, and the mother isn't cooperating, so we got a search warrant and found the same package in the kid's bedroom, along with drug paraphernalia. On the basis of that she's been medically examined. The doctor found needle tracks on her arm, and there are semen traces on her underwear that we expect will match wee Ryan's blood group, putting him in still more bother, even though he's under-age as well.'

'Where are they all now?'

Tommy replied. 'The McAlpine and Macbeth families are all in what I'll call informal police custody. We've got them all in a safe house, voluntarily, parents and five kids in total. The Alexanders, mother and daughter, have both been detained. They haven't been charged with anything yet, but they will be . . . at least the mother will, for I reckon that young Sherry's smart enough to put herself on the side of the angels. George Ramsay and Ryan Watson are still walking about in blissful ignorance, but we have to move on them fast, before wee Ryan finds out that his girlfriend's been lifted.'

'How fast?'

'This evening. They'll both be detained within the hour. But . . .' he looked me in the eye, and read my concern, 'they won't be charged formally until tomorrow morning, and they won't appear in court until ten at the earliest. You can run your story, but it has to be now. Can you?'

'Yes, but what about Mulholland?'

My stepfather smiled, 'Oh, we want him too, as far as we can nail him, but you're our only means of doing that.' He handed me a note. 'That's where he lives, and he's not on holiday yet. He's been golfing today; we've been watching him, and not making a secret of it. He's home now, and he won't be expecting you.'

'Thanks. What about Spreckley?'

'That's the one bit of bad news for us. We can't touch Spreckley, for we can't prove that he gave Ramsay the money to pay off the kids, or that it was his drugs his nephew was pushing in the school. The kid'll never shop him either, no chance.' He tapped the table. 'But you, you can touch him. You can print what you know about him, couched in whatever language you like; the Gavin Spreckleys of the world are not litigious people. He's not going to sue. And if he did, the evidence that you've got will be more than enough for a civil court, even if it doesn't allow a criminal prosecution.'

'And Perry Holmes?'

'No. Not a word about him. He really would sue, and he would win . . . that's if you were lucky. That's a nice girl you're with, and you don't want to put her in danger. That's the way Holmes works.'

That sent a chill through me, then a flash of inexplicable rage, but I tried to keep either from showing. 'Fair enough,' I said. 'I'll get on and see Mulholland. Ideally I'd like a pic of him, but I don't think he'll pose for me.'

Tommy laughed. 'Don't ask him. That photographer of yours has done a great job so far. Why stop now?'

Ricky had finished processing when I arrived at his place; he was keen for more action, particularly when the target was going to be a sitting duck. Mr Gerald Mulholland lived in a street of bungalows on the south-west side of Corstorphine Hill. The cars there were either garaged or in driveways, and John's clunker really did stand out when I parked it opposite his house, but not so close that Ricky didn't have a good angle. I walked up the head teacher's drive, rang the bell, and waited, notebook and pen at the ready, standing slightly to one side, to allow a clear view of the door, as it opened. Mulholland was a man in his early fifties, with a sallow complexion and big lugubrious eyes. They looked up at me, and didn't see any friendship in mind.

'Xavi Aislado,' I said, 'from the *Saltire*. I'd like a word with you, sir.' I spoke slowly, keeping his attention, allowing Ricky the time to do his work from across the street. 'It's about Mr Hugh Bracewell.'

The man's mouth tightened. 'He hasn't done it again, has he?'

'Done what, sir?'

'Molested young girls.'

'That's a very serious charge, sir. Mr Bracewell's a family man who's never been accused of anything like that in his life.'

'He did in my school. Damn it; I should have reported it.'

'Do you have any evidence of that, sir? Mr Bracewell's story is that he was assaulted in your school, slashed with a razor by a pupil named Ryan Watson.'

'Nonsense.'

'That's not what the doctor who treated him will say.'

'Maybe so, but three girls all reported him. He squeezed one of their breasts.'

'Would that have been Sherry Alexander's?'

Mulholland blinked. 'Yes, and the window was smashed. I saw blood all over it, and on his overall.'

'Maybe you saw blood from his overall, sir.'

'Maybe I . . .' he spluttered. 'Young man, are you saying I don't know what goes on in my own school?'

'The three girls, Sherry, Lana and Sandra. Did they come to you with their allegation, or were they brought to you by George Ramsay?'

'Neither. Miss Favor, the guidance mistress, brought me statements that they'd made, after Mr Ramsay brought them to her.'

'Mr Mulholland,' I said, 'if those three girls were sitting in my car over there,' he looked at the Allegro, giving Ricky a full-face shot, 'and I brought them over here, you wouldn't recognise a single one of them. Yet you damned a man out of fear for your own reputation. Sir, you don't have a clue about what's going on in your school. That's what my story's going to say tomorrow. You should read it. You'll learn a lot.' I turned and walked away.

I'm sure he did; he learned even more a few hours after it appeared when he was suspended from duty, pending a hearing that never took place, since he accepted an early retirement package from the Regional Council to minimise the damage.

We blew the rest off the street next day. John held back the first edition until the others were out, and it was too late for them to piggy-back us, then let it go as a three-page exclusive, by '*Saltire* reporter Xavi Aislado and staff photographer Ricky Thomas'. We invented names for the three girls and blanked out their faces, but we used everything else we had in a blazing, angry exposé of drug dealing and violence in a city school and of the attempt to ruin the life of 'Heroic ex-cop Hugh Bracewell'. Spreckley, Ramsay, Mulholland, they were all over the three pages.

The *Evening News* did its best to catch up, but Tommy sent Ramsay and Watson to court at ten sharp, and as soon as they'd been in the dock they were hamstrung in what they could report. We went national in follow-up, and I was asked to do an interview for ITN *News at Ten*, which looked slightly ludicrous on screen, since they sent a tiny woman to do the piece, which I insisted was shot with the *Saltire* office in the background, with its masthead above.

And in that follow-up, there was a degree of hell to pay, internally. It began with the invasion of the newsroom by 'The gang that can't shoot straight', all three of them, sober, if hung-over, and belligerent. I'd never seen them before, but I knew who they were without being told. They marched up to the headmaster's platform and confronted John Fisher. 'Who the fuck is this Ricky Thomas?' their leader demanded. He had an Italian name that I never did commit to memory. 'One of the printers told me he's an STA man. We'll go on fuckin' strike.'

'On you go then,' the chief reporter barked. 'But you'll be on your own. It'll be unofficial, because the chapel won't give it NUJ sanction. You guys have been on borrowed time for years, making a laughing stock of this paper. Ricky's transferring to our union, and he's got a staff job. And you know what? You three have just convinced me to do something I've been thinking about. We don't have an official chief photographer; I'm going to recommend to the editor that he's appointed. You'll be working for him from now on; if you don't like that, your resignations will be accepted.'

Within a year they had all gone, replaced by young people, recruited by Ricky.

The second protest was more discreet. It was by Doug McGrane, and I had anticipated that it would happen. As the gang slunk off, crushed, he approached John's desk, but stopped alongside mine, as he looked up at him. 'A word, please,' he murmured.

'Sure. Editor's room. Xavi, you're in on this.' I didn't want to be but I followed the two of them into Bannerman's office, empty even on the best day his paper had enjoyed during his tenure.

'John,' McGrane began. 'I'm supposed to be the crime reporter on this paper. Why was the boy given this story?'

'That's a reasonable question,' our boss replied. 'The answer is, because it was his, not yours. His contact, his tip-off, his initiative.'

'Still, I'm the senior man.'

'Since when was this job about seniority, Dougie? Xavi's source could have approached you. You were feet away from him when the contact was made but the individual chose not to talk to you, so no way was I going to impose you on him, nor could I, for that matter.'

'It makes me look like an idiot.'

John sighed. 'No, mate, it doesn't. It doesn't say anything about you. This is about the big guy here; it's his success.'

McGrane examined the floor. 'I suppose,' he mumbled.

'And you know the consequence, don't you?' the chief reporter added. 'After this, each and every cop who has something to tell the *Saltire*, they're not going to want to talk to you. They're going to want to talk to Xavi Aislado. So that's why he's got to be the crime reporter, and you've got to go back to general. Only not quite; your by-line will be special correspondent, and I'll wangle you a couple of quid more, to keep you happy.'

'John,' I intervened, 'I don't want to be crime reporter.'

He frowned at me. 'Son, we've been through this. Until this room is your room, you are what I say you are. Doug's not going to deny the truth in what I've said. And after you've done the best reporting job

277

anyone's done for this paper since well before my time, we'll be laughed at if we still call you a trainee.'

That's how my career, my meteoric career, according to a feature someone once did on me in the trade paper, got under way; through a succession of lucky breaks. When the smoke had cleared, I pointed this out to John Fisher.

'Sure,' he conceded, 'but good reporters aren't just good, they're lucky with it.'

He'd been right in what he'd said to Doug. After the exclusive that was christened 'The Redemption of Hughie Bracewell' by the *Daily Telegraph* in a catch-up piece, I did become the favourite reporter of the entire police service. I was the man who collared all the best tip-offs, and was given all the inside gen on cases before they came to court, and 'Exclusive' became a regular banner on the front page of the *Saltire*. The circulation saw a significant hike as well, in only a couple of months. We went from well under fifty thousand daily sales to above the sixty mark, and the entire tone of the paper sharpened up to justify it. The editor even began to show his face, occasionally, in the newsroom as morale improved. After the incident in the ladies' toilet, Mary Hackett's successor, a girl called Angie, recruited from the *Evening News*, transformed our features section, and gave John the confidence to press ahead with a Saturday pull-out section that he'd been considering since his arrival. The same positive vibes led Sandy Jeffrey to launch a dedicated Monday sports section, to which I was a significant contributor at the start of the rugby season.

The case against George Ramsay did not come to trial. He pleaded guilty to charges of perverting the course of justice and of supplying class A drugs to minors. The judge more or less laughed at his counsel's plea in mitigation. He sentenced him to a total of fourteen years. Eighteen months into that sentence he was stabbed to death in the mess hall of Peterhead Prison. No one was ever brought to account for his murder, but no prizes were on offer for guessing who was behind it.

Ryan Watson never made it to court either. In fact, he didn't make it to fifteen. When he and Ramsay made their first formal court appearance, no plea was sought or entered, and the janitor was remanded in custody and taken to the untried wing of the city's Saughton Prison. As a minor, young Watson couldn't be sent there, so the sheriff, after some persuasion by his solicitor against tougher alternatives, ordered him to be detained in a secure home for delinquent boys just outside Penicuik, a few miles south of Edinburgh. It wasn't quite secure enough.

On the Tuesday afternoon of the following week, I took a call in the office from DS Wallace. 'I thought I should let you know,' he said, 'that young Ryan absconded from detention this morning. He was being kept apart from the rest of the kids, and he exercised alone as well. He was out in the grounds this morning, his escort left him for a minute or two, thinking there was no way he could get away, but he found a hole in the fence.'

'Found or made?'

'He couldn't have made it himself, not without a wire cutter up his sleeve instead of his razor.'

'Could Uncle Gavin have made it for him?'

'Let's just say that's a possibility we're investigating. We're looking for Spreckley; I'll let you know when we pick him up.'

'Can I report this?'

'Please do. Obviously you still can't name the boy, since the court didn't authorise that and you can't mention that Spreckley's his uncle, 'cos that would identify him.'

I'd done a crash course on media law, so I knew that much, but I didn't tell him. 'I'll say you're keen to trace Gavin, without linking the two events. That won't upset anyone, will it?'

'No, that'll be fine. You appreciate that we'll need to tell the rest of the papers about the kid, but we'll wait till this evening. Hopefully he'll be picked up before then.'

'Do you see him as a danger, Bruce?'

'No, Xavi, we see him as a poor wee boy with a terrible family background that made him what he was. After it dawned on him that he was really done, he just collapsed; we had tears, we had the lot. He's pathetic.'

'Hughie Bracewell might not agree with you.'

'He'd be among the first to agree. Hughie has a grown-up son who's an engineer in Canada. There was a point in his life when he could have gone to the bad had his dad not sorted him out. I'll let you know if we find him; otherwise you can run the story, and nobody else will get the stuff about Spreckley.'

I wrote the piece up and added a bit to it by calling the head of the unit from which Ryan had done his runner. He was concerned, for his job, no doubt, but he was frank with me. He said that the boy had been well-behaved to the point of meekness from the time he had arrived there, and that his escort had seen no problem in leaving him alone for a few minutes. He also offered to swear on the biggest stack of bibles I could provide that the fence had been intact the night before.

There was no call back to say that the kid had been recaptured, so John ran the story on the front page next morning, with an exclusive tag, because of the Spreckley angle, and alongside it a picture of Jambo senior, cropped from the two-shot with Ramsay . . . under my new by-line, of course, 'By Xavi Aislado, *Saltire* Crime Reporter'. Doug McGrane caught me looking at it as he came into the newsroom. He gave me a grin and a quick thumbs-up: fences mended.

I had just taken a call from a woman detective I had met briefly the previous week at the Leith police office, when I had a signal from one of the general reporters . . . they were all fine with me, by the way; none of them was going to be a star and they all knew it, so there was no jealousy problem . . . that Hughie Bracewell was holding for me on another line. I arranged to meet the cop at the end of her shift in Skipper's, in Dock Place, then flicked the switch to pick him up.

'Hugh, how are you doing?' As I spoke I felt a sudden surge of guilt at not having called him the night before to warn him of Ryan Watson's escape. 'Listen, I'm sorry I didn't call you yesterday.'

'Why should you have? Wallace the Bruce let me know about the kid. They still havenae caught him yet, have they?'

'Not that I've heard.'

'You'd have heard.'

'You're not worried about him, are you, Hugh? Wallace says he's just a scared wee boy now.'

'Hell no, son. If young Ryan had another go at me, I'd have him between two slices o' bread. Ah'm no worried about the boy, I'm worried for him.'

'Why? Do you think he'll do something daft, like harm himself?'

Hughie chuckled, softly. 'Ach, Xavi lad, ye don't really get it yet, do ye? Never mind. Here,' he exclaimed, his voice brightening, 'you'll never guess. I had a call this mornin' frae the council. They've offered me Ramsay's job at Maxwell Academy.'

'That's the least they can do. Are you taking it?'

'No chance. I told the woman to stick it up her jacksie . . . politely, mind. Naw, I said tae her that I would take Broughton High School, across from the police headquarters. It's handier for the hoose. She said she would fix it, but Ah'm no going tae take that either. Ah've been offered a security job by Scottish Brewers; that's much more ma scene. Good money and Ah even get a beer allowance.'

'Good for you,' I laughed. 'I'll be in to see you when you start.'

I hung up and went back to consider my earlier conversation with the woman from Leith. She wanted to talk to me about street prostitutes. (Show me a Western city that claims not to have any and I will show you a public relations department that doesn't mind lying to press and public.) She didn't go into detail; all she said was that it was a matter of public concern but there was a passion about her that I had found convincing. I walked over to John's desk and told him about the contact. We were discussing it when Juliet, the copy-boy-girl, called out, timidly, 'Excuse me, Xavi.' I turned. She was holding a box, a cube of brown paper, tied with string. 'Someone left a present for you with the front office.'

'For me?'

'That's what they said.'

'Who was it?'

'The receptionist didn't know; only that it was a man in biker leathers and a helmet.'

'Put it on my desk,' I told her. 'I'll open it later.'

'Come on, Xav,' Doug called across the room, 'open it and let's see. It's probably the cops having a whip-round for you.'

'Not so fast,' said John. 'I'm not keen on mysterious parcels.'

I picked it up and shook it gently. It wasn't heavy, but I could feel something moving inside. 'I doubt it's a bomb, John.'

'Still.'

'Do we have a scanner?'

'No, but . . .'

'Then bugger it.' I picked up a pair of scissors and cut the string. 'Anyone who wants to get under their desk, feel free,' I told the room in general, then slit the paper. The box revealed was plain cardboard, with no marks on the outside that I could see. It was sealed on top by a single strip of Sellotape; I peeled that back, opened the two flaps and peered inside. There, I saw a copy of the previous Friday's *Saltire*, my big break, my three-page exclusive, carefully folded, like a wrapping.

'What is it?' John asked.

'Could be a fish supper,' I joked, 'but past its best.' I sniffed. 'No salt and sauce on it either.'

I lifted the parcel out and laid it, upside down, on the desk, then unwrapped it, carefully. I'll swear that my heart stopped when I saw what was inside, or maybe it was just one of those moments when time seems to hiccup. However long it lasted, I recovered, and when I did there was a picture imprinted on my mind, one that I can see with total clarity, even today, if ever it catches me unawares, one of too many in my personal 'X' file. I closed the paper as carefully as I'd opened it. The copy-person was still there, standing behind me. 'Juliet,' I said, without turning, 'leave us.'

'Pardon?'

I raised my voice. 'Get out of here, please; now!' If she'd seen what I had, she'd have run from the room, and she might never have returned.

I waited until she'd gone, and even then I didn't look at anybody, not even John, as I put my gift back in its box and closed it, as I walked round the desk, sat and dialled the direct number that my stepfather had given me. 'Tommy,' I said without preamble, as he answered, aware of the total silence in the newsroom that I was breaking. 'I'm in the office. You need to get here now, and you might want to bring forensic people.'

'Why, Xavi?' he asked me. 'What's up?'

'I've just received a box, dropped off by a biker.' My voice was matter-of-fact, as I knew it had to be if I was to keep my self-control. 'It contains two right hands, human; one adult size, one slightly smaller, each cut off at the wrist, possibly by a chainsaw, the two of them wrapped together in a copy of my story about drugs in Maxwell Academy. You can keep on looking for Spreckley and wee Ryan, but you're not going to find all of them.'

I hung up, and looked around. John Fisher's face was buried in his hands, and there was no one there who wasn't as white as a sheet. Angie pushed herself from her chair and rushed off in the direction of the ladies, but too late, judging by the trail she left behind her. Everyone else sat where they were, each one staring at the box. I thought about Bracewell, and of his strange concern for the kid. 'I get it now, Hughie,' I said aloud, as if he could hear me.

Tommy and DS Wallace must have left burned rubber all the way from police headquarters to the Royal Mile, for I'd hardly put the phone down before they were there . . . or possibly we'd all sat stunned for longer than we realised. By the time they arrived, I'd carried the box into the editor's office, where John and I sat, staring at it on the coffee table. 'Remember that Peter Lorre film?' the chief reporter had just asked me, as the door opened and Doug McGrane showed them in. *'The Beast With Five Fingers.'*

The detectives weren't in the mood for a movie quiz. 'Who's touched it?' Tommy asked.

'Nobody's even seen what's inside but me,' I told him. 'As for the outside of it, me, the copy-boy and the guy who dropped it off. But Juliet . . .'

'Juliet?'

'Don't ask. Juliet said he was wearing leathers, and I guess that included gloves. The brown paper it was wrapped in is still on my desk.'

'Let's have a look, then.' He nodded. 'Bruce.'

The sergeant opened the box as I had done, and took out the contents, then opened the package to reveal its contents. I'd been replaying it in my mind, over and over, so I was well prepared for a second look, but it was John's first. He struggled against throwing up but quickly lost the battle, vomiting copiously into the editor's waste-paper basket. Tommy waited for him to recover, before putting on a pair of plastic gloves and picking up the larger hand. He examined it, then showed it to me. The letters A, R, T and S were etched on it, left to right from the index finger in rough blue jailhouse tattoos. 'Gavin Spreckley,' he said. 'The clown had J, A, M and T on the other hand. If only he'd supported the Hibs; he could have had all of their name on each hand and it would have looked half sensible.' He put the severed extremity back on the table, picked up the other and showed it to Wallace. 'Remember when we interviewed Ryan?' he asked.

'Aye. His nails were bitten right down to the quick. The poor wee bastard.'

'Tommy,' I intervened, 'do you reckon they were alive when this was done?'

'I hope not,' he said. 'I'd like to think not. The guy who did this isn't insane. But the pathologist will tell us for sure.'

'Will he have anything else to examine?'

'Maybe.' He paused. 'But not any time soon. One of them might be fished up by a trawler some day, that's if they're not buried very deep, or been put through a tree mulcher. I wouldn't count on it, though.'

'So why do this?' John murmured.

Tommy looked at me. 'Tell him, Xavi.'

I didn't even have to think about it. 'This is a message,' I said. 'And I'm the guy who's been chosen to spread it, through this paper. That message is that selling smack to school kids will not be tolerated within the Edinburgh criminal community, and that anyone else who does it will wind up like these two, regardless of age or anything else. Can I use the sender's name?' I asked my stepfather.

'No way,' he declared, in a no-appeal voice. 'There's no prospect of anyone ever being convicted of these two killings, so it wouldn't achieve anything other than possibly some grief for you, and I'm not having that. The man will not be mentioned in the press, not in this context, until he's in our custody and charged. Be patient, Xavi. You'll get your shot at him in time.'

And so I spread the word for Perry Holmes, another exclusive in the next morning's *Saltire*, another scoop, another bite of the national news cherry. A pathologist confirmed within the hour that the two hands had been removed after death, and I was able to use the names of both 'Ryan Watson, aged fourteen, teenage drug dealer within the shamed school, Maxwell Academy, and his ruthless supplier uncle Gavin Spreckley, executed by their overlord for breaking one of his cardinal rules, no, not stepping over the bounds of morality, but bringing negative public relations down on the head of his mob.' That last phrase alarmed Tommy when he read it, but I told him that I might be a messenger, but I wasn't going to be a mouthpiece.

'The boy's done a good job for us.'

'That can't be denied.'

'He could be useful in the future.'

'You think?'

'He did what we wanted, didn't he?'

'He didn't have a choice. We gave him a big story; he had to report it.'

'Aye, we gave him a hand, eh!'

'Don't be an idiot, brother. There was no other choice to get the package; everyone was going to be reading him after that splash he got over Maxwell Academy.'

'Aye, okay, but, still. He's young and if we keep feeding him stuff, it could help us keep the opposition off our backs.'

'Give him misinformation, do you mean? Set false trails for the drugs squad?'

'That's what I was thinking.'

'Well, think again. The kid might be new on the block, but that doesn't mean to say that he's naive, or malleable. It took him about two days to nail that prick Ramsay and to uncover something that was going on under our noses without either us, or "the opposition" as you call them, having the faintest idea about it. That doesn't strike me as the act of someone we can control; it shows me someone who is out of our reach. What most of these so-called investigative reporters really want . . . and our friend McGrane's a classic example . . . is to snuggle up to the likes of us, so that one day they can write sanitised "true crime" stories about us that'll make them a few quid without us being locked up, or them winding up going into Johann Kraus's garden incinerator like Spreckley and the kid. Half the hoodlums in Glasgow get their rocks off being the heroes in crap like that. Young Aislado isn't one of those; he's shown already that he's got integrity. From what I gather, the boy has no detectable sense of humour, and he cares about nothing other than his girlfriend and his job. If he was ever forced to choose between them, it would be interesting to see who won. Add to that the fact that Tommy bloody Partridge is his stepfather, and all of it doesn't mark him out as someone who could be useful to us. It makes him bloody dangerous, someone we should keep at arm's length.'

'Should we get Johann to give him a wee warning?'

'Fuck me! The day I let you start thinking for me, Alasdair, I might as well walk into Tommy Partridge's office and give myself up. Let me tell you something that might get your attention. You were the guy who was supposed to be running Spreckley, and as such, you came very close to going the same way as him and the kid when I found out what they had been up to. It was only your inherent loyalty, and maybe also the fact that I don't have anyone I trust enough to replace you, that prevented that box being a wee bit heavier.'

'Aw, come on, Perry, this is me you're talking to.'

'Sure, brother, I know it is. But did you not tell me that when Johann took care of Gavin and the boy, Billy Spreckley, Gavin's brother, was there and didn't bat an eyelid?'

'Perry, chuck it.'

'Well, you chuck the helpful suggestions. Aislado's sacrosanct.'

'He's what?'

'Untouchable, Al, untouchable.'

'Okay. But McGrane, what about him? How come the boy got the tip-off about Ramsay and not him? And why didn't he fucking tell us that the boy was on to the story.'

'Now, those are a couple of good questions. If he had done, there wouldn't have been any story. Our Dougie's on the payroll as unofficial PR manager, and yet we wound up with a very public disaster. I reckon a spot of correction's in order there. Wait for a few weeks to let the smoke from this lot clear, then take care of it, will you?'

'A bit of a slap?'

'A bit more than that, I believe. He doesn't actually know anything that could incriminate us, but still, better be safe than to find ourselves staring at the same wall for twenty years.'

Twelve

My career settled into normality after that, or should I say I was able to define what normal was. For a while I harboured a degree of guilt for usurping the Crime Reporter slot, but that evaporated after Doug McGrane left the paper without warning, or notice. He didn't turn up for work one day, nor on any day after that.

When John went to his flat to roust him out, after a week of no-shows, he discovered that it was occupied by a new tenant. The landlady told him that she had gone in one day to clean it . . . she hadn't trusted him to do that himself . . . and found him and his stuff all packed and gone, and an envelope left behind on the table with a month's rent in lieu of notice. We never heard from him again, but a PC in Gayfield Square told me a few weeks later that Doug had confided in him that he was pissed off with his new non-job and was thinking of making a complete break with Scotland and heading for Canada, where he had family.

In truth, his departure barely registered with me; he and I had very little interaction in the office, not even casually, since our desks were in opposite corners of the newsroom, and I had other things on my mind. The story that the cop from Leith put me on to played out as another front-page lead.

As a woman detective constable in the male-driven world of the early 1980s she was as rare as hen's teeth, but she was a feisty girl who had joined the force to see justice done, and she was prepared to put her job on the line for her principles. I can't reveal her name even now, since she's still a serving officer, holding command rank in an English force. But she was an angry young lady when we met in Skipper's, and my mind was still scrambled from my close encounter that afternoon with two dead hands . . . before they disappear from my story, I should confirm that Tommy Partridge's fears were justified; not another trace of uncle or nephew has ever been found . . . but once we had sized each other up, she had decided that I could be trusted and I had decided that she wasn't a plant, she got down to business.

Over the past four weeks, she told me, there had been assaults on three prostitutes, but it was only after the last that the police had become involved. Some things were very clear to my informant. Each successive attack was more severe than the one before. Also, the descriptions given by the victims left no doubt that the same man was involved every time. Finally, her male colleagues were not about to burst their balls to catch him; that realisation had brought her to me.

'Prostitutes are at the bottom of the pecking order when it comes to CID time,' she hissed, 'unless we're locking them up. My bosses don't see this as the Yorkshire Ripper, so they don't really give a toss. Their attitude, unspoken, but still there, is that it's one of the risks a working girl takes, so let's not get excited, but if this man isn't caught, and quick, there will be deaths; trust me on that, Mr Aislado.'

'Could this be a domestic thing?' I asked her. 'Could these women have upset their pimp?'

'Their drug dealer, you mean? More than half the women on the street are there to feed a drug habit. But of these three, only one was a user, and her supplier wouldn't draw attention to himself. The other two have husbands, not pimps.'

'Husbands?'

She gazed at me. 'You're younger than you look, aren't you? You may not be ready to believe this yet, but there are men who're quite happy to let their wives earn the holiday money in the backs of cars or up against a wall.'

Yes, I was naive then, but she convinced me. We stayed in Skipper's long enough to have dinner on expenses, then, when she reckoned the time was right, she took me for a walk. We didn't go far, only across

Constitution Street and into Coburg Street. It was a sunny summer evening, but the ladies were there in numbers, ready for business . . . and less than pleased when they saw my escort. Before open hostilities could break out, she waved two of them across, a tall young blonde and an older redhead. She introduced them as Joanne and Mavis, the first two victims. She told me I could find the third, Wanda Crichton, in ward twenty-three of the Royal Infirmary, and then she made herself scarce, after warning me never to try to contact her.

The two women were willing interviewees, even more so after I'd taken them to a pub called the Cockatoo and bought them a couple of vodkas and tonic. The stories they told were identical, and grim. They had each been picked up by a punter, a man of medium height, late twenties, dark hair, non-memorable; he had paid them in advance, then had produced not what they had expected, but instead, a set of brass knuckles. Joanne, the first target, had been lucky. She had dug a heel into his instep and landed the first punch, hard enough to make him run for it. But Mavis had taken a couple of licks. A slight swelling showed under her left eye, and she lifted her white shirt, furtively, to show me two large purple bruises on her ribcage.

'What about Wanda?' I asked.

'Broken nose, and a few teeth missing,' Joanne replied. 'She was working Salamander Street. Somebody found her on the pavement just off there, outside a freight yard she used. They thought she'd been hit by a car at first. The Royal called the polis when she got there.'

'This guy,' I continued, 'did he say anything at all? Or did he just go straight on to the attack?'

The big blonde teenager frowned. 'He shouted something at me,' she recalled, 'but I was too busy gettin' stuck into him to pay any attention.'

'Polluting, plague-ridden whore.' We both looked at Mavis. 'That's what he called me,' she said. 'He shouted it when he started to hit me, and his face . . . It was, furious. I've never seen anybody look so angry.'

'That could have been it,' said Joanne. 'And you're right about his face. His eyes, too; he had these really mad eyes.'

'Did you tell the police this?'

'They never asked us.'

Next morning I visited Wanda Crichton at the Royal; the staff nurse wasn't keen to let me see her, but I persuaded her to give Wanda my card. When she saw it she agreed to talk to me. 'You're the guy that wrote that thing about the Academy,' she said, as I took a seat by her bedside. 'Ah was there. What a shite-hole the place is. And that Ramsay, he's an evil bastard. You did a good job, pal.'

She was recovering, but her injuries were even more serious than Joanne had known. She had a fractured skull, three cracked ribs and she had been kicked so hard that she had aborted the three-month-old foetus she had been carrying. Wanda was the addict among the three, but the hospital was giving her methadone, so she was calm and fully in control of herself as she told me what had happened to her. He had shouted exactly the same thing as in the earlier attacks, that and more.

'When you spread your legs you spread death,' she said. 'That's what he yelled at me. His eyes were wild, he spat at me, and he had these blotches on his face. He was terrifying, really awful, and yet . . . I had the weirdest feeling, that he was terrified himself as well. I had just shot up so I was in a strange state myself, not feeling all that much pain, and noticing the oddest things. Like those blotches on his face . . . they were purple, and they looked horrible. He was shouting about the plague; it was as if he had it himself.'

I stopped at that, as she was tiring. I promised to send her a big box of chocolates . . . 'Really big, ken, no' just a half pound of Cadbury's' . . . then left her to her recovery. I was leaving the ward when someone called out to me.

'Xavi!'

I turned and there, in the doorway of the sister's office, was Sheila Craig. She was still in uniform, but it was a different colour than the one she'd worn in Cameron Hill Hospital.

'What's this?' I exclaimed. 'What's brought you here?'

'Career move,' she told me. 'I applied for a staff nurse's job here and I got it. To tell you the truth I would have taken anything on offer to get out of that other place. The buildings here might be a lot older, but it's a proper hospital.'

'You're young to be a staff in a place like this,' I told her, sincerely.

She dropped a tiny curtsey. 'Thank you, kind sir, but I was twenty-one last March. You're young to be a crime reporter for a big newspaper.'

'I can't deny that,' I admitted. Then I came out with a question that was completely spontaneous, and for me, out of character. 'Fancy a drink after work? I owe you one, I'm sure, for looking after me so well back in that PoW camp.'

She looked up at me, and I realised what it was that had captured my attention. She had the kindest eyes I'd ever seen, neither blue nor grey, somewhere in between, unlike any I'd ever seen before. 'I've got a boyfriend,' she warned.

'Thank God for that,' I countered. 'I've got a fiancée.'

She smiled. 'Yes, I remember her. I don't think she took to me.' She chuckled. 'If you could kill with thought, I'd be dead now. The Doctor's? Six o'clock?'

'Deal.'

I headed straight back to the office and started work on my story. I didn't approach the cops, for a few reasons: I might have compromised my source, I didn't want to bring gender issues into the open air, and I didn't want to risk any of the goodwill I'd built up within the force by asking the questions that I'd be forced to put to them. Instead, I began, 'Edinburgh police are searching for a disfigured maniac . . .' then wrote what I'd been told by the three women. I invented names for all of them and concentrated on Wanda's account, as it had been easily the most detailed and the most gripping. I didn't leave anything out, not even the line about spread legs spreading death. I thought that John or the subs might amend that, but nobody was cutting my copy at that time, so it ran, intact. Yet another page-one splash.

Once I'd filed it I went off to meet Sheila. We had that drink, and another; she told me all about herself, and I told her a little about me. Then I went home, not too late, for a change, feeling impiously pleased with myself, had a fun evening with my little domestic group, then made love to my fiancée until we both fell asleep.

I was barely awake next morning when the phone rang. It was Tommy. 'Christ, Xavi,' he exclaimed, 'where did you get this stuff? The DS who's supposed to be on that case is a mate of mine. He's been on the phone to me shitting himself.'

'I got it from three women that he's already interviewed. Does that tell you anything?'

'It tells me plenty, but he wants to know who your source was.'

'So he called you to get it from me?' I asked, sharply.

'Don't worry, I told him to fuck off, and I don't really expect you to tell me either. It's a bloody good story, son, and you've made your point without making it, if you know what I mean. Lessons will be learned in CID, and arses will be kicked. As for the person who put you on to this, I can guess who she is, and so will other people, but even if it could be proved, no action would be taken against her.' He was right; we stood at the dawn of the age of political correctness, although I wasn't nearly smart enough to articulate that, even if I understood it instinctively. 'But,' he continued, 'this thing is about prostitutes, so be prepared for a backlash from the council, and a few others.'

'Do ships still dock in Leith, Tommy?'

'Yes, and they will for a while to come, and I understand why you're asking. But if you're thinking of yourself and your paper as a champion of these women, don't, because it's in their best interests to be left alone.'

'To be attacked in the street? Look at what happened in Yorkshire.'

'Sure, we should protect them better than that,' he agreed, 'and we will, but the majority, the people you're trying to sell to, they don't want to know about them, because if they did, they'd feel obliged to protest, and the council would feel obliged to put pressure on us to sweep them away. Understand?'

'I do,' I admitted. 'But you understand this too. Until you catch this bloke, or until he stops, this story isn't going away, and even if we don't report it, others will. So catch him.'

He laughed. 'You fucking catch him yourself. You're on a roll.'

'Me? No, that's your job, even if your DS pal doesn't seem to realise it.'

There was even more buzz in the office that morning, and not just because it was Friday. The horrors of two days before seemed to have faded from the collective memory . . . if not from mine, or John's . . . to be replaced by morbid fascination over the identity of the maniac with the ravaged face. Halfway through the morning I had a call from my informant's DS, a guy called Jeff Adam. He was civil, almost too eager to please as he told me that he was taking an artist to visit Wanda in the hope that she could recall him enough for a likeness to be formed and circulated. I suggested that a very large box of chocolates might help her memory . . . I'd given mine to Sheila the night before and asked her to deliver it.

Half an hour after that, I had a call from Sheila herself, on the direct number that I'd given her.

'Xavi.' She was keeping her voice down, even in her own room. 'I've just been speaking to a colleague, the sister on ward forty-two. She hasn't seen a paper this morning, but she told me a story about a man they've got in isolation in her ward. He was brought in last Tuesday. They're barrier nursing him . . . that means everything has to be totally sterile . . . and she doesn't know what's wrong with him, but she's seen him and she described him. His face, Xavi, it's covered in purple blotches. His name's Gunn, and he's very, very ill.'

I had been feeling drowsy, ready for a caffeine boost. Suddenly I didn't need it any more. 'Who's his doctor?'

'Professor Hanson. He's a virologist; a specialist in infectious and contagious diseases.'

'Thanks, Sheila. If this works out I owe you more than a drink.'

'A drink's all we can ever have, Xavi.' As she replied I could almost see her smile. 'I'll settle for that.'

I had meant dinner, that was all, but I didn't tell her that. Instead I found myself thinking about those eyes. 'Then call me when you're free,' I replied.

I thought about what she had told me, and made a decision. It was time to share. I phoned DS Adam; he was still trying to find an artist. I could have told him that Grace knew a few, and vice versa, but it wasn't relevant any longer. Instead, I suggested that he meet me at the Royal, ward forty-two. I was a lot closer, so I beat him to it by ten minutes. I spent the time watching a door. There was a sign on it, 'Isolation', in large black letters that could be neither missed nor ignored. And in a slot below it a card with the occupant's name, Millard Gunn. When Adam arrived, there was another detective with him, a woman. We'd met before but he wasn't to know that, so when we were introduced, the handshake we exchanged was on the edge of indifference.

I left it to them to ask for Professor Hanson, knowing that he couldn't tell the police to sod off. He arrived five minutes later, in the obligatory white coat, and with the air of someone who cannot be bothered with whatever is happening, permanently. That's what I thought at the time. Now I understand that it is the classic symptom of potentially fatal overwork. DS Adam introduced himself and his colleague, but the consultant wasn't really interested in them. He'd worked out that I was too young to be CID so his unwilling attention was entirely on me. I guessed that the man was far too busy to have read my story, so I handed him my copy of the *Saltire*, folded to page one, and said, 'I'm Xavi Aislado and I wrote that.' He took it from me, glanced at it, then took a closer look, then read the account of the prostitute attacks from start to finish. When he handed it back to me he seemed to have shrunk by a couple of inches, and to be even more tired.

'That's him, for sure,' he said, quietly. 'The marks on his face are signs of something called Kaposi's sarcoma. It's becoming a common manifestation in people with a condition that's been known until now as GRID, gay-related immune deficiency, but which the Americans want to rename AIDS, because we no longer believe it's confined to that community. Mr Gunn insists that he is not homosexual; he believes that he acquired the disease from a prostitute, on a visit to London. I don't share that view, for reasons that I won't disclose.'

'We need to interview him about these attacks,' Adam told him.

'Why?' the consultant argued. 'He's going to die, within a very few days.'

'We need to be sure it was him.'

'How did he get here?' I asked.

'He collapsed in George Street. He lives just round the corner, in Frederick Street.'

'Has his place been sealed and fumigated?'

'There's no need, Mr Aislado. The virus that gives rise to the disease can't survive outside the body for any length of time. Look,' said Hanson, 'if you want to talk to him, you can. He's conscious, and sedated, but he's not pretty. You'll need to be gowned and masked.'

Adam let me go in with them, but there was little point. Millard Gunn was in a room within a room, behind a glass panel in a space that was fed with filtered air. He looked like someone who was on the verge of losing his humanity. He was conscious, yes, but he seemed beyond understanding any questions that were put to him, far less giving reliable answers. In the end, Professor Hanson sent a nurse to fetch a Polaroid camera from the hospital's administration unit, the DS took a photograph and then showed it to Wanda, who was certain that she was looking at her attacker.

The identification was put beyond doubt when a set of brass knuckles, with her blood and skin on them, was found in his flat. Jeff Adam offered the Polaroid to me, for publication, but I told him to keep it. John Fisher had thrown up enough for one week, and I didn't want thousands of readers to be doing the same.

With everyone's agreement, I sat on the story until the following Monday, when Millard Gunn died, then we led with it next day, the biggest and the most momentous of my run of early exclusives. Nobody can ever be certain that he was the first person to die in Scotland from an AIDS-related illness, for diagnosis was still in its infancy in the UK, but I've never seen a claim made on behalf of anyone else. His death caused a sensation. The so-called gay plague had been a vague rumour from across the Atlantic; when it dive-bombed Edinburgh, the effect was dramatic.

The *Saltire* dealt with it by running a series of articles, written by John Fisher, with the cooperation and involvement of Professor Hanson. He turned out to be one of those medics who was not averse to the prospect of becoming a media star. He played that role for the rest of his career, and beyond. John was privately pleased too, for all the grimness of the subject. He told me that it made him feel like a real journalist again.

I bought Sheila that second drink on the following Friday; Grace had gone off on an unspecified modelling assignment in Glasgow that was going to mean an overnight stay, so I filled in my free evening. I even persuaded her to eat with me, in a Chinese restaurant called the Edinburgh Rendezvous. Her boyfriend? He was a lorry driver, and he lived in a place called Carluke, so she wasn't posted missing. Not that it would have mattered. We had a pleasant evening, then, since the empty taxis seemed to be hiding from us, I walked her back to her place in Lochrin, not far from the infirmary, and headed back to mine. She didn't invite me in, and if she had I'd probably have told her, 'Thanks, but I really have an early start in the morning,' or some other lie. We parted, promising to see each other again; and we did, eighteen years later.

After its tumultuous beginning, it came as a relief when over the next few weeks and months I became, maybe not just another reporter, for good tips and good stories kept flowing my way, but one of the crowd, a Member of the Press. The circulation increase that had been kicked off by the Ramsay scoop continued steadily, and within a couple of years we had overtaken sales of the *Glasgow Herald* in the Edinburgh area, if nowhere near overall. In his communicative moments Torcuil Bannerman was even heard to talk about surpassing the *Scotsman*; we all knew he was a clown so we let him dream on. In central Scottish terms, ignoring those strange tribal papers in Dundee and Aberdeen, the *Saltire* was the third broadsheet, and it seemed certain that it would always be so, since we lacked the physical capacity to print enough papers to catch the other two, and since our owners had no intention of funding a switch to modern technology.

In the spring of the following year, I asked John about them, one evening after the first edition had gone to bed. 'There's nothing to tell,' he replied. 'McCandlish's estate . . . the paper's only a part of it . . . was put in trust in his will. The trustees are three nominated partners in a firm of solicitors with offices in Charlotte Square and the beneficiaries are the old man's widow, who's in the grip of dementia in a nursing home in North Berwick, his son, who's a Methodist minister in Helensburgh, and his daughter who's married to a funeral undertaker in Cheshire. The paper's a limited company. As editor, Torcuil's a member of the board. The three trustees make up the rest.'

'So they take the investment decisions?'

'What investment decisions? The trustees are lawyers, Xavi, old school. They understand the world of trusts but not the world of business. Torcuil? He understands fuck all. Their role is to protect the assets and provide income for the beneficiaries, and that's what they're good at. If you're thinking that they'll fund a move into new premises with new equipment, forget it. There is an upside though; because the trustees are what they are, the *Saltire* pension fund is rock solid. The old family are all members, as well as the staff here, so old McCandlish stuffed it full of cash when he was alive.'

When you're twenty-one years old, provision for retirement doesn't dominate your thinking. John's good news was well outweighed by the downside of what he had said, that the paper was set on a course that would plough on through the dark ages, with little prospect of emerging into the light. I had seen the future in Girona, and so I found it frustrating, but by that time I was part of the very fabric of the place. My name was appearing on billboards and for the first time in my life, I understood what it felt like to belong. Money wasn't an issue for me. My trainee salary at the paper had been increased to match my status, my injury compensation payment would yield its modest income indefinitely, and, although I had told her to stop it, Grandma Paloma had ignored me and continued to send me the allowance she had been giving me since I left school. All that helped me to ride out the domestic crisis when it came.

I can't deny that my new career had an impact on life at home. My hours were irregular, and often they didn't blend too well with Grace's studying or with the Glasgow modelling jobs that seemed to be popping up more and more often. Some evenings I'd get back, still focused on whatever had been the story of the day, and it was as if I was interrupting the routine of the other three. On quite a few occasions it was the other four, because Jilly Hannah would be there, and still there when I left for work the next morning. I reached a stage at which I began to imagine that I was a lodger in my own flat. Oh, I did my best to give Grace all the time I could, and she rarely complained about my absences either. When I had a rugby match to cover at the weekend, I would always ask her to come with me. Occasionally, she did, but more often than not, she had an exam coming up, or she had to meet Magda in Jenners, or the weather was bad. We weren't growing apart, she and I, but I began to feel that not only was the time we had together being compressed, but so were we, into a smaller and smaller space.

I was irritated by the boys too; they seemed to be more distant, to have their own thing going on, that I wasn't a part of any more. One night as I lay awake in the dark, unable to sleep because of some crime scene photographs that Jeff Adam had shown me that afternoon, I even had the mad idea of finding another place, a smaller flat, or maybe a bungalow like the one where I'd cornered Mulholland, and running away with Grace to set up home there, leaving the other two to get on with it. Looking back, the truth was that while the others were still students, thinking like students and living like students, I had moved on. I was a working man, with the attitudes of a working man and with the stirrings of resentment towards those who weren't.

All these things were going around in my head, but they were never articulated. I had given a commitment to Scott, and later to Bobby, that they could stay with me until they had graduated and were ready to move on, and I wasn't about to renege on it, so when the . . . the thing . . . happened, it was as if I'd sleepwalked into it.

I didn't have many callers at the office. Okay, in the era when newsrooms were in city centres, there was always a steady stream of people wandering in off the street with stories to tell, but nearly all of them were gossips, malicious, unbalanced or after a free cup of coffee. Real sources, valuable sources, would not be seen dead walking into our reception area, some of them because they feared that's how they'd wind up shortly afterwards. So when Bruce Wallace walked up to the front office desk one morning in April 1983 and asked for me, I was taken by surprise. I told them to send him up . . . he'd been in the newsroom before, after all . . . but he said no, that he didn't want to do that. I was mildly annoyed, but intrigued, as I went through to meet him, but the annoyance vanished when I saw the expression on his face. He looked anxious, a bit strung out. 'Let's go for a walk,' he said, turning and leading the way before I had a chance to ask why I should do that.

It was cold outside; I was glad that I'd put on my jacket as we headed up the close towards the Royal Mile. 'Where can we go that's discreet?' he muttered as we reached the gateway.

I considered our options. It was too early for Gordon's, and there were too many toerags hanging around the court buildings; I looked around, saw only one possibility, and that was how I came to step into St Giles Cathedral, the High Kirk of Scotland, for the first time in my non-practising Catholic life.

The sergeant was wearing a hat, which he removed, respectfully, once we were inside. It occurred to me to point out that nobody had objected to the Pope wearing headgear in church when he'd visited Scotland the year before, but DS Wallace didn't look as if he was in the mood for levity . . . and anyway, in those days you had to be careful about offering His Holiness as an example, especially to a cop.

'Tommy sent me,' he said, in little more than a whisper, fearful of the acoustics. 'He doesn't like to be seen with you too often, and no way with this.'

'With what?' I said, not caring who heard.

'Shh. This is hush-hush; we shouldn't be doing this.'

'Bruce,' I exclaimed . . . in a suitably hushed tone, 'I get stories from cops all the time, not just from you two.'

'This isn't a story.'

'Then,' I looked up at the vaulted roof, 'God forgive me, what the hell is it?'

'We've had a guy under surveillance,' he replied, 'a street dealer called Greg McKinstry, who's a mate of a mate of a mate of Al Holmes.' I had done enough private digging into Perry Holmes by that time to know that he had a brother called Alasdair. (The *Daily Record* crime reporter once called him Mycroft, in a group in the Deacon Brodie pub, but only a couple of us got the joke.) 'We'd given up trying to connect the two of them, so we started taking pictures of McKinstry at work, so we could lift him and at least be sure we'd nail him. We followed him to a meet, a couple of nights ago. This is the best from the film we shot.'

He took a photograph from his pocket and handed it to me. It showed two men, dealer and buyer; their faces were recognisable and it was obvious which was which. The pusher was a greasy-looking guy, somewhere in his thirties. The casting agent who worked on *Trainspotting* could have used him as a template, but his young customer was cut from different cloth. He wasn't all that tall, but his frame was solid, contrasting with the slightly delicate features that showed up well in the shot. It was Bobby, Bobby Hannah.

'What are you going to do with it?' It was my turn to whisper.

'Nothing. We were going to arrest them both, until Tommy recognised your pal. We lifted McKinstry last night, making another sale. Your boy won't be involved, but Tommy says you should deal with it. If somebody else had got this, made the connection and tipped off another paper . . .'

He didn't need to spell it out. 'Thanks,' I said. 'And thank Tommy for me. Not just for this, but for not assuming that I was part of it.'

'How could we, after Maxwell Academy?'

'What was he buying? Not heroin, surely?'

'We don't think it was smack; more likely another class A drug. Cocaine. It's becoming very popular among the smart young set. No apparatus involved, you just lay it in a line and sniff it up your nose through a tube, or you take it off a wee spoon.'

'Can I keep this?' I asked.

'Yes, sure. Not for the paper though. We'll give you a better one when McKinstry's convicted.'

I drifted through the rest of the day, filing a couple of minor stories and writing my mid-week rugby column for the sports section, but thinking all the time about how I was going to handle things that evening.

I was still thinking about it when I arrived home, but no closer to deciding on my approach . . . until I saw Bobby. He was standing in the middle of the living room when I walked in, looking down at Scott on the couch. He hadn't been expecting me, and so a strange conspiratorial smile lingered on his face for just a fraction of a second too long, an expression that told me two things, that he and Scott were far closer than I had realised and that if one of them was into drugs, then in all probability so was the other.

He was still grinning as he looked across at me. 'Hey, Xavi,' he called out. 'Good day at the office? Exposed any more villains?'

Suddenly he was a stranger, this guy I had known since we were both five years old, this guy I had trusted and taken into my home, this guy of whom the only thing I'd expected was that he lived by my dad's reasonable rules as long as he was under his sheltering roof. I smiled back at him, but it was a smile of the deepest regret for that which I reckoned was lost and would never be found again, for that which was broken and could never be repaired. 'Yes,' I replied, 'but not for publication.'

Scott twisted round and looked up at me and it was as if I could see him properly for the first time in years. 'Deep dark secrets?' he chuckled, and I could hear the same patronising smart-arse tone that had irked me when we were at school.

'There are no secrets, you prick.' It came out as a snarl, as I stepped round the settee. 'There's only truth. It's just a matter of when it's discovered.'

He turned white as a sheet. 'What are you on about?' he said. He started to rise, but I pushed him back down, one-handed, easily.

'Shut the fuck up,' I retorted. I stared at Bobby. 'You know what this is about, don't you?' He took a step back. The grin had gone; he looked scared, downright terrified.

'Xavi,' he spluttered, 'this has nothing to do with me.'

'Nothing to do with you?' I shouted. 'Are you fucking kidding?' I took the photograph from my jacket and held it up, a few inches from his face. 'Are you telling me that's your sister buying dope off the white powder fairy?'

The kitchen door opened and I was aware of Grace standing there, but I was focused on Bobby. Scott tried to get up again and I slammed him back down, harder this time. 'Don't even think about moving,' I warned him. 'Did you bring drugs here, Bob, into my father's house?'

He mumbled a denial but his eyes wouldn't let him lie to me.

'Whose idea was it?' I demanded. 'Yours or his? Come on,' I sneered. 'Who's the daddy? Tell me. Is he shagging you, as well as your sister?'

I realise now that I wanted him to take a punch at me. I didn't realise then how scared he was of what might happen if he did. Even now, I don't know myself what would have happened if he had. It wasn't a Mulligan moment; that had been spontaneous, instantaneous and in hot blood. No, it was different; there was a fuse ready to be lit, and I had challenged Bobby to strike a match.

Grace ran across the room and put herself between us, pushing me away. I resisted her at first, but she whispered, 'Xavi, please.' I looked down at her and saw that she was frightened too; I couldn't work out why, but it was enough to make me back off. As I did, Scott finally made it to his feet, those bright staring eyes of his fixed on me, and stood alongside his friend . . . his friend, not mine, not any longer.

'Okay,' he shouted, 'so we smoked a bit of grass and we snorted a few lines. So fucking what? What the hell do you think this is? A temple? It's a flat, we're lads and that's what lads do. But a fat lot you'd know about that. You've been an old woman since you were born; hardly surprising, I suppose, since you were brought up by one.' Scott was a brave one, all right. He knew I wouldn't go through Grace to get to him.

'As for your father . . . "My father's house", indeed, as if he was God. You can't even stand him. Xavi, this last year or so, living with you's been like living . . . Christ, I'll bet they have more fun in Borstal. Bobby and I, we're out of here, right now. Grace, I don't know how you stand him.'

She turned and stared him down. 'I stand him,' she said, 'because he's everything you're not. I love him because he's what he is. You're a couple of fools who don't know what you're doing or where you're going in life. Wherever it is, it's not going to be here. So get on your way.'

Bobby looked at me, over her head. His eyes were misty. 'Xavi,' he mouthed, 'I'm sorry.'

I stared back at him, stared back at the stranger. 'Sure,' I said. I wonder if I sounded as cold as I felt.

They were gone within twenty minutes, without a goodbye, without any expression of regret beyond Bobby's attempted apology. I sat in my armchair gazing out of the window, hearing their muttered conversation behind me, then hearing the door close on a chapter of my life. Grace stayed in our room while it was happening. When we were alone, she emerged, curled up on my lap, and kissed me.

'Looks like we're a proper couple now, Xavi,' she murmured.

'At least a year later than we should have been,' I replied. 'I should have cleared Scott out when wee Dave left, and gone on with the two of us. I don't think I've truly liked him, you know. Everything's for Scott, everything's about Scott; he was just the same at school. He's led Bobby on.'

She shook her head. 'Inside that brash shell of his, there's a frightened boy hiding away, desperately hoping that nobody will see him. It's Bobby who's the dangerous one, gay Bobby; he's the manipulator, he's the controller, and Scott's always been fascinated by him.'

I peered at her, close up. I'd never seen Bobby that way before, but it was a day for shattered illusions. 'Fascinated?'

'Probably a bit more,' she said. 'I think the only reason he started going out with Jilly was to get Bobby's attention. And do you want to know what else I think? I think he succeeded only too well. I think Bobby seduced him. Now I think that's what he's frightened of; he's scared of anyone ever finding out. That's his secret.'

Anything was possible, I supposed, but right then I didn't want to think of Scott, or Bobby or any of them, not any more. 'As far as I'm concerned, my love,' I said, 'he can fuck the entire Hannah family, or vice versa . . . and isn't that an appropriate phrase? They are history; you and I, we're the future.' I ruffled her hair. 'We're engaged, and we're both twenty-one . . . or at least we both will be next week. Are you ready for the next step?'

'You mean getting married?'

'That's what being engaged is about, isn't it?'

'Yes, but there's plenty of time for that. Let me graduate, then qualify as an accountant. After that we can . . . move on. Meantime, let's just enjoy having this place to ourselves for a while.'

And that's what we did. I had what had been the boys' rooms redecorated, then turned one of them into a study, a quiet room where each of us could work in private when we had to (Grace had her finals looming; after those she would have professional exams, and with John's approval I still did occasional reports for the paper in Girona), and the other into a formal dining room. Suddenly we had a much bigger home and for the first time we were able to express ourselves in it. For example we were able to play our own music without worrying about anyone else, other than the neighbours. I spent more time on the piano, getting deeper and deeper into jazz, while Grace 'discovered', as she loved to put it, new bands, among them the newly formed Style Council, and an American group called REM, who developed, over the next few years, into an obsession with her. We were so liberated domestically that I let her talk me into buying a guitar. I knew a few chords and I could play the entire Neil Young repertoire on piano, so I picked it up fairly quickly. We even began to entertain other couples. We invited Rod and Magda for dinner . . . as a trial run, although we didn't tell them that. I did a Spanish starter, Grace did one of her mother's standard recipes as the main course, we bought the dessert from a cake shop, and it all seemed to work. It gave us a template for future events and in the time that followed John and Sheena Fisher, Ricky and Adrienne Thomas, and other friends from work followed them to our table. I'd have liked to invite Tommy Partridge, but he wouldn't have come on his own.

That doesn't mean that my stepfather wasn't an important part of my life in the years that followed. He made no secret within the force of our relationship. When he was promoted to detective chief inspector within the serious crimes unit, I began to have access to even more sensitive information. Two things might be read into that, but neither was true. I wasn't a stooge for the police, and I didn't go easy on them either. I was never given an advance on a general press release, and I never stopped or even held back on a story that put them in a bad light.

The most spectacular of these, three years into my *Saltire* career, involved someone I knew. I knew that Tommy suspected there was a

Perry Holmes mole in CID, and so when I had an anonymous call in the office from a source offering me his name, in exchange for a tip-off fee, I didn't dismiss it out of hand. I told him that if it worked out, we would pay out, but that the caller and I would have to meet. At first the man balked at that, but I told him it wasn't negotiable; I didn't want his name but I would have to sit down with him.

We got together early that evening in a pub at the end of Northumberland Street, well off the gangster circuit. He was a skinny guy, in his mid-thirties, with interesting fingers. We were the only people there apart from a blonde at a corner table with a guy I recognised as a PR executive. They looked to be doing some negotiating of their own; even I was invisible as far as they were concerned.

I bought the drinks, a pint of IPA for him, a bottle of Becks for me. 'Okay,' I said, 'down to business. How much?'

'Two hundred,' he retorted, firmly. 'Cash.'

I stayed impassive, but it was difficult. If he'd said two thousand, I wouldn't have been surprised, and I wouldn't have walked out either, without hearing what he had to say. 'Can be done,' I murmured. 'Depending on the quality of the information and whether it holds up.' I was actually carrying five hundred, expecting that he would want something up front. 'You give me the name, and if it winds up on page one with "Exclusive" alongside it, you get paid.' He nodded, and would probably have spilled it out there and then, had I not continued. 'But first, tell me why you're doing this.'

He looked at me, but his gaze stopped just short of my eyes. 'For money,' he mumbled.

'Bollocks. Nobody crosses the Holmes brothers for a couple of hundred quid.' I pointed to his hands. 'Do those run in the family?' He had rough tattoos on his fingers, a match . . . more than a match, since he still had all eight . . . for some I had seen before. There was a look about him too; a fraternal resemblance. His mouth tightened. 'Which Spreckley are you?' I asked.

'Billy,' he replied, reluctantly. 'Bastard killed my brother and my nephew . . . and it was your fault too. You owe me.'

'Are you telling me that Perry Holmes killed Gavin, and Ryan?'

'Himself? Of course not . . . it was . . .' He stopped. 'No, ye don't need to know that. Holmes has lots of people, but he's never near when that stuff happens.'

'Go to the police, if you know who did it. That's the best way to get even.'

'Are you fuckin' mad? Why do you think I'm here? Because anything that goes to them goes to him. I'll give you a name, but there are others, all over town, in the polis, and probably even in the fiscal's office as well. The fella I'm telling you about, he's the only one I know. He's a detective sergeant, name of Wallace.'

He went to pick up his pint, but I seized his wrist and squeezed it, hard. 'Are you setting me up?' I murmured. 'Because if I find out that you are, if I find out that this is bullshit, and that you're just trying to get back at this guy because he nicked you once, then I'll hand you over to Perry Holmes myself.'

He winced; I had made my point so I let him go. 'I'm not kidding,' he pleaded, 'honest. The man is on the payroll. I've seen him wi' Alasdair; I followed him one night and I saw them tegither.'

I found that hard to believe. 'You followed Alasdair Holmes?' I exclaimed. 'Why?'

Billy Spreckley seemed to shrink into his denim jacket. 'I was going to shoot him,' he whispered. 'It wasnae right what they did to Gavin and the boy.'

'What stopped you?' I asked, unconvinced.

'I realised what would happen to me if I did,' he replied. 'It wouldn't matter where I was. Look at what happened to Ramsay; being in the jail didn't make him safe, did it?'

He was right about that. I thought about what I was being told, I thought about what would happen if it played out as he feared, and I could see that Billy would surely wind up in the mortuary, sooner rather than later. I knew that wouldn't have sat well with me. I'd never felt a scrap of guilt about what happened to Gavin, but I didn't want to leave a trail of dead Spreckleys across town. I gave him the five hundred. 'Take that,' I told him, 'and fuck off. Get as far away from Edinburgh as you can and don't come back as long as the Holmes brothers are alive.'

He took the *Saltire*'s money, and my advice. I never saw Billy again, although I did hear from him indirectly, not quite ten years later. The way things panned out, he played one of the most important roles in the story of my life.

Nailing Bruce Wallace was so easy I was amazed that he'd got away with it for so long. I never even thought about tipping Tommy off that I was on to his sergeant. I was a journalist and I had a story. Obviously, knowing the guy, I couldn't handle the investigative work myself, but I directed it. I used Juliet Coats, who had stepped up from her copy-person role to become a junior reporter, and paired her with a new young photographer Ricky had just hired, also a girl. They did a damn good job. It took them a couple of weeks to establish Wallace's behaviour pattern, squash club on Tuesdays, pub every other week night, dinner out with wife Saturday, stay home Sunday, so when the first variation happened they were on to it quickly. On the third Tuesday of the surveillance he left home with his squash bag as usual, but he didn't go to the club. Instead he drove to Ratho, to a pub called the Bridge Inn. It was a summer evening and there were tables outside. The sergeant bought himself a pint and sat at one of them, but he was alone for only a couple of minutes before he was joined by a sallow individual in a dark business suit, balding, dark hair slicked back, rather outdated Mexican moustache, gold signet ring on the third finger of his right hand. I recognised Alasdair Holmes from Juliet's description before I'd even seen Denise's pictures, shot in perfect focus from the pub car park. They were so good that the handover of the envelope to Wallace might as well have been on film.

I wrote the story, and I gave Juliet a by-line, but after my own, just in case the aggrieved parties might think about making an example of her. We blacked out Al Holmes's face, and I didn't use his name. We couldn't prove what was in the envelope, and without that there was nothing to allege. All we did was report the fact; that a covert meeting had taken place between an Edinburgh detective and a man who was suspected of being a senior player in the city's organised crime.

That was all it took. A couple of hours before the story ran I met Tommy, told him about it, and gave him undoctored prints of the photographs. He was gutted. Bruce was his mate, and his confidant. When the connection to the Holmes brothers was made, he realised that some of those confidences had led to abortive operations and a couple of missing persons, as untraceable as Gavin Spreckley and Ryan Watson had proved to be.

Bruce Wallace was never charged. He had been smart enough never to bank any money, and there was no trail other than our photographs. Tommy told me afterwards that he had tried to claim that Alasdair Holmes was his tout, and that the stills actually showed him handing over an envelope, rather than receiving it, but when it was pointed out to him that they were in sequence on the negative, he collapsed. His resignation was accepted, the story went away, and so did he and his wife, to a bar in Tenerife that they bought for cash. The word went out, though, throughout the force: 'Be very careful in your choice of friends.'

My career was established from that point on. I was twenty-three years old, and I was recognised as the top crime reporter in Scotland, a distinction that was confirmed by two national awards in three years. I had offers from rival newspapers; the Glasgow giants the *Daily Record* and *Scottish Daily Express* were ready to start a bidding war for me, but I told them both that they were wasting their time. BBC wanted me to join their television news staff, but that didn't appeal either.

That's not to say that I settled for being what I was. I had told John at the very beginning that I didn't want to do crime, and while his decision to put me there had been vindicated, I didn't intend that it should be for life. And so I began to mix socially outside the cop-criminal world. Strangely, my rugby involvement helped me on my way. In those days, the game in Edinburgh was decidedly middle-class, and above. Even at player level, most of the people I met were plugged into the city's business and professional communities. I made sure that I accepted every club dinner invitation that came my way, and I was careful to take a supply of business cards to each one. Before long I had a second contacts book, almost as thick as the one that held the carefully coded details of my crime sources, and before long a different flow of stories started to come my way.

But it wasn't the rugby guys who gave me the biggest push. In the late summer of 1986, Grace passed her final professional examination, and became a fully qualified chartered accountant. We celebrated in a restaurant called Rafaelli's, a place in which boats were pushed out and gold Amex cards were flashed . . . although mine was a humble dollar-green at that stage of my life. Our table was in one of the quieter corners, almost out of sight. We were contemplating the dessert menu when a hand landed on my shoulder, and a voice behind me said, 'Xavi, Xavi, Xavi, well met.'

I looked over my shoulder, and found myself eye to eye with Alexander Draper. 'Is this your young lady?' he asked.

'This is my fiancée, Mr Draper,' I corrected him. 'Grace Starshine.'

'Starshine, Starshine,' he murmured. 'Lovely name, if unusual. But I know . . . Yes, of course, Rodney Starshine, one of our corporate members, a great supporter of the Hearts.'

'My father,' said Grace. 'You've made him a happy man.'

'I thought so. He's in the drugs business, isn't he?'

She smiled, and tossed her hair back. 'We prefer to call it pharmaceuticals.'

'We? Does that mean that you work for him?'

'Not right now. I'm with Bond and Rowan, the accountancy firm.'

He nodded. 'Outside experience. Good idea. Bring something new to the party when you do join.'

Draper had certainly brought something new to the Hearts party. The team had survived without me. The chairman had taken a moribund football club and restored its pride, and he was in the process of putting it on a sound business footing for the first time in its history. He had made a very large wave since his arrival in the city and he was riding on its crest.

He read my analogy. 'You're making quite a splash these days, Xavi. I'm sorry about what happened to you at Merrytown. Mind you, you don't seem to be missing football. Your name's all over the place.'

'I don't miss it a bit,' I confessed. 'I haven't been to a game in years.'

'In that case you and Grace must come tomorrow, as my guest. It's a UEFA cup qualifier, so the opposition won't be all that great, but the atmosphere will be good. You'll meet some interesting people too.'

I did. The football was poor . . . Hearts were playing a team from Finland, and they swept them aside . . . but I relished my return to the boardroom. The last time I'd been there, Alexander Draper had done a sales job and I'd signed on the dotted line for fucking Merrytown. He talked of nothing else as he introduced me around. (It was men only in there, of course; the chairman's wife entertained the ladies in a separate lounge.) I didn't see a single face in the room that I recognised from the old days. The members of the chairman's clique were all much younger, new money rather than old, business people rather than football people. At half-time he buttonholed one of them, James McLevy, the club lawyer, and drew both of us into a corner. 'Tell Xavi what you told me,' he murmured.

The solicitor must have been briefed in advance, because he didn't hesitate. 'A word to the wise,' he said. 'Do you know Fleming's?' Of course I did; it was one of the biggest furniture chains in the country, and it had started out as a family firm in George Street. 'They're about to be taken over,' he continued. 'Young Colin Fleming succeeded his father when he died last year and he's decided to get out before he makes an even bigger mess of things than he's done so far. He's selling to a conglomerate called Easdale; it specialises in out-of-town retailing, great big sheds, warehouses rather than shops. It's the coming thing, you know; you won't recognise the city centre in twenty years. The old

George Street shop will close and move to a new retail park that's going to be built to the east of the city, and the same will happen to all the Fleming stores.'

'More jobs?' I asked.

'The opposite; half the staff will go.'

'When's this going to be announced?'

'Midday on Friday, and nobody outside the loop has a clue.' He slipped me a card with a phone number on the back. 'That's the banker who's funding most of the operation. He won't tell you anything on the record, but he'll give you some of the headline cost figures. Don't pass this on to anyone else, though, Xavi. He'll only trust you.'

McLevy's tip held up. The financier gave me some very heavy investment figures, so willingly that I guessed he'd been expecting me. I called Colin Fleming and asked him for a comment. He panicked and referred me to his PR company. They panicked and threatened to sue me. Easdale were more cooperative; their spokesman told me that he couldn't confirm anything in advance of an announcement to the Stock Exchange, the equivalent of telling me to go ahead. I did. We splashed the story on page one and in the business section; a week later the *Scotsman* business editor was transferred to the features desk.

At the time I wondered why I'd been given this largesse, but it didn't take long for me to work it out. Fleming Furniture was the keystone of the proposed retail park; even before the Friday *Saltire* had become Saturday's fish supper wrapping, three other major companies had confirmed that they would be joining it. Full planning consent was granted less than a month later to the developer of the venture: Alexander Draper.

That's how I broke free of the criminal fraternity. Draper was the hottest ticket in town; nothing happened in the business community that he didn't hear of at its outset, and when it was in his interests to do so, he passed the news on to me. When it wasn't in his interests he didn't, but before long that didn't matter, as my networking in the rugby community had given me a list of friends who would. Business

Edinburgh split into two camps in those days, the nouveau like Alexander, the developers and the property professionals, and the old guard, the investment managers, the insurers, the stockbrokers and the lawyers: I had a foot on either side of the divide. There was a third camp, of course: it was the fiefdom of Perry Holmes and those who would ape him, but it was invisible.

On the day that I celebrated the fifth anniversary of my joining the paper full-time, John Fisher took me into the editor's office. It was just gone eleven o'clock, so I was astonished to see that Torcuil was there. 'Tell me, young Mr Aislado,' he said, as I sat, 'are you happy here?'

'Why do you ask?' I retorted. 'My happiness isn't the issue, is it? Are you happy that I'm here, that's the real question.'

'And why should I be unhappy?'

'Some of us are just born that way,' I replied. 'I don't know what happiness is,' I told him, candidly. 'I wake up in the morning and I see my girlfriend's face on the pillow and that gives me a good feeling. It tells me that my world is as it should be. Then I get up and I come in here, and if I'm lucky I'll phone someone to pass the time of day, and I'll pick up a tip. If I'm even luckier it'll be a really good one, I'll have another page-one splash and that will give me a real buzz. There is no story that I wouldn't report, and no story that I'll ever give up on if I know it's there. Perry Holmes, for example; potentially he is the biggest story in this city and one day I will report it.'

The editor frowned. 'Who's Perry Holmes?' Behind him, John Fisher rolled his eyes.

'Never mind. To tell you what you really want to know, I have a hard-on for this job. Do you, Torcuil? Maybe not, but that doesn't matter. The crucial point is that I do not have a hard-on for John's job, and least of all for yours. I'm a reporter, not a desk jockey.'

He blinked. 'Thank you for your frankness, Xavi. Does that mean that your ambitions lie elsewhere?'

'If they did,' I retorted, 'I'd have been gone by now. My commitment is to this job and to this paper.'

'In that case,' John intervened, 'we want to recognise it. Torcuil's agreed to give you a pay increase that'll make you the third highest earner in the place . . . and in this room,' he added. 'On top of that we need to give you a new title, one that reflects the job you're actually doing, but,' he grinned, 'doesn't give anyone the idea that you're more important than me. We're going to call you "Reporter Without Portfolio", if you're happy with that.'

'We're back to happy again, are we?' I retorted, but with a smile this time. 'I'm content with both of those proposals. Now can I get back to work?'

'Why are you doing this? Okay, stupid question; it's obvious why you're doing it. But what makes you think that you're going to get away with it? You come into my house, you hold us up at gunpoint, you bring me here, and of course I do what you say. But you're going to have to let us go, and when you do, that's when the hunt will begin. You think you're immune, you lawless ones. You hide behind your civilised exterior, your impeccable reputations, but you only get away with things because you intimidate others. Well, not me, not this one. People like me, we may seem meek and mild, but we're not. You can hide behind that stupid Ronald Reagan mask, you and your silent friend who's playing Margaret Thatcher. But they're not going to protect you. The police will find you: my son-in-law, he's good at hunting people, he'll find you. He's a quiet one too, but maybe you should hope that the police get to you before him, for you've scared my wife, and he won't like that. You're chicken, criminals like you. You have no morals, you have no standards, you have no courage, hiding behind guns and masks. And why have you brought me to this place? I know: now you're going to steal my car. You're going to leave me here to walk miles to call the police and you think that you'll get away. You won't. My son-in-law will find you and he will burn you. He will take everything you have.'

'Is that so?'

'Ah, it speaks. That is so. So go on, President Reagan, be on your way. You and your silly mask. You don't even have the balls to take it off and let me see your face, not even when there's only you and me here.'

'Oh no?'

Thirteen

My new designation at the paper gave me a freedom afforded to very few journalists. It meant that I could pick my own stories, and that I worked without direction. I didn't desert crime ... or rather it didn't desert me ... but I recruited Juliet Coats to take on much of the work, and took her around the police offices in the way that Doug McGrane, 'The Absentee', as he had become known, had taken me.

When I looked back then, as I still do, at my career, I was pleased with the way it had evolved. I had entered journalism full of zeal, inspired by Simon Sureda, but without anything resembling a plan, and there I was in my mid-twenties, if not a household name, at least a man of influence and respect. 'Happy?' Torcuil had asked. 'Content,' I had replied to John, and that's how it was.

My life at home was the same. Grace and I were both busy people, but we made allowances for each other. For example, she tolerated my weekend commitment to rugby during the winters. She even said that it allowed her personal space, although I had no idea what she meant by that, other than afternoons in John Lewis with her mum. In return, I tolerated her modelling assignments in Glasgow and the overnight stays that almost invariably they involved. When we were together, we tended to keep ourselves to ourselves, unless we were entertaining, or being entertained.

I'm not saying that I had a fan club, but my growing reputation, allied to my totemic appearance, made it difficult for us to go out without being interrupted, or imposed upon, and Grace didn't like that when it happened. The marriage question drifted on. Neither of us was in a rush, not being ready to start a family, but hints were dropped with increasing frequency, occasionally by Grandma Paloma, but especially by Rod, who took to referring to me as his 'son-in-law'. Eventually we gave in, and settled on June 1988, date to be determined by the availability of a suitable venue for the reception. We did discuss doing the deed quietly ourselves, since it was to be a civil ceremony rather than church or synagogue, but that would have denied Magda her big day, and I'd come to love her too much for that.

I wasn't cut off from Spain as my young life developed. We spent nearly all of our holidays there, summer and Christmas, although in 1984, our first full year of being a couple, we did fit in a spring week in Paris, following up in the three years that followed with trips to Rome, Florence, and Bruges . . . it's in Belgium.

For all that, it was very important for me to see Grandma as often as I could. Her confrontation with cancer had left more of a mark on me than it seemed to have on her. It was a warning, a long-distance forecast that promised bad weather down the line. I'd always known that she wouldn't go on forever, and I was no longer able to ignore the fact. To Grace and Carmen she seemed unchanged by time, as she insisted that she was, but not to me, and not, I believe now, to my dad. As time passed, while she remained outwardly robust, I thought I could sense a growing transparency about her, a little more each year, the intimation of inevitable mortality. Still, she entered her eighties in full sail, taking a growing interest in Grace and me as a couple, sending her flowers on her graduation and on her final qualification as a CA.

I wanted to spend as much time with her as my life allowed, and I sensed that she wanted that as much as I did. Every year, she spoke to me more, in private, as if she was preparing me for something, and knew that she had limited time left to finish the course. Two days after Christmas, in 1987, she and I sat together in the garden, beside the pool, which my Catalan-Scots dad never emptied for the winter because it would have cost too much to refill. It was mid-afternoon, the sky was one hundred per cent blue, and the sun was as high as it was going to get that day. I wore jeans and a T-shirt, she, a long skirt, a white blouse and a shawl.

'My husband wouldn't have believed this,' she said, breaking a silence that had lain comfortably between us. 'When we left I think he knew that he would never return, and although he made Josep-Maria promise that he would bring me back here when it was safe, he died without ever believing that it would happen. He assumed that after Franco, there would be another general, and so on and so on.'

'What was he like?' I asked her. 'Other than being a murderer, that is,' I added with a grin.

'He wasn't a murderer,' she protested. 'He was defending his family. But he was a very single-minded man. If he thought something was right, then he would do it and nothing would get in his way. He lacked imagination perhaps, he wasn't a natural businessman in the way that Josep-Maria is, but people respected him, and they felt they could trust him. Some tried to take advantage of that, but anyone who underestimated him usually came off worst, like those people in that awful football club you joined, when you were hurt, like they did with you. Yes, you're not unlike him, my boy. Maybe that's one reason why your career has gone so well, so far.'

I smiled. 'Maybe. And maybe the other is that I'm damn good at what I do.'

'No doubt. But be sure of one thing,' she murmured, her eyes misting as she spoke. 'Your life won't always be as uncomplicated. Things will happen to you that are beyond your imagination, and how you are in the years afterwards will be determined by the way you deal with them.'

'Are you sure you don't have gipsy blood?' I chuckled.

'Pah!' she spluttered, then smiled when she realised that I had played her. After twenty-five years of living with her, I knew how to push her buttons.

I had grown up thinking that Grandma Paloma was fey, that she had second sight, before it dawned on me that what she really had was a very good intelligence network, good sources, as the adult Xavi would put it. And yet now, as I think back to that afternoon in the winter garden, I'm not so sure. Yes, today, I know that she was warning me obliquely of the natural events that are lying in wait for all of us on our way through life, but I wonder whether she might have seen something else, had a supernatural glimpse of the horror and tragedy that were to come.

Although our wedding day was drawing nearer, Grace and I refused to be obsessed by it. We were both busy with our work . . . she had been made a junior line manager by her accountancy firm . . . and so we left all that to Magda. She had decided, finally, on the Norton House Hotel as the venue for the reception and had turned her attention to devising a menu that would suit the more orthodox members of the Starshine family . . . both of them . . . as well as a couple of Catalans. Grandma Paloma and my dad had both promised to come, the latter on pain of something or other, I guessed, as it would require the best part of a week away from his beloved business.

We were eight days away from the big day when it happened, on a Thursday. Grace had been growing more and more preoccupied, and edgy with it. Registry office or not, Magda had insisted that she would be married in white, and not in a rented dress either, but one that would be specially made, and put away for our daughters should they ever have need of it. She had a scheduled fitting with her mother after work, and came home from it full of hell. 'What's up?' I asked her. 'Is it too tight? Does your bum look big in it?'

'It makes me look like a fairy on a fucking Christmas tree,' she snapped. 'All thanks to my dear mother and her posh ideas. She even turned up for the fitting in that yellow Versace suit of hers.'

'Can you have Jewish fairies?'

'Very funny! You wouldn't be laughing if it was you.'

'I might not, but everyone else would be. And what about me? They don't have morning suits my size in Moss Bros. Mine's a tailor-made job too, remember.'

'Big deal. Measurement, one fitting, and that's it. Honest, Xavi,' she said, with a vehemence that set me back on my heels. 'I could strangle my parents. All my childhood they treated me like a little doll; they suffocated me.'

'Hey!' I protested. 'That's not the Magda and Rod I know.'

'Well, you know fuck all then!' she shouted. She was tetchier than I'd ever known her; I hadn't realised that the pre-wedding nerves were gripping her so hard.

I put my arms around her. 'I know one thing,' I told her, quietly. 'This event isn't about them, it's about us. Your mother may think of it as her big day, and if she does, let her; you're her only daughter. But we know different, don't we? We know that it's our day, and that everybody else in that hotel, them included, will be just spectators. For what it's worth, I'm in your camp. I'd rather get married in Levi's than in some poncy gear that's costing me a month's salary, but if it keeps a smile on Magda's face, and brings even a hint of one to Grandma Paloma's, then I will dress up like the head fucking waiter. For now, let's go up to the Bar Roma for a steak and however much Chianti it takes to get you over these pre-nuptial blues, or pre-menstrual tension, or whatever it is that's turning you from the goddess that I worship into a she-devil. Deal?'

She nodded. 'Deal.' She looked up at me. 'I love you, Xavi, really I do. It's jus . . . it's just . . . Och! It just is, okay?'

'Not to be understood,' I told her. 'Only to be loved, and that's enough for me.'

The chef in Bar Roma went some way to calming Grace down, and the Chianti did even more. When we arrived home she slurred her 'Good night' and went straight to bed. By the time I followed her, fifteen minutes later, she was lying face down, her right arm hanging over the side of the bed, out like a light.

She slept so soundly that she didn't waken when the phone rang, at just after four next morning. I did; I've always been a light sleeper, disturbed by the faintest sounds in the night. I snatched the receiver

321

from my bedside table. 'Yes!' If it's possible to whisper a snarl, that's what I did.

'Xavi,' said a voice I knew; not a prankster. 'You awake.'

'Stupid question, Tommy.'

'Get dressed. I'll pick you up in twenty minutes.' There was an echo, and background noise. I guessed that he wasn't calling from home.

'What the . . .'

'No time. Wait at your front door.' The line went dead.

'. . . bloody hell is this about?'

I slid out of bed, found some clothes in the darkness and dressed in the sitting room. I left a note for Grace on the kitchen table and made my way downstairs, wondering all the time what was important enough for any DCI, stepfather or not, to be digging me up in the middle of the night. He was a couple of minutes ahead of schedule when he pulled into the driveway of my block, not driving himself, but in a patrol car, complete with blue light. I slid into the back, awkwardly, my knees jammed into the front passenger seat until he slid it a little further forward.

'Are you going to tell me now?' I asked.

He shook his head. 'No. I need you to see this.' The car headed west, paying no heed to speed limits on the almost empty roads. The sun rises early in Scotland in June, and to the north the sky is never really dark. With Tommy staying silent, I took in the unfamiliar sights of the sleeping suburbs, until we left them behind, passing the airport and the Royal Highland Showground, as we headed into West Lothian, along what had once been the only road between Glasgow and Edinburgh, before the building of the M8 motorway. I checked my watch as we passed a sign that read 'Broxburn'; it showed five minutes before five.

'Look,' I began, frustration getting the better of me.

He turned in his seat and looked at me, properly for the first time. His eyes were slightly wide and his face was set. I'd never seen him so tense, not even when I'd told him that his pal Bruce Wallace was bent. 'Soon,' he said.

We had barely entered the small town before the driver executed a right turn, still at speed. There was a dark shape on the skyline ahead of us; I recognised it as one of the red shale bings that are dotted around the county, great waste tips that are relics of the days of James 'Paraffin' Young and the Victorian oil industry that once was its economic base. As we drew closer to it, I realised that it was our destination. As we reached it, I saw another police car parked at the junction with a track that led to its base, and a uniformed officer standing guard. As he waved us through, I tried again. 'Crime scene?' My stepfather nodded. 'Tommy, why am I getting this treatment? If the other papers hear about this, there'll be hell to pay, for me as well as you.'

He put a finger to his lips, just as our driver pulled up at a blue tape that had been stretched across the rough road. 'Looks like we walk from here,' he said.

As we stepped out of the car, another cop approached, Jeff Adam, who had taken Bruce Wallace's place on the Serious Crimes squad. 'It's up here, sir,' he said, then nodded to me, grim-faced. 'Xavi.'

He had the same look as Tommy in his eyes. Their tension invaded me like a fast-acting virus, racing through my body, chilling my stomach, tightening my scrotum. We walked up a rise, the red shale beneath our feet, until we reached a bend, and a plateau that lay beyond it. About fifty yards ahead of us I saw a car, a Volvo estate, red, like one I knew very well. Its back number plate was towards us. My eyes are good even now, but when I was twenty-six my vision was scalpel-sharp. I recognised it; it was Rod Starshine's car. Several other people stood around. One of them, a man, was standing by the open driver's door, camera raised, taking photographs of something at his feet. Or someone.

Tommy and Jeff each sensed that I was about to break into a run, for they held me back, by my elbows. I struggled for a second or two. I reckon that if I'd really wanted to break free I could have, even from two of them, but I let myself be restrained.

'You're not here as a journalist, Xavi,' my stepfather said. 'We need you to make a formal identification.'

I felt ice-cold, and it had nothing to do with the slight sharpness of the morning air. I was speechless; I could only nod. Jeff stood aside, and Tommy walked me towards the car then round it. The photographer stood back as we approached.

The sun was still too weak to cast shadows but it was bright enough for me to make out, all too well, what they had brought me there to see. Rod's body hung half out of the car, twisted so that he was face up. He was in shirtsleeves and flannels; no jacket. His right eye was staring at the sky. His left eye was gone; where it had been was a red, mushy mass.

I photographed the scene too, without a camera. I still have the image, in my mental chamber of horrors, alongside that of the hands of Gavin Spreckley and Ryan Watson, and others, worse, even worse, that have joined it since. Even today, if I close my eyes and concentrate I can see every detail. His mouth hung open and the expression in his remaining eye seemed to be one of surprise, as if he had been unable to contemplate what was about to happen to him. I looked inside the car and saw red streaks on the windscreen and on the window of the driver's door.

'Well?' Tommy whispered.

'That's Rodney Starshine,' I confirmed. 'By this time next week, he'd have been pacing the floor, getting ready for his daughter's wedding. So why should he kill himself?' I added . . . to myself, but my stepfather replied, and it stunned me.

'He didn't. He was murdered.'

'What?' I went from cold to hot in a second. 'Why?' I growled, feeling unfamiliar rage well up.

'We've established that there's been a robbery at Starshine Pharmaceuticals,' Jeff Adam told me. 'The first thing we did was to check there. We found the safe open, and the dispatch area, where they keep drugs that are ready for shipment to the wholesalers, had been stripped out. We've got the night security man helping us. I've spoken to him, and I've got a couple of DCs taking a detailed statement from him now.'

'Are you saying that he . . .'

'I don't imagine so, not for a minute. He's an ex-cop, and he was vetted for the job. But we have to interview him before we can eliminate him as a suspect. So far all he's told us is that Mr Starshine turned up very late at the factory, alone, as far as he could see, drove inside, stayed for a while, then left again. My feeling is that if the guy had been in on it, he'd be long gone.'

'What else?'

'The doctor says that he appears to have been shot only once, at close range. The forensic people say that the bullet's lodged in the door arch, which means that whoever killed him was sitting in the back seat. There's a travelling rug on the floor. If he hid under that it would explain the security officer not seeing him.'

I was surprised. 'They don't search all vehicles on the way out? They make diamorphine in there, and all sorts.'

'They don't search the boss's car.'

This is strange but it was true: I knew that Rod's factory produced class A drugs as well as milder pharmaceuticals, but he had never taken me there, so my knowledge of its supposedly iron-clad security was built on scraps dropped by him and by Grace.

'Who found him?'

'A man and his girlfriend,' Tommy told me. 'They came up here for a bit of this and that. He saw the Volvo's door open and thought it looked a bit odd, so he checked it out. He went straight to the Broxburn police office. Many another guy would have done a runner, since this one has a wife as well as his bird, and he knew they'd both have to give us their details.'

'Have you got a name for him,' I asked, 'and an address and a number?' As I realised what I had just said, I buried my face in my hands. I was thinking like a reporter. Witness, therefore get a quote; beat the opposition to it. 'Oh Jesus,' I whispered. My fiancée's father, a man I'd known since my adolescence, was lying dead at my feet, and all I could think of was another fucking headline with 'EXCLUSIVE!' in a banner above it.

My stepfather understood. He patted me on the shoulder. 'Easy now, mate,' he said, gently. 'We'd best get you home to Grace. I'll call John Fisher and let him know what's happened. I've got his number. I'm the polis; I've got everybody's number.'

I recovered myself. 'What about Magda?' I asked him. 'Who's going to tell her?'

'I'll get a woman officer to go to the house.'

'Like fuck you will. You'll take me there. I'll tell her, then your officer can stay with her while I break it to Grace.'

'Okay, Xavi. If that's what you want.'

He led me back to the patrol car. He slid into the back seat alongside me, as sombre and lost in thought as I was. We hadn't gone far down the road back to Broxburn when I saw a car heading in the opposite direction. As we passed each other I recognised the driver as a *Daily Record* reporter. My professional instincts awoke again, a wholly involuntary reflex, breaking through the shock. They told me that there had been a leak from within the force; if the tip-off had included the name of the victim, then Magda's phone might ring at any moment. I told Tommy as much, and he ordered the driver to put the hammer down again. He cut through the suburbs, took the Western Approach Road, then turned up Lothian Road, heading for the Grange.

The Starshine place was in a cul-de-sac called Copper Lane. It was a large stone villa of conservative design, set well back from the road and hidden discreetly behind a large hedge. It was the house of a wealthy family who didn't want to be ostentatious about it and it had been home to three generations since Rod's grandfather had bought it during the war years of the 1940s. Tommy told the driver to stop at the entrance, and to wait there, on guard against callers. I didn't want any other journalists on the doorstep, to protect Magda's privacy rather than my exclusive access to the story . . . at least I hope that was why.

There were no lights showing as we approached, but that meant very little, since the daylight was growing ever stronger. I looked up at Rod and Magda's bedroom window and saw that it was still curtained. As was normal, the double storm doors that gave entry to the vestibule were open. I led the way in and rang the doorbell. As I did, I noticed that my hand was rock steady, and felt another wave of guilt pass through me. I had just seen the murdered corpse of someone very close to me and yet I was still functioning, still in control, still razor-sharp and on the job.

My stepfather may have read my thoughts once again, for he put a hand on my sleeve. 'I'll do the talking if you want,' he offered.

I shook my head. 'Tommy,' I told him, 'I don't even want you in the room when I tell her. I'm sorry, man, but this is family.'

'Sure,' he murmured. His tone told me I'd made him feel that as far as I was concerned, he wasn't, but I had no time for guilty self-recrimination.

We waited for the door to open, but it didn't. I rang again, but there was no response. 'She's probably asleep,' Tommy guessed. 'I can give her a wake-up call through the car.'

'No need,' I replied. 'I can get in.' In my rush to be ready for my pick-up, I had snatched the wrong keys from the dish in the kitchen, where we kept them, taking Grace's instead of my own. Her collection included one for her parents' house, just as they had one for ours in case of emergencies when we were away. I dug it out of my pocket and found the one I needed without difficulty. It was a brass Chubb, unlike any of the others.

I slipped it into the keyhole, but when I tried to turn it, nothing happened. The front door was unlocked. I stepped into the hall, and called out loudly, 'Magda! It's Xavi. Are you there?' I didn't expect an instant reply, knowing that if she slept anything like as soundly as her daughter, it would take more than that to waken her.

'Wait here,' I told Tommy. 'I'll go up to their room.' I climbed the stairs, up to the half landing and round then on to the upper floor. As I turned to my right I could see my future in-laws' bedroom door, and more; it was still gloomy in the upper hall and a strip of light showed clearly beneath it.

I was there in two strides. 'Magda!' I shouted again, turning the handle as I spoke. There was no response, but by that time I didn't expect one. I stepped inside.

Magda had a thing for chandeliers, even in the bedroom. It was lit up like a football field, but the thick black-out curtains let nothing through to the outside. The bed hadn't been slept in, but the satin cover was rumpled as if someone had been sitting on it. There was a jacket hanging on Rod's Corby trouser press, which stood in the far corner. Close by, another lay on the floor, discarded. The first shiver ran through me then, for it was Magda's yellow Versace, and she was as neat and tidy as her husband. She'd been there, but . . .

The door to their bathroom was in the furthest corner of the room from where I stood. It was open. As I walked round to check it out, I caught the smell for the first time, acrid, odd, like the aftermath of a garden firework display, but before I could consider what it might be . . .

Magda was in the bathroom. She was lying on her side on the floor, in front of the toilet and bidet, her head and shoulders in the tray of the shower cabinet. There was blood on the floor where she lay and in the shower, blood on the walls, blood on the bathroom fittings and on the bath panel. There was a trail of it from the doorway; the trousers of the yellow Versace, and her white blouse, had red rose smears all over them, and her hair, blonde like her daughter's, was mostly dark and matted. I stood and stared, aware that my mouth was hanging open but unable to close it, wanting to scream, but incapable of making a sound. Somehow, after Tommy's early hours summons, I'd been prepared for something very bad at the shale tip, but not that, not that, not Magda, not that bright, vivacious, kind, lovely . . .

I knew that she was dead; it didn't occur to me for one second that she might have been breathing. 'Deathly still' isn't just a simile, and she was. As I stared, frozen, details began to register with me. In the centre of the red roses, there were darker spots that I took to be bullet wounds. I noted one on her right thigh, from which a lot of the blood seemed to have flowed, one on her left buttock, two on her torso, and judging by the dark tangled mess of her hair, at least one shot had hit her in the head. Two of the floor tiles were shattered. Her killer had been no marksman, just a bastard with a gun, firing wildly but at such close range he had been certain to have hit more often than he had missed.

I didn't hear Tommy come up behind me, but I heard him gasp, and saw his right hand at the edge of my vision as he seized the door frame, then felt the other on my shoulder, gripping tight as if his legs had given way. 'Oh dear,' he moaned. 'Oh dear, oh dear, oh dear. Oh Xavi, son, this is the worst thing I've ever seen.'

'Me too,' someone else murmured. 'But it won't be, not after I've found the bastards who did this. I'm going to rip them to bits with my bare hands.' I was in a trance, hovering somewhere out of my body; the big guy in the doorway who had made that solemn promise looked just like me, sounded just like me, but I didn't know him.

Tommy drew me back, into the bedroom; he had to pull me pretty hard before I yielded, and came back within myself. 'Tell me what this means,' I whispered.

It took him a while to reply, but eventually he did. 'It tells us why Rod Starshine took the guy who shot him into the factory. Somebody else, maybe more than one person, was holding his wife hostage.'

'But why kill them both?'

He tried to look at me, but he couldn't, so he closed his eyes instead. 'With some people, Xavi, it's "Why not?" We'll find out when we catch them. Wait here,' he continued, then stepped back into the bathroom, stepping carefully, avoiding the blood, to do what I hadn't, put a hand to Magda's neck, feeling for the pulse that we both knew was gone but doing it anyway in case of a miracle. He didn't take long to satisfy himself, only a few seconds, then he was back. 'We have to get out of here,' he decreed, trying to sound businesslike, but with a tremor still in his voice. 'Hopefully these people have left a calling card for the forensic crew to find.'

We left the awful room and went back downstairs. 'Where's the phone?' Tommy asked, as we stood in the hall. I took him into the kitchen; he called the police control room and ordered that officers and a forensic team be sent to Copper Lane, but discreetly, no blue lights or sirens, then asked to be patched through to Detective Chief Superintendent Alf Stein, the recently appointed Head of CID. We'd met, Alf and I; he was one of the good guys, and I rated him.

Once he'd been wakened and was on line, Tommy told him in detail what had happened, then fell silent. 'Yes, sir,' I heard him say, 'both victims have been identified, by a male relative; Xavi Aislado, as it happens. I think you know him.' He nodded as he listened. 'Yes, I agree, but I don't reckon that'll be easy. The *Record* knows something's up in West Lothian even now. Yes, sir, I'll wait here for you.'

He turned to me as he hung up. 'The boss says he wants to keep a lid on the information,' he told me, 'until we know what's gone from the factory and we're ready to make a full statement.'

'I need to be home before that happens,' I replied. 'Christ, I need to be home now.' My stomach was beginning to churn at the thought of telling Grace.

'As soon as the first car gets here, and that should only be a couple of minutes, my driver will take you home. Don't worry; I'll still call Fisher for you.' I no longer gave a shit about the *Saltire*, or any news story that I'd ever covered; finally my news brain had been overwhelmed by what I had seen, on the shale tip and upstairs. 'Have you got anyone, Xavi?' he continued. 'Anyone who can be with you just now? Another woman to help you with Grace . . . because you're going to need some help.'

'Rod has an older sister,' I murmured, noticing my mistaken tense as I uttered it, but choosing not to correct myself, 'but she and her husband are very orthodox. They never really approved of Magda, and Grace can't stand them. They were only invited to the wedding because Rod felt he had to.'

'Nobody else?'

'There's only Grandma Paloma,' I said. 'And she's an old lady.'

'There is somebody else, son,' he ventured. We both knew that he was risking my wrath; I kept it in check.

'No, Tommy,' I replied. 'I'm sorry, but there isn't.'

As it happened, Sheena Fisher volunteered for the worst job in town. She's a good woman, and she made John call me as soon as Tommy told him what had happened. By that time, Grace was in the bedroom, screaming silently into her pillow. She'd been in the kitchen when I got home, brewing a pot of tea . . . she liked Earl Grey, in leaf form, not tea bag . . . and humming an REM tune. The note I'd left had read 'Work, urgent,' all I'd known myself at the time, so I'd given her no reason to suspect that something was wrong, but the look on my face changed all that, as I stepped through the door. She stared at me, and frowned. 'What's up, Xavi?' she asked. 'You look as if you've seen a ghost.'

'I wish I had,' I whispered, as the full force of the tragedy finally hit me, and my eyes filled with tears. 'It might have helped.' I drew her to me and held her, weeping into her hair, feeling her stroke my back, sensing somehow her growing fear as I tried to compose myself so that I could make it come true. She led me into the living room, sat me down on the couch and waited, until I was able to tell her, as calmly as I could, what had happened.

'There was a robbery, at Rod's factory. Your mother was held prisoner while he was taken there, and made to open the safe and clear out the despatch room. When it was over, and they'd got what they wanted, they shot them both. They're dead, love, our folks are dead.'

She stared back at me, wide-eyed with an expression I'd never seen before. Not disbelief, as I'd expected, but hate; hate for the person, whoever he was, who'd just thrown acid all over her life.

It passed, and became a bemused frown. 'They killed them?' she exclaimed. 'They killed them? They killed them? They killed them?' And then the scream erupted, a howl of the purest rage, unlike any other sound I've heard a human being make. 'Bastardssss!!!' but it wasn't a word, instead a pure roar of rage, and the look in her eyes matched it. I leaned over to pull her to me, but she hit me, battering my chest with her fists over and over again, her eyes fixed on nothing, her mouth as tight as a razor's edge.

I let her work out her horror and her shock and then I picked her up, carried her through to our bed and laid her down upon it. She lay rigid and I sat beside her, watching her lips move without sound, wincing at the grief and pain in her dry, staring eyes.

I don't know how long we'd been there, in those postures, when I heard the door alert; I don't even know how long it had been buzzing. My basic instinct was to leave it, but I thought that it might be Tommy Partridge, so finally I answered. It wasn't him, but someone he had sent, a doctor from the police panel, a chum he'd asked to do him a grim favour. I let him in. Grace didn't react to his presence as he took her pulse, nor flinch as he shot her with the sedative that I'd okayed. He offered me some of the same, but I declined. The day was going to be hell, Grace was going to need me, and I reckoned that I wouldn't be much good to her as a zombie.

The doc had barely gone when my boss phoned; he didn't really know what to say, so I helped him. 'I've been in the job for six years now, and I've seen some stuff,' I told him. 'You've seen even more. There's evil in the world, mate, no question; guys like us, we encounter a lot of it, so we build invisible walls between it and our own comfortable lives. Mine's been broken, John. It's got inside, and what it's done . . . what it did to those two lovely people . . .'

I felt the furnace light within me once again. 'I want to find them, Jock. I want to use every contact I have, every source, pull in every favour I'm owed, till I track down these bastards. Then when I've found them I want to sit down with them and ask them just one question. "Why?" It's something I haven't done yet. I've covered some bad stuff, and I've dealt with some crazy people, like that poor bastard with AIDS, but I've never confronted anyone like these people, cold, calculating and pure downright evil. I want to know what they're like. I want to know how to recognise it . . . before I rip its head off.' I sighed. 'But I can't do any of that, I know. I can't cover this one for you. I have to give everything I have to Grace, to get her through this. Anyway,' I admitted, 'I can't describe what I saw. I don't think I'll ever be able to write it down.'

'The day that you can unaided,' Jock replied, 'I will be truly worried about you as a human being. People like us, Xavi, and cops too, we who look over the edge into the nether world, we run the risk of losing our humanity. Too many of us do. The guy McGrane, maybe he got out because he saw himself heading that way. You're on leave, son, indefinite leave. Only come back to work when you and Grace are both ready for it.' He paused. 'Listen, will it be all right if I bring the wife over? She thinks Grace might need somebody about the house. You too, for that matter; you don't want to be answering your phone today.'

Gratitude washed over me like a warm wave. 'Please do. As long as she knows it's the shittiest job in the world.'

'No, Xavi. Mine is.'

'Then let me help you in the only way I can. There are two photographs in my desk drawer. I don't like to display them, but I keep them there. One is of Magda, Rod, Grace and me, taken at a Chamber of Commerce dinner dance a year or so back. Use that any way you like.'

Twenty minutes later, I saw the crappy old Allegro . . . he kept it until it died, in 1991 . . . pull into our drive. I was ready to open the door for Sheena as soon as she buzzed. I was slightly surprised that there were no photographers waiting outside, and that I hadn't had any calls from reporters. I guessed, correctly as it turned out, that Alf Stein had sent a 'Fear of God' message round the force warning against any leak of the victims' names until he was ready to announce them.

Sheena didn't look at her best when she came in, but she made me feel better for sure; not unburdened, but enormously relieved that there was someone there to help me bear it. 'Awful,' she whispered, as she gave me a quick hug. 'Where's Grace?'

'Bedroom. A police doctor knocked her out, and left me some industrial-strength sedative tablets for later . . . made by Starshine Pharmaceuticals, for all I know.'

'Let's hope she stays under for a while. Have you had anything to eat?'

'The thought of it's never occurred to me.'

'Then you should.'

Even with all that had happened, all that I'd seen, it was still just short of seven thirty. On a normal day I wouldn't have had breakfast for at least another half hour, and not much of one at that, but a bizarre shock-driven reflex must have kicked in, for the mention of food made me feel ravenous. I nodded. 'Yes please. There's stuff in the fridge.'

As Sheena went into the kitchen, I switched on the radio, and tuned to Forth, the local station, just in time to catch the half-hourly news bulletin. It reported police activity at both scenes, but there was no hint that they were linked. That was a relief, although I knew that it wouldn't be long before an enterprising reporter spotted my connection with the address of the city incident.

I felt becalmed, waiting for the storm to hit. I slumped into my armchair, picked up the phone and dialled the Spanish number. As it rang out, an hour later in Central European Time, I hoped that my dad hadn't already left for the office, and that he would answer rather than Grandma Paloma. She was eighty-four, and although she was still younger than her years, I didn't want to be telling her my story. Fortunately, he was there. It was Carmen who answered; all the pretence surrounding them had been abandoned. She put him on, and I told him the story, slowly, so that he could take it all in.

'Oh my,' he murmured when I was finished. It occurred to me that I'd never known him to be shaken by anything before then. 'Those bastard drug dealers,' he spat, in a fury. 'I'm not a butcher, Xavi, but I'd hang the fuckers, in a public place, in front of the people they victimise. You tell that poor girl I'm coming right over. I'm going to light a fire under the fucking polis.'

That was the very last thing I wanted, or needed. John Fisher was quite capable of doing that job, if the investigation lagged, and so was I for that matter, behind the scenes. 'No,' I told him firmly. 'Thanks, but please don't. You'll be more use to us in Spain than here. You stay with Grandma; she's motored through everything else in her life, but not this.'

'Stay with her? I'll need to tie her down to keep her off the fucking plane. I've got one booked for next Wednesday, for the wedding, but as soon as she hears about this she'll want to be with you by lunchtime.'

'Then tell her we'll come to her. This will break here very soon. And when it does, the story will be mega. You'll even be covering it in Girona. It won't matter if they make an arrest within the next hour or so, Grace is going to be mobbed here, even worse than anyone else because of who I am. I need to get her out of that.'

'Then I'll charter a plane for you. You'll let me do that at least.'

'Of course.'

'How soon?'

I had given no thought to any of the practical consequences of the murders. Funerals. How long would the police keep the bodies in the mortuary? For a while, I guessed; even after they'd done autopsies there was the possibility that defence lawyers, after arrests were made, might want to have another pathologist take a look. And then there was the factory. People worked there; hospitals and pharmacies depended on its output. It would pass to Grace; she'd have to take some quick decisions, but it would be a while before she was capable.

'I don't know. The police will want to talk to us again. And there are people I'll need to talk to myself. Two days, maybe; tomorrow if we're lucky.'

'Tell me as soon as you know. I'll have a plane on standby.' He paused. 'I'll need to go. I can hear my mother heading this way.'

I hung up, and went through to our room, to check on Grace. She was awake, sitting up, leaning against the headboard, her eyes red, puffy, and doped. She looked up at me. 'It's true?' she asked, throat dry, her voice a croak.

I lowered myself alongside her. 'Yes, *chica*,' I replied. 'I'm afraid it is.'

'Then my life's over,' she said. 'Everything there was before is gone.'

I took her hand. 'I'm not,' I whispered. 'I'll always be here.'

'I know. But everything changes. All my plans are gone up in smoke.' And then she began to sing quietly; one of her REM favourites, from their newest album, the one she'd been playing almost non-stop for nine months. *'It's the end of the world as we know it … and I feel fine.'* She slumped into me, her head resting against my arm, repeating the words, over and over again.

'You know what's going to happen to us, don't you?'

'Nothing.'

'You think? Life with a minimum of twenty-five years is nothing? We've pulled off an armed robbery, and we've killed two people in the process. We're wanted for the rest of our days, or until they catch us, or until . . .'

'Nothing is going to happen to us. We wore sterile clothing so we've left no traces. The guns are in pieces and the bits are scattered all along the Water of Leith. There's nothing to lead the police or anyone else to us. Mr Plod is going to be looking for the stolen drugs to surface locally, but they're not going to. We got what we were after, the payroll of one of the last companies in the country that still pays most of its wages in cash, but Mr Plod's going to be thinking that we went in there looking for dope and got lucky. We are lucky; we're free and clear.'

'I'm glad you're so fucking confident. Why did you have to shoot him, man?'

'So I'd feel so fucking confident. No witnesses.'

'That wasn't what we agreed.'

'We agreed that we would do what was necessary. And you did too, remember.'

'You left me no choice.'

'And you still have none. The sun will rise tomorrow as usual, and it will follow its usual pattern. So will we, tomorrow and every day, until we're ready to move on.'

'I want out of here now. I want my share and I want to go.'

'Not a chance. That would be weakness, and any weakness on anyone's part puts the rest of us in danger. Granted, killing the two of them changes things a bit, changes the timetable, but we stay the course. We have to. You run, you do it without money. But you won't, because if you show me weakness again, I'll kill you too.'

Fourteen

Willie Lascelles was by no means the only lawyer in Edinburgh. As a matter of fact, the city was, and still is, teeming with them. But Willie was the best, and all his clients were blue chip, so it was quite natural that he acted for the Starshine family as well as for the Aislados. I rang him at nine fifteen, after Sheena had made us eat breakfast, then persuaded Grace to go back to bed, and after I had showered until the water had run cold, and for a while beyond that. I shampooed my hair three times, used half a bottle of body gel, yet I still couldn't make myself feel cleansed.

I told the solicitor that I needed him at the flat. By the time he arrived, we'd had phone calls from reporters from the *Evening News*, the *Daily Record*, the *Scottish Daily Mail* and the *Herald*, each one of them asking if they could speak to Grace and each one of them stone-walled by Sheena. Ex-directory status means nothing to us journalists; it's an obstacle but not a barrier. Only one of them asked for me, Ross Roberts, from the *Herald*; I knew him and I trusted him, so I spoke to him. 'What have you got?' I asked, before he could say a word.

'Police activity at your in-laws' place,' he replied. 'White coats, mortuary wagon; typical murder scene set-up. What's happened, Xavi?'

'It's as it looks,' I told him. 'What have the police said?'

'Nothing, till ten thirty. We've been told to report to Fettes for a briefing.'

'Make sure you're there. Who have you got at the West Lothian incident?'

'The local freelance is covering it. One of the press office cops hinted that it was a suicide, so we all pulled out.'

I frowned; I've never approved of misinformation, under any circumstances. If you can't say anything, don't say anything, that's always been my idea of the way a good PR should behave. 'He lied,' I growled. 'Think bigger, think broader.'

'They're linked?'

'Yes, but don't you start the frenzy. Alf Stein will do that in an hour.'

'Can I have a quote from you?'

'Not a chance. Make one up, non-attributable, and make sure it includes "shocked and under sedation". Don't call here again, Ross. You want anything from now on, you phone Lascelles and Company.'

There were three photographers outside when Willie arrived, and a couple of reporters. As I lifted the intercom transceiver and pressed the button to let him in, I could hear the clamour below. He arrived at the door white-faced, out of breath and puzzled. I ushered him into the living room, and told him why he was there. Before I'd finished he was shaking; he almost fell on to the couch. I gave him as long as he needed to recover, then got down to business. 'Starshine Pharmaceuticals is going to need you,' I told him. 'The company employs over two hundred people, and they have to be looked after.'

'Too right they have,' he gasped. 'This is wages day. That safe would have been stuffed full of cash. I've told Rod for years to pay everyone by cheque or transfer, but he wouldn't have it. Normally the money would have arrived today in a security van, but this is a bank holiday, so . . .' He started to rise. 'Xavi, I'll need to get out there to sort it. They'll all be expecting their pay, and most of them will need it.'

I put a hand on his shoulder, making him remain seated. 'Then it'll have to go to their homes,' I pointed out, 'or they'll have to collect it at the gate. Nobody will be getting in there today. Who's in charge there, apart from Rod?'

'No one really. There's a chief chemist, a production manager, personnel manager, finance manager, but he was managing director and general manager all in one.'

'Then you have to put someone in there, or take over yourself for now. What's Grace's position. Were there wills?'

'Oh yes. I made him take at least that prudent step. Rod and Magda were co-owners of the business; each will leaves the testator's share to Grace, the rest of the estates to each other, then to her.' He frowned. 'Who died first? The Inland Revenue will want to know.'

'I'm not certain, but I'd guess it might have been Rod.'

'Either way, inheritance tax will be a bugger.'

'But Grace now owns the business?'

'Yes; lock, stock and barrel.'

'Then run it for her, until she decides what she wants to do with it.'

'I'll need a signed mandate from her.'

'She'll give you one as soon as she's fit. You get the staff paid first, and we'll do the paperwork later. I want to get her away from here, by Sunday at the latest. We need you to represent her in every respect, arranging the release of the bodies with the police, funeral arrangements, the lot.'

'What about the wedding?' He put a hand to his mouth. 'God, what an awful question.'

'Maybe, but a practical one. You'll find the guest list at Copper Lane, when the police let you in there. Magda's wedding papers are all in a file, in order; I've seen it. Sometime next week, ask your secretary to contact everyone and let them know it's postponed.'

Willie, with a sense of purpose, was a formidable being; he nodded, and left to set about his business with his jaw set and a gleam in his eye.

We had two or three more press calls, but things were mostly quiet after that, until Tommy Partridge phoned just after eleven. 'The boss wants to visit Grace,' he told me, 'but only if she's fit for it. If not, he can wait for a while.'

By that time she had risen again, and was sitting on my lap, her head on my shoulder, eyes fixed on a landscape painting that Carmen had given us. 'Are you up for the cops?' I whispered in her ear.

'No,' she replied, 'but I should get it over with.' I told Tommy that we'd be ready at midday.

I knew Detective Chief Superintendent Alf Stein well enough, and I had a lot of respect for him. He was a straight cop, tough, but not the sort to cross any lines, not the heavy-handed type, of whom there were still a few around in the eighties. But the man with him was new to me. He was taller than Alf, around six feet two, and a lot younger; he was my age, give or take a year or so. He was tanned and his hair was dark, with streaks that I thought at first were sun bleaching, until I realised that they were advancing grey. He was lean, with wide shoulders, but it was his eyes that caught and held my attention. They were ice-blue and managed to be both friendly and fierce at the same time; it occurred to me even then that I'd never seen anyone quite like the man, an opinion I've never altered.

'This is DS Bob Skinner,' the head of CID told me as we shook hands. I should have known, for I had heard enough about him. His reputation had gone before him like a warning; a graduate entrant to the force, in the days when those were still rarities, a legendarily hard man as a beat cop, transferred to CID as quickly as possible, and used by Stein to throw a scare into people who thought they were tough, something he could do, it was said, just by looking at them. And there was something else about him, something that I recalled being told by Tommy Partridge. Not long before, he had lost his wife in a road accident. He had known recent bereavement himself, and I wondered if that was why he was there.

That may have been the case, for he did most of the questioning, gently, sympathetically, giving Grace time to consider her answer to each one.

'Do you work in your father's business?' he began.

'No. I'm an accountant. I worked there when I was a student but his plan was that I should gain some experience outside, then join him in a couple of years as finance director, so that he could back off gradually.'

'You were to succeed him?'

'I was going to be running the business by nineteen ninety-five.'

'Did he discuss company matters with you?'

'All the time.'

'Has he mentioned anything to you recently that struck either of you as out of the ordinary?'

'Not that I can recall . . . so he can't have.'

'Would it have been unusual for him to turn up at the factory at a late hour, as he did last night?'

'Not at all. My dad was a bit forgetful, but he didn't like people to know.' That came as news to me, so I conceded that he must have been good at hiding it. 'If he couldn't remember how he'd left something in the factory, a file on his desk, say, or the safe lying wide open, he'd never think of asking the night security man to check for him; he'd always get in the car and go back to do it himself. Or if he'd paperwork to do: sometimes he'd go back in the evening when it was quiet. He never brought work home with him. My mother always said that there wasn't room in our house for the business and for her.'

'Did she ever go to the factory?'

'I suppose she must have, but I don't remember it. The place is top security; Dad didn't do guided tours for anyone. Xavi's never even been there. You only went there to work, and everyone was vetted by the police before they were employed.'

'Yes, I know that. Let me ask you about your family. You have no siblings?'

'No.'

'Who's your closest living relative?'

'My granny Jacobsen. But she doesn't know me anymore; she's in a nursing home. I should have them tell her about Mum, even though it won't mean anything to her.'

'Anyone else?'

'Auntie Rose. She's my dad's sister, but they haven't spoken a civil word to each other for fourteen years. When Grandpa Starshine died she tried to contest his will, but she lost.'

'Is she married?'

'Yes, to Uncle Bert. His name's Levin. I have two cousins, Leah and Joel. Leah's married and lives in Israel.'

'And Joel? Where's he?'

'No idea. Last time I saw him was at Grandpa's funeral. I was twelve and he was thirteen. He was about to have his bar mitzvah, and I'd just had my bat mitzvah. That's—'

'I know; it's coming of age in the Jewish faith; "bar" for boys, "bat" for girls.'

'Mumbo-jumbo,' Grace murmured.

'I wouldn't say so. It must give you a sense of belonging. My daughter isn't baptised; maybe she should be.'

'How old is she?'

'Five,' Skinner told her.

'Then let her decide for herself when she's grown up. Do it now and she'll hate you for messing her hair up.'

'You must have met her.'

'It's a girl thing.' She paused. 'If you want to get in touch with my aunt, or my cousins, you'll find their addresses in Mum's wedding file. Dad didn't want to invite them, but she insisted. She said she wasn't being blamed for anything else.'

He smiled; so did she, and a little of the tension that had been in the room all morning seemed to float away, through the open window.

Stein nodded to the sergeant and they both stood. 'We'll keep you informed of progress, Xavi,' the chief superintendent said as I walked them to the door. 'But you understand that some of it might be in confidence?' he added

'Of course. I'm on leave anyway. Do you have anything so far?'

'Only a feeling.' It was Skinner who replied. He looked at Stein. 'The boss doesn't agree with me, though.'

'No, I don't,' the head of CID confirmed. 'You bright young things with your theories,' he muttered. 'Ever since that fucker Morse appeared on telly ... He's to blame, you know, Xavi, for this new tendency to ignore the obvious. This is a drug raid, pure and simple. The payroll robbery's like a side bet to these guys; big bucks maybe, but the diamorphine, the pharmaceutical cocaine and the temazapam jellies are worth a lot more than that out on the streets. It won't be the local talent that's done it either. Perry Holmes is miles too smart for that, and so's Tony Manson. And it won't be the Glasgow boys. They're not that bright, but they've got the sense to know that if they piss on Holmes's doorstep, he'll drown them in it. These drugs will surface, but it won't be in Scotland. It might not even be in Britain.'

I stared at him. 'What you're saying, Alf, is that you're not likely to catch these guys.'

'No. I'm saying we might not catch them tomorrow, that's all.' He looked around the flat. 'Look,' he said, 'I don't want to scare you ...' He hesitated.

'You won't,' I told him.

'You might think about making this place a bit more secure. We're not talking about the odds against lightning striking again. Criminals have got a nasty habit of copying each other. I don't see an alarm system, so I assume there isn't one.'

'Correct.' I saw where he was heading. Grace had inherited the business that had killed her parents. 'Can you advise me?' I asked.

'Advise you?' Skinner exclaimed. 'We'll fit it for you. When we're done you won't even know it's there, but we'll be able to identify every person who comes to your front door.'

I wasn't sure that would be good for me as a journalist, but Grace's safety was paramount. 'Do it. If it's okay with you, I'm going to take Grace to my dad's place in Spain.'

'Good idea,' Alf declared. 'The lass is all right just now, but sooner or later she'll have to face what's happened without the support of medication. Go as soon as you can. Give Bob your number; he'll be your liaison from now on. I'm not shutting Tommy Partridge out, you understand, but he's too close to you personally to be involved.'

I had some business cards in my shirt pocket, where I always keep a supply, and a pen. As the senior cop stepped outside I dug one out, scrawled the Spanish number on the back and handed it to Skinner. 'Thanks,' he murmured. 'That wedding file,' he added. 'I'll find it at Copper Lane?' I nodded. 'Fine. Someone will have to break the news to Mr Starshine's sister and her husband, and it might as well be me. Tell me, has the factory been in the family long?'

'Rod's dad founded it,' I replied, 'at the end of the war, just as antibiotics were starting to be mass-produced.'

'And it was left to Mr Starshine alone?'

'So Magda told me. The old man didn't rate his son-in-law, she said, so Rod got the business and his sister got a chunk of money which the husband promptly blew on a chain of cheap clothing shops that went tits up about eight years ago. Auntie Rose blamed Magda; she more or less accused her of seducing the old man.'

'How long has the daughter been in Israel?'

'At least fifteen years; she's older than Grace. Magda said that her husband's a politician; he's been in government a couple of times.'

'And Joel; what does he do?'

'Sorry, Sergeant, I've no idea.'

'People I like get to call me Bob.' He smiled, and the exceptional eyes exuded warmth; but only for a second or two. 'Maybe I should find out. The boss is right about one thing, he and I do think along different lines. There's no harm in that in CID. But Inspector Morse! A boozy, intellectual snob, whose idea of a cheery night is listening to Wagner . . . and a university drop-out to boot. He'll hear more about that.'

I smiled too, for the first time that day. 'And what's your idea of a cheery night, Bob?'

'Any one that I spend with my kid. That usually involves listening to Abba. She says she'd like me to marry the blonde one . . . but I think maybe once is enough.'

I called my dad as soon as they'd gone. As I've said, he's one of those rich people who spend most of their lives oblivious to their wealth, until it's necessary to use it, and then they make things happen. The charter jet was on stand-by already at Edinburgh's general aviation terminal, and would be ready to fly by four o'clock that afternoon. I expected a little resistance when I told Grace that we were leaving, but there was none. She looked at me, gratefully, then went off to pack.

The photographers were still outside when we left, but the police had moved them back to Queensferry Street, and so we were able to leave without my having to clear a path through a crowd of people that I knew. Sheena came with us to the airport, then our car took her home. I'd have taken her with us to Spain if I'd thought John would allow it, so calming had her presence been through that awful morning.

It was the first time I'd ever travelled in a private jet, still the only time apart from the trip back home. We had our own stewardess, and I could tell by her expression that she had been briefed about the situation. She offered us a drink; I wasn't going to have one, but Grace insisted. We drank Chablis all the way through the flight. I watched Grace carefully and tried to ration her intake, worried that it might combine with the sedative and knock her out again, but if anything it seemed to waken her up, and to clear the fog from her brain.

'It really did happen,' she whispered, just before we touched down. 'They killed them. The mindless bastards killed them.'

My dad was waiting to pick us up at Girona Airport; there was hardly any flight traffic on a Friday in 1988 and so they'd let him drive right out on to the tarmac. He was alone. He's never been loquacious at the best of times; at the worst, he didn't know what to say. He looked at Grace, whispered, 'So sorry,' then looked away again as I tossed our bags into the boot of his latest modest Merc.

It was almost nine o'clock when we arrived at the big house. Grandma was waiting for us, as solemn and silent as my dad. She had salad in a bowl, and steaks ready to go on the grill, but neither of us was ready to eat. I told her that I would cook when we were. I was having the first of a lifetime of flashbacks to Rod's car on the shale bing, and to Magda's bathroom, and I wanted more alcohol to keep them at bay. I guessed that Grace was imagining what she hadn't seen; her defence mechanism was a need to swim. She took a suit and a towel and went straight to the pool house, where she changed and dived in, carving out length after length. I sat in a garden chair and watched her, with half a dozen Heinekens in a bucket of ice by my side, pursuing my remedy as assiduously as she was, by the neck.

I had just finished my second when Grandma took the seat beside me. My dad had retreated to his office. She held out her hand. I took it but she shook herself loose. 'No, stupid boy,' she exclaimed, 'give me a beer. There are plenty more where they came from.'

I was too drained to be surprised. I knocked the tops off two more and handed one to her. 'I'll get you a glass,' I said.

'No need.' She put the bottle to her lips and chugged away, then held it out and examined the label. I sat and watched her, fascinated. 'You have the demons, haven't you?' I nodded, then put away most of my bottle. 'Me too,' she murmured.

'You? What are yours?'

'Remember, Xavi, I was there when my husband shot that man, that Francoista. It wasn't nice, not like in the films. He didn't just lie down and die. He tried to get up the first time and Xavier shot him again. Then he started to crawl away. He took four more cartridges before he stopped moving. The last one blew his head wide open. I've revisited that scene many times, but after a while not so vividly, until today. What happened to Grace's parents has brought it all back, every small detail, right down to the colour of brain tissue, grey among the red.'

'I'm sorry,' I whispered.

'Why? You weren't even imagined at that time. What do you have to be sorry for? No, it's I who's sorry for you. I'll carry that scene to my grave, as you will carry yours, but my journey there is short, yours has many years to run.' She finished her beer, and waved the empty bottle at me. 'This Dutch stuff is okay,' she announced, as I uncapped the last two. 'Much better than our Spanish rubbish. I wish I'd taken to it when I was much younger.' She looked me in the eye. 'You know, I think I'll smoke a cigar before I die.'

'You'll smoke a whole plantation before you're done.'

She shook her head. 'No. We both know that I won't.' She must have caught a look of alarm in my eyes, for she went on. 'Not tomorrow, or even the next day, but in places my skin is starting to turn to paper, and that's part of the process of dying for an old lady.' She pointed across the garden. 'Josep-Maria is going to build a mausoleum over there, in the corner. Not into the ground but into a grave in a wall, Spanish style, like Marilyn Monroe did in Hollywood, in the year that you were born, that's where I'll go, and him too in his time, maybe even you in yours, so we'll make it extra thick. I'll miss this place, though,' she said, as I tried to fit Monroe and Grandma Paloma into the same mental photo frame. 'Do me a favour, will you?'

'It's yours. What?'

'Name your daughter after me.'

'What if it's a boy?'

'You will have a daughter, Xavi,' she declared, so firmly that for a moment or two I almost believed her, but before I could press her, Grace emerged from the pool and announced that she was ready to eat.

After the meal, Grandma, who only had a little salad with a third Heineken, went to bed on steady legs. Grace and I sat in the garden for a while, counting the stars in silence, postponing the moment when we would have to try for sleep that we both knew wasn't going to come.

'Let's get married, Xavi,' she said, suddenly.

'As scheduled?' I asked. 'Are you sure?'

'Not in Edinburgh. I could never do that now, without Mum and Dad. Let's get married here, as soon as we can.'

'I don't even know if we can. This isn't Las Vegas; there are rules, and different procedures for non-nationals.'

'You're an Aislado; you can make it happen. Please; it's what I want.'

Next morning I told my dad, and asked if it would be possible. That's when I found out that I have dual nationality.

'You're kidding,' I gasped when he told me.

'Seriously. The old bat registered your birth when we moved back here. You're Spanish; you've got a DNI number and everything. You'd have had to do military service here after you graduated, but I got you an exemption when you fucked your knee playing football.'

He took it on board and made it happen. Willie Lascelles had Grace's birth certificate sent from Edinburgh by courier and six days later, on the day that Rod Starshine should have been giving his daughter away in Edinburgh, we stood in front of the local mayor and made our simple vows, in Catalan, flanked by my dad and by Carmen, with Grandma Paloma a few feet behind us.

In that week of waiting Bob Skinner had phoned me a few times, out of courtesy more than anything else, for he had no progress to report. Alf Stein had rattled a few local cages, but he was standing by his theory that the stolen drugs would surface in time, and nowhere near Edinburgh. I asked the sergeant about his own lines of inquiry, but all that he could tell me was that Rod's sister and brother-in-law had been suitably shocked by the murders, and that he had found Joel Levin, Grace's cousin, who seemed to be making a small name for himself as an antique dealer in Glasgow.

Lascelles was in contact too, on the Wednesday. Grace left it to me to deal with him. She was spending much of her time with Carmen, and was taking the view that since the business had killed her parents she wanted nothing to do with it. I didn't either, but there were a couple of hundred employees to be looked after.

The solicitor told me that his first call on the Monday after the killings had been from Rose Levin. She wanted to know what she and her family could expect from the wills, and she had been mightily displeased to learn that they hadn't rated a mention. She had threatened to sue; Willie had told her to go ahead, but had warned her that her claim would be seen as vexatious by the court and that she would wind up liable for all the legal costs, her own and ours. The factory had reopened on the following Tuesday, after the police and section managers had conducted a full audit to determine the types and quantities of drugs that had been stolen, and their street value, which was reckoned to be at least ten times the hundred and fifty thousand stolen from the safe.

'I've intimated a claim to the company's insurers,' he said. 'There won't be any problems.' He paused. 'There's something else, though,' he continued. 'I've had a call from the managing director of one of the company's main competitors. He asked me about the ownership of Starshine Pharmaceuticals. I replied that I didn't need to tell him that at this stage and that I wasn't going to, but he said, "No matter," and that whoever it was, he was prepared to make a very substantial offer for the business.'

'Grace might listen to that,' I ventured. 'What's your advice?'

'Don't accept. If the estate sells the business, the proceeds will be liable for inheritance tax, whereas it's exempt as a trading company. If Grace chooses to sell at a later stage she'd be liable for capital gains tax, but there are ways round that. You could go offshore; stay in Spain for a couple of years.'

I didn't like that suggestion. 'She could also pay the tax,' I pointed out.

'Yes,' Willie admitted. 'There is that.'

'What about the funerals?' I asked him.

'I've been pressing the procurator fiscal about that. He's agreed that if, at the end of next week, there is no prospect of an early arrest, he will release the bodies for burial ... not for cremation; you'll understand why.'

When we were finished, I made Grace sit down with me, and listen to me. 'You've got three choices, love. Sell it, now or after probate, and let it all go away. If you don't, you either appoint a chief executive ...' I knew that the business was very profitable, from what Rod had let slip during his lifetime and from what Willie had told me about the estate,

'. . . and let him run it, or you run it yourself, with beefed up management support.'

'There's a fourth option.'

'What's that?'

'You could run it. Once we're married, in a couple of days, it'll be half yours.'

My reaction was immediate and firm. 'No way. It's not what I do, and anyway I'm not trained for it.'

'Nonsense, Xavi. Grandma's been training you all your life . . . and so has Joe, for the last few years, if you'd only noticed.'

'But not for that. It's a non-starter, love.'

She pouted, slightly, but I wasn't giving in. 'Okay,' she sighed. 'If you won't, I'll have to. It's what my dad wanted, and if he was still here, it would have happened in a few years anyway. Tell Mr Lascelles, and then let's forget it until we're ready to go home.'

We didn't have a honeymoon; we had planned to go to Mauritius, but that had been cancelled along with the Edinburgh wedding. Instead we did the usual, hung about the house, swam, Grace posed for Carmen and I drank some more beer at the poolside with Grandma. But we did one positive thing. My dad had installed a fax line at home; I asked Willie to send us the wedding list, with addresses, and the list of presents received. When he did, we sat down in the office at the new, if expensive and primitive, Apple Mac computer that had appeared with the fax, and composed a letter to the guests, thanking them for their gifts and for their understanding, telling them that we had been married in Spain and promising that at a time and place still to be determined we would hold a reception in celebration of our union and of the lives of Rod and Magda. I believe that it helped Grace move forward, for she seemed more focused afterwards. It helped me too . . . but it didn't make the demons go away.

We decided that we would go back to Edinburgh on the second Sunday after our wedding. I asked my dad if Esme would book us flights, but he insisted that we went back by the means of our departure.

'Call it my wedding gift,' he said. 'You're not going to have an easy time. There'll be the funerals, then Grace will have to pick up the pieces. Want me to come over and help you out?'

His offer took me by surprise, so completely that I almost accepted. 'Thanks, Dad,' I said, 'but what would you do? Grace has worked in the company before; she knows more about it than you do, and where she does need back-up there are lawyers and accountants she can call on.'

'I should go to the funerals. Grace is proper family now.'

'The funerals will be private. Rod's sister and her family are specifically banned and Grace's granny wouldn't know what she was at if we took her along. It'll be us, the Fishers and those of Magda and Rod's friends that we care to invite. If you came you'd just go to the casino afterwards and drop a couple of million.'

'More likely I'd win a couple,' he chuckled. 'But there's this paper of yours, Xavi. I'd like to take a look at that.'

I frowned. 'Why?'

He shrugged his shoulders, looking untypically diffident. 'Well,' he murmured. 'I know it's come on leaps and bounds in the last six years, but . . . you're still stuck in the dark ages technologically and in that museum of a building, you've got no fucking investment capital, your owners don't have a fucking clue and even less ambition. I could change all that.'

'No!'

'Why the hell not?'

'I don't want to work for you.'

'You wouldn't be working for me, not me alone. You'd be working for yourself. Look, man, Grace has just inherited a company from her parents. What the fuck do you think's going to happen when I die? Effectively you'd be buying it yourself.'

'And that's something I'd never do,' I retorted, stubbornly. 'It would change everything for me there, all my relationships, with Jock, with Ricky, with everybody there. And this too: if I was to come in with you and we were to buy a newspaper in Edinburgh, it wouldn't be that one.

I love the *Saltire*, but if my head was in charge and not my heart, I'd aim for the *Scotsman*. It has tradition, it has reputation and it's already got its modernisation under way.' I paused, aware that I'd revealed a side of myself that not even I had seen before. 'But I'm not, okay? You're fifty-six, a long way from the grave, or from retirement. The *Saltire* will move on, because there are other buyers out there. What we've really done, Jock Fisher and I, is put it in the shop window.'

He smiled. 'And what if I bought it anyway?'

I frowned at him. 'You know what would happen. I'd leave and you'd be fucked.'

He shrugged his shoulders. 'Okay, Xavi. But when you have strings in your hands, as you do, like it or not, then sooner or later you will pull them. You'll find that out for yourself. And you're right about one thing. There is a buyer out there, sniffing around, and if he does take a bite, you lot had better be careful.'

The flight wasn't the only wedding present we received in Spain. We had just finished packing when there was a knock at the bedroom door. I yelled 'Open!' and Carmen's head appeared round it. 'Could you come to the living room when you're ready?' she said. 'Both of you. Senora Puig would like to see you.' I was struck by the formality of the request, and by its bearer, but I was too busy to dwell on it, and still consumed by my conversation with my dad. When we were ready we reported as requested. Grandma was waiting for us, and so was Carmen. They stood on either side of a large easel, from the cottage studio, and on it was what could only have been a painting, even though it was draped with a sheet.

'This is our gift to you,' Grandma announced, 'Carmen's and mine. I still feel that it's presumptuous of me, but Carmen has persuaded me that you will like it. I have my doubts, but I hope you do.' She pulled off the covering. Underneath was a portrait, of her. It was as large as that of the naked Grace, the one that had caused a brief sensation in Barcelona, and it was every bit as good. It depicted her standing, dressed in her Spanish style, long dark skirt, white blouse open-necked, and a shawl. There was no background other than white, and yet the work was earthy rather than ethereal. Her silver hair hung down to her shoulders and her head was held high. It was a study of pride, authority and, I realised, as I looked at the subject objectively, for the first time in my life, extraordinary beauty.

'Wow,' Grace whispered.

'Not the comment I expected,' said Grandma, 'but it'll do.'

'Has he indeed? In the circumstances, I can quite understand his special interest in you, and in your connections, but I'm surprised that he's managed to tie the two of us together.'

'Nobody's listening in to your calls, are they?'

'Don't get paranoid on me, son. There are laws against telephone tapping in this country, and just in case anyone does decide to ignore them I have this place swept for listening devices at least twice a week.'

'What do you want me to do?'

'I want you to do nothing. Indeed I insist on it. I have an associate with me just now who'll take the matter further. Now go away and don't bother me again unless you have a bloody good reason for doing so.'

'Who the fuck was that?'

'Young Lovejoy through in Glasgow; Mr Aislado's been rattling his cage and he's getting nervous, although I have no idea why he should. Still . . . Until now I've preferred to keep the chiel at a distance . . .'

'The what?'

'Ah, you Germans! Robert Burns, Johann; from his poem about the peregrinations of one Captain Grose. "If there's a hole in a' your coats, I rede ye tent it. A chiel's amang ye takin' notes, and faith, he'll prent it." So far Mr Aislado's refrained from printing anything about me, or been restrained by his stepfather, and I'd like to keep it that way. Invite him to visit me here, please . . . politely.'

'What if he tells me to fuck off? I get less polite, yes?'

'There you go again, with that reflex violence. Big and all as you are, you might find that you don't impress this chap. Just do what I say, with discretion. He'll accept.'

Fifteen

The photographers were long gone when we arrived home. So were the police technicians, although they had left a few flakes of sawdust on the landing as evidence of their recent presence. After I'd carried Grace across the threshold . . . her idea; I've never done romantic gestures . . . I came back out with the vacuum and cleaned it up.

Bob Skinner came calling next morning, Monday; we'd scheduled the funerals for the Wednesday and I'd told John that I wouldn't be back in the office before then. Skinner brought with him a guy called Davidson, whom he introduced as head of the technical support department, to talk us through the installation. I didn't spot the pencil-thin camera until he showed me where it was, set into the door frame, looking like nothing more than a knothole in the wood. The wiring went to a transmitter on the roof that sent a signal direct to a monitoring station where images were recorded on tape. The system was cute in that it was only activated by movement towards the door, and not by guests leaving.

'You know what this means,' said Grace, as we inspected it. 'You'll never be able to sneak a bimbo in here when I'm at work.' The thought hadn't occurred to me . . . nor would it have. Inside, panic buttons were installed in every room, inconspicuous studs that it was virtually impossible to push accidentally. Push one on purpose, though, and an alarm would be triggered in the communications room at police headquarters.

Skinner stayed on for coffee after Davidson had returned to Fettes. Grace made it, then left us alone. She didn't want to talk about her parents' deaths any more than was necessary, and she didn't want to be briefed about the investigation. As it happened, he had nothing solid to tell me. There were no new leads, and every line of inquiry had run into the buffers. He didn't have to add that with every day that passed the greater the chance that the crimes would stay in the 'unsolved and open' box for ever.

'Alf Stein's theory wins?' I suggested.

'I hate to admit it,' he confessed, 'but it's well in the lead, even if the race isn't over yet. I've still got something nagging at me, though. As you'd expect from what it produces, the security system at Starshine is as good as it gets. Within the factory, there are keypads separating each section, and each one has a different six-digit code. Also, there's a failsafe built in. If a code is entered and it's wrong by more than a single digit, the keypad is disabled, and that door can only be opened by using a unique unlock sequence. Those are held by the security staff, under lock and key. So, when Mr Starshine was being forced to open each door by his captor, all he'd have needed to do to abort the whole operation was get two numbers wrong, on purpose. But he didn't. Something else, too. The buttons on the pads are very small, so we're only ever going to get partial fingerprints off them, at best, but we've found nothing that even resembles Mr Starshine's.'

'There was a guy in his house with a gun to Magda's head,' I pointed out. 'Rod probably realised that making a mistake would be putting her life at risk.'

'Agreed,' said the sergeant, at once. 'But under that sort of stress it's almost remarkable that he got everything right.'

'He could have read out the codes for the kidnapper to punch in.'

'Sure.' He didn't sound convinced.

'Are you saying it might have been insiders who did it?'

'I'm saying nothing for the record. Before you ask, every person with knowledge of those codes has been thoroughly checked out. My cop's nose is still a bit twitchy, that's all.'

I dwelt on Skinner's nagging doubts after he had gone, but not for long. As he had admitted unprompted, all the potential insiders had been checked out, and if one had gone missing, that would have sent a very large flag up the signal pole. I had walked the police beat for the *Saltire* long enough to have become a pretty sound criminologist, and that put me firmly on the Alf Stein side of any lingering debate.

The funeral passed us by in a blur. Grace found a black dress in Jenners and I had a suit that was fit for purpose. She was tearful but strong throughout, in the synagogue and at the burial in the Jewish cemetery in Piershill, off the Portobello Road. I was aware of no-one but her at the service, but I was able to look around during the interment. I didn't recognise many of the few people there, but John and Sheena Fisher stood out, as did Alexander Draper, who had called me to ask if it would be okay to attend, in his own right and as a formal representative of the football club. Tommy Partridge was there too. That didn't surprise me, but Bob Skinner's presence did. I wondered if he was looking for possibles among the faces in the crowd.

The cops didn't come to the reception in the Caley Hotel, but everyone else did apart from John and Sheena, who had both to go back to work, and Alexander, who offered his condolences at the graveside, and excused himself. I'd have done without it, but Grace insisted. She said she wanted to hear people say nice things about her parents, as she might never have the chance again. They did, but not for long. Since then, I've been at post-funeral gatherings that turned in to carousing wakes that lasted for hours, but that crowd stayed for no longer than the minimum period required by respect, then buggered off, most of them forever.

We walked home, just another couple among the summer crowds. Grace put the black dress away, I hung up my suit until the next time, and we set out on the rest of our lives. There was nothing for us to say, even to each other. I played solemn music on the piano, 'to draw a line' as I put it, then we spent the rest of the evening listening to our favourites, turn about, some on vinyl but most on the compact discs that were taking over our library. As always, Grace was in an REM mood; I found myself leaning towards a guy called Michael McDonald, and Chet Baker, who had died in Amsterdam a month earlier. We spent the evening sprawled on the settee, with Grandma Paloma looking down on us from the illuminated place of honour we had given her on the wall. When we had heard enough we went through to the bedroom and made love, for the first time since the murders, for the first time in our married life. There was something different about Grace, something that couldn't have been attributed solely to the new ring on her finger. From our earliest days, ten years in the past by then, she had always been a vigorous lover, throwing her hips into it, hyper-energetic, mounting as often as she was mounted, driving on, long after I was spent, relentlessly, often until she had aroused me anew, but the woman who lay with me that night was different, quiet, submissive, waiting until I was ready to enter her rather than throwing herself on me, responding to me slowly, gently, until we climaxed in perfect unison, for the first time that I could remember.

'You're the only one, Xavi,' she whispered, as we came out of it.

'You too,' I replied. 'Always have been, always will be.'

Next morning we went to work; Grace took our car to the factory, and I took my bike, as usual. When I walked back into the newsroom, the atmosphere was as I expected, strained, awkward, nobody knowing what to say apart from John, who'd said it by then anyway. I called for attention. When I had it, I said, 'Colleagues, it's happened, we're dealing with it, and we're moving on. We know we've had your support, and we thank you for it. By the way, for the information of those who don't know, Grace and I were married while we were away, so don't be looking to get the office wedding present back.'

While I was dealing with that, Grace was doing something much more difficult: she was settling into her dead father's chair. I'd offered to take an extra few days and help her, but she turned me down. 'If you're going to stay, yes. If you're not, no thanks, I'll start as I'll be going on.'

I was home before her that evening; I'd had the first of what were to prove to be quite a few quiet days. It seemed that if my circle of contacts and secret sources knew I was back, they were hesitant to intrude. 'How did it go?' I asked her.

'I'll get there,' she told me, 'but it's not going to be easy. Dad took a lot of stuff to the grave with him in his head, plus he did the work of at least two people. I'm regretting ever bitching at you about the hours your job makes you keep, because I fear that mine's going to be worse.'

'In that case, you're going to need an extra staff member.'

'What do you mean?'

'You're going to add one more to your security department. He's going to pick you up in the morning and he's going to bring you home at night. Wherever you go on business, he takes you there.'

'Are you suggesting that I have a bodyguard?'

'No, love, I'm insisting on it. I don't have to spell out why.'

She gave in without a struggle. 'Okay, I'll tell personnel to advertise for someone.'

'No, you won't. I'm going to handle his recruitment myself.'

Next morning I called Tommy. 'I need a minder for my wife,' I told him. 'He doesn't need to be Brain of Britain, but he needs to be bright, brave, willing to work all the hours it takes and fucking lethal if he has to be.'

'One of ours?'

'That's why I'm calling you.'

He thought it over. 'There's a new kid in Gayfield, called McGuire. But no, he's going to be a career cop and anyway, he's probably too fucking lethal. Xavi, your problem here is that if anyone here is that good we're going to want to keep him. You don't want your own private police officer, you want your own one-man army.'

I was still considering the best way to recruit Rambo that evening when the phone rang. Grace had just arrived home and she picked it up on the move, as she came into the kitchen. 'Yes,' she answered, and I saw her expression change, and her face blanch under the tan. 'You'd better ask him,' she murmured, with an odd tremor in her voice, and handed me the receiver.

'Ask me what?' I said.

'Whether I can come to see you, with a peace offering,' Scott Livingstone replied.

I gasped. 'Are you kidding me? "An old woman" you called me, the last time I saw you.'

'Yes, I know and I'm sorry. I was off my fucking head then, screwed up with Bobby's dope, but I'm not any more. I've changed, I know what's happened, and I want to make it up.' I thought about it and asked myself a question. Did I have so many friends that I could afford to banish one forever? 'Okay,' I sighed, 'get your apologetic arse up here.'

He must have been phoning from close by for the buzzer sounded in less than five minutes. 'Will we tell him the police are watching him?' Grace murmured, as he was making his way upstairs. She wasn't smiling.

'No, we don't tell anyone that.'

When I opened the door to him, I saw that he had dressed for the occasion. Or had he simply changed for the better? The old sloppy Scott had been replaced by a mature twenty-something, clean-shaven, well groomed and wearing razor-edge trousers and a jacket that could only have been Daks. He was carrying a bouquet, and a box. 'Hello, Xavi,' he said, looking up at me. 'Not a bit like an old woman.'

'And you're not a bit like a dope-snorting tosser either,' I conceded. 'Come on in.'

I was ready to give him a hearing, but when I led him into the living room, I wasn't so sure about Grace. Sunny June outside, snowy December inside; you could have cut the atmosphere into blocks and built an igloo with them. She tore straight into him. 'Our life's been perfectly fine without you in it,' she snapped. The strength of her hostility took me by surprise. 'What makes you think we want to welcome you back?'

'I don't,' he responded. 'I'm here to tell you how sorry . . . no, that's not enough . . . how devastated I am by what happened to your mum and dad, to give you these.' He offered her the bouquet and the box, but she wouldn't take them so he laid them on the coffee table as if they were offerings on a shrine. She was trembling; I was ready to ask Scott to leave, but he went on. 'And to apologise to the both of you for the way it ended with all of us. I was completely out of order, and I've been ashamed of myself ever since I got my act back together. I should have done this long ago, and I'm sorry as well that it's taken me so long.'

'What about Bobby?' I asked him. 'Where's he these days? He hurt me more than you did, for what it's worth.'

'Fuck Bobby,' he said.

'But you did, didn't you?' Grace hissed.

He glanced at her with that sheepish sideways smile of his, a bit of the old Scott still in evidence. 'Well, maybe once or twice,' he replied. 'He's a perverted bastard, is our Bobby. He was all for a threesome, me and him and his sister, but even in those days I drew the line at that. You asked where he is, Xavi? The last I heard he was working on an oil platform in the North Sea; usual deal six weeks on, six weeks off. No women; that should suit him.'

'He'd better not try it on with the wrong bloke there,' my wife observed, icily. 'I imagine they'd chuck him over the side and say he jumped . . . although I'd go for the Edward the Second treatment, myself.'

I winced; we'd seen the Marlowe play at the Traverse Theatre, and the scene with the red-hot poker had been very well staged. 'What are you doing these days?' I asked him.

'Stationery supplies,' he replied. 'I'm the Edinburgh branch manager of a national company.'

'That's a long way from your degree,' I pointed out.

'Who does what they're qualified for these days, apart from doctors? I was with a photocopier outfit before I landed this job.'

He had a point. Even in the eighties I knew quite a few bankers who had law degrees, the younger, thrusting, cut-throat types who would eventually land the global economy in the shit.

Finally Grace relented enough to open Scott's wedding present; it was half a dozen Edinburgh crystal wine glasses, quite a gesture from someone who couldn't have been sure he'd get over the door. He didn't get to try them out, though. It was Friday and we had a table booked with Alexander Draper and his wife, at Umberto's, in Dublin Street.

Welcome or not, Scott's visit was helpful to me. I recalled that Billie, his sister, had married wee Dave's dad. He gave me their phone number, and I called him next morning. Retired from the army, Lieutenant Colonel Colquhoun had not only kept his links there, he had set up what he labelled a 'defence consultancy'. He gave me three potential candidates for the job of looking after Grace. A week later we hired one, an ex-para named Clinton Storm, a name I wouldn't have believed if I hadn't been shown his passport.

We knew that our lives had entered a new phase, but we came to terms with it over the next couple of weeks. I got back into the swing and racked up a couple of exclusives, one a takeover in the investment management sector, and the other involving a scam run by the photocopying company that Scott had worked for. It was legal, but some supposedly clever people were left egg-faced after being talked into signing escalating leasing contracts that would lead to them paying six figures sterling for equipment that they could have bought from the manufacturer for a couple of thousand. Grace, on the other hand, was coming home a little later each successive night, and was spending most of the weekends on paperwork.

Eventually, I persuaded her to stop, for long enough to tell me about the trouble that clearly she was having. 'I don't know how my dad did it, Xavi,' she confessed. 'He ran everything; buying, manufacturing, packaging, sales, distribution, they were all under his personal control. As a result, I have no adequate support. The finance manager's a glorified bookkeeper; I'll have to replace him. The rest of the department heads are adequate, but I'll drown if they all report directly to me. I need someone there as a second in command, someone I can trust to supervise production, sales and delivery, so that I can handle the top-level stuff, including the new internal audit system I've set up to keep a track of every last capsule and grain of product that we manufacture.'

'Then recruit someone,' I told her. 'Instruct a head-hunter to advertise and fill the job.'

She looked at me, hesitantly. 'I've got someone in mind already. Telling you is partly what's been worrying me. It's Scott Livingstone. He's exactly the sort of person I want. Since he's got over his student nonsense, and got away from Bobby's influence, he's built a pretty decent CV. I know, because I asked him to send it to me a couple of days ago.' I knew part of it, but I couldn't tell her. Scott had given me the low-down on the photocopier company; he'd shown me a typical contract, and given me a list of the clients who'd been taken in. Still . . .

'You're sure we can trust him?' I asked.

'What's to distrust? He'll be a manager reporting directly to me, he's smooth enough not to ruffle feathers on the shop floor, sharp enough not to be fooled, and if he's nothing else, he's an open book to us. We've known him for most of our lives, love.'

I couldn't counter her arguments, although it occurred to me that there were bound to be people out there who ticked all the boxes at least as well as Scott did, and maybe better. But I judged that Grace was in the process of building self-confidence in her new role, so I nodded and told her that if she was happy, it would be okay by me.

And so it was. Scott served a month's notice with the office supplies company and joined Starshine Pharmaceuticals plc as general manager. It took him very little time to settle in and soon Grace and I were back to the old pattern of me being the one who was late home, most evenings.

There were no positives on the murder hunt. The investigation was still live, and Bob Skinner called me or visited me at the paper at least once a week, to give me what we soon began to call 'lack of progress' reports. The only change was to his hair, which seemed to have more grey in it than when we'd first met. Eventually, the calls became fortnightly, then, after four or five months they stopped.

When he phoned me again, in March the following year, I was surprised. I'd heard on the grapevine that Stein had moved him within CID, to a squad that was monitoring the growing number of east European gang-bangers who were showing up in the city, and so my first reaction was that he had a tip-off about them for me. He wanted to meet away from the office. I suggested that he come to my place in the evening, but he turned that down as he had to go home to his daughter. We settled for lunchtime, and a pub called the Doric, down in Market Street.

'How's life?' I asked, as he broke with normal press-cop procedure by buying the drinks.

'Not so good on the private side,' he told me. 'My father died. You know what I found among his effects, Xavi? The fucking George Cross, and he never told me. I still don't know how he got it; he never talked about what he did during the war, never, but I know he wasn't in the army.'

'Jesus,' I murmured. 'My old man and I don't talk much, but I can't imagine him keeping that big a secret from me. How's your mother taking it?'

His face twisted into what might have been a smile. 'With tonic and a slice of lemon if heaven's licensed. She's gone too.'

'Sorry about that, Bob.' I didn't want to get into a discussion about mothers.

'Anyway,' he continued, changing the subject, 'I've been on a bit of compassionate leave. When I got back I picked something up. Maybe nothing ... certainly nothing for me to act on ... which is why I'm passing it to you.'

'Intriguing.'

'I have a pal in Customs and Excise,' he told me, 'VAT division. Last year I suggested to him that if he ever inspected the records of an antique dealer called Joel Levin, through in Glasgow, I might be interested in seeing what it showed up. By happy chance, that inspection took place six weeks ago. Levin passed with flying colours; his records are immaculate and the Customs actually wound up giving him a rebate. But there were a couple of names among his customers that intrigued me. One of them is familiar to you: Starshine Pharmaceuticals.'

'What?' I exclaimed.

'That's right. A couple of years ago, he sold a set of four antique prints, framed, very expensive, to his Uncle Rod. I guess that they weren't on as bad terms as we thought.'

I searched my memory, and recalled Rod telling me early in 1987 that he was having his office refurbished. 'I think I know where they might be,' I told him. 'I'll ask Grace.'

'Do that, but you won't want to mention this. Another client, supplied with a full Georgian dining room set for ten thousand quid, is Pentecostal Estates Limited. It's a holding company for a group that includes hotels, pubs and office buildings, and it's owned by one Perry Holmes. So you see what intrigues me; we've got an unsolved drug robbery and murder that might just be an inside job, a supposedly estranged member of Mr Starshine's family, with connections to him, and to a guy who is believed to be the king of organised crime in Scotland. Make no mistake, Xavi, Perry Holmes is national. He's a level above our local guy Tony Manson and the like, and he's even cleverer than Manson, who's not dumb. He never leaves a trace behind him, not a one, but you've seen close up what he can do . . . or rather cause to be done.'

'Why is he so good?'

'Because he never takes chances. There's a tale about Holmes, from thirty years ago, when he was our age. One of his lieutenants tried to betray him, but the cop he approached was on Holmes's payroll. The historic penalty for treason was hanging, drawing and quartering; the story goes, that's what Holmes did to the man, and he did it himself, as a statement. But from that day on he has never been within three stages of any crime, and each order is passed on without witnesses, so we'd need to suborn at least three people to get anywhere. Holmes is never in a room with more than one person, that's how careful he is.'

'Does Alf know about this?' I asked.

'Of course he does; I wouldn't go behind my boss's back. He hasn't changed his mind, we can't go waltzing into Strathclyde territory, and anyway, I can't expose my VAT contact. But if you want to visit cousin Joel, he's fine with that.'

I had stayed on the Alf Stein side of the debate and was resigned to the growing likelihood that the drugs were long gone and the money had been laundered, but the mere mention of Perry Holmes was enough to stir me. I was on the Glasgow train next morning, heading for an appointment with Mr Levin that I'd made with his assistant, as a potential corporate buyer. I'd called myself Francis Saint, a pseudonym I'd used a few times in my career when dealing with people who might not have been too keen to talk to Xavier Aislado.

The premises of Levin Fine Antiquities were located in Woodlands Road, about halfway between Charing Cross and the Gothic tower of the university; they were a double-fronted shop in a sandstone tenement building. There was a red-haired, busty woman front of house, the assistant, presumably, but nobody else; it didn't look like the sort of business that pulled too many customers off the street, although for all I knew there might have been a big turnover in Victoriana in the traditionalist west end of Glasgow. 'Mr Levin's expecting me,' I told her.

'Mr Saint? He's in his office. I'll show you through.' She led me into a passageway, stopped at one of three doors and knocked. 'Visitor, Joel,' she called out.

'Moment!' We waited, not speaking but listening to the sound of the morning traffic and, I thought, to that of a door closing. 'Enter!'

The hub of Joel Levin's empire looked out on to a communal courtyard that was seriously in need of taking in hand. It was big enough to have housed a block of flats but all I could see were overgrown grassy areas with clothes poles, and a flat-roofed building in the centre that might have been a working wash-house before John Bloom revolutionised the white goods industry by putting washing machines within everyone's reach. There was nobody there, apart from a man walking away, across the nearest of the drying greens. The office itself was well-furnished. It reminded me, faintly, of my dad's study in Spain, although without the modern trimmings of computer, printer and fax that had crept in there. Its owner was seated in a green leather captain's chair that was almost certainly not antique, the kind with plastic casters, and cross-grooved screws if you look underneath. He didn't rise from it as I entered, simply extending his hand across his desk as I took a seat facing him. I let it hang there until he withdrew it.

There was no doubt about the family relationship; he looked a lot like his late uncle, although I realised quickly that he was much smaller. Happily he didn't look at all like Grace, and he didn't have Rod's natural charm, or the same warmth in his eyes. They were narrowed as he looked at me. 'There's something familiar about you, Mr Saint,' he said. 'Have we met, in synagogue, perhaps?'

'I'm not Jewish, I'm afraid,' I replied, then stood again, to my full height, six feet and sevenish inches barefoot, add on a couple for my sturdy shoes, spreading my arms out as I gazed down. 'Am I the sort of person you see and forget?' I smiled as I sat down. 'I've spent my whole adult life wishing I was inconspicuous. No, we've never met. We are related, though; we're cousins by marriage. I'm Xavi, Grace's husband; sorry about the subterfuge, but sometimes I don't like to give advance warning of my arrival.'

I hadn't gone to Glasgow with any hope of justifying what wasn't even really a theory on Bob Skinner's part, only an apparent circumstantial link between people whose paths should never have crossed. When I told Joel who I was, I'd expected him either to be annoyed by my game, or to laugh it off. What I wasn't prepared for was the sudden flash of fear that shone in his eyes, or the way that he seemed to recoil into the green leather. It only lasted for a second but I didn't imagine it.

'Well,' he exclaimed, after another couple of seconds, 'this is a surprise.' He mustered a smile. 'What brings you here, "Cousin" Xavi? I hope Grace isn't still pissed off at my mother for threatening to challenge Uncle Rodney and Aunt Magda's wills.'

'Grace never even knew about that,' I said. 'It's history now anyway. No, I'm here as a journalist.' I handed him a business card. 'You'll see from my job description that I'm free-ranging in what I cover. Right now, I have an interest in a man called Perry Holmes. I don't need to tell you who he is. He's a real business success story; started in the taxi business, then expanded into bookmaking. Now he owns hotels, nightclubs, and commercial property, all across Scotland. He's everywhere; I'm told you've even done some business with him.'

The eyes narrowed again. 'Have I?'

'So I'm told. You sold some very expensive antique furniture to one of his holding companies, Pentecostal Estates. Or am I misinformed?'

'Xavi, Xavi, come on. I have a lot of corporate clients. They're the bulk of my business.'

'I know. Rod was a customer, wasn't he?'

Joel nodded. 'I doubt if he ever told Aunt Magda, but yes, he was. He told me that it wasn't fair that my mother's dispute with him should affect me, and so he made a point of buying from me, personally and through the company.'

'Through the company?'

'Yes. He bought an office desk from me when I started out five years ago. More recently I supplied him with a set of antique prints for his office. Military scenes, limited edition, very rarely on the secondary market.'

'Did you hang them for him?'

'Of course.'

'So you've been to the factory?'

'Oh yes.'

'More than I have. Rod didn't invite anyone who didn't need to be there.'

His little chest seemed to puff out. 'He gave me the full guided tour,' he exclaimed.

I raised my eyebrows. 'Lucky you.' I paused. 'Going back to Perry Holmes; too bad you can't remember dealing with him.'

'As I said, Xavi, I have a lot of clients.'

'I'm sure, but this one's your landlord. When I looked into the Pentecostal Estates holdings, I discovered that they own this building. Now there's a coincidence for you.'

His eyebrows ridged. 'Indeed,' he said.

'Never mind.' I smiled. 'You don't live above the shop, do you?'

'No, no. I have a flat in the Merchant City; I took a chance on that years ago, and it's worked out. It's a good place to be. There'll be a lot more happening there over the years. And I have the house near Loch Lomond, as well.'

He was out to impress me. 'Business must be good, then,' I retorted, rising from my chair. 'I'll let you get back to it. Nice to have met you.'

The train back to Edinburgh was delayed, and so I had time to think about my family visit on the way home. Joel's link with Perry Holmes: it could add up to nothing, or it could add up to everything. But . . .

Back in the office, I called a contact in the property records office, then rang Bob Skinner. 'Can you remember,' I asked him, 'what Joel Levin's annual turnover is?'

'Off the top of my head, about three hundred thousand, gross.'

I did some sums in my head, thinking aloud. 'Net around a quarter of a million; let's say his mark-up is a generous one hundred per cent, down to a hundred and twenty-five, then there's overheads, office rent and rates, and wages for Titsy the Redhead, leaves him maybe seventy-five thousand for himself before tax, eighty tops.'

'He's doing all right,' said Skinner.

'Yes, but would it cover a four hundred grand property on Loch Lomondside, as well as his flat in the Merchant City?'

The detective sergeant whistled, and I could see him grin. 'Good question, Xavi. My friends in the Strathclyde force might be interested in finding that out.'

I left it to him. There was nothing more I could do. That same day another story, about a dodgy pest control firm that had probably increased the number of cockroaches in the Royal Infirmary rather than eradicate them, threw itself into my lap and demanded all my attention.

It took me until well into the evening of the next day before I signed it off and sent it to print. I was feeling pretty pleased with myself as I unlocked my bike from the rack, when a voice sounded behind me. 'Mr Aislado.' There is never a question mark when people address me for the first time.

I turned to see a large man, a very large man, looking at me. He wore a grey suit over a collarless grey shirt. His fair hair was crew cut, his forehead was heavily ridged, and his thick nose had been broken at one point and reset not quite straight. We were eye to eye, but we were standing on a slope and he was slightly higher up than me. Even so, he had to be at least six feet four. I stared back at him. 'Yes?'

'My boss would like to meet you,' he said. There was an accent: it could have been German, Polish, maybe even Russian.

'My wife has the same expectation. Who's your boss?'

'Mr Holmes.'

'Give me a clue. Is he real or fictional?'

The big man didn't do banter. 'Mr Perry Holmes.'

I wanted to smile, but didn't. I looked over my shoulder, down the close, to check that there was nobody else there, behind me. 'Then he can come to me,' I retorted.

'He would rather that you came to him.' Maybe I ought to have felt fear, but even then I didn't. Instead I felt intrigued, excited, and slightly amused. The big man's eyes showed me nothing. 'He said that you would,' he continued.

'Then I will,' I told him, 'but at the first sight of any person other than him, you are going down, my friend.' It wasn't bluster; I knew that was how it would be if it came to it, and because of that, I was certain that it wouldn't.

He had a car parked illegally in our loading bay, with its hazard lights flashing. It was a people mover, some sort of a seven-seater, and high in the roof, fortunately. I didn't ask where we were going, for I knew where Perry Holmes lived, on a small private estate not far along the Biggar road. There was no conversation on the journey there. The big guy was a taxi driver, but not the kind who gives you his life story along the way.

It didn't take us long to reach our destination, since we were travelling across what little commuter traffic there was left at seven on a Thursday evening. The house was at least half a mile off the road; it was big, built from a stone that I learned later was called Rattlebag, and a favourite of its architect Lutyens. It looked as if it was listed to hell and back. We stopped at the foot of a flight of five steps that led to the entrance. The driver gave the horn a long blast, then nodded to me to step out. I did, looking around, expecting, I don't know what, swarthy guys with luparas, maybe, but there was nobody else in sight. 'This way,' said my escort. He led me up to the front door, which wasn't locked, into a hallway that reminded me of the Caley Hotel foyer, and through into a room at the back of the house, which opened on to a conservatory.

My host was waiting for me. 'Thanks, Johann,' he said. 'I told you he'd come.' As the big man left, closing the double doors behind him, he extended a large meaty hand. 'Mr Aislado. We should have met before now.'

Perry Holmes was fifty-eight years old when I met him that first time. He was a year older than my dad, but looked a few years younger. He was around six feet tall, wide in the shoulders and almost as thick in the waist. His hair was dark, like his brother's, but it was more sparse. A mark on the bridge of his nose told me that he wore glasses, but, I guessed, only when he had to.

I shook his hand. He smiled as mine engulfed his. 'Glad you could come,' he beamed. 'Can I offer you a drink?' There was a bottle of champagne in an ice bucket on a table in the centre of the glass room. I let him pour me a flute.

'What would you have done if I'd refused?' I asked him as I accepted it.

'I'd have been surprised, but that's all. You're not a man to be brought. That said, I never doubted it. You have an innate curiosity that you'll never be able to overcome.' He took a step back, and looked at me, appraising me, and then he nodded. 'My God, yes.'

I smiled. 'Indeed?' I murmured.

'Indeed. I've seen you before, from a distance, Xavi, just out of curiosity. Close up, you confirm the impression of you that I formed.' He gestured towards a couple of cane chairs; we sat. 'Before I get there, though, there's something I want to clear up. One of my tenants from Glasgow called me, a couple of days ago. You paid him a visit, I believe, and after it he was shitting himself.'

'I don't recall saying anything to scare him. In fact, I don't recall ever setting out to scare anyone.'

'You don't have to, my friend. It's in your blood. Anyway, wee Joel: he told me everything you asked him, everything you talked about, and everything he said to you, including the fucking stupid part about having had a guided tour of the Starshine factory. I see where you're going with it, so it's best I tell you something now, openly and on the record, if you care to report it in your paper. I had nothing to do with the robbery at your father-in-law's factory, and I had nothing to do with his murder or your mother-in-law's. I have no idea who did it, but I will tell you . . . and this is strictly off the record . . . that if it was anyone in my team, even Alasdair, my brother, they'd be fucking dead by now. I've already made inquiries among the Scottish talent, and I'm satisfied that none of them had a finger in it either. A few facts to support my position. One, I don't need a ton and a half in payroll cash, or factory drugs that would stand out a mile as soon as they appeared on the street. I would never stir up a hornet's nest like that. Two, the last thing I want is to get Mr Stein and his colleagues, especially your stepfather and that new guy Skinner, any more excited than they need to be. Three, I would never harm your family; I like to sleep at night and I plan to waken up for a right few mornings yet. You believe me?'

I took a sip of Krug as I returned his unwavering gaze. 'Yes, I do. But tell me about reason three, and about your impression of me.'

He nodded and leaned back in his chair. 'Okay,' he said. 'I haven't always been like this, Xavi. There was a day when I was much less cautious, reckless, in fact. That's a long while back, though. I had associates in those days who were the sort of people you read about in true crime stories. You know the type; you've probably met a few. Some of these people were moving certain goods around the city, rather openly, I'm afraid, although I was unaware of that. One of them pushed some stuff in a particular pub; the manager caught him and called the police. The next day, the same manager had acid thrown all over his front door, and a visit from another associate of mine, who told him that if he ever did anything so public-spirited again, the stuff would go in his wife's face. I promise that threat wasn't made with my knowledge or authority, but that's no more relevant now than it was then.' He paused. 'A couple of days later, I was in my office. It was in Rose Street Lane in those days: I'm talking thirty-four years ago. A man walked in. My minder of the time was meant to stop him, but he was too busy crying and holding on to his balls, worried that they'd been ripped off. The visitor was a very large man, not as large as you, or even as Johann Kraus, but that didn't matter. He could have been five feet four and he'd still have been the same. He sat down and he told me that I had offended him. I had done something that he interpreted as a threat to the business that supported his wife and family, and that, by extension, he interpreted as a direct threat to them. I hadn't, of course, but as far as he was concerned I was where the buck stopped. He told me that if it happened again, or if a single hair on the head of any of his family or employees was as much as disturbed, one thing and one thing only would follow it, without warning. He would kill me, me, personally. Not my wife . . . not that I've ever had one . . . not my brother, not my people, but me, Perry Holmes. And I believed him, because when I looked at him, I knew for sure that he'd done it before and that it had been no big deal for him. You know what I'm going to say next, don't you?'

I did. I nodded, realising that even if I'd wanted to blink, I couldn't have.

'That man was your grandfather.' He seemed to shiver. 'God, you're like him. He said what he had to say, and then he got up and left. I had a fucking gun in my drawer. I could have shot him in the back . . . only I couldn't, because it was for show, that's all. There's a story about me, I'm sure you've heard it. But it's not true. It's an urban legend, but it's always suited me to have people believe it. Yes, things have been done in my name.' His eyebrows rose. 'You have first hand . . .' he leaned on the second word, '. . . experience of that, but only ever as matters of discipline, the setting of fearful examples. I've never personally killed, or even bloodied, anyone. Your grandfather knew that when he looked into my eyes, and I knew that I'd never be able to stop him if he came for me. He taught me a huge lesson that day: never to be so arrogant as to assume that I could do anything I wanted to anyone I wanted, without the risk of any personal consequences. He also made me realise that I should never become a despot, a bully, because if you do, there's always someone who'll kick the crap out of you eventually, or just put a bullet right in your fucking head.' He poured me some more champagne. 'Whoever did that thing to your in-laws, Xavi son, I hope you never catch them, because you won't be able to help what you do to them, and it will change your whole life.'

Some time passed before I was able to respond. 'I'm two generations removed from my grandfather,' I told him, when I could. 'Worse, I went to fucking Watson's and had all the Spanish lawlessness drained out of me. You misjudge me.'

'That's one thing I never do,' he countered. 'I know people better than they know themselves. That's why I am where I am.'

'She's sure?'

'Yes, she's sure. She's a very fine doctor, she's looked after me for years and she knows my body better than I do. The test results are in and she's not surprised by them. It's back and it's evolved. It's in my blood; leukaemia, she said.'

'I'll have you taken to Barcelona. They can treat you there.'

'And turn me into what? A drooling old vegetable having my arse wiped every day by paid young women, joking among themselves as they do it? You'll take me no further than the garden. I will never leave this masia again, not even in my wooden overcoat. Josep, I'm eighty-eight. Most of the women of my generation are dead, and all the men, even old Dali. Hire a nurse, yes, but that's all I want you to do for me . . . all but one thing. Send for him. It's time.'

'You don't need to tell him.'

'I do.'

'He never needs to know.'

'He does.'

'But how will he take it?'

'Like the man I've raised him to be. Besides, in his secret heart, he knows already.'

Sixteen

My encounter with Perry Holmes didn't leave me liking the man. Far from it; for all his wealth and his involvement in legitimate business, there was an amoral glibness about him that disgusted me. It had enabled many people to take a view expressed roughly as, 'Well, old Perry may have been a bit dark in his youth, but he's up front now and what's in the past . . .' They chose not to look under the rock on which the empire stood, for they feared that if it did come tumbling down, it might drag a sizeable chunk of the financial establishment with it. Even the police were stymied by his cleverness in distancing himself from all the corruption, drugs and darkness that he still directed, with a word to one man, who would pass it on to another, and so on.

I told Tommy Partridge about our meeting, a couple of days after it happened. He agreed with my analysis of the man. 'Holmes's secret is that he doesn't have a fixed chain of command, as such,' he explained. 'He doesn't have a right-hand man, as such; he has three or four people who think they're his closest confidant . . . his brother Alasdair, Johann Kraus, the guy that you met, and a couple of others, depending on what the job at hand is . . . but he never brings them all together, so none of them can really get a handle on where they stand with him. Ultimately everything's deniable, right down the line.'

'What about the brother? From what Holmes said to me he sees even him as expendable.'

'He is. To Perry, everybody is. They're set up like department heads, each one replaceable by the guy below him. Alasdair runs the criminal side, the drugs, the art thefts, the blackmail rackets. Kraus, you might call him head of security. What happened to Gavin Spreckley and the kid, Johann probably did himself, and for sure he arranged for Ramsay to be chibbed in prison. He's an intimidating bloke.'

'He didn't seem intimidating to me,' I said, 'just a bully; the sort of guy that Holmes said he'd never become.'

'Maybe not, but he knows the value of having some around him. Bottom line, Xavi, do you believe that Perry ordered the robbery and the murders of Grace's parents?'

'No. I'm pretty certain that he didn't.'

'Then forget about him. He's out of reach. You'll never get to write the big exposé that'll bring him down. I'll never get to put my hand on his shoulder and say the magic words, "You're nicked." Get on with your life and don't be obsessed by him.'

'I could say the same to you.'

'I am getting on with mine. Detective superintendent next week; my promotion's just been approved.'

And we did move on, both of us; all of us, indeed, for Grace began to emerge from the solemnity that had enveloped her as she dealt with her double bereavement. She seemed to recover some of her old vivacity, and if she wasn't quite the same as she had been, I put that down to the inescapable truth that she and I were both marching steadily towards our thirtieth birthdays, the age at which 'start a family' was marked in the life plan we had drawn up in our teens. Of course, we hadn't anticipated that she'd be running a multimillion-pound business by that time. I began to raise the subject tentatively after her twenty-ninth; she didn't rebuff me, but she wouldn't set a date for coming off the pill. I didn't press her; truth be told, for all Grandma Paloma's prediction, I was pretty set in my ways too, and couldn't quite get my head round the idea of a small person joining the party.

There was another reason for my not pushing her for a decision. I was distracted at work. For most of April 1991, John had been acting as editor of the paper, and I'd been his designated second in command. It had made no difference to the way we worked since Torcuil's approach to his job had never changed over the years; he rolled in, Dalek-like, after midday and rolled out again at six, but his total absence that month was unexplained. If he'd been going on holiday, he'd have told John, and if he'd been ill . . . he'd been known to pull a few sickies . . . he'd have called in. Still, we carried on regardless, until the first of May, a Wednesday.

I was first in the newsroom, as usual; I left home at the same time as Clinton Storm picked up Grace, and she was an early starter. To my surprise, when I sat down at my desk and switched on my computer, to finish a rugby story I'd left the night before, I saw a light shining under the editor's door. The day had started dull, and I assumed that the cleaners had been forgetful, so I went to switch it off.

To my astonishment, Torcuil was in his office, at that unprecedented hour, and he wasn't alone. He was seated at his beloved coffee table as usual, and the chair next to him was occupied by another man, a total stranger. I'm not saying that I knew everyone in Edinburgh by that time, but I could recognise all of the senior players in the business community and the guy wasn't one of them. He confirmed that as soon as he opened his mouth. He stood, as I was about to withdraw with a muttered apology, and thrust out a hand. 'Hello,' he said, 'I'm Marat Petrov. I'm the new owner of the *Saltire*.' Just like that.

We shook hands. 'Xavi Aislado.'

'I know. You are star turn. The man we must keep at any cost, Torcuil says. Pleased to meet you. I'm going to double your salary.'

I had heard of Petrov. His name featured regularly in the London broadsheets; most of them portrayed him as a modern business phenomenon, apart from the *Financial Times*, which treated him with disdain. He was a man ahead of his time: the Soviet Union was still alive at that point, if very ill, but he had emerged from behind the Curtain three or four years earlier with access to funds that seemed to come from Switzerland. He had begun in transport, air and sea freight, then had bought an ailing Sunday title from its ailing proprietor, and used that as the vehicle to take over the *Journal*, a Fleet Street tabloid that was ripe for the picking. That was his power base, the tool he used to build his reputation.

'That's damn good of you,' I replied, then was overcome by a strange flush of loyalty, 'but I report to Torcuil, and my pay negotiations have always been done through him.'

'Of course, of course,' he rushed to say. 'And that will still happen, I promise; I'm speaking on his behalf. Torcuil will continue as editor . . . that is part of the deal. I've been looking at this for two years now; finally all is agreed and everything will be as it was before.'

He outlined the rest of the agreement at a mass staff meeting at midday, when everyone but the printers were at work. The McCandlish Trust had agreed to sell the *Saltire* to him, on the basis that its editorial philosophy . . . and its editor; nice one, Torcuil . . . would remain unchanged. He alone, not one of his companies, would own the paper and it would remain as an independent Scottish entity with him as chairman, Torcuil as a director, and a new man, unnamed, brought in as finance director. But everything else would be different. We were moving to a new production centre on a site he had found in Fountainbridge, a mile away, the technology would be state of the art, and our printing presses would be able to produce as many papers as we could sell. I spent the rest of the day with John, trying to pick holes in the set-up, but we couldn't, not after we had been shown the purchase agreement for the new site, and the bank guarantees that would underwrite the construction of the new headquarters. The first sod was cut the very next day.

Petrov's revolution was completed on 30 September 1992, when the new building was opened, by the Tory Secretary of State for Scotland, who'd obviously have done anything for a headline, since the paper had been set up to oppose everything his party stood for. I wasn't there; I was in Spain, and my life was being turned upside down, all my certainties cast aside, my most private fear confirmed.

It began with an interrupted phone call, on a Monday, two days before the official move to our new glass palace. I'd been in the newsroom for an hour when Tommy Partridge rang me. We had remained in regular touch, but usually after hours. For him to be on the blower at that time, I thought, as I picked up, it had to be business. 'Something for you, Xavi, that should really go on general release, so if you use it, be careful.'

'As always.'

'Last week, some building contractors broke ground on a new site for private housing out in Tranent. When the diggers went in, they turned over your classic shallow grave, occupied. A male skeleton, still in its clothes, back of the skull smashed in. It had been there for at least ten years. It's on land that was rezoned last year, after a bit of local debate, so whoever buried the body may have thought it would never be discovered there. We don't have a clue who it is, but there's one interesting thing that we do know. The scientists have been over the clothes, and what's left of the tissue. They found semen traces and reached the conclusion that the victim was sodomised. Whether it was before or after he was killed they can't tell, but . . .'

I had a morning news conference looming, plus we were all preparing for the move; I was less patient than I might have been. 'Gruesome, Tommy,' I interrupted, 'but what's the hook?'

'I'm getting there,' he chuckled, and I realised that whatever his news was he was looking forward to telling me. 'There's this new technique,' he continued, 'that's going to revolutionise identification. It's called DNA profiling.'

'I've heard of it.'

'Yes, well, we've got a woman in our forensic lab who's very keen on it. She's been building a record, database she calls it, using forensic samples taken from crimes that are still unsolved. When she adds a new sample, she runs comparisons across what she's got, looking for a match. She did that with the scrape she took off our body, and guess what? She got a result, one that's close to home for you. Remember your Chinese friend, Lina?'

'Of course, but . . .'

'I know what you're going to say,' he declared. 'She wasn't raped, and it's true there was no penetration, but the attacker did ejaculate. He came all over her, and over some of her clothing. We kept them, as we do in cases like that. I've been waiting years for this guy to resurface; now he has.'

'I don't know whether that's good or bad, but if the body's ten years old . . .'

'If we can identify the victim, we can look at his associates, and if it wasn't random . . .'

He had my attention, but at that very moment it was taken away from him by the telephonist, standing in the doorway of the newsroom waving at me. I cupped the phone. 'What?' I barked.

'Xavi, it's your father. He's on another line and he says it's urgent.' Something jumped into my throat from the pit of my stomach. If my dad called me at the office, and insisted on being put through . . . I started to list possibilities, but didn't get past one. 'I'll take it,' I said, removing my hand off the phone. 'I'll need to get back to you on this,' I told Tommy. 'Family business.' I killed the connection, and the waiting call came through instantly. 'Dad,' I snapped. 'Tell me. Is she . . .'

'Not yet,' he replied. 'Not tomorrow either and not the next day, but soon.'

'She was fine in the summer.' She had been. Older, and a little more transparent, but still mobile, hearty and vocal, even more so after her third Heineken of the afternoon.

'Yes, but at her age, that can change quickly. She's had a recurrence.' He gave me her diagnosis, and prognosis. She might just make it to October, but not Halloween, no chance. 'She wants to see you.'

'We'll come at once.'

'Just you, Xavi. She says it was just the two of you at the start and that's what she wants at the end. When can you leave? I'll charter a plane.'

'No. If you do that she'll see you're scared, and that wouldn't help.'

'I am scared, Xavi. She's my mum.' He sounded ready to cry.

'And she'd be quick to tell you,' I said, her thoughts in my head, as so often they were, 'that this is something all children must expect, and should experience; their parents are supposed to die first. I'll call our travel agent now and book the first available flight. When I give you my arrival time, have me picked up at Barcelona.'

When I had to I could make things happen just as fast as my dad could, even then. I went home to pick up some necessities, called Grace's secretary to let her know what was happening, then caught an afternoon shuttle to Heathrow and connected with an early evening service to Spain. A limo picked me up at the airport and I was at the masia by ten thirty.

I'd expected Grandma to be asleep by that time, but she wasn't even in bed. She was sitting by the window in her upstairs perch, a robe over her nightdress, looking down at the garden and pool. She'd probably seen me arrive. Her window was open, but that didn't mask the clinical smell that pervaded the room. It was lit only from the outside as I entered, and I left it that way. I walked across to her, knelt beside her and kissed her on the cheek, rare behaviour between us. 'Now I know I'm dying,' she murmured, with a sidelong grin.

I sat on the floor, so that I could look up at her as I did sometimes when I was a kid. God, but she'd been a different woman then, severe, black-clad, bun-bound, olive-skinned, with a smile for Christmas if I was lucky. As she approached her end, her complexion was yellow, for the renewed cancer was affecting her liver, but her hair was loose, silver and shining, there was a radiance about her and her severity had turned to serenity.

'I'm glad you could make it,' she said. 'There are things I have to tell you. Doors I have to open, so you can see what's inside.' She patted me on the shoulder, her touch feather light. 'But not tonight. We'll do that tomorrow; I'll still be here then, don't worry. For now, go and get us a couple of beers. Josep-Maria has been rationing me,' she chuckled, 'as if he's afraid I'll drink myself to death.'

I did what she asked. She sipped hers slowly, I noticed. She didn't really want it; she was putting on a show for me, to make me feel better. We sat there and watched the moon rise. 'When I'm gone,' she said suddenly, 'you must be good to Josep-Maria. He's going to miss me, and he's going to need you on his side, not against him.'

'I'll never be against him, Grandma Paloma; he's my dad.'

'He has done a lot for you,' she continued, as if she hadn't heard me, 'much more than you know or can understand yet. Promise me that as he gets older you'll look after him. Yes, I know he's still full of life, he has his business to keep his mind active and he has Carmen for companionship, and to keep other things active. But inside, it's only ever been the two of us. With me gone . . . you have to fill my place with him, Xavi. I don't want him to die of loneliness. Promise me. I don't ask you to build your life around him, just to be there for him, as he has always been for you.' She took my hand; hers was warm, slightly feverish. 'Promise me, son.'

'I do, Grandma Paloma.' I said the words in Catalan, in the same tongue, and tone, as I had made my wedding vow.

She made it halfway through her Heineken, before deciding that she should sleep. 'I need to be clear tomorrow,' she declared. She belched as she pushed herself slowly out of her chair. 'It's good, that Dutch beer,' she laughed, 'but anti-social.' She walked unaided to her bed, but let me take her robe from her shoulders, then help her into bed. As she lay down, my arm was across her back, and I could feel the sharpness of her vertebrae.

My dad was waiting for me when I went downstairs. Carmen had been cooking since Grandma's illness had re-emerged, and there was a meal ready for us, welcome after the minuscule in-flight trays I'd been offered. She set it out and left us to it. 'What do you think?' he asked me, tentatively, as I cut into my steak.

'I think she's really going to die,' I replied. 'She didn't finish her beer.'

'Christ, you didn't give her a beer, did you? Her nurse is a nun; she'll go fucking spare if she finds the bottle.'

'I'll charm her,' I growled. 'She says I have to look after you when she's gone.'

'I can look after myself.'

'Tough shit. She made me promise.'

He grinned. 'That's me stuffed then. I can get my fucking bath chair out right now.'

'Maybe not quite yet.'

'That's all she said?'

'Yes.'

'Mmm. How's Grace?'

'Grace is fine. The company turned in a record profit last year. She's working hard at it, doing a lot of travelling to keep existing customers happy, and to sign up new ones. She's away at least a couple of nights every week.'

He raised an eyebrow. 'Does that not piss you off?'

'Not really.' I shrugged. 'It makes her happy, and that's the main thing.'

'What do you do when she's away?'

'Watch some telly, play the piano, a bit of guitar.'

'You never go out? With the boys?'

'Did you?' I countered. 'As I recall, you went out with the girls, when you weren't at the casino.'

'True; I admit it. But don't you have any friends?'

'Lots,' I told him, 'but I don't want to go boozing with them.'

'Maybe we've failed you, Xavi. You've become a solitary man.'

'You haven't. I like who I am, I like what I am, I like sitting by myself, making music . . . and I love my wife. Where's your failure in that? Music's part of our life, hers too. Grace is obsessed with this band, REM.' I smiled at the thought of her addiction. 'There's a song of theirs . . . "Country Feedback", I think it's called . . . I haven't a fucking clue what the lyric's about but she's been singing it around the house for months.'

'And babies?'

'Some day. Soon. When we're both ready.'

'But you are ready, Xavi,' he countered. 'I can see; it's what you need in your life.'

'Like I said, when we're both ready. Now, how's business?'

'Growing, hand in hand with Spain. How's yours?'

'About to be revolutionised. The new paper will be full colour, almost unlimited in its scope. We've done test runs on the presses. They're better than yours.'

'You've still got that fucking useless editor, though.'

'He's a figurehead. Even he knows that now. He doesn't come close to understanding the new technology. John's head of editorial, and I'm his number two, well, two equal, with Sandy Jeffrey the sports editor.'

'Xavi, you're number one; everyone knows that, including Fisher. You don't realise how much you're carrying on your shoulders.'

'Don't overrate me, Dad.'

He shook his head, then leaned forward. 'Listen, Marat Petrov bought that paper without using any of his own money. It was all borrowed. The new place is funded by more borrowing and by substantial government and European grants. The *Saltire* is doing well now, but its success began with your arrival. Test him. You tell him you want more money and a seat on the board. He'll give you all the money you like, but he'll resist making you a director.'

'Why?'

'As a director you'll have access to all of the company's financial affairs.'

'Torcuil's on the board,' I pointed out.

'Because he's a fool. Whatever they told you, there was no deal guaranteeing his job when the *Saltire* was sold. Petrov uses him as a buffer between himself and you guys on the staff with brains.'

'Okay,' I conceded, 'Petrov's a chancer, but the paper would have been doomed without him. We'd never have funded the move, and we'd have been left behind by the competition. I'll go along with him.'

We finished off our meal making small talk, then I turned in for the night. After all that had happened, I slept fitfully, but I was sound asleep at eight forty next morning when I felt a hand on my shoulder, shaking me awake. It was my dad.

'Xavi. Ma's taken a turn for the worse overnight. The nurse has given her a shot, and she's perked up, but the doctor's been in; it's the beginning of the end. She wants to see you, now, while she's still lucid, she says.'

I jumped out of bed, pulled on a pair of jeans and a polo shirt, and walked along to her room, nodding to the black-clad nurse who was sitting in a chair beside the door. Grandma Paloma was sitting up in bed when I went in, her eyes just a little bit glazed, but aware. She looked up as I approached her. 'Carry me across to my chair, son,' she instructed. 'I'm a little shaky on my legs this morning.'

I did as she asked, settled her down gently in the old Parker-Knoll chair she had brought from Edinburgh, then covered her legs with a blanket that lay folded at the end of her bed, and settled on the floor beside her. She weighed nothing. 'That's better,' she whispered. She smiled. 'Maybe I shouldn't have had that beer after all, but what the hell. I smoked my cigar, you know. Last week, when I knew this thing was running after me. Overrated. I don't know why your father was so keen on them.' That was a surprise to me. I'd seen my dad smoke the odd panatela but I didn't know he'd been an addict.

'At least you got to find out for yourself.'

'And now, so must you,' she replied. She took my hand. 'I'm going to tell you something now. After I have done, you may hate me. If you do, feel free to put a pillow over my face and send me on my way. No one will ever be any the wiser.'

'Grandma,' I murmured, 'what is this?'

'I'm not your grandma,' she said bluntly.

I stared at her, all the breath left my body in a single gasp and for a second or two I neglected to replace it. 'You . . .' I spluttered. A wave of cold and dread swept through me. My head swam. If I hadn't been seated, I might have fallen over. I steadied myself; the coward in me wanted to get up and run from the room, but I didn't give in to his urging.

'Around thirty-one years ago,' she continued, '. . . and please don't interrupt me, Xavi; if I stop I may not have the strength to go on . . . I had a phone call, at home in Edinburgh. It was from a girl, a young girl, I knew from her voice. She told me that her name was Mary Inglis, and that she worked for my husband. She said that she had been "going out with", as she put it, my son, and that she was pregnant. She said that when she had confronted him with it he had told her to, and here I use her words, "fuck off".

'I was enraged. I never went into my husband's place of work . . . that's not to say I had nothing to do with the business; Xavier the First had great strengths, but I was better at thinking than he was . . . but that morning I broke my rule. I dressed and I went in there. I found the girl Inglis, and I marched her into my husband's office. He was there; he looked bewildered, but I ignored him. Instead I sent for my son. When he came in he was angry, to see her there, but he was embarrassed too. I asked him if it was true that he'd had relations with the girl, and he said that he had. They had been "seeing each other" for a few months.

'She smirked at him then, looking pleased with herself, until I asked Josep-Maria if he had told her about his medical condition, about the mumps he had had when he was twenty, the disease that had spread to his balls and had left him as infertile as a lump of wood. She stopped smiling then, did young Miss Inglis. She stopped smiling and she looked at Xavier, my husband. And he looked back at her, his face paler than I'd ever seen it, that great lump of an idiot who could never resist a pretty smile cast his way or pass by any twat on offer when we were younger and living here before the beast Franco.

'I had put that down to growing pains, to a Spanish male being what he is, and it hadn't worried me too much, for to be honest, my boy, I was never too interested in that part of my womanhood. But because of it I knew then, knew what had happened. "You little whore," I shouted at her, "you conniving little whore, with your eye to the main chance. You rode two stallions, father and son, to better your chances."

'Xavier threw himself on my mercy. He told me that it had only happened once, that he had been working late and she had been helping him. He had made a remark and she had smiled and made one of her own. He'd fucked her on his office table and he'd thought no more of it, until it came back to bite him.'

She stopped, to gather her strength, holding up a hand to still any interruption from me. 'I decided there and then what was to be done. She would have the child, and it would be Josep-Maria's for the world to know. I was rather hard on him I'm afraid, for he'd given the girl hope of advancement. She would live with us, as man and wife with Josep, if only in theory, for I wouldn't allow her the security of marriage, in their own accommodation that we would build for them in the garden. I wasn't having her within a cock's length of my husband again.

'But that house was never built, for as you know, three months later Xavier died, of the same sort of disease that is claiming me, but it took him much, much more quickly. So they, and you when you were born, lived in the big house, although I hated her, as I hate her now. It's a terrible thing to die in hatred, Xavi, but I'm doomed to it, because that greedy little whore took my husband from my affection, because she made me hate him too, for the last weeks of his life.'

I could see her weakening. She stopped again, for breath, and I let her recover. I let her take all the time she needed, for I was consumed myself by what she had told me, overwhelmed.

'So you see, my boy,' she murmured, 'I am not your grandmother. I'm nothing to you. I am no relation at all. She put a curse on me for life, that girl, and yes, every day she was under my roof I treated her like shit. But she deserved it, all of it. She never took any interest in you as a child. You were no more than a commodity to her, a means by which she would get what she was promised. Money.

'Every month she lived under my roof I gave her an allowance of a thousand pounds, ten years in all, around a hundred and twenty thousand pounds. When the time came that I wanted rid of her completely, for her presence was impeding your upbringing, I doubled it. Over the last twenty-two years, I've paid her over half a million pounds. I'm a wealthy woman, it was little to me. So now she is rich. She got what she wanted, unless she's thrown it all away.

'So there you are; that's the truth. You can hate me now, you can get that pillow. But don't hate your half-brother, please. He's always been a good man, and he's always loved you as if you really had been his son. He went along with my pretence because it was what I wanted, and because he felt, as I did and still do, that it was best for you, that we treat you in the way of a child that had been born out of wedlock and adopted by a privileged family.

'But I find that I cannot bring myself to die without telling you the truth about yourself. It's your right to know; it's always been your right, and I've sinned by keeping it from you. You are part of that privileged family, by blood, even if it's not mine. And that last truth, Xavi, that's the only sadness I take to my grave, when I look at you and see the man you are. With your father's strengths, and your brother's.'

'And yours, you old love,' I whispered, behind my tears, 'for you put them there.'

'What I tried to do, my son, was to take their weaknesses out of you. Only you know for sure if I've succeeded in that, but as far as I can see, I have.'

'You call me your son,' I said, 'and that's as I want it. For in my eyes, you are my mother, and you always have been.'

She smiled, that of an angel, floating away. 'That's good,' she whispered. 'It's a fine thought to die with. Now you'd better fetch the other one.'

Joe was waiting outside as I emerged, looking at me as if the sky might fall on him in human form. Instead I hugged him, and it was all right.

I left him to sit with her alone for a while. The nurse wanted to go back in, but I forbade it, until she was needed. She was, later that morning, when Grandma's breathing became laboured, and she showed signs of pain being resisted. She accepted another shot of morphine, but only on condition that we left her in her chair, and she died there just after three o'clock in the afternoon, with Joe and me sat on either side of her, him in a chair, me on the floor, my half-brother holding her left hand and I her right. Afterwards, the two of us who were left walked in the garden, looking at a house that somehow seemed to be much bigger without her massive presence to dominate it.

Joe told me that she'd said she'd never leave the house again, but she was wrong about that. Her funeral service was held within forty-eight hours, as Spanish law requires, in the church in the local village, where she had shopped, gone to market and danced in Plaça Major. Grace was there, of course. She had flown over the day before, and she had dug the black dress out of her wardrobe. I asked her not to wear it, though, but to opt for bright colours instead. Willie Lascelles was present also, invited by Joe, I'd assumed, for I hadn't thought to ask him. The service was informal. We had no requiem mass; she'd made it clear more than once that she didn't want to be seen to beg God to let her into heaven. Instead, the priest said a prayer, my half-brother delivered a eulogy, and so did I, a very brief one.

'I called her Grandma all my life,' I said in Catalan, 'but she was even more. What I am, she made me.' Then I walked over to the piano that had been placed beside the altar. I played some Scott Joplin, whose music she'd liked, then a blues called 'She Moves Me', because it always had. I finished with 'Els Segadors' which became the national anthem of Catalunya a year later. Most of the congregation were puzzled by the first two, but they stood and sang the third. When it was over we took her back to the masia. Joe and I slid her coffin into its place in the family mausoleum, and then we stood back as she was sealed in there forever, however long that may be, by the mason who had built it, with a single stone that bore the inscription, 'Paloma Puig I Garcia. 1904–1992.'

That was a day devoted to Grandma, but next morning my dad . . . after the funeral I told him that's how I'd always think of him, and what I'd probably still call him most of the time. He was fine with that, slightly touched even . . . told me that we had to have a meeting. I thought it was just the two of us, but no, when I went into his office at the appointed hour, Willie Lascelles was there. I frowned. 'What's this?' I asked.

'This,' said the lawyer, 'is what's commonly known as the reading of the will. It was made in Scotland, but it's been notarised here too, so it's equally enforceable and entirely taxable here.'

And this is how it turned out. When my father, my real father, that is, died, he had left his property equally between her and their son, Josep-Maria Aislado. But then I was born, a second son to him, post mortem, so to speak, with rights under Spanish law, which doesn't allow a son to be completely disinherited. I never knew about that provision, but it was irrelevant anyway, for Grandma took the view that both her husband's progeny should inherit equally. So, in that room, Willie told me that I had come into half the Aislado empire.

'Fuck me, Dad,' I gasped, 'that isn't fair. You've built the business, it should be all yours.'

He shook his head. 'It's eminently fair, Xavi. It was hers to dispose of as she pleased. But there's more to it than that. She didn't just sit in the house and knit all the time she was here. Well, she did knit a bit, and she never went further than the village, but by God her brain was active. First, she made it clear when I moved out here that I wasn't going to spend my life getting under her feet. Then she made me sit down and look at opportunities. The media business wasn't my inspired whim, son, it was a decision jointly made, and every step I've taken since then was discussed with her. So don't feel awkward that she's passed her share on to you. She told me long ago she was going to do that.'

'But Joe,' I protested, 'I don't want to be involved in running your business.'

'Then don't be involved; go back to Scotland, carry on with your life as normal, until you're ready to make the move out here; she said that you will one day. If I'm ever thinking of doing something crazy I'll talk it through with you first, just like I did with Ma. I'm sixty; I've got years ahead of me, my doctor says. When I am knackered, and I can't go on any more, we'll talk about you taking over then. Deal?'

'The monster's loose, and he's coming to get you.'

Seventeen

'Deal.'

We shook hands on it, and next day Grace and I went home. I had the office move to contend with and she said that she had 'meetings all week'. But before I did anything else, I had business to do: more family business. Willie had briefed me on my inheritance. It included all of Grandma's personal wealth as well as her share of the business, and that was considerable, the old fox having taken very good tax advice and hidden most of it offshore. It was the pot from which she had been paying my natural mother. I instructed the solicitor that should stop. Whatever formal agreement might have existed would have died with Grandma, and she was getting not a penny more out of me.

I phoned her to tell her, from one of the quiet rooms in the new building, choosing a time when I knew that Tommy was at work. She didn't like it. 'She said it would be for life,' she protested, 'hers and Joe's.'

'Hers and my father's,' I countered. 'And we both know who that was. Sue me if you're bothered. But you won't do that, will you? You know what I reckon?' I asked. 'I believe you were blackmailing her, all along, using the fact of my true parentage as a lever. She was too proud ever to admit to that, but I know that's how it happened.'

'You'll never prove that,' she said, icily.

'I'll never have to. I'll simply have to whisper it to Tommy, and you are done. Grandma was right about you. When you were a girl you were a greedy wee whore with an eye to the main chance, and you never grew out of it. You should think yourself lucky I don't come after you for the money you've had. But if I ever find out that it hasn't been used for the benefit of my half-sisters, then I will. Goodbye.'

I haven't seen her since, and I never will. Maybe, as you read this, you believe that I was too hard on her. Maybe you find me a little self-righteous. I concede that you might, but I can find no regret or apology in my heart. All I can do is hope that the woman who's married to Tommy Partridge shows him a kinder face than the one she showed to me, and that with him it isn't all about money.

Apart from my fortune, I had another inheritance to consider. I was no longer the person I'd thought myself to be; that's a hell of a large adjustment for a thirty-year-old to make. With the truth revealed, things began to make sense to me, small things, but significant. The greatest of these was the complete absence of photographs around the house, either in Edinburgh or in Spain, of the man I'd thought of as Grandpa Xavier. The only one I could recall was that indistinct family group I'd seen in Joe's office, and that had been removed the next time I'd gone in there. In Spain, before I left, I asked for a couple, and he gave them to me. One had been taken when he was twenty, and the other when he was fifty-two, a couple of years before he died. (He hadn't been that old, you see: at first I'd been disgusted by the thought of some grey-bearded, toothless lecher fucking an office girl, but when I saw that second photograph I realised that I was looking at a big, lusty guy, in his middle age, not all that much older than I am as I write this, and still attractive to women, as I've been told I am.)

When I looked at the two images, my father in his youth, and my father in his prime, I saw a tall, strong man, not quite as big as me, but still well over six feet, who carried himself assertively and gave the impression that it would take a steamroller to move him from any place that he chose to stand. I recognised some of his physical features as my own, the thick black hair, the full mouth, the dimple, things I'd thought had come from Joe, not from a common parent. But my jaw is bigger than his was, my nose is narrower and I'm even wider in the shoulders than he was.

However, there was no doubt about his dominant feature. There was something about his eyes, at twenty and at fifty-something, that reached out of the photographs and grabbed your attention, a little like Bob Skinner's had grabbed mine. They were uncanny. They seemed to express both the heat of the furnace and the coldness of dry ice, and they told you everything of which he had proved himself capable. This was a man you did not mess with, not at all. As he looked out at me, I imagined myself as the young Perry Holmes, and I understood the profound impression that his unexpected visit had made upon the fledgling gangster.

But they weren't unique, those eyes. I had seen them before, that very morning, and I would see them again, next time I looked in a mirror. When I did, I saw the man I'd grown into, someone I regarded as moderate, broad-minded and a pacifist at heart. That's what I saw, but when other people looked at me . . . did they?

I didn't tell Grace any of it. Why not? Well, we had carried our beliefs and certainties with us since childhood, and although mine had been revised, I could see no reason to alter hers. My birth certificate still showed Josep-Maria Aislado as my father, and it always would. If I'd told her it shouldn't have, everything would have changed. I would have become a different person in her eyes, and she might have looked at that man differently. That was a risk I didn't want to take, for I loved that woman even more than I had ever told her, and with Grandma Paloma gone from my life, I needed her more than ever I had, as my rock, my mooring point when the sea turned angry.

So we carried on with our lives as before. I threw myself into the task of reshaping and developing the *Saltire*, and Grace . . . with Scott keeping production running like clockwork, she told me . . . set her sights on ever-higher turnover and profits and on more awards to follow the 'Female Director of the Year' accolade she picked up at the end of 1992. A family was still not a subject for discussion, but I wasn't pressing that any more. I knew that when we had a child I'd feel compelled to lay its entire genetic history on the line, and I wasn't in a rush to do that. In any event, our prospects of conception weren't helped by our lifestyles. Grace was away even more often, we were producing much later editions of the paper, and so it was quite common for a month to go by without our ships docking, rather than merely passing in the night.

In fact, business success aside, 1993 was a barren year for us. Petrov's finance director, a Dane called Hans Andersen, was pushing us for profits and I found myself tied to Edinburgh for the first six months. When I did tell him forcefully, in July, that I was going to visit my dad in Spain for most of that month, Grace declined to come with me. She said that she had new products coming on stream, and needed to be on hand to market them. She even asked Clinton Storm to drive me to the airport when I left.

The masia without Grandma was hard to take at first. With the rest of it, I'd inherited her suite in the house, and that was difficult too, but I cured my blues by spending a little time each day standing at the mausoleum, making small talk, hearing her responses, and occasionally her questions, in my head. 'Yes, I'm content,' I told her. 'Honest.' I'm not sure that she believed me.

Joe, my dad, was fine, though. As I'd said to him the year before, losing a parent is a natural thing, and while it's meant to hurt, it's meant to happen also, and our emotional structures recognise that and deal with it. His had adjusted, and he and Carmen were turning into a contented middle-aged couple who might as well have been married, so amiably did they bicker from time to time. InterMedia Girona was doing well also, established as the biggest newspaper and magazine publisher in Catalunya and expanding its radio division across the whole of Spain.

One night, over dinner, he asked me what I thought of the potential of 'this thing called the internet'. I told him that a man who worked in Heriot Watt University, in Edinburgh, had assured me that open computer systems and the World Wide Web would change everything beyond most people's imagination, and that the media potential was endless. 'In that case, we'd better go there,' he declared.

I went home after three weeks, on a Friday, back to Grace, who actually collected me from the airport, alone. We spent much of the weekend in bed, then resumed our largely separate lives. We cruised into our early thirties, each of us finding fulfilment through work. While I may have asked myself whether that was enough, I didn't put the question to her. I kept focused on my day job, and took what I could from my marriage. Yes, we cruised.

Until October 1994. That's when everything changed.

The First World War began when a teenager named Gavrilo Princip assassinated Archduke Franz Ferdinand of Austria and his wife Sophie. Contemporary accounts indicate that he succeeded more by accident than design, but nobody could say that about the gunman who sparked the global upheaval in my life.

Billy Spreckley had summoned up all of his suicidal courage and was quite determined when he stepped into Perry Holmes's unguarded outer office, in a new block just off Lothian Road, walked through to his inner sanctum and shot him and his brother Alasdair. The latter was hit in the throat and died instantly as the bullet shattered his spinal column. Perry took four bullets, in the head, chest and abdomen. That's as many as Billy got off before Johann Kraus, who had been taking a leak when he'd arrived, blew his skull apart from the doorway.

Johann rather lost it after that. He killed a secretary from the neighbouring office who had come running to see what the noise was about, then barricaded himself in, starting a one-hour siege which ended when he was taken out by a bullet from a police sniper on the roof of a building across the street. Perry was still alive, and conscious, when the paramedics got to him, but the surgical team that operated on him discovered that while the chest and stomach wounds were survivable, the bullet that was lodged inoperably in his brain would leave him paralysed for the rest of what, they estimated, would be a very short life. When he was told this next day, he thought about it for a few minutes, then uttered four words. 'Get me Xavi Aislado.'

Jeff Adam, still a detective sergeant, as he remained for the rest of his career, came to collect me from the office. I commuted by bike whenever I could, so my car was at home. 'Why, Jeff?' I asked.

'Haven't a clue, big man,' he replied cheerfully. 'Maybe he wants to give you the keys to his kingdom.'

'I don't need them,' I murmured. 'I have enough already.'

The stricken crime lord was in a private room, on drips, tubes in and out, propped up on a mound of pillows to help his chest wound drain, his head swathed in bandages and fastened to all the machinery the Western's neuro unit had at its disposal. He couldn't move at all, so I stood at the head of his bed. 'You're still as scary looking as your grandpa,' he hissed, after Adam had left us alone, as instructed.

'It turned out that he was my father after all,' I told him.

'No surprise, that. I know Joe; I couldn't imagine him spawning you.'

'He's a better man than you, Perry, and he's still all in one piece. What is this anyway? A dying declaration?'

'I'd like to think not, but just in case, there's something I have to square with you.' His voice was weak; I moved closer and sat on the side of his bed. 'When we met, what I told you, it was the truth. I had no part in that robbery and I didn't know who did. Then last year, last January, a guy came to see Alasdair. He told him that he had a consignment he wanted to sell. My brother was smart enough to think he might be a plant. So he sent big Johann with him to check the stuff out, and to do him if he as much as suspected that he might be. It was straight up, though, and they brought it back to Alasdair. It was a whole fucking pile of factory drugs, diamorphine, cocaine, temazapam jellies, and some softer stuff, piles of it. It could only have been the take from your wife's factory. Alasdair said to me that the jellies even had "Starshine" printed on them.'

'Did you buy it?'

'Like hell,' he whispered. 'I told Alasdair to burn the lot in big Johann's incinerator on his smallholding, and to tell the guy that if he had a problem with that he'd be going in there too. He left, alive and unhappy.'

'And?' I asked, my eyes narrow.

'I never met him, but Alasdair knew him; he'd been a customer over the years. His name's Bobby Hannah. Pal of yours, they tell me.'

I stood. 'Is this a game, Perry? Remember I'm within reach of all that equipment that's keeping you alive.'

'No game,' he croaked. 'True bill. Hannah had the gear. The rest . . . that's up to the polis, or to you. But take my advice, Xavi; leave it to them. He's not worth fucking up your life over.'

'I'll bear that in mind. Stay well.' I turned and walked out.

Jeff Adam was waiting for me outside. 'Well?' he asked casually. 'What was that all about?'

'Nothing,' I replied, taking a chance that the room hadn't been bugged. 'He wants me to ghost his life story. I told him I'll write it my way and run it in the *Saltire* once he's dead.'

I asked the detective to take me home, rather than to the office. There, I did some checking, then got in my car and drove to an address out in Balerno. As I'd found out, Mr and Mrs Hannah still lived in the house I'd visited as a kid with Bobby, for tea. She still taught in a primary school in Dreghorn, but he had retired from his bank job, one of a host of early departures that had followed the appointment of a new and ruthless chief executive, one of the guys who set us on the way to our global fuck-up.

I came up lucky; Mr Hannah was in when I arrived. He opened the door of the family bungalow, lamenting the midday rain, which had caused his opponent to back out of their golf tie. He knew me at once, as a *Saltire* reader, but also, he claimed, because he recognised me from my school days. He asked after my family; I told him that Grandma had died, but that my dad was well. Then I asked after his. I told him that I'd been passing and thought I'd take the opportunity to try to catch up with Bobby. Somehow we'd managed to lose touch.

'It's not a problem to give you an address,' he said, 'but you might have trouble with the catching up part.'

'Is he offshore?'

'No, not at the moment; he's on shore leave, but he's in Australia, working out of Perth. He moved there eighteen months ago.'

Indeed, the late Alasdair and Johann must have made an impression on him, I thought. 'Is he, by God?' I exclaimed. 'Lucky him, in this weather. Never mind, Mr Hannah. It was just a notion.'

'Next time he calls I'll tell him you were asking for him.'

'If you can give me an address, I can drop him a line.'

'Of course.' He invited me into the hall while he found a pad and scribbled down Bobby's contact details, address and phone number. 'There you are,' he said. 'They'll reach him.'

I drove straight to the office and into John's room. 'I've got a story,' I told him, 'a big one. The kind that will have the opposition banging their heads off walls.'

'That's my man. I've been thinking that we need a boost; the circulation's stalling a bit and that shit Andersen's breathing down my neck.'

'I'll be off the pitch for a while,' I warned him.

'If it's that big, take as long as you need. Do you need travel arrangements made?'

I frowned. 'No. I'll do that. It's that secret.'

I called American Express from my desk and booked myself a business-class open return ticket to Perth, Qantas through Singapore, using a credit card that drew on a private bank account, one I'd set up but hadn't used before. I'd never been out of Europe before, never been further afield than Rome, but it didn't occur to me for a second that the trip was an adventure in any way. I was on a story and I'd do what it took.

I was packing that evening when Grace came home. Scott was with her. I'd forgotten that we were having dinner that evening with him and with Jilly Hannah. Their relationship had been on and off for years but

Grace had told me they were solid, and that marriage was on the horizon. 'Where are you going?' she asked me.

'Story,' I muttered.

She peered into my case. 'You're going to freeze if that's what you're taking,' she remarked.

'True,' I agreed, kicking myself as I reached for something warmer. 'I'm used to packing for Spain, that's my problem.'

'So where are you going?' she pressed.

'London.' It was partially true; I was routed through Heathrow. I didn't want to lie to her, but no way was I going to tell her what I was up to. Grace couldn't know anything about it until I'd caught up with Bobby and had the truth out of him. 'I'll be away for a few days; not sure how long exactly.'

She gave me the sort of smile I hadn't seen for a month or two. 'In that case,' she murmured, 'I'd better fuck your brains out before you leave. I'll tell Scott that he and Jilly are eating on their own.'

She did, then she did her best to live up to her promise. I woke up slowly next morning, to find her bustling around, dressed for the office, ready for her pick-up by Clinton. She leaned over me and kissed me. 'Call me when you can,' she murmured. 'When you get back, I want to talk about babies.'

I was still thinking about that bombshell as I checked my bags in at the express counter and as I hurried down the air bridge, catching my flight with a couple of minutes to spare. I was still thinking about it as the 747 took off for Singapore from Heathrow, wondering how Grace would react when I told her that if we had a girl, she would have to be called Paloma.

It takes a long time to go to the other side of the world, especially when not even Australian business class seats are big enough to let you rest comfortably. I watched movies all the way to Singapore, when I wasn't being fed by the attentive crew, and I didn't really start to think about Bobby until I was heading for Perth, on the last, five-hour, leg of the epic trip.

I couldn't believe that he and I had grown so far apart. I couldn't say that we were absolute best friends at school, for Grace always filled that slot, but he was next on the list, an open-hearted friendly kid it was impossible not to like. How had he fallen so far, changed so much? I asked myself. Had his gayness unsettled him? Or was it just the drugs, pure and simple, that had turned him full circle, from poster child to man beast? Whatever it was, childhood Bobby was gone. It wasn't him I was going to find, but what he'd become, and when I found him . . . What was I going to do? I didn't know. I hadn't thought that far ahead. I had made some preparations, but they weren't that sophisticated.

I still didn't know, when the taxi picked me up from the Hilton and took me to the address in Raglan Road that Bobby's father had given me. I'd dressed Spanish style for the searing late afternoon heat, white shirt, light trousers, sandals, no socks. I surveyed the place as the cab drove off. Unlike most of the larger brick houses in the street, it was white timberboard, built to repel sunshine, I imagined. There was a big blue Dodge truck parked in the driveway, with kangaroo bars front and back and massive wheels, a proper off-roader. I rang the doorbell; a young guy answered, early twenties, straggly blond hair, muscled up, everyone's idea of a surf bum, if they have them in Perth . . . I don't know; I wasn't there long enough to find out. 'Bobby in?' I asked.

He looked me up and down. 'Who the fuck are you?' he drawled.

'I'm the guy who's going to crumple you up and flush you away if you don't answer my question,' I promised him.

For a moment I thought I might have to, until a Scots voice came from within the house. 'Dennis, will you chuck it with the attitude, before it gets you hurt.' Bobby stepped into the hallway. 'You find a Hearts supporter, even here, and ask him about Big Iceland. Then you'll behave yourself.' He beamed at me. 'Sorry about this idiot. His parents named him after Dennis Lillee and he thinks he has to live up to the image. Xavi, this is fantastic. What brings you here?'

'Qantas, and a story that I'm working on. Your old man gave me your address.'

'How is he?'

'Cherishing Arnold Palmer dreams, I'd say.'

'That figures,' he chuckled. 'How much free time do you have?'

'The rest of today and tomorrow.'

'Great. You want to go for a beer and something to eat, then we can plan tomorrow?'

'Fine by me.' We got in the truck and he took us to the waterfront, Riverside Drive, it was called, and to a colourful drinking place called the Lucky Shag ... they could have called it the Lucky Cormorant, same bird, but that wouldn't have pulled in so many punters. They were out of Heineken, so we settled for Victoria Bitter.

'I can't tell you how glad I am to see you, mate,' Bobby said, as he watched my first one disappear. 'I'm sorry about what happened between us. I was bang out of order.'

'I'm sorry too,' I responded. 'Maybe I was a bit hard-line, but my old man laid down some pretty firm ground rules about the flat. I might have taken him too seriously.'

'No, you were right. Drugs fucked me up big time. But I'm clean now, I promise. That's why I got out of Edinburgh, to get away from all that shit.'

I looked out of the window, across the Swan River. 'You couldn't have picked a better place.'

'Lovely, isn't it? Gay-friendly too, for all they say about the Aussies. You know the one about the queer Australian? "He preferred women to beer." That's not true; this is a liberated place.'

'Fucking *Neighbours* by the sea,' I grunted. The VB was tilting me a little. I had no idea what time my body thought it was, but I realised I had to stay sober.

'Yeah, nice one.'

'Show me some of it then, tomorrow. I'm going to have to crash soon.'

'Sure,' he said. 'What do you want to see?'

'The Outback, the Outhouse, whatever it is they call it. Show me fucking kangaroos.'

He nodded. 'I can do that. I'll pick you up early tomorrow and we'll head inland.'

'Fine. But leave that cunt Dennis behind, will you? I've been a moody guy since Grandma died and he doesn't want to push his luck with me.'

Bobby frowned. 'Yeah, I heard about that, Xavi. I'm sorry, mate.'

'Mate,' I repeated. 'You'll be calling me fucking "cobber" next.' I held up my empty bottle. 'One more of these and maybe a koala-burger, or whatever else is on offer, then I have to go.'

We had the second, and a shark steak each, then he drove me back to the Hilton. I set my alarm for seven next morning, but I wakened at three and that was me for the night. The hotel catered for jet-lagged insomniacs, for the gym was open round the clock. I did some cardio work on a static bike, then spent half an hour on weights, rounding it off with a swim in the outdoor pool. By the time Bobby called for me at eight, in the blue Dodge, I was showered, shaved, and as sharp as I was going to be that day.

I had asked the hotel for a supply of takeaway food and plenty of water. As I tossed these into the back seat, I saw several jerrycans in the platform space, and a shovel. 'What are they?' I asked.

'Petrol,' Bobby replied, grinning. 'We're going a long way, beyond the fuel stops, and this thing likes a drink. The shovel's in case we get bogged down. It's easy to do that when you go off road.'

As I slipped into the passenger seat, I saw something else that hadn't been there before, a rifle, resting in two clips above the windscreen. I pointed to it. 'And that?'

'Wildlife.'

'Hey, I want to look at kangaroos, not shoot them.'

'There's not just them, there's dingoes. They hunt in packs. You don't go out there unprepared. You're not squeamish, are you?'

'Not if it's necessary,' I said. I'd been hunting that summer, in fact, with Pablo, Carmen's father, who'd decided that he had to reduce the local bird population to protect our fruit crop. We'd discovered that I have a natural eye, and after a while he'd left the shooting to me. 'Where are we going?'

'I thought we'd take the Great Northern Highway for a while, a couple of hundred miles, and then go off road.'

'You're the tour guide . . . mate.'

We set off, Bobby giving me a running description as we made our way out of Perth. It was a sprawling city with around one and a half million inhabitants, around three-quarters of the population of the state, but it wasn't long before we were clear of it and, so the compass on the dashboard told me, heading north, along a blacktop road with only ourselves for company. I pointed eastwards. 'What's out there?'

'Hundreds of miles of fuck all. The nearest big city is Adelaide, and that's around a two-thousand-mile drive.'

'People do that?'

'Only after a lot of thought and planning. The sensible ones fly.'

He kept up the commentary until he had run out of things to tell me. After that we talked about the old times; our school days, the way we'd been. 'How's Grace doing, after what happened to her parents?' he asked.

'She's turning into a typhoon.'

'You mean a tycoon.'

'No, I mean what I said. She's a real fucking whirlwind. She runs that factory better than her dad did, with Scott acting more or less as her body slave. Funny that,' I mused. 'Scott's such a fucking misogynist that I never imagined him taking orders from a woman, any woman, but there he is, Grace says jump and he's in mid-air.'

'Do you see much of him yourself?'

'A bit. We were supposed to be having dinner the other night, the two of us, him and Jilly, but this came up and we'd to call off. Yes, he's still banging your sister, boy.'

'Steady on, man.'

'Keeping it in the family,' I added. 'Literally.'

He stared at the road ahead for a minute or so. 'Scott's been talking?' he murmured, eventually.

'Only to us . . . as far as I know. Anyway, that's all past history. You're gay, and if he fancied you, there's no law against it . . . not any more.'

'Scott's a bastard,' he growled. 'He collects people like trophies. I love to think of Grace having him by the stones, pulling him along after her like a toy.'

'I'm not sure I like to think of it that way,' I said, quietly.

'Figure of speech, Xavi, figure of speech.'

We drove up the endless highway for three hours. In that time we'd seen two trucks and one car heading south, towards Perth, and overtaken none. When we reached the next of the rare junctions, Bobby slowed us down. 'Okay,' he announced. 'This is where the fun begins.'

He swung off to the right on to a road that was tarmac for only a couple of miles, then compacted red dust. Until then the terrain had been flat and civilised, some of it cultivated, but as he swung the Dodge off the track, I had a sense that we were entering another place, more rugged, almost mountainous, the real Red Continent, where man is at the mercy of just about everything. And it was hot. Even in the air-conditioned vehicle, it was hot enough to fry a steak on a stone.

'Where's the joeys, then?' I asked after twenty minutes of bumping and shaking, of me clutching the seat tight to stop my head from banging on the roof. 'Where's the bloody 'roos?'

'They'll be further on up the road.'

Oh yes, I thought, *along with their food supply*. I've never been a naturalist, but I do absorb and retain facts, and I knew that kangaroos are herbivores and that their diet is mainly grass, with the occasional shrub thrown in. Where we were headed there wasn't a blade to be seen, and not as much as a green twig.

Ten minutes later, my friend, driver and escort brought the truck to a halt. 'Comfort pause,' he said, opened his door and jumped out, into the blazing heat. 'Got to take a piss.'

I watched him in the wing mirror as he walked to the back of the vehicle, and as he reached not for his zip, but into his incongruous and wholly unnecessary denim jacket.

Quickly, I took the rifle from its place, and checked that it was loaded, opened my own door and slid out, finding the safety and flicking it off. I crouched and took two long duck-walk paces towards the tailgate, then stepped out, weapon raised, just as Bobby turned, with a pistol in his hand.

'You need to drop that, mate, inside two seconds.'

He looked up at me, his tanned face frozen. He stared into my eyes and he made the right decision.

'Now back off,' I ordered. He obeyed and I walked towards him and retrieved the silver, oily automatic. 'You know, Bobby,' I told him, 'ever since I arrived, I've been waiting for you to ask me one question, but you never have. Just this. What's the story that's brought me here? Come on, man, I come halfway round the planet and turn up on your doorstep in the land that time forgot, I tell you that I'm following a lead and you never even ask me what it is. Really?'

'Well?' he spluttered. 'What—'

'You didn't ask, Bobby, because you know what it is. You set up that scene yesterday with your current bum boy to impress me with the spontaneity of your reaction, but you weren't surprised at all. You knew I was coming. And you know what the story is. You are the story, yourself. You, the guy who tried to sell the stolen Starshine drugs to Alasdair Holmes, then ran for your life when he took them off you and destroyed them.'

'Bollocks!' he protested. 'That's pure bollocks.'

'Are you calling Perry Holmes a liar?' I laughed. 'You'd sat on your haul for over three years, you and your partner, until you thought it might be safe to move them on, only to find out that nobody in his right mind would have taken them off your hands. You reckoned you'd get

409

maybe a million, and instead you actually got fuck all, and out of there with your life only because the Holmeses had no reason to have you killed. You probably know by now that Alasdair and big Johann are dead, and that Perry's heading for a vegetative state. Yes, all that happens,' I told him, 'and next thing you hear, I'm heading for Western Australia.

'There could have been only one conclusion possible: that I know. Me, Xavi Aislado, the man who will learn, sooner or later, about everything that happens in Edinburgh, I've found out and I'm coming to get you. So, you were warned. You were told I was after you. It's ironic. I made you bring me out here so I could get the whole story out of you. You brought me out here so you could kill me, and bury me in this wasteland, with the fucking shovel.' I sighted the rifle, taking a bead right between his eyes. 'Leaving the dingo gun in the car was a big mistake, though, Bob. And you didn't even have the sense to keep the ammo in your pocket.'

I wasn't going to shoot him, at least I don't think I was, but . . . Bobby really should have taken that piss, for he wet himself. He dropped to his knees, crying, his hands on his head, and then he fell on his face. 'Xavi, please,' he whimpered.

'Don't give me that,' I said, coldly. 'You were brave enough to kill Magda. Don't let yourself down now.'

'Please!'

'I've worked out how you got the tip-off,' I told him. 'I made a mistake. I asked your father for your address, he told Jilly, and she told Scott. And . . . Scott . . . told . . . you. Your partner in fucking crime. That's the only way it could have happened.' I sighed. 'Aw, Bobby, for Christ's sake, I'm not going to kill you. Just tell me why the two of you did it. I deserve it; I've come a long way to take your confession. Get up, man.'

He pushed himself upright, the wet legs of his jeans muddy with red dust. 'Money,' he said. 'What the fuck else? It was Scott's get-out money, and me, I was so bad on the heroin then I'd have done anything. It was Scott that made me kill her, Xavi, honest,' he pleaded. 'I didn't want to, but I had to. He called me at the house, on Rod's car phone, and told me I had to shoot Magda, because he'd shot Rod.'

I stared at him; I'd guessed as much, but it still numbed me to hear it. 'And you just did it?' I roared at him. 'You could have said no. You could have stopped. You could have turned yourself, and him, in. But no, Bobby, you didn't. You had a choice and yet you pulled the trigger, over and over again, until she was bleeding and dying at your feet.' I had to pause, to gather myself, and to control the rage that I'd been suppressing from the moment that Perry Holmes had let me in on the secret.

'Go on,' I growled, when I was ready. 'Let me hear all of it.'

He nodded, shivering even in the blazing heat. 'We'd planned to do everything without speaking. We wore sterile suits, like they use in the factory, and masks.' His confession flooded from him. 'He was Ronnie Reagan and I was Maggie Thatcher. The idea was that we were going to tie them up and leave them, Rod at the bing, her in the house, then meet up somewhere to stash the money and the gear so we'd both know where it was. But Rod got to Scott, he challenged him to take his mask off, and that got him killed. And her.

'Scott's a fucking psycho, man,' he wailed. 'Surely you realised that. He's afraid of only one person in this world, and that's you. Remember Lina? It was Scott that attacked her. Remember that toy boy of his mother's, the one that vanished? Blake Seven, we called him? Scott killed him, and he raped him, then buried him out in East Lothian. We'd stashed the drugs and the money out there too, but we'd to go and dig it all up when we heard that the land was being used for housing.'

My conversation with Tommy Partridge, the one about the mystery corpse that had been interrupted by the bad news about Grandma, hit me like a ton of bricks. I'd forgotten about it, completely. If I hadn't, if I'd thought it through . . .

'But there's one thing I promise you,' he told me, 'if you've got the wrong idea.' He had recovered some control, if very little dignity. 'My sister had nothing to do with this. Scott's been using her, for years now.

She's been a smokescreen, although she's never known it. I did though, from the start, but I was too scared to say anything.'

'Scared of Scott? You've got as much on him as he had on you.'

'Not Scott!' he shouted. 'Scared of you!'

'Me? Why me? Why's everybody in fear of me?'

'Because that's how you are, man, fucking scary. Scott calls you "the monster". You're this big, serious, respectful, gentle guy to the world, but there's something about you that makes people wary of you too.' *People like Perry Holmes*, I thought. *They fear me just as he feared my father.*

'Look at the time you went at us in the flat, when you found out about the drugs. I thought you were going to slaughter me, man, but I didn't know you were on about them, not till you said. Xavi, if I'd told you the truth, I don't know what you'd have done to me. I still don't, but it's too late not to.'

'What fucking truth, Bobby, for Christ's sake? What are you talking about?'

His desperation was written on his face. 'Man, this is how it is. Scott and Grace have been doing each other since we were all at school. It goes back that far, and it's still going on. Those so-called modelling jobs of hers? She was meeting Scott, usually in her cousin's flat in Glasgow. Nowadays, those business trips? On most of them she goes through to Drymen, near Loch Lomond. There's a house there, Scott told me, a place the cousin has, that she bought for him.'

The cousin she said she hadn't seen since they were kids. I felt my forehead creasing, felt my hands tighten on the rifle, as I started to raise it again. 'Bobby,' I growled a warning.

'I'm not lying!' he screamed. 'She's been controlled by Scott all along. It wasn't Jilly who found out where you were off to. Grace took a look at your airline ticket when you were asleep. She told Scott and he phoned me. "The monster's loose," he said, "and he's coming to get you. Time to slay him." And then he hung up.'

Bobby looked up at me. I'm sure he really did believe I was going to kill him, but he was past caring. I wasn't thinking about him at all, at that moment, only about myself, the big scary monster whose wife and friend had been deceiving him for years. 'Why didn't she leave me?' I murmured, not to him, to myself.

'Because she loves you,' he answered nevertheless. 'That's what the fucking robbery was about. Four years ago, she told Scott that it had to end, that you and she were getting married, that she wouldn't be able to keep up the pretence any longer and that if it came to a choice between the two of you, Scott was a bad second place.'

He peered at me, trying to read me; looking for signs of belief. 'He was rough trade to her, Xavi, always; the roughest sort. He's AC-DC; he's anal, man. When she told him they were done, he didn't like it. He threatened to tell you, but she knew that was bluff, a double bluff, because truth be told he was a bit scared of Grace as well. She has power over you and because of that, she worried him.' He paused, and I had the impression that he was summoning the last of his courage.

'The robbery was her idea,' he told me. The rifle was back at my shoulder in an instant, and my finger was on the trigger. 'It's true!' He screamed the words, for his life. 'I swear it. She told Scott how it could be done and she even said that if he did it on that Thursday, it would net him enough money to set himself up, wherever he wanted to go. The robbery wasn't about the drugs; that part was a cover, but I persuaded Scott that if we'd destroyed them, and traces had been found, the whole thing could have been blown. Plus, yes, okay, I got a bit greedy.' He paused. 'Scott knew his way around the place from working there in the summer, and Grace gave him all the codes, and even the safe combination, just in case her dad played the hero. Then he did of course, and it all went fucking pear-shaped.'

As he spoke, I thought back to what she had said over and over again after I'd broken the news of her parents' death. 'They killed them. They killed them. They killed them.' I recalled her rage, and realised that all the time she'd known who 'they' were.

I didn't need him to tell me the rest, but he did.

After that Grace and Scott had been tied to each other by their own guilt, secret partners in a journey that might have ended at any time, or might not. Bobby had been held prisoner for a while by his addiction, until finally, cleaned up, he'd tried to escape by selling the drugs to the Holmes family, then had run off anyway, after his failure, to Perth.

With his confession to me, Perry had created both a danger to them and an opportunity. If I found Bobby and forced the truth from him, they were all fucked. But if he shot me and hid my body where it would never be found, they'd all be free.

'Quite a deal,' I murmured. 'Close call, Big Man.'

'I'm sorry, Xavi,' Bobby said. 'I can just about remember being an all-right kid once.' And then he started to run, not back in the direction from which we had come but onwards, past me, then away from me, towards the red hills and the places that go on forever.

As he raced off, I took the tiny dictating machine that I'd bought in Heathrow from the pocket of my shirt, and checked it for clarity.

I was satisfied, and so I let him go; I walked to the top of a nearby ridge and watched him as he made off, without water or food, suicidally, into the distance, across a flat plain, in the full, burning desiccating heat of the day.

When he was out of sight, I refilled the Dodge's fuel tank from the cans in the back, then took the shovel and buried the guns and the wrappings of the sandwiches that I'd brought and consumed. I could have driven after him, but the thought didn't even occur to me at the time. Instead I used the compass to guide me westwards, towards the highway that would take me back to Perth.

I left the Dodge at Bobby's house in Raglan Road, and walked down William Street towards the city centre, until I hailed a taxi to take me back to the Hilton. Next morning I caught a flight back to Singapore. My ticket allowed me a stopover and so I used it. I checked into Raffles Hotel and stayed there for three nights, mixing with the Aussies in the Long Bar, drinking Tiger beer and crunching the peanut shells under my feet. On the second evening I allowed myself to be picked up by a dark-haired tourist from Taunton, took her back to my suite, and sent her on her happy way next morning after breakfast, no harm done to either of us; only the second woman I'd ever slept with.

I did consider staying there for a little longer, but I knew what I had to do, sooner rather than later. So, as planned, I caught my midday plane to Heathrow, and managed to sleep through most of the flight. I had an hour to wait for the Edinburgh connection. I could have used the British Airways lounge in Terminal One but instead I chose to stay among the business-suited punters, where I'd sat with Grace once before, when she was fourteen years younger but not as innocent as I'd thought. On a wicked whim, when the flight was called, I took out my contact book, walked to a public telephone and dialled Scott's home number. He was there. Whether he was alone or accompanied I knew not, but it didn't matter to me. 'Yes,' he answered, sounding slightly irritated.

'The monster's loose,' I said, 'and he's coming to get you.' As I hung up, I was smiling.

My good humour had worn off by the time my taxi dropped me at the flat. There was no sign of Grace, no cup in the sink with coffee stains, no toast crumbs on the work surface. I showered and changed into heavier clothes, then got into my car and drove to the factory, arriving there at twelve thirty. The gate security men were uncooperative when I asked them if Mrs Aislado and Mr Livingstone were there, until I followed by asking them whether they wanted to be on the payroll at the end of the day. They sent for Clinton Storm, then directed me to a reception room for visitors; looking through the window as I waited for him, I could see the senior staff car park.

'Where are they?' I murmured, as soon as he entered. 'My wife and Mr Livingstone?'

'They're not here, I'm afraid,' he replied, all crisp efficiency.

'But their cars are. Since you're Grace's chauffeur, that means you've taken her somewhere. I'm prepared to bet that Scott was with her. So, where was it?'

'I can't tell you that, sir,' he replied.

I seized him by the throat with my right hand, lifted him clear of the ground and held him against the wall. 'I don't think you've got a choice,' I told him, quietly, as his eyes popped.

'Drymen,' he wheezed. 'I took them to a house just this side of Drymen, on the Stirling Road, earlier on this morning. It's called Aitkenhead.'

I put him down. 'You're fired,' I said. 'It's probably unfair, I know, but just on general principle, you're fucking fired, because I'm quite sure that you've known the score all along.'

I knew how to get to Drymen, up the M9 and then on to the A811. It didn't take me long, and it didn't take me any time to find the house called Aitkenhead; it had its own sign, on the road, about a mile short of the village. It was Victorian, a villa with wide windows to the front, in the style of Alexander 'Greek' Thomson. The driveway was red gravel, big granite chips that crunched under my wheels, announcing my arrival to anyone inside. That didn't concern me. Scott knew I was on the way, and he knew me well enough to be sure that I'd find them.

The wooden storm doors lay open and the stained-glass door within the porch was unlocked when I tried it. I didn't see any need to ring the bell. I stepped into the house, then paused. Years later, I still find it difficult to describe how I was feeling, or what. 'Out of body' might fit best; yes, I was an emotionless observer of events, in which I was the central character.

I waited in the gloomy hall. I didn't want to find them in bed together; it was important to me that I remained dispassionate, and let's face it, I'd been excessively good at that all my solitary life. So I gave them time to dress, if they had to, and join me. But they didn't; I allowed two or three minutes to pass, but neither of them appeared. Eventually I moved. I opened the nearest door, on my left; it revealed a drawing room, but it was empty. So was the dining room on my right. I was heading, reluctantly, for the stairs when I saw a sliver of light beneath a door towards the rear of the house. It was the kitchen, and they were there.

Grace was dead; I could see that at once. She was seated at a heavy farmhouse table, leaning back. Her head lolled on her left shoulder, her eyes were dull, and there was a small hole on the right of her forehead, from which a single line of blood ran down the side of her nose, then added even more redness than usual to her full lips.

My heart was pounding in my chest like a piledriver. I felt my face twist into a snarl. I wanted to cross the room, take her in my arms, and shake her awake, but I wasn't sure that my legs would work right at that moment. In any case, Scott stood beside her, his eyes wide and mad, and he was pointing a black gun at me.

'I wanted to run,' he exclaimed, before I'd had a chance to speak. 'When I told her you were back and that Bobby wasn't answering his phone, I wanted her to come away with me, as far away as we could get. But she wouldn't; she said that finally I was on my own, that she was staying with you, and that if it came down to it, that nobody, least of all you, would believe that she had anything to do with her parents' deaths, whatever story I came up with.'

I don't think that I'd really believed that she had, not until that moment; but Scott hadn't known what Bobby had been forced to admit, yet here he was corroborating it.

'The job with Starshine,' I murmured, leaning on him with my eyes. 'Her idea or yours?'

'Mine.'

'You and her: how long?'

'Since we were all in the flat, when you were so busy being a fucking bore with your football and your obsessions. Even had a threesome once, Grace, Bobby and me . . . not that Grace and Bobby got it on, mind; she watched the two of us and got a great kick out of it. Then she made me fuck her the same way. From then on, she was mine. From then on she was under my control. A word, a hint, from me to you . . .'

'Until now?'

417

'That's right. I made her come here with me, to talk it through. I thought I could persuade her to run with me, but finally she said no more, that I could go if I liked but if I did, it would be on my own.'

'So you killed her?'

'Yes,' he hissed, and at that moment I knew what I had come to do, to reach out, grab hold of him and squeeze the last breath of air from his rotten evil lungs. I would have too, but . . .

'You had it all, you bastard,' he screamed, 'you've always had it all, including Grace, when it came to the crunch. Well now, you've got fuck all!'

'Yes,' I agreed, 'but I'll be leaving this room alive.'

I didn't think he would shoot me, but he did. Not very effectively, though. The pistol was small calibre and its bullet didn't even knock me off my feet. It caught me on the upper right side of my chest, just below the collarbone. Some of its impact was absorbed by the padded jacket that I was wearing, one made of fine, heavy leather that I had bought in Spain years before. It rocked me back on my heels, but no more than that. Most important of all, it missed the voice recorder, which hung on a lanyard round my neck.

He stared at me. 'You really aren't human, are you?' he murmured.

He aimed at me again, at my head, and for the first time I did think that I was going to die. I know with certainty that I wouldn't have cared, but it didn't happen. Instead, his eyes filled with tears, he put the muzzle in his mouth, and he pulled the trigger.

'It's time, Dad, I reckon it's time.'

Eighteen

There was a phone in the hall. I thought about calling Tommy, but I decided against it. For all that I had resisted the notion, we had a family connection, and I didn't want to compromise him professionally. So I found Bob Skinner's number instead, and rang him. I told him where I was and explained the situation. I added that at some point I was going to need surgery. He didn't hesitate; he said that he'd be on his way, as soon as he'd alerted the locals.

I was sitting on the front steps, pressing a towel inside my jacket to my wound, when a squad of Strathclyde officers from the Dumbarton office arrived fifteen minutes later. I described what had happened inside, but I didn't tell them why, other than that I'd found out that my wife and her works manager were having an affair, that I'd traced them there, and the rest had exploded upon me.

A couple of paramedics arrived soon afterwards, in an ambulance. The cops were happy to let them take me, with a police escort, to the Vale of Leven Infirmary. There the bullet was dug out, under local anaesthetic, and I was stitched up, but only after a crime-scene cop had swabbed my hands and taken my jacket for gunshot residue testing. They're suspicious by nature in the Strathclyde force; they had to rid themselves of the notion that I might have shot both Grace and Scott, and then myself.

That's where Skinner found me, at the hospital. That's where I told him the whole story, and that's where I played him the recordings that proved it. I hadn't told the Strathclyde cops about those.

The blue eyes were icy for a while; he was a DI by then, with even more clout and even more menace near the surface. 'You should have left it to us,' he told me. 'You could have wound up dead . . . twice.'

'I'm a reporter, Bob.'

'And that calls for objectivity,' he countered. 'You were about as objective in this as a heat-seeking missile.'

'How objective would you have been in my shoes?' I asked him. 'Would you have gone after Hannah when he ran off into the wilderness?'

He looked back at me for a while, pondering. 'I can't be certain without having been in your size sixteens. I'd like to think that I would have, but possibly, yes, quite possibly . . . in the circumstances I'd have shot the fucker, just as soon as I turned the recorder off.' He sighed. 'Anyway . . .'

'Anyway I got a result,' I concluded for him.

'You did,' he agreed.

'And a story.'

'You're crazy,' he gasped. 'You can't . . .'

I could, though. I'd already written most of it on an Apple Mac laptop I'd bought in Singapore. There was no legal constraint on my running it. All the leading players were dead, apart from me and maybe Bobby Hannah, although by that time he was about five days through the survival window in the sort of country into which he'd headed. And even if, by some miracle, he was still alive, no arrest had been made; the sub judice rule didn't apply. The only name I didn't mention was that of Perry Holmes. He was refusing to die with a stubbornness that astonished his doctors and annoyed the police, and he'd have denied telling me anything about anything. 'Drugs?' I could hear him say, incredulously.

My right arm was immobilised, so Skinner took me back to Edinburgh, home to collect my new computer, and then to the *Saltire* as I insisted. I finished my story one-handed, printed it out then handed it to John. He read it through, three times, and when he had finally taken it all in he was as pale as Grace had been in death.

'Do you actually want me to run this?' he asked.

'If you don't,' I replied, 'I'll buy this paper and shut it down.'

'Xavi, you're in shock.'

'That's the bugger of it, Jock. I wish I was, but I'm not. Being a journalist, the job won't let me. It overrides everything.'

The story ran next morning, three pages under my by-line with shots of the Starshine house, the villa in Drymen, the factory, the shale bing and, of course, of Grace, Scott and Bobby Hannah . . . 'reported missing in Australia' as he had been by that time. There was also a supporting, illustrated feature on Grace the businesswoman, and the bonus of a second day follow-up story on the attack on Lina Chan, and the murder of the mystery man dug up two years earlier on an East Lothian building site. The blame for both was laid firmly at Scott's dead feet.

The story of a lifetime; and yet, in writing it I betrayed myself, and my profession. My reportage made no mention of Grace's involvement in the robbery. It did not reveal that she'd known who had killed her parents all along. It said nothing of her long liaison with the psychopath who had been our friend. Instead it portrayed her as the tragic victim of Scott Livingstone's last act of malice, as a heroine, as my lost love.

In its most important element, my story was, well, not a lie, but it was fundamentally economical with the truth, as some guy would say a few years later. So, why did I allow it to be told that way? To spare myself from being revealed as a cuckold?

No, I did so because at the time I thought that's what Grandma Paloma would have expected. It's taken me years to realise that the opposite is true. She lived with a secret for thirty years; it's the last thing she'd have wanted me to do.

And so here, on this page and with these words, I set it right, and put myself at one with my conscience.

Back then, in the knowledge and light of my duplicity, I gave Torcuil my resignation two days later.

'I'm done,' I told him. 'It's like the Nobel Prize,' I excused myself, laying deceit upon deceit. 'Everything's an anti-climax after that.' John pleaded with me to change my mind, and even our editor backed him up. As for Petrov, he panicked when he was told. Eventually I agreed to stay on, as deputy editor, but well away from the front line. I had no intention of ever writing another news story.

Having played the major part in persuading me to remain, John more or less forced me to take a couple of weeks off. That wasn't so difficult, for there was a hell of a mess to clear up. The prudent Willie Lascelles had insisted that Grace make a will, 'against unforeseen illness or acts of the Deity' as he had put it. It named him as executor and left everything to me.

I owned Starshine Pharmaceuticals. Shit.

My first act was to confirm my vengeful sacking of Clinton Storm, albeit on generous terms. My second was to install Willie's son Niall, a partner in the family law firm, as acting general manager. I didn't keep the company long; I didn't like the feeling of being responsible for the livelihood of over two hundred people in an industry I didn't understand, and so, as soon as probate had cleared, I sold the company to the predatory competitor who had sniffed around after Rod's death, and took the capital gains tax hit.

There was Grace's funeral to take care of also. On the day, there were probably more press outside the synagogue than mourners inside, for all that it was filled with civic and business dignitaries. The workforce was represented by a delegation of a dozen, and even wee Joel Levin had the courage to attend, although he must have known he was risking my wrath, given that he had gone along with the arrangement that had given Grace and Scott their meeting place. (He wasn't a player in the Holmes organisation, by the way; I'd been wrong about that. He was a fence, and he might have handled a couple of stolen treasures for Alasdair, but no more. The guy I'd seen leaving when I visited his office had probably sold him a piece of contraband, or tried to.) The service was short. With the rabbi's consent the music was limited to two REM songs of my choosing; 'Country Feedback' . . . that line she sang over and over, 'It's crazy what you could've had'; *I had it,* I protested in my head, *but you took it away* ... and one other, 'Everybody Hurts'.

I did hurt, make no mistake about it. Widowhood is awful. Within my great impassive shell, I was in agony. There were times when I thought I could not stay in that flat, or in that city, for a day longer. More than once I found myself with the phone in my hand, ready to call a travel agent and book myself a one-way flight to nowhere. Singapore was a possible, the far side of Australia was another. 'Where's further away than Australia, Xavi? New Zealand. Why not?'

'Why not?' was Grandma Paloma. What did she do when her life was taken away from her? She looked at what she had left, namely me, and her natural son, and she made the best of both of us.

So that's what I did; I followed her example. I carried on at the *Saltire.* I was a conscientious deputy editor, then Torcuil's title was changed to 'managing editor', and my 'deputy' tag was dropped. I went to work every day, and I made a name for myself as a curmudgeon, as I set standards for my reporters that bordered on the cruel. I'd probably have ruined quite a few young journalists but for John's ability to rein me in when I threatened to tear a strip off someone that might have proved career-ending. Yes, I went to work, and then I went home. I sat by myself in my lofty apartment, I played my piano and I played some guitar, blues, always blues. I might still be doing that, if I hadn't been saved.

Fate's wicked when She puts Her mind to it. Five years after my threat to John, as the century drew to a close and we were gripped by the uncertainty of the millennium bug, I did wind up buying the *Saltire* ... okay, InterMedia Girona did, but that was much the same thing.

It all started when I attended, grudgingly, a civic lunch and found myself placed next to a chartered accountant named Ronald McSkimming. We exchanged the usual polite but meaningless remarks, yet all the while I could sense a familiar tension in the man. I'd been through the same routine a thousand times before. He had something for me, a story, a hot one. I knew that if I waited, it would be offered, and it was.

'I'm on your audit team,' he whispered. 'Your pension fund, it's . . .' Then the Lord Provost's hand fell on his shoulder and that was as much as I got.

It was all I needed. Over the next few days I did some digging. First, I pulled the last three years' published accounts of the *Saltire*'s holding company. I looked at the profit figures, then I looked at shareholders' funds. They didn't square. Next I examined the overall salary costs. I knew what the total payroll was, including national insurance, and I knew what the employer's pension contribution should be. It wasn't there.

In theory, the company's pension fund was ring-fenced, and overseen by an actuary. There was a name shown in the fund's annual report to members, but when I tried to track down its owner through the actuarial professional body, I discovered that he didn't exist.

There was one door open to me, and I stepped through it. Torcuil was a trustee of the fund; I cornered him in his room and asked him, 'How much is in the pension account, right now, invested and in cash?'

He looked back at me, nervously. 'There is no cash,' he told me. 'Marat ordered the brokers to invest it all in a company that he bought last year. It's how he funded its takeover.'

'What does it do?'

'It's in oil exploration and production, somewhere off the African coast.'

He gave me the name of the enterprise and the state in which it was based. I recognised it; three days before, I'd read a report in the *Financial Times* of the seizure by that great nation of all foreign-owned oil and mineral assets.

There was more, and it didn't take long to find it. In addition to raping everyone's pension pot, Petrov had put all of the *Saltire*'s available cash into the doomed business. I visited my new auditor friend and told him what I had.

'You're bust,' he told me. 'Petrov's done this without the approval of the company's bankers, and without board or trustee authority. It's a massive fraud.'

I went back to the office, wrote the story myself and told John to run it, front page. Next day, Hans Andersen was arrested at Gatwick Airport, on his way to join Petrov in North Cyprus, three hours after our bank sent in the receivers.

Did that put me in a difficult position? No; there was no subtlety, there was no quandary. I had a straight choice to make. I could walk, or I could act. I could retreat into my wealthy cocoon, washing my hands of the personal tragedies that I'd be leaving behind me, or . . .

I called my dad. He told me to do the best deal I could with the bankers, and the other creditors. I did, and that deal was ninety pence for every one pound of debt; I agreed to it, and within days, the paper to which I'd devoted my working life belonged to my family. Torcuil left, voluntarily, and I assumed his title 'managing editor'. I replaced Andersen as finance director with Ronald McSkimming, reporting not to me, but to Girona.

I'd saved the paper, but the pension fund was stripped. Since then, every penny of profit made by the title has gone back into it, and it's all but restored; the pot is full enough for Jock Fisher to have retired a few months ago. The *Saltire* is what it is, what it was set up to become. It may not have seen its founding purpose, independence, delivered, not yet at any rate, and maybe it never will, but it has realised its potential, for the moment at least. It's respected and popular, even if it is still regarded as the newcomer in the capital city. It's taken me nine years, but now I can go. I've even secured my succession, my dynasty, if you like.

Five years ago, in 2003, a job application landed on my desk, with a full CV. It was from a 27-year-old woman named June Crampsey. She was widow, ever so young, and I empathised with her. She was also an exceptionally good journalist, with a first-rank international experience. She had taken a degree in journalism in Glasgow, worked for a couple of years on the *Glasgow Herald*, then followed her fund manager husband to New York. She'd found a job on the *Wall Street Journal*, and so she'd been on hand when he was killed in the Twin Towers on September 11, two years before her approach to me. She'd stayed on in the USA for a while, in her job, until her continued presence there had come to the attention of an unsympathetic idiot in the federal government, and she'd been asked to leave the land of the free.

Most employment applications were nodded through to John, but I handled that one myself. I invited her to meet me, gave her a grilling, and set her some really wicked practical tests. When she sailed through them all, I employed her.

Since then I've been grooming her, in a wholly acceptable way, as my successor in charge of the resurrected *Saltire*. She picked up usable Spanish in America, and that allowed me to send her to spend most of 2006 in Girona, as Pilar Roca's assistant, and although she didn't know it, her pupil.

And now she's ready. The moment has come. Finally, aged forty-six, Xavi, this loner, is off to find companionship, and a life.

'Who are you?'

'My name's Niall Lascelles, Mrs Crampsey. I'm the company's lawyer.'

'So? Where's the boss? Where's Xavi?'

'He's gone.'

'Where?'

'Away, that's all you need to know. This is your office now, and this is your contract of employment as managing editor, made out in the name of Mrs June Crampsey, née Partridge. Please sign where indicated.'

'Are you serious?'

'I'm a lawyer, Mrs Crampsey, I'm always serious.'

'Xavi's gone without a word?'

'No, he did leave me two messages for you. One, you're going to be a great success, in building on what he's begun. Two, you're his sister.'

Co-author's postscript

When my work was finished, I sent Xavi an email and told him. I offered to forward what I had done as an attachment, but he said he'd prefer it if I brought it to him as a printed manuscript. He sent me a plane ticket to Barcelona, and he met me himself at the airport.

Two years had flown by since our last meeting, yet Xavi looked younger than I could ever remember him being during our acquaintance. As we shook hands, I noticed that his were hard and calloused, those of a man who did a lot of manual work ... a gardener, perhaps. He had dropped about twenty pounds in weight, and that lugubrious, jowly look had gone, but the greatest change was in his eyes. Their intense, probing, intimidating, seriousness had disappeared completely; they had acquired laugh lines and a gentle, serene expression, even if there was still evident sadness there from time to time.

Our destination was no surprise. He drove me to the masia, set in the majestic hills west of Girona, where Paloma Puig lived and died and where she's entombed. As we pulled up at the front door, an old man came out to meet us. He looked like Xavi and yet not like him, white hair, not black, the same body shape but much smaller, the same eyes but without any of the joy.

'This is Joe,' said my host. 'My dad.' The older Aislado greeted me warmly, saying nice things about my work, and we made a little polite conversation, before he retreated, back to his lair, where Xavi says he's most comfortable. He explained that he rarely visits Girona these days. Esme Waller died in 2005, and since then he's preferred to stay at home, with Carmen.

'He still plays a part in the running of the business,' Xavi told me.

'He's its chairman, but most of the executive decisions are mine now, with Pilar Roca to advise me on editorial matters. We're the biggest independent media group in Spain now, would you believe, and the internet edition of *GironaDia* has more paying subscribers than any other online publication in Europe. Hector runs it.'

'Who's Hector?' I asked.

'Hector Sureda. He's Simon's son; his and Pilar's.' He caught my expression. 'Ah,' he exclaimed, 'I had a feeling I'd forgotten to mention that they're husband and wife.'

He led me inside. The house is bigger than he had described it in his document, especially the great drawing room. It was dominated by three portraits. The one that hung over the fireplace was of an old lady, white-haired, tall and utterly majestic. From the wall to the right a much younger woman looked down, blonde, nude, and incredibly sexy.

'Grace,' Xavi murmured. 'After she died, I found the man who owned it and I bought it from him. I had intended to destroy it, to reduce it to ashes . . . out of grief, I explained . . . but Carmen wouldn't let me. She said that I had loved Grace, and that I shouldn't hide from her memory. She didn't know the whole story, but what she said was true nonetheless. She pointed out that it was the work that had made her reputation as an artist, and said that if I did, she would paint another, and keep on doing them if necessary, until we were both exhausted.'

I was about to ask about the woman in the third portrait when she walked into the room.

Xavi beamed. 'And this is she who saved me,' he declared, as she and I shook hands. 'This is Sheila Craig, my second wife, as of two years ago. I have all my weddings in Spain,' he chuckled.

'We met up again ten years ago; I did something damn silly on my bike on the ice and wound up in the Royal A&E with my good knee twisted. She was the sister on duty. When she saw me, she said that I looked in a bad way, and she wasn't talking about my sprung cartilage.

She decided that I was a long-term care job, and we've been together ever since.'

'I needed him as much as he needed me,' Sheila told me. 'My first husband drove off in his lorry one day and never came back. He left me with a broken marriage and a thirteen-year-old son, so I wasn't too clever either. Xavi and I formed a mutual support group, but we kept quiet about it, for all the time we were in Scotland. We didn't want to involve anyone else in our business, so we each got on with our jobs, we didn't live together, and we kept our relationship entirely private.'

'Until I was ready to move here,' Xavi added, and walked me out through patio doors back into the garden. 'We came together . . . or rather all three of us came.'

As he spoke, a child, a girl, rose from a chair beside the pool and laid a book on the ground. She was only eight years old, I learned later, but she was tall for her age, straight-backed, with dark hair, although her mother's was auburn. As she drew closer her resemblance to the old woman in the central portrait made my spine tingle.

Xavi knew that it would, of course.

'She was a late baby,' he told me, 'for both Sheila and me, a real surprise. Remarkable, isn't it? She doesn't have a trace of her genes, and yet . . .' He smiled. 'There are still mysteries, my friend, waiting to be uncovered by people like you and me, the seekers.'

He held out a hand to his daughter. 'Come here, Paloma,' he called out to her, in Catalan, 'and say hello to our visitor.'